✳︎⤳ THE ⤳✳︎
LISTENING SKY

Lesley Denny

C̲

CENTURY PUBLISHING

LONDON

First published in Great Britain in 1985 by
Century Publishing Co. Ltd,
Portland House, 12–13 Greek Street,
London W1V 5LE

ISBN 0 7126 0860 5

Printed in Great Britain by
St Edmundsbury Press, Bury St Edmunds, Suffolk
Bound by Butler & Tanner Ltd, Frome, Somerset

*To my Mother
and the courageous women
of her generation*

M ✗

THE
LISTENING SKY

Chapter One

It was the coldest winter for 45 years. 1940 roared in with savage fury: blizzards cut off towns and villages, roads were blocked, the Thames froze hard for eight miles. Four months into the war, it seemed as though the weather had conspired to add to the confusion and disruption of daily life.

Huddled in a corner seat in an unlit, draughty train heading into the night, Eileen Howard felt uncertain about the choice she had made. Her whole way of life would be different now. It was no light decision she had made.

With her coat collar pulled high under her hair, she turned her face to the dark window ghosting her outline against a featureless landscape. At the time there had seemed no alternative. In her desperation to find a place to go, the Women's Auxiliary Air Force appeared to offer a chance for freedom, a new beginning, the opportunity for adventure, and for security such as she had not known for years. The WAAF had seemed the answer to all her problems.

But sitting here in the creeping train in the blackout, reassurance seeped away. Although the carriage and the corridor were tightly packed with people both in and out of uniform, she felt immeasurably lonely. She was on her way to the WAAF intake camp in Gloucestershire to begin her training. It would be a new life full of challenge and fresh opportunities, just what she had been looking for. So why did she suddenly feel this wave of depression and anxiety? All the other new recruits would be as apprehensive and nervous. It was like the first day at a new school all over again. Perhaps there were even some of them here on the

1

same train, travelling as she was on a rail warrant and trying to look out for their station in the grey-white obscurity of the night.

The train was already running two hours late. There was no hope for it; conditions were so bad that railway staff told complainers that they would be lucky to reach their destinations at all. Hardly the most auspicious start to a new life.

The flash of the guard's lamp lit up the figures in the corridor as the burly uniformed figure squeezed and jostled his way forward down the train. He was calling out something indistinct and Eileen quickly got to her feet and went to the door of the compartment.

'Your stop next, miss,' said the guard, forestalling her question. His dim lantern lit up the lines of his weary face in dramatic silhouette as the train rocked from side to side. 'About two minutes.'

Eileen thanked him, holding on to the luggage rack to steady herself as the engine slowed down on its approach to the station ahead. She took hold of her worn leather suitcase and heaved it down on to her seat. Her movement and the changed rhythm of the train stirred a couple of her companions from their sleep in the cramped, uncomfortable compartment.

'Is this Gloucester, love?' asked a khaki-clad corporal sitting bolt upright and searching anxiously in his tunic pocket for his rail warrant.

When she told him it was not he groaned, blowing out his lips, and then settled back down in his seat, arms folded, and shut his eyes again.

With her suitcase in one hand and a small holdall in the other, Eileen edged her way out of the narrow compartment doorway into the crowded corridor. There was scarcely room for another body, but the occupants of the freezing corridor eagerly made way for her. There was an immediate movement behind her to grab her vacated place.

The train was slowing right down now, pulling into a darkened station banked high with fresh falls of snow. Opening the stiff carriage door to a faceful of icy air, Eileen peered anxiously out into the gloom. When the train finally pulled up, she stepped down cautiously on to the ice with her luggage and noticed that other women were following her example all along the winding length of the train. A sense of sudden excitement seized her and she made her way with renewed confidence towards the tiny shuttered station, blinking in the light as she entered the busy lobby.

There were already 20 or 30 women packed into the close area, shuffling slowly through the ticket barrier and showing their crumpled rail warrants as they passed. They wore civilian clothes of all colours and styles. Eileen could tell from one glance that here were women from all walks of life, from all classes. Here and there a woman of real elegance stood out from the crowd wearing a hat or coat in the very latest London style. She felt a moment of surprise to think that any woman of means would choose to volunteer for the Forces, to leave a comfortable home background where they did not have to work for a living for the discipline and rough and ready nature of communal life. It was different for a woman who was used to hard work. Eileen wondered what could have motivated a wealthy woman to join the WAAF.

She saw that the women were all looking round at one another, their faces etched with undisguised curiosity as they acknowledged their sudden sense of community.

'Well, I'll be darned,' declared the ancient station-master as he piled up the warrants at the barrier. He scratched his head under his cap and gave a sour smile. 'Going to beat old Hitler single-handed, are you? Must be barmy! Women in the Forces, whatever next?'

One of the women looked round as she passed through the barrier.

'Don't you worry, Grandpa! You stay safe and sound in your bed and we'll protect you!'

There was a general chorus of laughter as they all spilled outside into the darkness of the station forecourt. Fresh snow was falling quite heavily and the freezing air stung their bright, eager faces. Snow was stacked high under the flimsy iron canopy over the entrance which offered little protection. The women all huddled deeper into their coats and their eagerness visibly began to wilt.

'All right! Over here, you lot. Speed it up!'

The parade-ground voice cut across the bustle of new arrivals and all heads turned in the direction of a tiny figure in a military greatcoat stamping across the yard towards them. In coat and peaked cap, face half shadowed, it was difficult at first to detect the sex of the sergeant but the voice was deep and authoritative enough to command instant obedience, even among those without experience in taking orders.

'Come on, double quick. Into the first truck. The first one, I said.'

There were two RAF vehicles parked just out of the yard, canvas-topped and snorting clouds of filthy exhaust fumes. An impatient corporal was stamping her feet up and down, urging the newcomers to get inside.

A couple of women had come in trousers. Eileen had never seen a woman wearing trousers before, though she had seen pictures in magazines. But the radical new fashion had hardly hit the small provincial towns which she had always been used to. Uncertain whether she really liked the look of them, Eileen had to admit that they gave women a new freedom of movement. She envied the ease with which they clambered aboard the high truck. A woman in a tight-fitting tailored skirt had less luck. She laddered her silk stockings as she tried to get up the side of the vehicle, and in the end had to be pushed inside by friendly if over-familiar hands.

When it came to Eileen's turn she handed up her bags first and then reached out for a hand which was extended to her from inside the truck.

'Put your foot flat against the side,' she was advised and, unthinkingly, did as she was told and felt herself pulled up and over the tailboard into the dark interior.

'Thanks a lot,' she told the brown-haired woman who helped her. 'But wouldn't you think they'd just let down the back of the truck?'

'Oh that would be too easy, dear,' said a voice from the deep recesses of the truck. 'First lesson in the WAAF: make even the simplest little job twice as hard. They get a thrill out of it.'

'That's wonderful,' added another voice caustically, 'but I've ruined my last pair of stockings!'

Eileen settled herself on the hard wooden bench which ran down the inside of the truck, her bags round her feet. The brown-haired woman sat next to her, and in the fitful light from the station entrance she saw that she was younger than she had first thought, younger even than herself.

'Were you on the train?' asked Eileen quietly, feeling she should make some friendly gesture towards her.

'No, no, we've been here half an hour or more,' said the woman. 'One truck went away full to the camp, but we were unlucky. We had to wait for another train to fill up.'

'You must be frozen.'

'Well, yes, it is rather cold,' she answered apologetically as though she feared to offend anyone by criticising the weather. 'Do you think they will give us something to eat when we get to the camp? I haven't eaten since leaving London.'

'Is that where you're from, London?' Eileen asked politely.

'Yes, well, no, from Kent, actually.' She was clearly extremely nervous and unsure of herself and sat there twisting the corner of her scarf in her hands. But there was no more time for further conversation as they had to move along the bench to make way for other women. The truck was already quite full, but they kept on climbing up over the tailboard until there was no more room to sit down.

'OK,' came a shout from outside, 'that's it! Take her away, Mavis.' The side of the truck was slammed, the engine coughed abruptly and they rumbled forward.

Away from the station, they were plunged into almost total darkness. The women had to brace themselves as the truck rocked and jerked its way through the narrow Gloucestershire byways. In such a rural setting the wartime blackout was complete, although Eileen was doubtful whether Hitler's bombers were really interested in targeting such isolated regions of the country. Four months into the war and no one had even been bombed. In fact there were times when you wouldn't know there was a war on. It was crazy, really.

A fine spray of ice from the country lanes showered the canvas sides of the truck and icy draughts whistled through the gap in the flapping tarpaulin over the entrance.

'Bloody Hell! We'll all be frozen statues before we get there.'

'Laid it on specially, I shouldn't wonder. Fucking weather.'

Eileen bowed her head in embarrassment, but she saw that her shy neighbour was shocked, eyes wide with surprise.

5

The camp was about fifteen minutes away. It would probably have been a quick journey in less treacherous conditions, but on the icy surface of the roads they seemed to crawl along. The driver struggled bravely with the gears of the old vehicle, and they slowed right down to manoeuvre up the icy ramp by the gatehouse. Inside the truck the women listened as words were exchanged between the WAAF driver and the camp sentries on duty.

That's what I will be doing soon, Eileen realised as she became aware of their driver forcing the ancient vehicle up through the gates of the camp. Driving a truck! I must be mad, she thought.

They pulled up abruptly outside a large hangar of a place. The tailboard was lowered this time and a voice told them all to get down.

'This is the cookhouse. Get inside, all of you, and get fed. I'll be back to pick you up in 30 minutes.'

'Do you mind if we stay together?'

Eileen looked round into the face of the woman who had sat by her in the truck. They stood in the doorway of the cookhouse, where the women were piling their luggage in one corner. Eileen saw that she was short and nervous as a schoolgirl, her chestnut hair parted in the centre, framing a delicately pretty face. Her large frightened eyes compelled Eileen's pity.

'No, of course not,' she replied, feeling oddly protective towards her new friend. 'My name is Eileen, Eileen Howard,' she volunteered.

'And I'm Veronica.'

'Veronica what?'

She saw a spasm of embarrassment cross her face and she wondered what was wrong now. But Veronica said quietly,

'Veronica Darling.'

Eileen felt sorry for her. She could see at once that having such a name must be a real burden in life. Everytime she had to give her name or fill in a form she must meet the same jokes and snide comments from people who thought they were wonderfully original and witty. Eileen wondered what she should say to her, but the problem was thankfully taken out of her hands by the growing queue that was forming to get supper.

It was not a great deal warmer inside. The cookhouse was an

6

enormous shell of a building full of long trestle tables and benches. At one end a series of shutters were pushed back to reveal a glimpse of the kitchens, separated off by a long low counter on which piles of plates were stacked in readiness for them. Two or three women in white overalls and white caps hovered on the opposite side of the counter, grim-faced and unsmiling. As the line of recruits moved forward, the women thrust the plates forward impatiently, as though they bore some grudge against them.

'It's cold food!' exclaimed someone at the front of the queue in dismay. 'Fancy giving us a salad on a night like this.'

'If you don't like it, you complain to the CO,' retorted one of the white caps. 'What else do you expect at this hour? We've been hanging around waiting for you when we should have been off duty.'

The angry words were accompanied by such a glare of resentment that the newcomers quickly picked up their plates and moved on.

With a wilting spam salad in one hand and a mug of tea in the other, Eileen and Veronica made their way to one of the tables. All the women were looking at one another apprehensively, prodding the limp vegetables with their forks, wondering just what they had got themselves into. They were rookies, raw recruits, the lowest of the low, and within ten minutes of their arrival at camp there was not one of them who did not feel exactly that.

The huts were all in a row. The new recruits had been collected, together with their luggage, and marched down the line, picking their way across the icy ground only by the white-painted stones which edged the slippery path. Women were directed towards the huts in order, but counted off at random. Veronica kept close beside Eileen as they were allocated to the first batch, just getting in before the sergeant cried,

'That's all. Move on to the next hut and be quick about it.'

The Nissen hut had double doors at the entrance, forming a kind of lobby with a door to a small separate room for their corporal. After the women had struggled into the hut with all their bags it seemed wonderfully warm and welcoming. There was a strong odour of floor polish and the pungent smell of burning coke from two iron stoves spaced out along it. Eileen saw that there were fifteen metal beds on each side and that one of these was already occupied.

She was a startling red head. She sat up in bed wearing a white nightdress and a loose, filmy wrap-over that would have cost Eileen at least three months' wages. On the locker by her bed were a collection of make-up and scent bottles, a mirror and a framed photograph. She had made herself completely at home, and had probably arrived on the earlier train.

'Well, hello there.' She put down her magazine and looked over at the new arrivals. 'Whatever kept you?'

'It's all right for some,' said a cheery voice. 'Picked yourself the best bed, did you?' Certainly the bed was right opposite a stove, strategically placed away from the draughts of the doorway.

'Well, naturally.' The large bright eyes regarded her bedraggled audience with amusement. 'Better take your coats off before you flood the place out.'

Eileen had found herself closest to her and therefore staked her claim to a bed by depositing her bag on the folded coarse grey blanket. Veronica quickly followed suit, taking the next bed, sitting down abruptly, as though to dare anyone else to try and take it from her.

'That's a nice dress,' came the voice from the bed.

Eileen turned to look at Veronica and saw that under her heavy winter coat she was wearing an expensive and well-cut dress in soft green wool that must have cost a pretty packet. The plainness of her coat had given no hint of what was obviously a very exclusive outfit and Eileen felt rather taken aback at the discovery that her new friend was well off.

'It's all I had,' explained Veronica obliquely, leaving both of them feeling even more curious.

'Well, if that was all I had I certainly wouldn't complain.' She pushed aside the bedcovers and swung her long legs over the edge, obviously eager to talk. Eileen noticed that her toe-nails were painted a brilliant red. 'Might as well get to know each other,' she suggested. 'My name's Moira Adams and I'm from London.'

8

'Eileen Howard. From Ross.'

'Where's that then?'

'On the Welsh border. It's very small really.'

Moira stared at her shrewdly. 'Yes, thought there was a bit of the old sing-song in your voice.' She passed her over and looked at Veronica. 'And what's yours?'

Eileen saw Veronica positively hesitate before she told her, but she need not have worried. Whatever curiosity and self-importance there was in Moira's nature she was not vindictive. Eileen saw that at once, and Eileen was now an expert at spotting the kind of trouble-maker who enjoyed slyly stirring the situation. She knew that Veronica Darling was safe enough, at least for the present.

'I used to know a bloke called Darling,' Moira told them. 'Quite a looker he was. Can't remember his name. Pete or Paul or something like that. Got any commercial travellers in your family, have you?'

'Not as far as I know,' Veronica said delicately, a pretty blush coming to her cheeks. Eileen, with a smile, saw that commercial travellers were likely as not the last people she would have in her family. Vicars were far more likely.

'So what does your old man do?'

'Daddy's in banking,' she replied, still embarrassed. 'And what do your people do?'

'My people?' Moira frowned. 'I live with my grandmother, so I suppose that doesn't count. And she does so much that I can't keep up with the old girl.'

'How do we make up these beds?' Eileen asked her suddenly, speaking up before their attention came round to her. She had discovered that a change of subject soon diverted interest.

'God knows,' said Moira. 'I just put everything on at once it was so bloody cold in here.'

Eileen found that what she presumed to be the mattress to the bed came in three attached sections. It looked pretty uncomfortable.

'I thought at least they would make up the beds for us,' said a woman on the opposite side of the hut. 'Whatever do they think we are? Housemaids?'

Eileen turned sharply aside and began to unpack her bags. She

9

emptied the old suitcase in a state of high agitation, unable to say a word.

'You'll have to change your ideas here,' someone told the woman who had complained. 'Just wait till you see the ablutions.'

'The what?'

'The karsie.'

'Blimey, where is it? I've been cross-legged ever since Wapping!'

'It's outside and to the right. It stands by itself, you can't miss it.'

'Outside?'

'No bathrooms en suite around here, ducks. Thirty cubicles in a row. And they've got half-doors so they can tell if you're skiving in there.'

'My dear, how primitive!'

'My dear!' aped the cockney, 'you ain't seen nothing yet.'

'OK, what's all this noise about then?'

The room fell silent and the women turned to see the newcomer in the hut, in battledress uniform with two stripes on her arm. She was no older than many of them, but she held herself erect and her voice was bossy.

'I'm your corporal and it's my misfortune to have to sort you out during your stay here.' She began to patrol down the centre of the hut, glancing from side to side and frowning. 'And what's all this?' She had stopped right in front of Moira's bed. 'Quite comfortable, are we?' The sarcasm in her voice matched her fiery eye. 'What's all this?' She flicked a hand in the direction of the locker. 'Not a blooming boudoir, you know. All that will have to go. Strictly regulation here. And those clothes. As from tomorrow you all get pyjamas, regulation striped pyjamas.'

There was a universal groan of disappointment.

'OK, OK, that's enough. I'll sort you all out in the morning. Reveille's at six sharp.' There was more outcry and the corporal actually grinned. 'So you better get your beauty sleep. Lights out at ten.' She turned back towards the door. 'And no hanky-panky. Because I've got my room just down there.' She indicated the room between the inner and outer doors. 'Get some shut-eye.'

Eileen's sudden apprehension was clearly mirrored now by her companions. A thoughtful silence fell over the hut as the women quickly made ready for the night. There were hurried and experimental manoeuvres with the bed and speedy visits across the white outside to see the ablutions in the snowlight. The lights went out automatically at ten, although some of the beds were still in chaos.

Eileen felt her way to the head of her bed and climbed inside, glad of the darkness which masked her. Although the hut was still full of movement it did not bother her as much as being overlooked by strangers. She knew that there were women from all kinds of diverse backgrounds there, that some of them would even have their own secrets to conceal. She guessed that the fact she did not want to talk about her own background did not make her unique. In her heart she already knew that she would have to learn to hide her feelings, to become less sensitive to stray remarks if she was to survive there.

In the night there were sounds of other restless bodies, of heavy sleepers and deep breathing. There was even the sound of faint sobbing from a bed near the door. Eileen finally drifted off to sleep with the comforting realisation that she was not alone in her depression over her past and her apprehension about her future.

When she woke again she thought the faint light of dawn was seeping under the blackout curtains and it was bitterly cold. But turning in the narrow little bed, she saw with astonishment that it was not the dawn at all. Moira Adams was already sitting up, a mirror in her hand, a torch on the cabinet, concentrating as she applied her make-up. The glow of the torchlight gave their part of the hut a rosy glow which suggested warmth although the temperature was down to zero. As though she sensed that Eileen was awake, Moira suddenly turned and gave her a radiant, wide-awake smile. One cheek was rouged, the other pale as marble. Eileen just gaped at her.

'Morning.'

'What time is it?' Eileen whispered, aware of the sleeping hut.

'Four-thirty.'

Eileen groaned. The woman was mad! She stared in undisguised amazement as Moira calmly went on making up her

11

face, putting on her lipstick and setting it with a powder puff. Then she turned her attention to her hair. Eileen snuggled down under the blankets and watched her from her nest, but Moira seemed unaware of the freezing temperature. She vigorously brushed her thick auburn hair and then drew a dark velvet ribbon round her head. With deft fingers she then rolled her hair round the ribbon, using great skill and precision as she smoothed and tucked, securing the creation with a fistful of hairpins. It took a good fifteen minutes, but looked magnificent. Eileen had seen the style on models in the latest magazines left lying around the house, but she had never seen anyone actually perform the ritual.

She must think a lot of herself, thought Eileen, half in admiration, half in amusement. I wonder why she does it?

Her thoughts about Moira were the last she remembered until an appalling metallic clanging noise woke her later. She opened her eyes to find the grinning corporal moving swiftly down the length of the hut, rattling the bed legs and shouting, 'Wakey-wakey, rise and shine!'

After trooping out again to the misery of the ablutions hut to wash and dress, they followed their corporal once more to the cookhouse. The vast building was teeming with women in uniform eagerly collecting plates of porridge and mugs of tea. It was so cold and they were so hungry that they would have eaten anything. Eileen saw that even the woman who had made the comments about housemaids did not complain.

The morning was a busy one, spent in learning how to make and stack their beds according to RAF regulations, learning that the sectionalised mattress was known in RAF slang as biscuits. They had to parade out in the falling snow before an officer who hid her face behind a high collar and then sent them off to collect their uniforms. Tunic, skirt, shirts and battledress. Greatcoat, peaked cap, rain cape. All piled up and carried on down the line. Not forgetting the infamous blackouts and twilights - enormous elasticated knickers, WAAF regulation, hideous. Striped pyjamas, thick lisle stockings and finally, on top, the black clodhopping shoes, hopefully the right size, stiff as boards, bound to cripple anyone for the first few weeks.

Back in the hut Eileen put her collection down on the bed and her eyes met Moira's and Veronica's and all three burst out laughing. Moira held up her skirt and groaned in despair. The waist was barely on her hips.

'Look, try mine.' Veronica held out the skirt she had been issued. 'You'd have to take in the waist but it's certainly long enough for you.'

They exchanged skirts and shared a grin.

'God knows what we'll look like in these,' said Moira cheerfully. 'What about the caps?' There was more laughter as she caught sight of Eileen almost drowning in hers. 'Come on, let me try. It might fit with my hair.' She took the cap and carefully put it on the back of her head so that the roll of hair fitted around it perfectly. 'Not bad, eh? I think I'll look quite something when I've done.'

All the badges and buttons on the uniforms had to be cleaned. They were an appalling green colour and it looked as though it would take hours to make any impression on them. The corporal hovered between the beds, showing them how to use the button-stick. Four or five buttons could be slotted into the stick at a time and then cleaned with Brasso.

Sitting around on their beds there was a clicking of buttons and a buzz of friendly conversation. Veronica, Moria and Eileen sat together taking up hems and taking in waists, using the regulation needles and thread from their canvas roll called a 'housewife'.

There were all kinds of women there from all classes. Many had volunteered through patriotism, wanting to do their bit for the war effort, but Eileen was interested to find that quite a number of them had joined simply out of economic necessity. They were down to train in all manner of jobs, and it was obvious that they would have to split up into their groups at some later point.

'We only stay here four or five days,' someone told them. 'Then we have basic training – that's square-bashing.'

'I wonder when we get round to learning our jobs? I'm going to be an R/T operator.'

'What's that?'

'Haven't a clue, but it sounded interesting when they told me I'd be working with the pilots!'

In their small groups they were tentative about getting to

13

know one another, aware that they might be separated again.

'What did you do before?'

'I was a typist. It was just something to do until I get married.'

'So what did you put down for?'

'Clerk, what else can I do?'

'What about driving?'

'Oh, I didn't think they'd take girls.'

Eileen saw the smug expression on Moira's face. 'Are you going to drive, too?'

Moira's face lit up. 'You bet. Anyone else?'

They were both rather pleasantly surprised when Veronica said that she too was going to train as a WAAF driver. Her nervousness had obviously misled them because she added humbly,

'My father taught me to drive last year. Only a small Austin, of course, but it's good fun.'

Moira and Eileen exchanged looks of envy. It was unsettling to think that timid Veronica was already one step ahead of them. But none of the other women had thought of driving. Eileen was shocked. She did not agree that war work should be defined by sex. She sincerely thought that anyone who was young enough and capable of learning a trade should be where there was work to be done. The Government had said that no skilled person was to do what could be done by an unskilled person, and that no man was to do what could be done by a woman

To Eileen the war offered a chance to try new things, an opportunity to get on in life. She could not understand those women who had opted for jobs like cooking or typing which were traditionally women's work. Surely, she thought, in wartime things should change? All those old ideas should go by the board and women ought to get a chance to show just what they could do.

The next day they paraded before the officer in their new uniforms. They were all terribly proud of the work they had done in order to make their uniforms more fashionable. Some women wore their peaked caps jauntily at an angle or, like Moira, on the backs of their heads. The officer, whom they had to call Ma'am, just walked down the line of recruits and yanked their caps straight down on their heads.

14

Something about Veronica's appearance seemed to set Ma'am off in a temper. She stopped when she came upon her in the line-up and made some quite inaudible remark which caused Veronica to blush to the roots of her hair. Watching out of the corner of her eye, Eileen felt for her friend, though she thought the officer had probably picked her out at random in order to demonstrate her authority to the rest of them. They had quickly discovered that in the Forces life could be very far from just.

The four days at camp passed in almost sub-zero temperatures. By morning the stoves in their huts were dead and the air was freezing from the ice which had formed inside the windows. One morning they had to dig their way out through the main door after an especially heavy snowfall. Coal was rationed as supplies could not get through on blocked roads after the blizzard. It was so cold that at night, as soon as the lights went out, they would leap out of bed and get dressed in their greatcoats, balaclavas and socks before getting back in to try and sleep.

Their days were spent in attending endless lectures on everything from air-raid precautions and the merits of secrecy to long and boring talks on daily routine orders, called DROs. More illuminating were the medical lectures, especially on the dangers of VD. For many women from sheltered backgrounds this was a first insight into sex, and seemed to raise more questions than it answered. Of the trio, only Moira seemed to think VD had its humorous side.

'Some chance round here,' she said gloomily. 'Not a man for miles.'

It was therefore nothing but a relief to everyone when they were told by the officer that they would be travelling the next day by train up to Morecambe in Lancashire for their initial training period.

'Old Jenkins told me we've got nothing to smile about,' said Moira once they were back in their hut packing. 'She says it's worse than here.'

'Impossible,' they all said together.

The prospect of Morecambe, which some of them remembered from holiday posters, gave them all considerable cheer and they were in high spirits as they began to pack up their kits for the next day's journey.

★

15

All Morecambe Bay stretched before them, a desolate and frozen wasteland as far as the eye could see. The bitter north wind cut through their uniform greatcoats and they were chilled to the bone long before they reached the house to which they had been allocated. It had come as something of a surprise to discover that in Morecambe they were to be divided out into small groups and billeted among the seaside landladies on the front. Veronica had clung protectively to the side of Eileen and Moira as the sergeant from the local depot marched them down the wind-blown street in a ragged line.

'What a shower!' she exclaimed at the sight of them. 'Try and keep together, for Crissake. I've got no bloody time to come looking for stray sheep. If you get lost, you blooming well stay lost as far as I'm concerned.'

All along the route she stopped to consult a clipboard with lists of boarding-houses and the number of recruits each landlady could take.

'You, you and you,' she announced, separating the nearest with an ungentle shove. 'Eight sharp tomorrow morning at the depot. Got it?'

When it came to Eileen and her little group they were lucky.

'Three of you,' said the sergeant, stopping outside a green front door with a brass letterbox which had recently been polished.

Moira pushed Eileen and Veronica forward until they were all three right under the sergeant's nose and could not be ignored.

'Righto, you three. Tomorrow eight sharp.'

Their landlady was a Mrs Nightingale, a cheerful widow. She was a dwarf of a woman who wore her colourful hair piled high on her head to give the impression of another five or six inches of height. Eyes of a startling blue blinked up at her three frozen lodgers full of eager curiosity. She bustled them inside and their eyes opened in surprise at the Aladdin's Cave of her home. The sitting-room was a treasure house of souvenirs and mementoes. There were shell baskets from Brighton and clay pipes from Cornwall, garishly bright dolls dressed in national costumes and glass cabinets full of glass and ceramics inscribed with place names.

'From my guests,' she explained humbly, beaming at them over the teacups. 'Won't you have some more tea, girls?'

They successfully fended off her interrogation without giving offence. Mrs Nightingale was enjoying their company immensely. They could almost see her boasting to her friends and neighbours of her wartime lodgers. Overall, she gave Eileen the impression of a good natured dormouse, bustling round her guests, asking interminable questions.

They found that they were to share one large bedroom on the second floor under the eaves of the house. It was clean and comfortable, over-decorated in homely chintz, but they were pleased that they already knew one another because of the closeness of the space.

It was only that evening, as they sat in this room taking refuge from the gale blowing outside on the seafront, that Eileen realised how little they had told one another of their backgrounds. She mentioned this almost without thinking but the others gave her rather sheepish smiles. She saw that now they would all be required to say something about their former lives, and already she regretted her easy remark.

Typically it was Moira who volunteered to tell them something about herself. She said she was from London, from a district called Finsbury which neither of the others knew. To Eileen, who had never been to the capital city, this conjured up an image of immense sophistication and worldliness. She knew that Londoners had all the opportunities, that everything was available to them from a real choice of jobs to all kinds of entertainment and education. She could not imagine what it must be like to be brought up in such a place, somewhere where everyone really had a chance to make something of their lives.

Moira had been brought up with her grandmother, whose photograph she carried around from place to place to sit proudly on her bedside table or locker like a religious talisman. Eileen imagined that Moira's parents must be dead, although she never said as much. She said nothing at all about them or the circumstances of her going to live with Lily, this marvellous woman who was almost seventy. Moira obviously loved and admired her very much and called her Lily, which Eileen thought was very unusual and rather progressive. Moira told them that Lily had been a rebel all her life, that she had once been a suffragette and was now a local councillor and very active in the

17

borough. The image of the one solitary lady councillor in Ross sprung immediately into Eileen's mind, with her large flowery hat and long white gloves and handbag. Was Moira's Lily just like that? Formidable, ample women, poking their noses into other's business, do-gooding and sanctimonious, all Tories, of course. Looking at the photograph next to Moira's bed, Eileen could not reconcile this image with the intelligence and humour of the face staring back at her. Lily Cox looked like a woman she would want to meet.

'So why did you join up, Moira?'

'To get a husband.' She spoke without hesitation but she was laughing as though it was a joke. Yet there was something in her face, something in her eyes that told Eileen to tread warily, that to Moira this was nothing to joke about. To her it seemed that the subject was a serious matter, perhaps even of desperation.

Eileen saw that Moira was hiding something from them under her mask of brash confidence, that she used her looks and assurance to keep people at a distance. This seemed in marked contrast with Veronica, who always seemed very tense and shy but was adept at pulling surprises out of the bag. Eileen asked her about her own background.

'My family live in Tunbridge Wells,' she replied after a moment's thought, as though she was trying to give a compact answer. 'I didn't go to school but had a governess who came to the house every day. I suppose we were well-off.' She looked up at them suddenly. 'But don't think I had an easy time of it. My parents were very strict. They believed in self-sufficiency and discipline. They had rules about everything. I suppose I had rather a sheltered childhood.'

She sat back on her bed and they assumed that she had finished her account. Certainly they did not expect anything more; her information fitted in perfectly with the impression they had formed of her in their minds. But Veronica, as ever, surprised them. She reached inside the collar of her shirt and pulled out a fine gold chain on which hung a ring, the diamonds flashing in the lamplight.

Moira's eyes opened wide at what was obviously an engagement ring.

'Tim and I got engaged last Easter,' she told them. 'His family and mine know one another, so I suppose you could say it was all arranged for us. It's my luck that we really do like each other.' She blushed again. 'I don't know how I could be so lucky.'

Eileen could see that Moira was looking rather cynical. A photograph of Tim Barton was duly produced and as they gathered around it was a handsome and friendly face which smiled out at them above a Territorial Army uniform.

'It was taken just before he was called up.' A shadow of sadness had fallen over Veronica as she hunched forward on her bed.

'He's a smasher.' Moira whistled in respect, somewhat awed by Veronica's catch. 'What are you doing in this place when you could be with him?'

'He's in France,' said Veronica in a low, painful voice that said it all.

To break the uneasy silence which had suddenly descended, Moira turned her attention to Eileen, seemingly unaware of her reluctance to talk.

'And what about you then, Eileen?'

'There's not much to tell,' lied Eileen with a self-deprecating shrug of her shoulders. 'I'll be twenty next month, and I come from a small country town. My Dad used to work on the railway but he had this accident and now he stays at home.'

'And your mother?'

'I don't remember my mother at all. She died a long time ago.'

There was a moment's silence.

'Is that all?' Moira did not disguise her disappointment. 'Didn't you work or do anything?'

'I used to keep house,' Eileen answered evasively and lapsed again into silence as though to show them that she was not prepared to say anything more.

But that night she felt a pang of conscience that she had not been more honest with them. They were her friends, after all. And even if they had not been totally honest themselves, she was certain that they had not actually lied to her. She was overcome by an uncomfortable sense of guilt that kept her from sleeping. She was suddenly irrationally homesick for Ross and the open countryside as she had not been for a year or more.

The thought of the Wye bounded by lush meadows, green forests and sandstone cliffs filled her head as she tossed and turned in the sleeping room. She saw again the view from Symonds Yat, she remembered the slender spire of St Mary's and the bustle there had been on market days. She saw herself, tearful and yet half-excited by the prospect of leaving Ross behind her, sitting on the steps of the Plague Cross in the sheltered churchyard, wondering when she would ever be back again.

She almost fooled herself that she loved and missed her father. Suffering all the sharp intensities of childhood, she suddenly found herself longing for the sight of her mother. Tears filled her eyes, anger mingling with pain at her own perversity. Her mother had been lost long ago. There was no way of ever bringing her back.

Her mother was a memory which could only be conjured by a great concentration of will. Faint images flickered into view and then were gone. Like a magic lantern slide show the pictures were there, faint and tantalising on the edge of her memory, to haunt her. She remembered her most of all in the cluttered little kitchen of their home, bent over the scrubbed wooden table, shelling peas into a colander, peas drumming against the metal. Or basting meat on a Sunday after chapel, or the click of her needles as winter approached. But it was always a back view, always her back hunched over some domestic task, or the sight of her frail figure, the sound of her cough. Never a glimpse of her face. Her mother's face always eluded her, as though to reject her all over again.

Then there was only Dada.

Eileen knew that her whole future could have been eaten away with looking after her father, had not Rose Williams turned up and relieved her of this burden. Rose was the sister of an old family friend, a trained nurse who was used to looking after rich geriatrics in their own homes. She had made a tidy little sum in this way it was said, what with being left bits and pieces in their wills after they died. She was between jobs when she was introduced to Eileen's father and began to look in on him daily.

Eileen could not help feeling that this other woman, so much older and more experienced, was stepping into her home and taking over. In her crisp white dresses, Rose Williams intimidated her. She criticised the way she ran the house, she moved the furniture and ordered special food for Dada's diet, and told her that he must have his room always at a certain temperature. She was constantly fussing about him, straightening his sheets and rearranging his bolsters and pillows. Everything that Eileen did never seemed quite right and always needed Rose's final touch of correction. She felt a sense of rivalry, of growing outrage that this prim and officious woman was trying to take over from her mother.

Only now did Eileen realise that without Rose Williams she might never have had the chance to break away from that restrictive home life.

Just before she had joined up Eileen had received a letter from Rose Williams announcing that she and her father had married. Eileen was surprised by her own reaction to the news. Coming when it did in her own life, her father's remarriage was less of a shock and no longer a betrayal. She found that she was even grateful to Rose for taking on the burden of looking after her father, leaving her free to do as she pleased with her own life, to join the WAAF. Although she knew that Rose had been contriving to marry her father all along, she now saw that she did so to get out of service in other people's houses. She could now sympathise with her, knowing that her own problems were resolved, knowing that the WAAF and the war had given her a similar chance.

The WAAF was to be a new beginning for Eileen and she had consciously made the decision to break off old ties. She did not write any more to her father and Rose, or to any of her relations. It was therefore something of a shock to receive a letter the following evening at Mrs Nightingale's with a Buckinghamshire postmark.

Turning over the letter in her fingers, she recognised Aunt Meg's fine handwriting at once and hesitated before opening the envelope. A sense of deep foreboding made her hesitate, a feeling that her past had returned to haunt and torment her, even here in the incongruous setting of a boarding house overlooking Morecambe Bay.

She eventually tore at the envelope, deciding it was wiser to know the worse at once in order to dismiss it more quickly from her mind. This intrusion from the past alarmed and irritated her, but as soon as she saw the contents she knew there was little to fear.

Her aunt had written just a brief line or two, a simple covering

21

note to explain the letter she was forwarding to her. Eileen turned the second envelope over. The familiar blue paper and its markings reawakened sudden, bitter memories which banished any fear. She was angry now and for a second was tempted to throw his damned letter away unopened and unread.

Instead, hearing Moira and the others coming down to supper, she thrust the crumpled envelope deep into her skirt pocket, out of sight but not out of mind for long. Over boiled egg and toast, the letter lay next to her flesh, almost physical in its presence at the supper table.

'Are you feeling all right, my dear?' It was Mrs Nightingale, always so quick to notice the least little change in 'her girls'.

'Oh yes, I'm fine, thanks. Just a little tired perhaps.' But she saw that her lame excuse had not satisfied her landlady and was aware of the old lady's sharp blue eyes coming back to her throughout the meal.

Later she went upstairs and locked herself in the cold and cramped little bathroom at the back of the house. She drew out the letter and stared at it with undisguised hostility. From the postmark she saw that he was still at Chester, or had been when the letter was posted, because it had clearly been some time on its travels. Unfolding the thick wad of closely-written pages, she saw at once that he knew nothing of her recent history, that he had assumed her life continued in a constant pattern of drudgery.

His pleasant and open style irritated her where once it had delighted her, taking her out of her surroundings and sharing experiences that she could only dream about. He sounded self-assured to her now, complacent. His news and views were suddenly bitterly unwelcome as she recalled with burning resentment the trouble his letters had caused her.

So, he was flying solo, and it was a wonderful experience to be free. So, he felt 'at home' and had found a natural skill in flying, a sense of purpose. She was unmoved.

She scanned the pages with a cold eye, uninterested in Mr Gareth James. She saw that the war had touched him lightly, that the RAF were now turning out pilots with an increasing sense of urgency. He said that the whole process was being speeded up. So different, he wrote, from the leisurely club days at Cambridge. As she scanned the pages she found herself seeking news, not of his day to day activities, that did not interest her at all, but news that would awaken all the old memories. And finally she found it, the one word she had been looking for:

'Jonathan has already received his posting,' he wrote. 'They won't let me say where but it doesn't look as though we will stay together now' – and that was all.

The bitter irony of it all made Eileen sick with shame. She crumpled forward, leaning over the hand-basin, and let the cold water run. The sight and sound of the water swirling in the chipped basin was a strange comfort. She dared not look in the mirror, knowing already that her face burned with the force of her renewed memories as she relived that time over again. She did not know how long she stood there, watching the water, lulled by the soothing sound. Finally she forced herself to move. Raising her head, she ran a hand over her fevered face, scarcely recognising herself. She dashed her hot cheeks with cupped handfuls of freezing water and instantly felt better. But she knew that it was not over. She knew that she would remember, and go on remembering, the nightmare of her life at Charnwood.

Chapter Two

She first saw him that Christmas of 1938, just weeks after she had arrived at Charnwood. The Pemberleys were holding a grand festive house party. Everyone who was anyone in the county would be there. A steady procession of cars began to arrive on Christmas Eve and there was an air of expectation as the house began to fill with strange voices.

For a lowly third housemaid the sight of these guests drew Eileen like a magnet to the upper windows of the house. Dot was at her side. Dot, the second housemaid and her immediate senior within the service hierarchy. They watched with awe and a kind of incredulity as a succession of Rileys and Bentleys deposited the chosen ones at the pillared porch of Charnwood House where Schofield the butler was poised to greet them.

These fine, powdered ladies, well-wrapped in a variety of handsome animal pelts against the cold, accompanied by their starkly dressed escorts, husbands, fathers or brothers, were like nothing Eileen had ever seen in her life before. Pale face and scarlet lips were the fashion among women as strange to her as alien and fantastic beings. Piles of monogrammed calfskin luggage were waved away with the dismissive and unseeing calm of a class which has never doubted its right to attention. While Schofield led the way up into the main entrance hall, the footmen were left to struggle in their careless wake with all the necessities of the life led by their masters. Colonel Pemberley had arranged a shoot for the gentleman and his guests had come prepared.

Loud snorts of laughter and exclamations floated upwards from the frivolous pleasure-seekers to the housemaids fetching and carrying above. Dot was the herald, announcing every new arrival. She could recognise the majority of guests and gave potted histories which included all the scandal and a great deal of innuendo.

Eileen stared with envy and admiration as the Pemberleys' daughter Honor stepped out of her car trailing a silver fox fur and paused, waiting for her husband to escort her into the house. She was as perfect as the faded picture Dot had clipped from the Tatler had suggested. Her blonde hair was waved and as she moved there was a flash of jewels. She stood there, curling the high collar of the fur against her pale cheek, her eyes languorous. Eileen could not imagine what life must be like for a woman like Honor Pemberley, or Honor Darcy as she must now be called following her recent marriage.

From the other side of the car came a large man in a dark city suit, large in every way, tall and powerful yet moving with fluidity and complete self-assurance. For a brief moment his glance flashed up across the façade of the house as though some movement had caught his eye. Although she knew it was impossible, Eileen felt that their position had been observed and she hastily drew back from the window and continued sorting the laundry.

This uneasy sense of guilt, at having been found out, was not easily dispelled. She left Dot at the window to record the next arrivals, but eventually her curiosity was caught by her sudden excited cry,

'Look, Eileen, it's him, it's Mr Jonathan.'

Below in the courtyard a smart little MG sports car had pulled up and two young men were busy unloading their luggage even before Schofield and the footmen could hurry down the steps from the house.

The two young men could scarcely have been more different in appearance. One was as dark as the other was fair. His face was gaunt while the other's was broad and tanned, undeniably healthy. One look at his blond athleticism left Eileen in no doubt as to his identity. Jonathan Pemberley was as perfect as his elder sister, his light brown hair flecked with gold as though he spent his time at Cambridge out of doors, not cramped over his books in some dark library like his friend.

He strode across the courtyard carrying his own luggage, moving with easy graceful strides, broad-shouldered and loose-limbed, a real sportsman. His was a strong face, rather blunt in feature, not the finely boned face of an aristocrat. All Mrs Pemberley's blue blood must have gone into her daughter, for Jonathan had all the style and physical presence of far humbler origins.

As one of the footmen insisted on relieving him of his bags, Jonathan's face broke into an infectious smile and, watching him from above, Eileen's heart stopped. The broad grin took her breath away. He was undeniably the most handsome man she had ever seen. It was corny, it was ridiculous, but as she stood there just staring down on him she knew there was some significance in this first sight of him.

Compared with him his unknown friend, so dour and dark, faded away into the background. She had eyes for no one else, and yet she was horribly embarrassed by the realisation that he attracted her. She knew she was being absurd but her awareness, the impact of his magnetic draw, struck her with a strange sense of *déjà vu*. She had no wish to be the butt of jokes. She was already acquainted with Dot's ready tongue and knew that she must hide her interest from everyone round her. They must never suspect what she already knew instinctively was no shallow emotion.

'Have you ever seen anyone like him?' Dot fairly drooled with enthusiasm and undisguised admiration. But Eileen's silence seemed to irritate her. 'Well? Cat got your tongue?'

'He's all right,' Eileen said with measured reluctance in what she hoped was a neutral tone of voice, but when she saw Dot was looking at her strangely she decided she had not been casual enough to deceive her. 'He's all right if you like them fair,' she added carelessly, 'but I like them dark.'

'Then you can have his friend,' Dot told her with a broad grin as if her fantasy was one enormous joke.

Eileen had joined the WAAF to get out of service at Charnwood. A year in service had been ample time for her to discover that her father, however well meaning, had made a mistake in sending her there.

Her father had put her into service in the same household where her aunt, his sister, was the cook. He told her that it would be a good opportunity for her. Yes, he said he was doing the best for her. At home, trapped in a tiny house looking after an invalid father was no kind of future for a young girl, and when her aunt suggested the situation as third housemaid at Charnwood House, Eileen had jumped at the thought of going to Buckinghamshire.

Arriving at Charnwood station in the weeks before Christmas 1938, Eileen had felt she was on the threshold of a new life. Clouds of white steam billowed out over the tiny railway platform as the local train shunted off down the line, leaving her standing there with her luggage. Eileen had never been away from her home in the Welsh border country but there was no fear or hesitation as she set out along the platform with her bags, ready for her first adventure.

Outside, in the station forecourt, a large black limousine stood waiting for her. Her heart beating wildly, she saw a smart young man in soft grey uniform and peaked cap move forward to meet her. His face was shadowed, his expression hidden, but there could be no doubt about the sullen contempt in his voice as he addressed her.

'You for Charnwood? You're late.'

He grasped the bags out of her hands and tossed them into the cavernous boot of the car, slamming it closed and stalking back across the gravel to the driving seat.

'Well, get in,' he told her abruptly, but made no attempt to open the door for her.

She had scarcely seated herself before the powerful engine burst into life and the car was jerking forward out of the station yard and into the busy main street of the country town.

Nothing had prepared her for the grandeur of Charnwood House. The two mile long drive afforded ample opportunity to take in the rolling parkland beyond the lodge gates and the expanse of shining water of the manmade lake. Set on a hill in the midst of this beauty stood the house, a square Georgian mansion with bold colonnades supporting a majestic portico. Charnwood House dominated the Buckinghamshire landscape, dwarfing the estate cottages and farm buildings at the rear, lording it over the town in the valley.

As the car drove past, Eileen saw the enormous main doors were firmly shut, She was taken round the side of the house to the servants' entrance. Here was another courtyard with stables and old coach-houses. Thomas, for that was the chauffeur's name, fetched her bags from the car and deposited them at an open doorway and then drove the car out of sight.

Eileen was reunited with her aunt in the kitchen. It was a long room dominated by the massive kitchen range. It was many years since Eileen had seen Meg Howard. Not since her mother's funeral, when her aunt had come down to take care of the child. At home she was always mentioned with warmth and respect ever afterwards. Although she had never married – a fact which would have earned her pity or scorn had she stayed in her home town – she had a reputation in Ross because of her professional status. Everyone seemed to know that she worked for the best of families and Eileen was proud that she should be given the opportunity to join her aunt in whatever capacity. But Eileen was soon made to realise her lowly position in the hierarchy of servants at Charnwood. She was third housemaid, with two others above her. There were also three kitchen maids, two parlour maids, a head housemaid, one lady's maid – Miss Hunter – as well as Schofield the butler, Meg the cook, Thomas the chauffeur/valet, two footmen, one kitchen boy, an odd man to do the rough work like bringing in wood and coal for the fires, eight gamekeepers and many other daily labourers.

Aunt Meg welcomed her very formally before Schofield the butler, aware of her own favoured position within the household, but privately she softened considerably and Eileen came to call her Meg. In the kitchen she was queen. Among the huge copper pans, the larders and the range, she commanded her staff with all the precision of a military leader. Her timing was the result of years of experience of the whims of the Pemberleys, and her cooking was deservedly famous.

Eileen shared a tiny room with Dot, the second housemaid, up in the roof of the house, and it was the friendly local girl who put her wise about the ways of service. Fear of Schofield and deference to Miss Hunter were early lessons that kept Eileen out of too much trouble in those first hectic weeks.

Leading the way up the staircase to their quarters, Dot pointed

28

out the other rooms on the servants' floor. From the kitchen a long corridor led to the staff hall where the servants all ate together. The butler's pantry was off this room, along with rooms for cleaning the silver and arranging flowers. All these quarters were divided from the main house by huge doors, as though they inhabited a separate world. Neither were there carpets on any of the stone floors or staircases. It seemed as though the Pemberleys had one standard for their part of Charnwood House and quite another for their servants'.

The maids slept two to a room. Only Miss Hunter and Meg had their own rooms. Schofield had his own flat at the top of the house, well away from the rest.

Eileen found her uniform laid out for her in the bedroom. She eagerly held up the black dress with its long white apron and frilled cap.

'Don't get carried away,' said Dot. 'The cost of that lot will come out of your pay.'

Her thirty shillings a month suddenly did not seem such a fortune any more.

On her first morning at Charnwood, Eileen was taken to a huge room with a massive bed under a lace canopy. Across the vast distance between the door and the bed, Eileen saw a figure lying propped up among the pillows. Mrs Pemberley was taking breakfast in bed and hardly looked up as Schofield announced that this was her new third housemaid.

'Are you afraid of hard work?' She was an angular woman with long pale hair crimped into rippling waves. She was frowning, concentrating as she decapitated her boiled egg. She clearly did not require a reply and continued smoothly, 'You will have a good home here as long as you prove to be satisfactory.'

Schofield tapped Eileen on the shoulder and Eileen bobbed a curtsey, mumbling, 'Thank you, Madam,' before she was hurried out of the room by the butler.

That was the only time that Eileen actually talked to her employer for more than a year. Her duties were designed to make sure their paths never crossed; it was as though they inhabited separate worlds. The servants were never allowed in the main house when the family were about. Eileen only got a glimpse of the world upstairs, seeing Madam out in the grounds whistling up her dogs, all chows.

According to the gossip in the servants' hall, Mrs Pemberley came from a minor branch of an ancient ducal house. She was by all accounts cold and hard but as Miss Hunter pointed out to anyone who would listen, life had not been easy for the colonel's wife.

Colonel Pemberley was in a wheelchair as the result of an accident when playing polo in India. Madam had brought husband and children home and started a new, more isolated life. She had brought their daughter Honor out into society by herself and never let her husband forget it. She treated the colonel with open contempt but icy politeness. The colonel was very bad tempered. You could hear him bellowing all over the house, Dot said. He could not move without Thomas the valet. He had to be carried down stairs and put to bed. It was hard on Thomas but he had a good life, travelling everywhere with the family, spending months abroad.

Life at Charnwood was a hard round of drudgery for Eileen. Her day began at six am and went on until nine thirty at night with only two hours' break in the afternoon when she was so tired she had to sleep. She had just half a day off a week, but had to be back by eight thirty unless she was accompanied by another member of staff. She got a half-day Sunday once a month.

Eileen could remember the routine in every detail: housework all morning, laying fires before breakfast, then after the family was up, making the beds and cleaning bathrooms. The drudgery of cleaning with harsh, homemade mixtures, using her bare hands, of scrubbing acres of stone-flagged floors, of polishing miles of corridors and hand-brushing acres of carpets on one's knees. Madam was a terror. She checked the house personally, using a white lace handkerchief to find dust on the top of cupboards or under plant pots. If there was any, the housemaids were in trouble. But why spend money on the new household machines when servants were so cheap and when there were still a million unemployed after the recession. Jobs were hard to find.

It was the same routine every day – even Christmas. When there were guests the huge banqueting hall was opened up for grand dinner parties, and extra bedrooms had to be made ready. All the rooms were known by their colours: Green, Blue, Amber, Wedgwood, Black Lacquer, Chinese Lacquer. All the rooms had Adam ceilings and fireplaces, though the dining-room was the most famous. In the gallery hung four tapestries depicting spring, summer, autumn and winter, but so dark with age that the designs were virtually indistinguishable.

Everywhere there were flowers. One of the under-gardeners brought fresh-cut flowers to the house every day, no matter what the season. Sometimes Madam would arrange them herself. The grounds were always bright with blooms, and were especially noted for their azaleas in the springtime.

All the food at Charnwood came from the home farm. In season, pheasants were shot and brought in to hang until they were 'high'. Similarly, it was the tradition to leave Stilton cheeses covered in cloth which had been soaked in stout until they seethed with cheese mites. To Eileen this was disgusting, but Meg assured her that the family considered these delicacies as a natural part of their standard of living.

This standard included a round of regular society events: the hunt gathered outside to drink the stirrup cup once a month, there were bridge nights, tennis and shooting parties. But at Christmas the houseparty was something special. Family and friends assembled from far and near for a week or more of extravagance, as though they all sensed that this Christmas was one to remember, the last of the old style, the end of an era.

After dinner had finished upstairs and coffee and liqueurs had been served, Schofield would join the others in the servants' hall to carve their own joint. The food was very good. When too much was served upstairs they often had the left over turkey or side of beef at supper. Often only a couple of slices had been cut from it. The family would never have the same food served to them twice. To Eileen this was almost wicked. She was horrified to discover that there were people who were so wealthy that they could afford to throw food away.

Eileen could remember the night the butler had returned to the supper table in a high temper, his face indignant as though he personally had been abused.

'What's the matter, Mr Schofield?' asked Meg on behalf of the

31

rest of the table, the only one with status to approach him.

He attacked the beef aggressively, still rigid with anger. There was very little Christmas cheer about him.

'Oh, Mrs Howard,' he began – all cooks were 'Mrs' in respect of their position – 'Mrs Howard, you have no idea of the scene I have just witnessed upstairs. That so-called friend of Mr Jonathan's talking back to his betters.'

Eileen was immediately interested, hearing him mention Jonathan Pemberley's name.

'You would think that a gentleman up at Cambridge would know how to conduct himself at table instead of attacking Miss Honor's husband.'

'Attacking Mr Hayden?' It was Miss Hunter who spoke, her tiny eyes eager for scandal.

'Verbally, of course. Over politics.' He spoke the word with extreme distaste as though such a subject was something disreputable, too vulgar to be mentioned amid the crystal chandeliers and candles in the Adam dining-room. 'They were discussing Spain,' continued Schofield. 'Mr Jonathan's friend said some dreadful things about our Members of Parliament letting down the Spaniards. He said they had cheered when they heard that ships taking food to Spain had been bombed. Of course, Mr Hayden put him right.'

'Mr Hayden will know what he's talking about, as he's from London,' Miss Hunter announced authoritatively. Eileen remembered that she was a Londoner. 'And he has been abroad. He and Miss Honor took their honeymoon on the Continent.'

'In Germany,' said Meg, dropping the word coolly into the conversation.

Eileen looked from her aunt to the butler and back again. Schofield started passing plates piled with beef down the table, concentrating on his task and scowling.

'Well, Mrs Howard, let's not be hasty. Now that Mr Chamberlain has got the better of that Hitler person I'm sure everything will come out right. From what I've heard the Germans are a civilised and decent people. I'm sure none of us wants a war.'

'No, there are some of us who seem quite happy to join up with Hitler and his gang,' retorted Meg, going red in the face. 'Look at that dreadful Mosley man, not to speak of some who ought to know better.'

Eileen realised she was referring to some very notable people in the Royal Family and in Government, but the innuendo was enough.

'Really, Mrs Howard, I hardly think this is the right sort of thing to discuss in front of younger, more impressionable members of the staff.' He cast a warning eye round the lower end of the table. 'Just get on with your dinner, all of you. We at least know how to behave at our meal.'

'Well,' said Miss Hunter acidly, 'what can you expect from the son of a draper? Mr Jonathan should pick his friends with more care. One of his own sort.'

The servants never got their Christmas until three or four days after the rest of the world. The family joined in this belated event, trooping downstairs to the servants' hall with set smiles to stare at their servants all dressed up to eat their Christmas pudding, and to pour them a glass of wine so that they could drink the health of their employers. The Pemberleys and their guests would stare at them as though they were beings of another world. Which indeed they were.

Over Christmas Eileen was constantly aware of Jonathan Pemberley although their paths never crossed. Occasionally she would catch a glimpse of him from a window on his way somewhere in his smart MG, or hear a voice in the house which she believed was his. She knew he was there and the thought was tantalising. Her fascination was as remote and improbable as a crush on a film star and yet she nursed her passion to herself in dread that Dot or Meg would one day discover it. But the divisions of class were quite enough to keep them apart, their worlds divided although in the same house.

It was part of Eileen and Dot's duties to make up the bedroom given to Miss Honor and her husband, Hayden Darcy. They would take the opportunity to gaze in rapture at the gowns in the wardrobe, a fantasy of silk and chiffon far beyond their dreams. Miss Honor was known to be especially finicky about her clothes. She was waited on by Miss Hunter when she stayed at

Charnwood and as she insisted that everything was pressed before she wore it, the lady's maid was very busy, ironing even her silk stockings. Miss Hunter took pleasure in making herself out to be a martyr to everyone below stairs.

Just off the Amber bedroom was an adjacent dressing-room where Mr Hayden hung his clothes. In this small room there was a divan which he could use if he was not sharing his wife's bed. Dot took a wicked pleasure in noting how many times during their visit Miss Honor had thrown her husband out at night, for she had to make the dressing room bed. She pointed out a glass jar on a shelf in this room and nudged Eileen in the ribs.

'Looks like those are a waste of time here.'

It was some time before Eileen had understood the purpose for which Hayden Darcy kept his jar full of French letters.

Summoned by the bell in Miss Honor's room Eileen had no idea of what awaited her. Of Miss Honor there was no sign but her husband was there, resplendent in a quilted brocade dressing-gown and, as it turned out, nothing else. The brocade swung freely about his oddly smooth legs as he moved in on her. As he leant with his hand against the wall beside her head she had a glimpse of heavy white thighs as unappetising as uncooked chicken drumsticks. His handsome face hovered just inches from hers and his breath smelt of violets. For the rest of her life the smell of violets was enough to conjure up the whole incident again and to nauseate her.

Later she could not even remember what it was he had whispered in her ear. Probably she had not really understood his suggestion, but she was certainly left in no doubt of his intentions. When his hand touched her she jumped as though from electric shock, but for a moment it seemed he was oblivious of her horror, taking her reaction blindly for consent. Her cap slid off her hair as he strained her backwards against the wall and she thought he mumbled something about her age as he bent to kiss her. But that was too much. She thrust an arm up across his throat, pushing him aside.

She was well aware that it was an awkward situation. This was no village boy trying it on one night after the pictures. This was

Mr Darcy, son of an important banker, Miss Honor's husband, one of the Family. No telling him to get lost. One word to the Pemberleys and she would be out of a job. He had all the power, and of course he knew it. No doubt that was part of the attraction. Perhaps he even saw it as part of her duties, or had found others more accommodating. Perhaps even Dot...

'What's wrong?' he had asked her. 'What are you afraid of?' He stood looking down at her but he was not angry. Rather he seemed to find her confusion amusing and as she wrenched open the door into the hallway his laughter rang in her ears. He stood there in the open doorway, holding out her cap, mocking her, so that she had to turn back and seize it out of his hands, hurriedly trying to readjust her uniform.

She felt ashamed, alarmed. She knew that she would tell no one, that any attempt to explain the incident could so easily be turned on its head against her. It was ironic to think that even then she had instinctively realised the whole business could reverberate on her, the innocent party. She knew that in future she would take the greatest care to avoid any compromising situations.

What she did not know then was that she and Hayden Darcy had been observed, and that already a false connotation had been put on the incident.

But the repercussions of the affair were to come later. Eileen saw Hayden and his wife drive away after the New Year with a feeling of relief. She even felt some sympathy for the Pemberleys' elegant daughter who, according to Dot's tally, had kept her husband out of her bed every night of their stay at Charnwood.

She was less content to see Jonathan go. As 1939 arrived Jonathan and his university friend made ready to return to Cambridge. The draper's son, Gareth James, had done nothing to rectify his reputation below stairs and was generally regarded as an oddity. Jonathan seemed to like him though. They were always in each other's company and Eileen felt a pang of jealousy when she saw them together as they left.

After the guests had all gone the house was uncanny in its silence. For a complete week activity slowed down, but it was not for long. The Pemberleys always went away to Switzerland from January to April to stay at the lakes, taking enormous quantities of trunks and cases with them, not to mention the indispensable Thomas and Miss Hunter. The staff had to work hard to collect together all those items which were regarded as essential on such a journey. To Eileen, who had only ever travelled from Ross to Charnwood in her life, and had never seen London, Switzerland seemed such a huge adventure that she was almost as excited as if she, too, had been going. She spent her time packing and unpacking as Mrs Pemberley changed her mind at the last moment.

Only when their car had disappeared down the drive with Thomas at the wheel, could the household relax. Even the unbending Schofield took a moment to get his breath back before once more forcing his staff on to the mammoth task of spring-cleaning.

When the house is as large as Charnwood, this is no simple matter. Scrubbing miles of paintwork and concrete floors, Eileen was left in no doubt that there were two very distinct classes. The memory of Honor Darcy's easy freedom rankled. Now that she knew these people really did exist and they counted their privileges and pampered lives as their God-given right, nothing could ever convince her that the wide gulf between them was just; it seemed obscene.

As she scrubbed, she had ample time for thought. Hours when she was left on her own, with her mind free from the sheer physical grind of her daily life. Eileen now felt that all her hopes had been betrayed. Her father had always urged her to get on in life, to strive for independence. Her interest caught, Eileen had dreamed of financial independence, of having her own money to do with as she pleased. She had seen so many women who were little more than unpaid servants in their homes, completely beholden to the men in their lives for every penny. When her father was ill, young as she was, Eileen had held the purse-strings, managing his paltry pension as best as she could, making the decisions herself.

Getting employment outside the house had given her the hope of earning her own way in the world, of climbing up the ladder. She had seen herself putting aside a little money, even opening a bank account, and saving for the future. Perhaps she would even do as her father had suggested, half in jest no doubt, and get herself a small car. To them both a car was the symbol of complete freedom. Cars were such a rarity on the roads that they were status symbols of the modern age, an unbelievable dream for the railwayman and his daughter.

But now the move to Charnwood seemed like a betrayal of all her dreams. She knew that her father could scarcely afford to keep her on his pension, but was he just a double-dealer or did he really think that taking this job in service would be the first step up for her?

Letters from home showed that her father was increasingly under the influence of Rose Williams. Eileen found that her hostility to Rose was waning as she came to understand what being in service meant. Rose had spent almost twenty years in other people's houses, taking orders, scarcely better than a servant. She could no longer blame Rose for wanting to get out of service and make a new life of her own before it was too late. Whereas before Eileen had only seen the nurse as a schemer and interloper, she now discovered fellow feeling for another woman in her circumstances.

But 1939 was to change this lifestyle, perhaps for ever. The war which everyone had thought averted once again raised its cobra head. On March 10th Chamberlain had pronounced the international situation satisfactory. Five days later Czechoslovakia was invaded. Hitler entered Prague. On the last day of the month, on the day the Prime Minister gave Britain's guarantee to Poland, the Pemberleys came home unexpectedly, sending the servants into panic as they sat on the lawn enjoying afternoon tea in the spring sunshine.

The situation in Europe had made even the colonel and his lady uneasy. The inevitability of war could no longer be ignored. In April conscription was announced, the first time ever in peacetime. A ripple of panic ran through the male members of the staff. Men aged eighteen to twenty were to be called up for training; 300,000 would be in arms by autumn. But Thomas did not have to worry. The authorities were only too conscious of their loyalties to the status quo: chauffeurs, valets, gardeners and greensmen were all exempt from conscription. Come hell or high water, privilege must be maintained.

This release gave Thomas a new sense of power. He moved

about the house with more than his usual degree of self-confidence, curbing his insolence only when Mrs Pemberley was present. For his master he had total contempt. The cantankerous old colonel made a less than sympathetic patient. He required Thomas to wheel his chair everywhere and could scarcely do a thing for himself. When the colonel's moods and demands became too much, Thomas would get his own back by leaving the old man in the bath, often for hours, pretending to have forgotten him.

His particular position in the house kept him safe from Schofield's wrath if not his reprobation. Thomas nonchalantly shrugged off criticism and swaggered on his way, as smart as his dove grey uniform.

He thought highly of himself. Eileen knew that he had a reputation to keep up. The village girls would queue for the chance to dance with him at the fortnightly local hop and he could take his pick. Of course, he was good looking. If Eileen had not known more of his character and had not been wry of all contact with the male sex, she could possibly have been attracted. But Thomas had certainly not recognised her indifference and preferred to take his chance.

He caught her one evening just after dinner had been cleared away in the servants' hall. He must have followed her down the long corridor, observing how she lit a lantern and went armed with her basket to fetch firewood ready to light the fires in the morning. Perhaps he even guessed how much she hated this task, fearing the rats which skulked in the cellars below. He was sure to catch her off guard.

In the cellar old Tom the handyman had stored firewood bundles almost to the ceiling. By the light of the lantern she placed on a shelf, Eileen could quickly fill her basket and escape back upstairs to the light. But some sixth sense made her stop work as though she sensed his presence in the cellar behind her. When she turned round he must have seen the trace of fear in her startled eyes as she said,

'I didn't know you were here.'

'I have been wanting to talk to you.'

'Oh yes?' She could think of nothing he needed to say.

'You know, you're really quite pretty.' It was said grudgingly, as though against his better judgement, and she felt insulted. 'I don't suppose I would even have noticed if I hadn't seen you with old Darcy.' He instantly caught the panic in her eyes. 'Thought you got away with that, didn't you? Sneaking out of his room in the middle of the day like that.' His voice was full of snide innuendo. 'And him in his dressing-gown.'

'You've got it all wrong.'

'You should have let on earlier. Then we could have had a go before I went off abroad with the colonel.' He leant towards her, his face very close, but he did not touch her.

'Look, you don't understand. It was all his doing.'

'Really?' he said with a look of amused scepticism.

'Yes, look, he got me up there. I didn't know anything about it.'

'But you led him on. I saw you.'

'No! You're crazy!' She lurched past him and tried to reach the door, but he was there before her and slammed his arm across the exit, blocking her escape.

'Come on, let's not play games.' He took her face between his soft hands, but she struggled, trying to turn her head aside.

His fast disappearing control snapped and he grasped her painfully by the shoulders. 'What's got into you? Come on, you want me, I know it.' His warm wet mouth descended on hers in the semi-darkness, as unwelcome to her as the advance he had so clearly misconstrued at the New Year. But her alarm and obvious distaste was something he was plainly not expecting and soon convinced him that she was serious. He thrust her away furiously.

'So who the hell do you think you are, Miss High and Mighty? Some high-class tart who can pick and choose?' His eyes held hers, bright with offence. 'Not good enough for you, is that it? I know your sort. Always on the lookout for the nobs, just some little slut on the make.' He slammed his fist into her shoulder so that she fell back against the cold brickwork. It was painful and clearly meant to demonstrate his superior strength as a warning. 'Well, who needs you, darling? It's your funeral. But just you remember, I'm wise to your little game now, so you'd better watch your step. Don't try it on round me. Understand?'

When she looked up she found herself once more alone in the cellar with the flickering lantern light the only proof that he had been there.

She was suddenly trembling from head to foot. The injustice of

39

his accusation made her sick with shame. She could scarcely have felt more humiliated if his words had been true.

It was as she had feared. Hayden's assault had been turned on its head and she had come out of it looking guilty. For a man like Thomas, cocksure in his own powers to attract women, what he had seen in the corridors at the New Year could only mean one thing. It had doubtless never occurred to him that any woman in such a situation would be unwilling. A man like that would naturally assume that women accepted and enjoyed 'a bit of a lark' and would even boast of it. It was natural, it was human nature, just a bit of fun. The thought that it was harassment would never occur to him.

Her rejection could only mean one thing to Thomas. He was so conscious of his good looks, his smart uniform and powerful position in the household that he could only take it as an insult, as a deliberate slur on his class. He thought she only went with the gentry, and the implication was therefore that she was no better than a common whore, selling herself to the highest bidder, far worse than any fun-loving woman won by a handsome face.

It was unjust but she could not defend herself. There was nothing she could say which could prove her innocence. To try and explain would be simply to get deeper into trouble. How could she go to Schofield or even her aunt and say that Thomas had propositioned her? Thomas was outside their authority and so far in with the Pemberleys that no one would listen to the word of a third housemaid.

The cruel injustice appalled her. She could see no way out of the terrible situation without creating even more havoc. Thomas had warned her that if she gave him any trouble he would settle with her. He was not used to being turned down and his vindictive stream of abuse gave her warning that it would not be forgotten. Eileen had made a bitter enemy.

In the weeks which followed Eileen kept a low profile. She moved about the house carrying out her duties with unvarying diligence, unwilling to provoke the slightest comment. Only her aunt noticed her unusual silence and asked if she was quite well. Meg's sense of good nature might have provided Eileen with a confidant

40

in any other circumstances, but as cook in the household she had a position to keep up. Eileen had no illusions that if it came to a confrontation her aunt, out of a sense of self-preservation if nothing else, could not have defended her.

She gave Thomas a wide berth at all times, although she knew that he took a callous delight in placing himself in her path or making snide comments over the dinner table.

Her reticence continued throughout the spring and for weeks she never went anywhere off duty, preferring to stay behind with Meg and listen to Henry Hall on the radio. But with summer Eileen was at last tempted out by the arrival of the two undergraduate friends down again from Cambridge for the vacation.

The summer of '39 was one of the wettest on record. After a lovely June, the weather broke and all through July Jonathan Pemberley and his friend Gareth James haunted the library and drawing-room in boredom. Sometimes they played billiards by the hour while thunder rolled overhead and the rain lashed the tennis courts outside.

Below stairs they speculated that it was more than boredom which caused the uneasy atmosphere in the house. A sense of foreboding had overtaken Charnwood as the prospect of war loured on the horizon. Everyone felt it, but Schofield reported that the two young gentlemen seemed particularly on edge, rushing every morning to the post the moment it arrived, but always going away disappointed.

At last speculation was satisfied when it was discovered that Mr Jonathan and his Welsh friend had both joined up and had received their postings in the morning mail. Their studies were to be disrupted and they were off soon to become officers in – of all things – the RAF.

'Training to be pilots,' said Schofield across the table at lunch. 'Apparently they have both been learning to fly through the university. They have their own Reserve Air Squadron at Cambridge and Mr Jonathan has been with them all the past year. Since Munich he said. And without telling his father.'

Miss Hunter sniffed with disapproval.

'The Colonel is most displeased. He thought at least Mr Jonathan would have joined his old regiment. To carry on the family tradition. It hardly seems right, does it? New-fangled nonsense.'

'We must go with the times,' said Meg. 'They say this war will be won in the air.'

'We still need the Army, Mrs Howard,' declared Schofield, wiping his mouth delicately with the corner of his napkin. 'And it looks very bad form for Mr Jonathan to upset his father like this. I daresay it's the influence of that Mr James.'

'Not quite top class,' said Miss Hunter enthusiastically. 'A draper's son, you know.'

Meg clucked her tongue in annoyance. 'Well, I say good luck to them both. Fine young men like that risking their necks – which is more than can be said for some as I could mention.' She had no need to flick her eyes in the direction of Thomas as he sat nonchalantly chewing away across the table because every other eye at the table looked his way. The subject was quickly dropped.

The local paper soon caught on to the story. Jonathan Pemberley's picture appeared on the front page, dressed in white sports clothes smiling out at Eileen as she read the breezy report underneath. Fawning to the Pemberleys, the editor was clearly set on promoting the heir to Charnwood as a hero. The handsome face certainly fitted the image of a dashing RAF pilot but the prospect of war only caused Eileen dreadful anxiety about his safety. She secretly tore off the front page of the newspaper and in the room she shared with Dot, when Dot was absent, cut out the item very carefully, putting it safely away as a consolation. She did not analyse why she did this, knowing in her heart that her love was foolish, but in her isolation since the incident with Thomas she could not help herself. Depressed and lonely, she aroused Dot's sympathy and one Saturday she was finally persuaded to put on her best dress and go along to the dance held in the local village hall.

The servants were allowed out once the dinner had been served and they had rushed through their duties. Dot and Eileen hurried into outdoor clothes and made their way running and laughing across the park by eight-thirty to stay an hour or so at the dance. They had to be back by ten sharp or risk Schofield's wrath.

Eileen had just one decent dress. It was white with puff sleeves and a tight waist. She had prettied it up with a satin bow in dark blue which threaded round the neckline. It might not have been very fashionable but it was classically simple and suited her dark colouring very well. Dot had looked at her rather enviously, smoothing her own pink skirts uneasily.

When they arrived at the dance everything was already in full swing. All the locals were there, the farmers' lads and their girls in their weekend finery. The air was humid and inside the village hall the temperature was high. There was a great crowd round the refreshment tables but as only tea and lemonade were being served throughout the evening men would slip away in ones and twos to the pub next door for a pint.

There was a three-piece band playing a Cole Porter song, or what should have been Porter, but it was good enough to set feet tapping and to fill up the dance floor with eager couples. Eileen stayed close to Dot as she saw with dismay that Thomas was there. He had caught sight of the new arrivals and was making his way across the room towards her. From the light in his eyes she knew that he had singled her out. It could only mean trouble.

In his shirt sleeves he cut a handsome figure as he grasped Eileen by the arm with a grin and a perfunctory, 'Let's dance.' She found herself forced out amongst the dancers, clutched tightly about the waist and manoeuvred into the densest part of the floor.

'Come on, smile,' he told her, holding himself against her. 'I'm sorry we couldn't supply any titled gentlemen for you this evening. You'll just have to put up with me – excusing the expression,' he added with a leer. ' Come on, let your hair down. You don't know what you're missing.'

His coarse assurance was not only offensive but frightened her. Anyone who could be so certain of their own attraction had never received a rebuttal to dispel illusions. She was sure that Thomas was acting out of pure spite. He had tried his luck with her, thinking she was easy, and she had wounded his pride, but that was the only emotion involved. He cared nothing for her except as the object of his vindictiveness and revenge, but that was quite sufficient to make her life at Charnwood a misery.

As the music died there appeared to be some sort of commotion at the entrance. Absurd though it seemed to her, Eileen felt with a shaft of certainty that Jonathan Pemberly had just walked into the hall. A heady lightness made her break away from Thomas and she made her way quickly between the press of dancers to see for herself.

There was an uneasy silence as the local lads took in the sight of Jonathan and Gareth on the threshold. No one from Charnwood House, from the Family, had ever gatecrashed the village hop and feelings were clearly mixed about their presence. Everyone there knew that Mr Jonathan and his friend from the university had joined up and there was a ripple of excitement among the women and of resentment among the men. As the music swelled the two young men were surrounded and the moment of tension was broken, though not forgotten. Set faces watched as Jonathan and Gareth had their pick of the local girls and joined the dancers on the floor.

From the line of wallflowers Eileen saw him. He was grinning at his partner and his face was a familiar and sweet anguish. For a large man he moved well, holding the girl easily as he twirled her round. She stood watching, never taking her eyes off him, drinking in every little detail. He must have been saying something to the girl – who was she to have such luck? – because his full and mobile mouth smiled, revealing strong white teeth as he talked. He was very fit and looked tanned and healthy in his casual clothes. He wore nothing ostentatious, nothing that would be too out of place among the farmers' sons, but even so there was a quality about the cut of his jacket and the fit of his twill slacks. His body was well-developed, his chest broad and his arms muscled from athletic workouts. She had heard that he rowed at Cambridge though his interest was not serious. Nothing he seemed to do appeared serious. He was easy-going by nature, always ready with a smile, the most amiable and likeable of men. And Eileen admitted to herself that she really liked him. She found herself attracted to his little boy smile and the quizzical tilt of his great blond head as he stooped a little to catch something that was said to him.

The music stopped and in the wake of the dancing he had released his partner and stood for a moment adrift among the milling crowd. Eileen's heart went out to him as he stood there, apart and apparently at a loss, out of place. If she had been able to will him to come to her by sheer force of concentration she would

44

have known a power capable of lifting her out of her fear and loneliness.

Another tune was struck up and he was looking round for a new partner. But in that instant when it seemed he must look in her direction, Eileen's willpower wavered and she turned aside, blushing furiously, sure that everyone must have noticed her strange interest. She gave all her attention to the unlikely items on a trestle tea-table and she waited. Scarcely breathing, it felt as though her whole world rested on this simple choice. Surely he was meant to dance with her?

A hand came to rest lightly on her shoulder. She turned at once, her eyes already bright with relief, only to find the lad from Emmitt's farm – she did not even know his name – standing before her asking her to dance. If he saw her bitter disappointment he said nothing. She was shaking slightly as he led her among the other dancers. But she was no partner for him. She scarcely gave him a glance as her eyes searched the hall for Jonathan. If he spoke a word to her she never heard him, for all her thoughts were with another man.

She saw him at once. He was with a dark haired girl now, a brash girl in a striped dress, a common girl who wore her hair in loose curls caught up with a diamanté slide, vulgar. She must have forced herself onto him. Surely he would never have picked her out on his own? As the dancers manoeuvred round the floor she was given many opportunities to take in his polite smiles as he held that dreadful girl with the lightest of touches. She felt sorry for him. Coming here, hoping for a good time and then having to put up with all the village girls throwing themselves at him. Just because he was off to join the RAF. It was rotten of them.

Even with her back to him, she was aware of his presence. In the close pack there was some jostling and they bumped together briefly, separating with quick apologies, though their eyes never met. Her skin tingled and her head felt light as she veered between ecstasy and dreadful depression, never caring where her unknown partner led her in the dance.

All at once the beat of the music changed into a swing and the bandleader announced brightly that it was time for a Paul Jones. Amid the buzz of excitement, Eileen found herself next to Dot as two huge circles formed, the women on the inside. At her side

Dot was red-cheeked and laughing as the music began and they moved in opposite directions to their prospective partners.

Eileen could see Jonathan's bright head moving towards her as the wheeling circles swung round. Dot's bright eyes caught hers with a flash of surprise and she realised that her own desperation must be written plain on her face. She summoned up a weak smile in return, but Dot still looked at her with concern. And then the music stopped.

Jonathan was just three dancers away to the left. He was already taking his lottery partner in his arms and swinging her away into the crowd. Eileen turned aside and found herself looking into the face of Mr Gareth James.

His hands were light on her body as they danced gently. Although she recognised him at once, she had never really taken any notice of Jonathan's university friend. But now she was surprised to discover that his face was oddly familiar. Dark, slightly curling hair framed a strong sculptured face. There were stark hollows under his cheekbones, shadowed as though he had been ill or unhappy. Yet his dark eyes stared back at her serene and alert, interested in her appearance.

'What's your name?' he asked her, and at once she knew what she had recognised. The Welsh draper's son, of course. His accent instantly recalled the sing-song of voices in the villages back home, his dark hair and skin the people of the valleys. With a pang she smiled back at him.

'Eileen,' she said.

The furore he had caused at Charnwood House had almost passed her by. But here he was, the outspoken trouble-maker who had offended Miss Hunter and Schofield with his political talk. And yes, the unsuitable friend who had dared to confront Mr Hayden Darcy over the dinner table about Oswald Mosley. Her smiled broadened. Anyone who attacked Darcy and the Fascists could not be all bad.

'Whereabouts in Wales do you come from?'

'Neath.' His sharp eyes held on to hers and a slight frown puckered his brow. 'Aren't you a local girl?'

'Wye.'

'What's that?'

'No, Wye, the Wye Valley.' She laughed, the first time all

evening. 'My family straddle the border.'

'That sounds painful.' He smiled with his eyes. 'Poor you, a hybrid. And what are you doing here, so far from –'

He was cut short by a sudden silence as the music changed back again to the furious beat of the Paul Jones and Eileen was pulled away into the woman's circle.

Twice more the music broke and Eileen found herself with different partners, separated by the crush from both the gatecrashers. Only when the women joined hands again for the last round, did hope surge at the sight of Jonathan Pemberley moving down the line in her direction.

He was just four away, no three, and the music kept on playing. He was just two away, and still it played. He was one away and now, now, let it stop! But the beat continued, loud and raucous as Jonathan briefly stood before her and then moved on. The music ceased with an abrupt wheeze and Eileen saw that the woman next in line had won her prize.

Despair hit Eileen like a blow in the stomach. She almost stumbled, and her new partner caught her by the arm and saved her. He obviously thought she was not feeling well and led her off the dance floor to the side of the hall. He would even have stayed with her but she told him she was feeling better, sounding almost rude in her hurry to get rid of him.

With her back to the cold wall, she watched in stony silence as Jonathan danced in and out of the crowd. She could have wept with disappointment at the bitter trick fate had played her. She stared at him scarcely giving a thought to anyone else. So near and yet so far. It was savage and humiliating and she knew she was a fool.

'Don't waste your time,' said a voice near her ear. 'He doesn't even know you exist.'

She turned in horror to face Thomas's hard eyes and smiling mouth. He had no difficulty in reading her expression and putting two and two together. He had guessed her secret. The very worst had happened.

Knowing the threat which now hung over her, Eileen had almost thrown caution to the wind. If Jonathan Pemberley had suddenly recognised her existence and asked her out in his MG she would willingly have gone with him, regardless of the comments at Charnwood House. But it was Gareth James, with his unconventional behaviour, heavily criticised below stairs, with whom she was thrown into contact.

Gareth's path crossed her own as she carried out her duties round the house. She constantly came across him, although whether this was by accident or design on his part, she was not sure. He seemed out of place there, lonely perhaps. He seemed pleased to have found her again and there was nothing mocking or patronising about his recognition, nothing to make her ashamed of her position in the house. Alone with him in the early morning library while the house was at breakfast, she had no qualms in picking up their conversation from the previous Saturday night.

He seemed pleased to discover that her home was not so very different from his own in South Wales. He kept his questions to safe perimeters, never venturing into the personal, as though he shared her uneasiness. On the third morning that he waited for her in the library, he told her he was glad he was going off to join the RAF and not returning to Cambridge. He said he would be glad to get away and do something with his life. He had smiled wryly as he volunteered this information, noting her reaction carefully as though he was frightened of scaring her off. She thought that he would have liked to make friends except for the restraints imposed upon them both by the traditions and values of Charnwood House.

So when he asked her to come to the cinema on her next free evening off, she felt guilty about bridging the gap between upstairs and down. But she said yes. There was a defiance about her, and a need to show Thomas and the others that she was not intimidated, not beaten.

But they set about planning their outing with all the secrecy of a military operation. She met him outside the grounds of the house, down the lane a bus stop further on than the usual one by the lodge gates.

There was time for tea and buns at the cinema before the film, but they bought their tickets beforehand as the show was 'Pygmalion' with Lesley Howard and Wendy Hillier and was sure to be packed. Sitting in comfortable armchairs in the circle restaurant overlooking the High Street, they both visibly relaxed. The barriers imposed on both of them by Charnwood and its stifling atmosphere and conventions could be let down for a few hours and they could be themselves.

Compared with Jonathan, Gareth James would not be considered good-looking. He did not fit the romantic image she had read about or seen at the cinema. When she looked at him there was no quickening of her pulse or sense of danger, no excitement. She felt safe, able to respond naturally. In some ways he reminded her of the local boys back home, though of course he was far cleverer than any of them, winning a scholarship to Cambridge like that.

Yes, his father was a draper. But he actually owned three shops and had made himself some money in spite of the recession. He was strict chapel, a hard-line Methodist who saw work as the answer to everything. If there was trouble, or illness, to his father the solution was 'to work it off'. Gareth told her that he had always been studious as a child as there didn't seem anything else to do. When he won the place at Cambridge it was his father who was over the moon because he had never had the opportunity himself. He wanted his son to get on in the world, but Gareth wasn't sure that he could live up to his father's expectations.

His professors all seemed to have it in for him as a scholarship boy, and his fellow students saw him as an interloper, a social climber. Of course, they were all pretty wealthy while Gareth's father kept him on a shoestring budget – 'He thought it formed character,' he told her with a wry smile. 'If it hadn't been for Jonathan's friendship...'

Eileen's interest picked up as he described how he and Jonathan had come together through boredom with their studies.

'It all seemed to have nothing to do with reality. There we were discussing Greece and Rome while all around us Europe was erupting. We were on the brink of a holocaust and no one seemed aware of it.'

He said that his father objected to his friendship with Jonathan, and thought he ought to be studying and thinking about making a secure future.

'A future!' Gareth was cynical. 'With Hitler seizing countries right and left, how do we know we'll even have a future?'

Eileen was irritated by this sudden gloom. That wasn't to say that he hadn't got the right idea about Hitler and everything, but the last thing she wanted to hear was that there wasn't going to be a future. Why then was she putting up with the drudgery of Charnwood if it wasn't going to lead to a better future?

Eileen could sympathise with Gareth while at the same time she was astonished by his openness. He was talking to her as though he had known her for months rather than days. She felt flattered yet also regretful. She could not prevent herself from thinking how different her reaction would have been if it had been Jonathan sitting there instead of Gareth.

They sat side by side in the darkness watching the B film. It was cops and robbers and a bit corny. She and Gareth laughed together at the cartoon which followed and then grew tense as the Pathe Gazette newsreel came on. The sonorous voice of the commentator got on their nerves and his snide comments seemed to annoy Gareth. When the pictures of Chamberlain came on the screen there was a general outbreak of catcalls and ribald remarks round the hall. No one trusted that man now.

When the big film started the whole place grew quiet and Eileen sank down in her seat, conscious of Gareth's arm against hers on the arm-rest. As Leslie Howard's conversion of Eliza Doolittle progressed, she thought with irony that her own situation was not so very different. The bridge between Gareth's world and her own was almost as wide as between Gareth and Jonathan. That proved that Jonathan Pemberley was no snob and the thought cheered her up immeasurably. She was pleased to be there with her new friend, even if he was only second best.

After the show they had to hurry in order to catch the last bus back to Charnwood, but when they arrived at the bus stop in the High Street there was no one waiting there.

'Have we missed it?' Gareth asked, looking at his watch doubtfully. 'I don't fancy a walk home. Is there a taxi service?'

Eileen told him that she didn't know. She didn't add that taxis were quite beyond her tiny pay packet and that she had never been in one in her life.

'Well, let's give it another few minutes,' she suggested, 'and then we'll just have to start walking.'

But as it turned out there was no need for any of that. The lonely noise of a motor heralded the approach of a low sports car. Within yards of the bus stop it pulled up with a dramatic screech at the same moment as Gareth exclaimed,

'God, it's Jon!'

It was indeed Jonathan Pemberley in his MG. Eileen was covered in confusion but the roving eye the driver cast in her direction betrayed no sign of recognition.

'You old dog, Gareth,' he declared with that famous grin, 'so this is what you've been up to!'

'Shut up and give us a lift, will you? We missed the last bus.' Gareth seemed as embarrassed as Eileen. Only Jonathan was having a good time. He pushed open the passenger door and indicated that she should get in.

'You'll have to squat at the back,' he told his friend, 'but hang on for Christ's sake.' He turned back to smile at Eileen as she sat rigidly beside him. 'Don't I deserve an introduction?'

'Just shut up and drive,' Gareth told him good-naturedly, as though he was jealously guarding Eileen's identity. But Eileen was grateful for anonymity.

Jonathan obligingly started up and decided he would drive at top speed, out to impress Eileen and to give his friend a bit of a shakeup as he sat propped on the hood of the little car. Eileen was thrilled and exhilarated, not only because this was her first trip in a sports car but because it was Jonathan Pemberley who sat beside her.

In the darkness of the country roads she could flash him occasional glances, aware of his outline half in shadow. He drove in his shirt-sleeves as the night was warm and the white silk shirt showed up in the gloom. She knew that he was also looking at her, obviously intrigued by Gareth's secret liaison with a complete stranger. Of that there was no doubt. Although he must have seen her round the house many times he clearly had no idea that she was one of his family's servants. If he saw a housemaid at all it was certain that he never looked close enough to recognise one out of uniform. He was used to servants, he had always been surrounded by faceless creatures who got on with their work and did not speak unless they were spoken to.

What would he say now if she told him who she was? It would

shock him and humiliate Gareth, but how was she to get out of the situation? The car was already approaching Charnwood village.

As though he had read her thoughts Jonathan said suddenly, 'Where shall I drop you?' He was under the impression that she was a village girl or from an outlying farm.

'Keep going,' Gareth commanded from behind. 'She lives at Charnwood House.'

The grin died on Jonathan's face as he realised it was not a joke. Frowning, he turned the MG up through the gates of the estate and started up the drive in grim silence.

'What's the matter, Jon? Don't be such a bloody snob.'

After a moment's silence, Jonathan turned to Eileen and said gently, 'I apologise. It was rather a shock, that's all. What do you do here?'

'I'm a housemaid.' She had almost added 'sir', such was her nervous and agitated state of mind, all her thoughts in turmoil.

'And – do you like it? I mean, do you like your work?'

'Oh, for God's sake, Jon! Don't be so bloody condescending. Of course she doesn't like it. Just get us home, will you?'

Jonathan drove on in silence, pulling past the main doors into the courtyard at the side of the house where the servants' entrance was. He pulled up abruptly, but kept the engine ticking over as Gareth jumped down from the back of the car to open the passenger door and help Eileen out.

She smiled her thanks, unable to speak in her terrible embarrassment, but Gareth gave her hand a squeeze before getting back into the car, this time beside Jonathan. As they reversed and drove off with a roar towards the main entrance, Eileen made her way into the kitchen, very conscious of the lateness of the hour, praying Schofield would not still be around to catch her.

'So you've come in at last, have you?'

It was Thomas's voice speaking from the shadows. He sat in a chair at the far end of the long refectory table watching her.

'And that was Mr Jonathan's car I heard, if I'm not mistaken. Well, well, well. You are full of surprises, aren't you?'

★

52

It was a week later when Jonathan and Gareth left Charnwood for their RAF posting. Eileen heard of their impending departure the night before and the news upset her. She thought of the house after they left it and felt very depressed. She knew that Thomas was watching her every move and that he took pleasure in hurting her. Eventually he would try and get her into trouble with the Pemberleys and the prospect terrified her.

On the morning of their departure she found Gareth waiting in the library while the others were down at breakfast. He looked sheepish and regretful, and immediately apologised for not seeing her over the past few days.

'I wanted to say that I really enjoyed meeting you. And to ask you something.'

She looked up cautiously, a little surprised.

'If I wrote to you from the RAF camp, would you mind very much? I mean, would you write back to me, as a friend?'

'Of course,' she replied, although she was a little doubtful. 'But I'm not a good letter writer. You see, I'm not used to...'

'Oh that's all right,' he said, cheering up. 'Look I've written my address down here. That ought to find me.' He thrust a folded piece of paper into her hand, and then held on to the hand. 'I'm really grateful.' He hesitated, his eyes liquid with concern. He would have said more but something stopped him. Still clasping her hand, he pulled her towards him instead and kissed her lightly on the lips.

And then he left her.

Jonathan and Gareth's departure seemed to herald a change of mood not only at Charnwood but in the country as a whole. A sense of inevitability about war was now prevalent. False optimism and jokes vanished as people began to take the threat of hostility seriously.

They had all seen the newsreels of German and Italian planes bombing the cities of Spain. There were few illusions about the death and destruction on a vast scale that a modern war would bring, with civilians in the frontline everywhere. They had seen for themselves that war was no longer a chivalric duel between hostile armies. If war came then the cities of Britain would face immediate attack from enemy bombers and thousands would die. Look at Guernica. They didn't stand a chance. The Stukas caught them in the market place. Barbaric. No wonder that children were being evacuated out of London.

Taking his cue, Mr Chamberlain announced that blackout regulations would be enforced from Friday September 1st. The staff at Charnwood were immediately set to the task of making up yards of black material as blackout curtains for the 73 windows of the house. It was estimated that it would take up to twenty minutes every night to check that all windows were covered. The penalty for showing a light was £2 fine in the local police court, and Mrs Pemberley duly warned her staff that they would have to pay for any negligence out of their own wages.

At the height of the Munich crisis the year before, the Pemberleys had offered Charnwood to the Government if war should break out. The prospect of little cockney kids running wild through the Adam dining-room did not thrill the colonel and his lady, and they had opted for expectant mothers as the lesser of two evils.

This burst of patriotism had died with the crisis but had evidently not been forgotten by the government. On August 31st the Pemberleys received official notice that Charnwood House was to be requisitioned as a maternity hospital from September 4th.

To their credit the family took the news on the chin. There was little panic although it was rumoured that Mrs Pemberley had spent an anguished morning on the telephone to her great-aunt the Duchess trying to reverse the decision. But the old order was already crumbling before the onrushing impetus of war. The Pemberleys were obliged to put a brave face on it and to look for alternative accommodation.

They found it by ejecting one of their tenants from the estate lodge, but this house was an appalling come-down for the Pemberleys. There were just four bedrooms, so only the indispensable Thomas was taken together with Meg the cook and Eileen to do all the housework. The rest of the staff would be released to join the Forces or to seek work elsewhere; there were still many advertisements in the newspapers for valets and domestic staff. Only Schofield the butler would stay at

Charnwood House, remaining in his flat in order to supervise the occupation by midwives, mothers and babies.

War had not yet been declared, although an attack on Poland was imminent. People could not understand the reason why Britain should go to war over Poland, whose Government was not exactly renowned for its democratic methods, while poor old Czechoslovakia had been sacrificed so readily.

'A war might not be such a bad thing,' Schofield announced from the security of his fifty years. 'I envy the young men going into the Armed Forces. They may learn a bit of discipline there.'

'It will solve the unemployment problem,' added Miss Hunter loyally, although she herself was shortly to join their ranks. 'Give them all something to do.'

That night they heard the news that Poland had been invaded. On top of this, it was the first night of the blackout restrictions with total confusion everywhere. Road casualties doubled as people tripped, fell and smashed into everything in range. Dot had sprained her ankle over a milk churn and Meg apologised to a post box down in the village. Soon everyone had their own blackout story to tell.

Cinemas and theatres had closed down and there was nothing to do in the evenings. Boots Lending Library did a roaring trade. But at Charnwood House the servants were kept busy moving furniture into the estate lodge and tidying away all art treasures into the famous dining-room which was then sealed up for the duration. Then the rest of the house had to be cleaned and made ready before the arrival of an advance party of medical staff on the Monday morning.

On Sunday September 3rd Eileen was on her knees scrubbing the floor in the entrance hall of Charnwood House as war was declared. Meg shouted out the news and everyone rushed into the kitchen to gather round the wireless set.

'This is the National Programme from London.'

After Chamberlain's voice had wavered away there was complete silence as they stood solemnly looking at each other. There was no relief, no jubilation, only a grim acceptance of the inevitable. After two years of scares and crises it had come at last.

All at once there was an incredible noise far off from the village. A warbling, wailing noise which rose and fell like an animal moaning in pain. They hurried outside, the noise continuing, panic growing as they realised it was the sound of the sirens fitted on the roof of the village pub to give warning of an air raid.

'The bombers! They're coming!' screamed Miss Hunter white-faced. 'Where do we go? We'll all be killed!'

'I don't have my gasmask,' exclaimed Dot helplessly. 'Where did I put my gasmask?'

'That will teach you a lesson for the future.' Schofield wagged his finger in her face, although he too had forgotten his square cardboard box like everyone else.

At that moment Sid Byfield, the local policeman, appeared puffing and sweating up the drive on his old push-bike. He waved his hand frantically at them, too out of breath to blow his whistle, although it dangled out of the corner of his mouth as he pedalled towards them.

'Take cover, take cover!' He was gasping, red-faced and furious. 'Don't you know there's a war on?'

It was the first time that Eileen heard that remark but it was certainly not to be the last.

Even as they all began to move towards the cellars the village sirens changed their note. The seething wailing noise changed to one long continuous blast, the All-Clear.

'Well, that was quick,' said PC Byfield, disappointed.

'Must have been a practice run.' Schofield looked at the staff and actually smiled. 'I'm proud of you all. It's a relief to know that you won't get hysterical when the bombing starts.'

The women stared at each other after the back-handed compliment and decided that as the fun was all over they had better go back to their work.

In the proximity of the small house the relationship between staff and family changed overnight. Eileen knew that she had only been kept on because she was Meg's niece and because she was cheap. More experienced members of staff would have been able to demand an increase in wages for the extra work involved. Eileen soon found herself obliged to carry out tasks that would normally have fallen to the butler or footman in the old house.

She remembered one morning just after the move when she was in the tiny hall of the lodge and the newspaper arrived. She was just about to put it on to the hall table when Mrs Pemberley came downstairs and Eileen went to hand her the paper. Madam had raised herself to her full commanding height and looked through her as though she was sub-human. She said nothing. Only later had Meg explained that Eileen should have used a silver salver when handing anything to Madam.

The problem was that Mrs Pemberley just could not adapt to the move. She simply could not bring her style of living down to the lower level. She expected the same service from one servant as from seventeen, and she criticised everything that was done for her with regular monotony.

Eileen had her first chance to study her employers at close quarters and any illusions she might still have had were quickly dispelled. There were no great house parties now, no gatherings of friends or family. The Pemberleys were on their own, often scarcely speaking to one another, their true natures revealed in all their selfishness. But worst than the increased pressure of work for Eileen was the almost continuous presence of Thomas about the house.

Thomas had his own room, unlike Eileen who had to share with Meg. The new arrangements gave him considerable freedom. There were few places where the Colonel wished to be wheeled in such a small house, and with the new restrictions on petrol Thomas hardly ever took the car out of its garage. This meant that he had considerable amounts of time on his hands and he seemed to take a perverse pleasure in using it to taunt and intimidate Eileen.

He would frequently lie in wait for her, try to touch her or fondle her, so that before September was out Eileen was already going crazy in the confines of the small house.

'I can't stand Thomas,' she told Meg one night in their room. 'He's really got it in for me. Please don't leave me alone with him.'

Meg had looked at her in surprise but sympathetically, and she had not asked further questions. They shared their evenings together, often sitting in the homely kitchen listening to the wireless. Meg's favourite programme was 'Bandwagon' on

Saturday evenings. She and Eileen took to going out together in their free time – which was not much – and often went up to the big house to give a hand with the mothers and babies.

It was amazing to see the transformation of the past weeks. The bedrooms had become wards full of regulation metal bedsteads and movable screens. There were strange women moving down the galleries and grounds in their cheerful smocks and nurses in starched white aprons in the library.

Air-raid warnings were becoming more frequent although they were all false alarms. They were being conditioned to a state where a real attack would meet with an automatic response. The trouble was that the longer these false alarms continued, the more probably a genuine attack would be treated as a cry of wolf.

At the hospital there were even gasmasks for the babies. They would be strapped into the contraption with their heads completely enclosed. A rubber tube was connected to a bellows which somebody had to pump continously to keep the poor mite alive. No turning away for more than a second or the effect could be worse than Hitler's bombing. Even so, the babies emerged from their ordeal red-faced and screaming with rage at such indignities.

Most of the women came from London and were deeply concerned about the families they had left behind in the city.

'They gave us one of those shelters, an Anderson, but I know my Mum will never use it. Not on your life.'

Eileen was fascinated to sit and listen to tales about the London she had never seen. She heard them talk of trenches which had been dug in the London parks and sandbags piled outside official buildings. Now that the war had come Eileen feared she never would see the capital. She was certain that when the war began in earnest bombs would destroy it all before she could get there to have a look. The way the women talked about getting back home, war or no war, made Eileen all the more discontented with her life at Charnwood.

Of course, there was nothing to keep her there. Like Dot, she could have volunteered to work in a munitions factory. The girls were earning a fortune it was said. Or there was the Women's Land Army, except that on the BBC they were always making disparaging jokes about it, putting the women down.

About that time the first of Gareth's letters arrived. It flopped

58

on to the doormat just as Thomas was crossing the hall. He snatched up the post and held it above her head, refusing to hand it over to her until he had had a good look. When he saw the letter addressed to her he made some comment about the postmark. Gareth was at RAF camp near Chester, but nothing would have made her disclose to Thomas anything about her correspondence.

She was delighted to hear from Gareth. Although the letter was clearly censored, he succeeded in telling her a considerable amount about his training and what life was like in the Forces. Of course, she had an ulterior motive for answering the letter. Gareth was her only source of information about Jonathan Pemberley.

As the November fog closed in on Charnwood and the only topic of conversation seemed to be the scarcity of torch batteries for the blackout, Gareth's letters were a blessing. They were full of surprisingly funny anecdotes which gave her a new insight into his character. He was training on something called a Miles Magister and had just got his confidence in the air. Eileen thought that the experience sounded thrilling. She envied men for their freedom to go and do exciting things which were denied women.

Constantly under a barrage of criticism and bad temper, Eileen suspected that Thomas was spreading rumours about her. Mrs Pemberley had commented on the frequency of her visits to the hospital, as though she had not been going there to do voluntary work but for some other, less commendable, less respectable reason altogether.

'And are there only nurses at the hospital, Howard?' Madam inquired. 'Are there no doctors at all?'

Answering truthfully Eileen could have sworn that Mrs Pemberley looked disappointed. It was some time before she realised that to her employer all doctors must be male, and that her questioning took on a different meaning.

'Just because we are at war there is no excuse for a general lowering of moral standards,' Mrs Pemberley told Meg in Eileen's hearing. 'I truly believe that these evacuee women have a bad influence on our local gals. I am told that some of the women actually go to the Clifford Arms unaccompanied.'

She added that she would continue to expect a high standard from her household and she would not condone any loose behaviour. She had looked at Eileen as she said it and the cold

59

expression in her eyes quite unnerved her.

Mrs Pemberley had taken to wearing Red Cross uniform. Although she only went there for an hour once a week she thought she was doing her bit for the war effort. Being in uniform brought out all her authoritarianism which seemed directed against Eileen in particular.

Matters came to a head one day in December. Mrs Pemberley had made a habit recently of coming downstairs early in the mornings and taking the post herself the moment it arrived. Any letters that were for the staff she left on the hall table. Day after day, watching her, Eileen felt that she was annoyed or irritated by something, perhaps a letter which had been delayed.

She learnt the truth the morning that one of Gareth's letters fell through the door. Mrs Pemberley saw the postmark and summoned Eileen with a gleam of satisfaction in her eyes. Eileen knew that she meant trouble as soon as she saw her.

'This letter is for you, Howard,' said Mrs Pemberley holding it out to her. 'I demand that you open it in my presence.'

Eileen just stared at her.

'I don't understand.'

'Kindly do not argue with me. You will open the letter at once. I wish to discover who sent it.'

After a moment's weighty silence, Eileen shook her head.

'I'm sorry, Madam. I'm sorry, but my mail is a private matter. It has nothing to do with you.'

'Insolent gal, open that letter at once!'

'I will not, Madam.' Seeing her unreasonable anger, Eileen grew all the more determined. 'You have no business reading my mail.'

The argument had drawn both Meg and Thomas into the hall to see what was going on. Meg looked worried, confused by the scene, but Thomas had a knowing look in his eyes.

Aware of her audience, Mrs Pemberley played up to the occasion. She suddenly reached out and seized the letter from Eileen's hands and jabbed at the postmark with a fingernail.

'Chester,' she hissed passionately. 'Don't think that I don't know what has been going on. I have been warned against you for some time but I chose to give you the benefit of the doubt.' She arched her back, tilting her chin. 'But here is proof. Please don't shame yourself further by trying to deny that you have been consorting with my son, because I shall not believe you. It is disgraceful, quite disgraceful.'

A dread silence hung over them all. Eileen simply could not believe her ears. Consorting – with Jonathan? Was this some kind of wicked joke at her expense? But one look at Mrs Pemberley's tense white face was sufficient to show her that she meant every word, however unjust or ironic to Eileen.

'Now open that letter.'

Eileen saw that she had no alternative. She took back the envelope and slit it roughly open, pulling out the thick wad of closely-written pages in the familiar handwriting. But before she could say anything, Mrs Pemberley once more pounced on the letter. She frantically unfolded the pages and discovered the RAF censor's mark at the top with a great audible sigh of relief.

'Now deny that you have been corresponding with my son!'

'Turn to the last page.' Eileen's voice was quite calm although her anger mounted. 'You don't even know your own son's handwriting, do you? Just look at the signature.' She watched as the older woman turned to the bottom of the final page, watched as Mrs Pemberley's face paled with shock. 'Go on, read it out,' said Eileen bitterly. 'Let's all hear who it's from.'

Anger twisted Mrs Pemberley's upper lip as she fought to control her fury and embarrassment. She said nothing but thrust the crumpled letter back at Eileen in disgust.

'Tell them, go on, tell them it's not from your son!' Eileen turned towards Meg. 'It's from Gareth James. He's serving at the same unit as her son, that's all.' She was shaking with emotion and the effort to control her tears. She looked back at Mrs Pemberley. 'I think you owe me an apology.'

'An apology!' Mrs Pemberley could barely contain her fury. She was appalled at the ignominious position in which she had been placed. She struggled to retain her composure as the bitter words came tumbling out. 'You are shameless, shameless! Whether it is my son or his friend, it is unjustifiable. Your class appears to consider this war as an excuse for every kind of moral laxity. I know the type of gal you are, and I will not permit such loose behaviour on my staff.'

'Loose behaviour?' Eileen was stunned. 'How dare you say such a thing!'

'Let me tell you, my gal, I only took you on in this household on

61

the recommendation of your aunt. I knew nothing of your background. The very least I would have expected in the way of gratitude is that you would know your place. Members of my staff do not enter guests' bedrooms.'

There was a gasp of dismay and shock, and Eileen turned to look at Meg in desperation, but she had lowered her head. Mrs Pemberley saw her falter and swooped to consolidate her position.

'Never in my experience have I had to deal with such wanton behaviour. This is a Christian household. I am well known for my charity and understanding but I will no longer tolerate a Jezebel under my roof.' She turned her head, as though to dismiss the subject from her mind. 'You have 48 hours to pack your bags and leave.'

She closed her mouth with all the finality of a steel trap, her chin raised high. There was no possibility of breaking through her steely self-righteousness. To cover her false accusation she had brought out every rumour and insinuation Thomas had poured drop by drop into her ear over the past months. She had fallen back on this store of maliciousness in order to save face, pushed into this position through her hasty misinterpretation of the postmark on Gareth's letter. Only Eileen's dismissal could now eradicate the humiliation of this scene.

Eileen looked from her to her aunt. Meg hung her head low, appalled by the outrageous confrontation she had just witnessed, unable to conceive how this had come about. She was shaken that her relative, for whom she felt responsible, could have caused such strife with her longstanding employer to whom she owed her livelihood. Being uncertain of Eileen's honesty concerning her relationship with Mr James and any other guest at the house, she dared not risk the security of her own position in the household for a niece she had not really known since childhood. Eileen realised that Meg would deplore her familiarity with Gareth which broke all the bounds of convention and acceptable behaviour between upstairs and down.

Finally, Eileen turned her attention to Thomas, expecting to find his cat-like smile of gratification mocking her shame. But Thomas had the grace actually to look uncomfortable and quickly slipped away towards the kitchen without saying a word.

Unjustly accused, Eileen had no way of disproving the slander against her name. Her attempt at defence had been regarded as insubordination and had earned her instant dismissal.

To leave Charnwood was no hardship, but to leave under the bitter stigma of a ruined reputation was a terrible legacy to carry with her. She had almost made up her mind anyway to volunteer to join the Women's Auxiliary Air Force, but now her visit to the local recruiting office in the nearby town was marked by a desperate determination to be accepted.

At the interview the WAAF officer had asked which trade she wanted to follow. She was offered a place as a cook when she explained her previous experience at Charnwood, but Eileen wanted to do something quite different with her life; she wanted to drive. The idea had been latent in her thoughts all the time. It was part of the old dream of independence, of getting on in life and making something of herself. She wanted to be free, to have a little car and to go where she pleased.

The officer had looked at her with surprise but duly filled in the application form with the proviso that if she failed her driving test she would be posted wherever she was sent. Eileen readily agreed.

She supposed that Gareth's letters had a great deal to do with her decision to choose the WAAF in preference to the Wrens or the ATS. But any gratitude she may have felt towards him previously was now outweighed by a sense of resentment because his letters had caused her so much trouble.

Receiving his letter now via Meg had brought back all the misery and pain of her life at Charnwood which she had pushed aside and tried to suppress since joining the WAAF. She thought she had freed herself from the memory of that bitter experience by creating a new life for herself.

There were still minefields in her memory: places she no longer dared to tread, people she dared not think about. She had tried to cut herself off from Meg, from Gareth and from the emotional sway which Jonathan Pemberley held over her even there.

*

After Moira and Veronica had gone to sleep, Eileen was still restless. She sat up in bed in a state of nervous and miserable discontent, quite unable to sleep for the tumultuous thoughts whirling round inside her head. She had set out to make something of herself, knowing her own worth, ambitious to do things few women of her class or background had done before. If anything, the injustice of her dismissal from Charnwood had made her more determined. But there were moments when an overwhelming sense of grief washed over her, flooding her with memories both welcome and unwelcome.

She reached into the bedside cabinet and produced the old chocolate box in which she kept all her personal and private things. The cardboard was somewhat worse for wear, battered at the corners, but the lid was as pretty as ever, a thatched cottage and country garden full of blooms. Among the letters and ancient Christmas cards was the newspaper cutting.

She carefully unfolded the paper, yellowing now, the print of the caption smudged and faded, but his photograph was just the same, as good as her memory.

Chapter Three

Their time at Morecambe was largely spent in learning how to march up and down to the satisfaction of their sergeant. This torture was repeated daily on the open seafront where they struggled to fight the wind, marching in unison, swinging their arms as a snowstorm beat and battered them. And if this was not sadistic enough, there were also gym sessions held at the far end of Morecambe pier, an island marooned in a frozen sea which stood up stiff as white meringue peaks across the bay. Wearing only shirts and blackouts, the WAAF rookies turned blue as the icicle fringes which frosted the old penny arcade.

The waiting for their postings exasperated them. It seemed such a waste of time.

'It's all so petty,' they grumbled continuously. 'I joined up to do something really useful.'

The Bore War or Phoney War as some were calling it, dragged on and on. It was now February and yet it was hard to know they were at war. There was a feeling that they were being pushed into dreary jobs while the men got all the excitement. There had to be excitement somewhere, surely? Veronica's fiancé was out in France, but you could bet that they would never send women out there.

But one bitter February afternoon their sergeant posted up a list of names for transfer. Eagerly crowding round the noticeboard, Eileen found their names: Adams, Darling, Howard, all listed for motor transport instruction at Weston Camp.

'Weston? Where's that?'

'Ah, the bright lights for you girls,' grinned the sergeant

amiably. 'Just down the road from Blackpool.'

Going into camp at Weston was an experience. The huge RAF complex occupied an old aerodrome with large concrete hangars and lines of uniform Nissen huts. Back in a hut with fifteen beds a side, they began to appreciate their fortune in having had a room to themselves in Morecambe.

'It's huge,' admitted Veronica anxiously looking around, her face pale and pinched. 'I'm sure I'll never find my way round.'

'Don't you worry, we'll all stick together,' Moira told her cheerfully. 'I can't wait to have a crack at those cars the officers go round in.'

'Or the officers themselves!' added Eileen drily.

Moira made no secret of her interest in men. Weston plunged them all in the deep end: you had to sink or swim. The fact that women were so scarce at the camp suited Moira perfectly. Her warm but often alarming confidence still had the power to shock Eileen. Besides Moira she felt naïve and unsophisticated. She and Veronica would often exchange delicate glances whenever Moira went into action, though Eileen was certain that Veronica herself must have some experience.

'What? Just because she got engaged?' scoffed Moira. 'Don't you believe it! The nearest she's ever got is probably a peck on the cheek and a quick fumble in her Dad's Austin.'

'Moira!'

'Well, that's all right. He's just the type for her, and good looking too, but I couldn't do with that.' She paused and looked away, not smiling now. 'No, I'm looking for a man with prospects. I'm looking for someone who has it all sewn up. Things are going to change, mark my words, Eileen. You've got to know where you're going, you've got to know what you want. OK, of course he's got to be good in bed, but that's not all, is it? I'm not going to miss out on anything and when this lot's over I intend to come out of it a lot better off than when I started out.'

Eileen gave a lot of thought to Moira after this. From her brief account of her early life in London she was surprised that Moira seemed so desperate to change her status, to get on in life. Her home background had seemed happy enough, progressive even, with her grandmother being such an unusual woman. There was no suggestion of privation or serious money worries. Eileen would have thought that with the example of her grandmother, Moira would have had more personal ambition, more drive to make her own way, but all of Moira's energies seemed channelled into getting herself a husband, as though only a man could improve and complete her life.

Moira said that if and when the war really got going then there were bound to be casualties. Every war meant the loss of thousands of young men, the creation of thousands of widows and women who had lost fiancés. As she saw it, her chances of finding a good catch were vastly reduced by this prospective man-hunting competition. There was obviously no time to be lost.

Eileen was amazed at the speed with which Moira ingratiated herself at Weston. Within days she seemed to know every man on the camp by his first name.

'You know Jimmy?'

'Who?'

'Jimmy, the depot flight officer.' Ignoring their puzzled stares she would go on to describe how Jimmy or Harry or Frank had asked her to meet him outside the NAAFI that night. But she was openly contemptuous of non-commissioned ranks. It was an officer that she was after and the higher the rank the better. She knew that the RAF would give her the chance to meet someone really special, the kind of man she would never have had the chance to meet in ordinary life.

'Don't get grand ideas,' one of the other women told her. 'I've seen it all before. You'll get nothing but grief from tangling with an officer.'

Moira was busy ironing pleats into the straight A-line regulation skirt to give it some flair. She did not even look up.

'Look, dear, I mean this kindly. Get yourself a boy of your own kind.'

Moira's red head jerked up. 'My own kind? And what kind's that? You don't know anything about me, so why don't you just mind your own bloody business and shut up?'

The woman instantly cowered away, mumbling something under her breath about 'touchy bitches'. Eileen noticed that Moira was visibly upset by the casual remark. She wondered how much she really knew about Moira's life before she joined the WAAF and how much she too had been hiding from them.

Moira's confidence was often taken for granted and got her into trouble more than once with Corporal Brittain, who was responsible for their hut. But being Moira she could usually talk her way out of a charge, unlike poor Veronica. For some reason the diminutive Corporal Brittain took an instant dislike to Veronica. It could have been her air of quiet panic which drew the scent of her tormentor, but once the corporal had discovered her name there was no hope for her. The mellifluous tones of Corporal Brittain could be heard all over the camp crying in high-pitched outrage,

'Darling, come here!'

From her arrival at Weston Veronica seemed to be a marked woman. On kit inspection it was discovered that her blackouts were missing. Pilfering was very common, and as long as all the regulation underwear was available for inspection usually no one cared whether they really wore silk. Someone had clearly taken Veronica's blackouts to escape a charge and thereby had landed her right in trouble: two days jankers.

Jankers at Weston were a torture to the punishment squads, a pleasure to sadists of Corporal Brittain's ilk. All the filthy jobs round the camp were saved for those poor souls sentenced to jankers, their names inscribed in the Defaulters' Book. Jankers could range from chipping ice off the fire buckets right round the camp, cleaning and polishing, scrubbing and whitening, to emptying the dirty sanitary towels in the boiler house to the amusement of guffawing male stokers.

Veronica was soon familiar with every humiliation that Corporal Brittain could devise for her. The other women in the hut realised that while she drew the fire away from them they were safe, but Eileen and Moira were deeply angered by this attitude and took it upon themselves to try and steer Veronica away from the more obvious pitfalls.

On the driving course it was more difficult. They were split into teams of two assigned to instructors from the British School of Motoring, and as it turned out, Veronica was separated from them. She took her lessons in the mornings and had practical instruction in maintenance in the afternoons, while Moira and Eileen's schedule was vice versa. In spite of the advantage of driving lessons from her father, Veronica was soon reduced to tears by her morning sessions. Her instructor was a little man with a pencil-thin moustache and sandy hair, a civilian who could not understand what women were doing in the Air Force. He had derided her knowledge and made her look a fool, not because of her driving but because she was a woman.

There was some surprise at the ease with which women picked up skills previously monopolised by men. Some men at the camp, including Veronica's instructor, thought that women were doing these new tasks only because the country was at war and that this would be a purely temporary phenomenon. They were continually pointing out that a woman's place was really at home and the sooner they were back there the better.

'Just like a bloody woman!' he would exclaim if she crashed a gear. 'My God, whatever are they thinking of – putting women into responsible jobs. Things have come to a pretty pass when we need women in the Armed Forces.' And so on, in an unrelenting stream.

'Ignore the bugger,' advised Moira. 'Or tell him where to get off. Miserable little squirt.'

'He saps my confidence,' Veronica explained. 'I know I can do a manoeuvre – it's something I've done dozens of times back home – but he gets me so muddled that I just go to pieces. I'll never pass the test!'

'At this rate, none of us will.' Moira looked bleak. Her own introduction to driving had been a severe blow to her confidence. It had all looked so easy when other people drove her round, but once behind the wheel all her natural co-ordination seemed to disappear and her feet seemed determined to act independently of her hands. Changing gears and double de-clutching were skills that suddenly seemed far beyond her capabilities, wearing down the saintly patience of Mac, their own placid, worldly-wise instructor.

Only Eileen nursed her own pleasure in the driving lessons. She had been delighted with her first taste of the masculine world of engines, 60-foot long-loaders and heavy transport lorries. Something that had always been designated as a purely male reserve was now wide open to her. Eileen surprised herself and Mac with her own abilities. Driving came naturally to her and gave her a new confidence. She was learning all the time, discovering her own strengths.

The contrast between the freedom discovered on the road with Mac and the spite and authority exercised by Corporal Brittain in her own domain set Eileen on edge. The rules and petty regulations of the WAAF were not so dissimilar to her life in service with its tradition of doing the simplest tasks the hardest ways. It seemed like a continuation of the public school-big house system all over again. Didn't they see that the war was bound to change everything? The system was designed to demonstrate that life was far from fair. The ruthless discipline demanded the submission of all individual initiative and imagination.

'What they want are machines, not human beings,' Veronica groaned over dinner in the cookhouse one evening. 'How can they expect us to eat this?' She moved the cold mashed potato to one side of her plate, awash with damp cabbage spreading over the edge. The pieces of cheese which were beaten into the potato winked obscenely out as Veronica stabbed the mess with her fork. 'Three times this week. It's disgusting.'

The WAAF officer was moving down the line of tables with Corporal Brittain in tow. 'Any complaints?' She moved on without even waiting for an answer. 'Any complaints?'

Eileen felt Veronica tense as the procession approached. She put out a hand to prevent Veronica from rising.

'Don't be a fool. Brittain will put you on a charge for speaking out,' she hissed in a low urgent voice, and Veronica fell back in her seat.

There were other traps awaiting the unwary. Sitting in the NAAFI with steaming mugs of cocoa they saw two or three of their number fall easily.

'Anyone here like music?' asked a cheery voice round the door. The gullible volunteers raised their hands. 'Rightoh, you lot, come and shift the piano.'

As they progressed in their training from cars and trucks to heavy transport lorries, they were introduced to driving in convoy. Out on the country roads round the camp they learned to manoeuvre the heavy vehicles past obstacles which blocked the highway in case of German invasion. There were tank traps and 500lb cylindrical blocks of cement which reduced the width of the road to a single lane. Round the camp and at the entrance to large towns were pill-boxes and concrete abutments manned by troops and homeguard volunteers. To prevent enemy gliders landing in the fields or on golf courses there were improvised obstacles of every kind, from derelict cars and barbed wire to abandoned bedsteads. There were no signposts on the roads. Every single name plate had been covered up or taken down. Milestones and war memorials were mutilated. Every name was obliterated, even local vans had their exchange telephone numbers painted out. It was a country playing at war, even though the fun was palling.

People were sick of the blackout. Six months of darkness and accidents had spoilt the fun, the novelty had worn off. For Eileen driving in the blackout was no joke. Headlights were fixed with a mask which left only a tiny slit and gave virtually no light at all. Street kerbstones and lamp posts in the towns were painted with white circles to aid pedestrians, but there were still accidents. The wise took to wearing something white or carrying a newspaper in the dark so that they could be seen, but it was still a damned nuisance when Hitler quite obviously had no intention of bombing Britain.

Driving at night along deserted country roads, Eileen thought she had never seen the sky more beautiful or mysterious before. Without street lamps and brash headlights to break down the darkness, her eyes became accustomed to the velvet blackness of the sky spangled with myriad stars.

With confidence running high, Eileen was almost arrogant about her ability to pass the driving test. As the date approached and the last snows began to melt, she set out with Mac for a last lesson driving into the outskirts of Blackpool. She sat jauntily behind the wheel of the old Bedford, slamming the gears and settling comfortably into top as they cruised along the country lanes. It was a bitterly cold day and there was still ice in the puddles. As they sped along, Mac dourly watched the pheasants fly screaming into the hedgerows as Eileen showed off her new skills.

In the town there was very little traffic. Since petrol rationing had been introduced late in September, there were few private cars on the road except for doctors and farmers. Even in a town the size of Blackpool, Eileen had an easy passage.

At one point her route passed across a steep hill, a side street lined with suburban houses, still covered in ice. Eileen had the right of way, but a heavy coal truck, coming down the hill towards her, could not get his brakes to work on the slippery surface at the road junction and plunged downhill straight towards her. There was an almighty crash as the coal truck hit the Bedford in the side, missing Mac in the passenger seat by inches. The force of the crash sent the Bedford sideways, ramming into the corner grocery shop and shattering the glass window inscribed 'Roberts Provisions'.

Eileen sat clutching the steering wheel, shaking with shock after the accident. Mac had abandoned the cab and gone to check that the truck driver was all right and to see to the damage. The coal truck's brakes had failed; it was clearly no one's fault really and there should not be too much trouble over the incident, but it took Mac some time to convince Eileen that her future as a WAAF driver was not over. She was still shaking as Mac told her to get back into the driving seat and take them home.

'I can't,' she said lamely, demonstrating her quivering hands. 'I'm sorry, Mac, you'll have to drive us back.'

For once his placid face darkened and real anger showed in his blue eyes as he glared at her. 'Now listen to me, young lady, you get back in that cab and you drive, because if you don't start driving again now then you're never going to want to drive again. Do you understand me? You'll be finished, it will all be over with you.'

Eileen just gaped at him. She was suddenly terrified of sitting behind the wheel, her mind traumatised by the thought of another accident and the memory of metal sheering off metal. But she did as she was told, although her hands shook as she switched on the engine and kept it ticking over.

'Well, come on,' said Mac impatiently. 'What are you waiting for?'

'I think I've lost my nerve.'

'Codswallop! Don't talk so daft, woman! You're my star pupil and I'm not having you let me down now. So get your finger out and get us home sharp. I don't know about you, but I'm bloody freezing!'

Once the van was moving Eileen was astonished at how smoothly her hands and feet took over the controls. All her instinctive skill reappeared and by the time they were out of the town she was smiling again. Mac's admission of his judgement of her driving ability now cheered her as the freezing miles stretched before her. Mac thought she was good, Mac thought she was the best! Even after the shock of their accident, he still believed she could do it!

It was dark and a fine freezing drizzle was falling fast all round them as they displayed the 658 Motor Transport Authority form at the camp gates.

'Drop me here, Eileen,' Mac instructed her, 'but the Bedford must go to the MT.' He clambered out of the cab. 'You did well, young lady, very well indeed. Leave me to sort out the details with the bods in there. I'll see you tomorrow afternoon – for the test.'

The test. Eileen tingled with excitement and apprehension as she locked up the van and dropped the keys in to the MT section. It was so cold that she hurried back to the hut, grabbed her towel and bag and raced for the bath hut to thaw out. It was deserted so she assumed that the others were still at dinner or in the NAAFI. She lay back in the huge steaming bath, stretching her aching and bruised back, revelling in the glorious heat, when suddenly there was an ominous crunch of footsteps outside the cubicle door.

'Who's that woman inside?' demanded the booming un-mistakable voice of Corporal Brittain. 'Who dares to take a bath today?'

Eileen started up, splashing water over the side. She stared at the flimsy door, imagining the red-faced fury of the corporal on the other side. 'It's me, corporal. Howard. It's Howard.'

'Howard!' The searing voice held an hysterical note of betrayal. One of her own flock daring to have a bath! 'What are you doing in there, Howard? Get yourself out here instantly!'

Eileen grabbed her towel and hurriedly clambered out into the freezing passage, coming hurriedly to attention in her bare feet and toga. The famous Brittain leer took in all her misery.

'You miserable woman, don't you read your DRO's? Don't you know that the bath hut is out of bounds today? No, don't say a word. Get yourself dressed, Howard, and report at once. It will be jankers for you for the rest of the week, just you wait.'

For her sin, Eileen found herself treated like a criminal. No one bothered to read DROs but it had just been her luck to get found

73

out by someone as heartless as Corporal Brittain. She was marched before an officer and given three days' jankers and told to report the next morning to the kitchens. Eileen spent her last three hours before the driving test washing mountains of cabbage, her hands wrinkled from the cold water.

By the time she arrived at the MT section, Veronica had already gone back to the hut after taking her test. There was no way of knowing if all had gone well for her, but Eileen saw her tiny, rat-faced instructor standing side by side with Mac with the examiner, clipboard in hand. Moira stood together with the other candidates, huddled in a corner of the open hanger in their battledress, watching what was going on with pinched, nervous faces.

'Did you see Veronica? Was she all right?'

'She came straight back to the hut and threw up,' Moira said bluntly. 'One look at her was enough to put me off for life. I just don't know why I ever put down for a driver.'

My God, poor Veronica, thought Eileen, that means she would not be with them, she would be assigned to some other dreadful job that no one else wanted. Only those who passed their test would go on to join stations as staff drivers; there was no second chance.

With a sudden start she heard her name called and felt Moira give her a little push forward. She hurriedly presented herself to the stern-faced examiner and gave a little salute. There was no turning back now. Behind the examiner's back she caught sight of Mac and she almost gave the game away by smiling when she saw him give her a sudden wink of encouragement.

After that the test itself was a dream. She barely remembered getting into the vehicle beside the examiner and starting up. It seemed to her that it was all over in an instant and she was back in camp, drawing up outside the hangar, aware of a row of curious faces demanding to know her fate.

'I'm pleased to tell you that you've passed,' said the examiner, scribbling on the clipboard at her side, 'but you'd better turn off the engine now.'

Eileen stumbled out to join Moira and clutched her hands.

'My God, was it awful? You look dreadful.'

'No, it was simple. I passed, I actually passed!'

'Well, you might look a bit pleased about it,' Moira said resentfully. 'It's my turn next. Wish me luck – I'll need it.'

Back at the hut Eileen found Veronica lying flat out on her bed, her face as pale as death. Eileen felt guilty about her own success, not knowing how to tell her friend, but Veronica had heard her come in and sat up on the bed, propping herself up on her elbow.

'Well?'

'I passed,' Eileen confessed, shame-faced. 'And you?'

'I passed too,' came the reply. 'I was so shocked that I came straight back here and was sick!'

Fifteen minutes later they watched the doorway for Moira's return, biting their nails. If she had passed there was a chance that they could all stay together for a while. None of them wanted to be split up now.

The door to the hut opened furtively and Moira's red head appeared, grinning from ear to ear. A surge of relief ran round the group and Veronica and Eileen let out a cry of joy as they ran forward to meet her.

To celebrate they hitched a lift into Blackpool on their next pass, determined to have a good night out. Veronica's cheeks were bright with relief and a sense of accomplishment. In her best blue she looked smart and pretty as she brushed her hair with vigorous strokes so that it shone. They had all pressed their skirts into shape under their mattress biscuits and had made a conscious effort to look good, but Moira was more than usually dazzling. Her make-up was sophisticated, her hair perfectly in place. She wore her sharply pressed uniform with unique style, knowing that there would not be a woman in town to match her.

'There'll be some action here tonight,' she promised them, flashing her bright eyes around the entrance to the Tower Ballroom. 'The RAF's in town!'

The dance floor was already packed with couples. Most of the men dancing or sitting at tables around the edge were in uniform, predominantly blue. Moira's self-confidence had proved to be correct. It was already obvious that women were clearly in the minority, about three to one, and as Moira had predicted most of the competition were local girls.

'Let's get a table,' Veronica suggested, becoming aware of stray glances in their direction.

'No, not yet.' Moira smoothed her skirt. 'Let's take a stroll and show ourselves. I want a chance to inspect the goods.'

She moved forward from the entrance with supreme self-assurance, her walk exaggerated by the tightness of her skirt. Following her between the tables, Eileen thought she would be on jankers for a fortnight if the corporal got hold of her.

As they progressed around the edge of the room, Eileen became aware that Moira was closely observing their audience as much as they were staring at her. Heads turned in their direction as they passed and Moira was carefully categorising each and every one. But only the officers stood a chance with Moira Adams tonight.

Satisfied at last that she had publicised her arrival sufficiently to bait the trap, Moira gathered her companions about her and selected an empty table on the fringe of the dance floor. Eileen and Veronica seated themselves, very conscious of the aura of interest all round them.

'Are you ladies out all on your own?'

Moira slowly raised her eyes. A fresh young man in a smart blue uniform with pilot's wings hovered over her, dark hair smoothed back, eyes bright with mischief.

'No one here to look after you?'

'We can look after ourselves,' she told him, raising an eyebrow. Her mocking gaze held on to his to let him know that she was only goading him on to further sport. His smile broadened in open appreciation.

'I bet you can,'.he murmured. 'Why don't you – and your friends – come over and join us? No point in being all alone and miserable.' He saw the look that passed between them, the hesitation in Eileen's face, the reluctance in Veronica's. With a devastating smile aimed directly at Moira, he added, 'That's our table over there.'

Looking in the direction in which he nodded, they saw a large table already well stacked with bottles and glasses, round which eight young men in RAF uniform lounged easily, laughing and talking. It took no more than a glance for Moira to discern the silver wings on their chest and the officer rings on their sleeves.

'How kind,' she said. 'We'd love to join you.'

Moira's unilateral decision left them no alternative. Their own table was abandoned as they followed her over to the pilot officer's group. An array of eager grinning faces turned their way and there were hurried movements to bring extra chairs for their guests. Eileen soon found herself sandwiched between two solicitous young men scarcely into their twenties. They were both fresh-faced and confident, wearing their uniforms with a casual lack of formality. She was offered a glass of beer or whisky, and quickly chose the former although she would have preferred to be offered something else. But it was a happy, friendly group. The pilots were all from a nearby flying school and had just passed out after their training. The wings on their uniforms were all brand new.

'What a coincidence,' said Moira brightly. 'We're here to celebrate our passing out, too!'

Eileen saw that Moira was drinking whisky and, as they had not eaten that night, thought perhaps it was not wise. Veronica barely sipped at her beer and looked rather shy and uncomfortable at so much attention. Moira was just lapping it up. It seemed to Eileen that her friend changed subtly in the company of male admirers, that she forgot any loyalties that were due to her female friends. Down the table she could hear Moira telling the tale of Veronica being sick after passing her test and of Eileen herself being on jankers all morning. It was designed to put Moira into a good light by comparison and was therefore thoughtless rather than cruel, but from the expressions on the faces about her Eileen saw that they found her a little vulgar.

Eileen could tell at once that Moira was out of her depth among men of this class. Even though they were so young, the stamp of wealth and easy living sat comfortably about them. Behind her back she saw the exchanged grins and laughing eyes. For all her high fashion and grooming, Moira could not fool them. Whatever her life had been in London, she had not mixed with the class of people with whom Eileen had been familiar at Charnwood. Eileen had observed and learnt from her observation the deep and bitter divide which separated one class from another. It would take a woman more determined or blind to all outside pressures to attempt to cross that divide for the sake of a man.

Looking around the table, Eileen saw that even the oldest of

77

the pilots was twenty-one or twenty-two. Most of them it seemed were straight out of public school or university, although some had flying experience before joining the RAF.

Like Jonathan, thought Eileen, and regret flooded in. It was several weeks since she had allowed thoughts of him to trouble her, but the sight of these young men, out to celebrate their own success, turned her mind to thoughts of Jonathan.

The lighting was soft and the music began to play again. Eileen watched as Moira was taken off for a dance, followed by a rather humble Veronica on the arm of a boy younger than herself. As though in a trance, Eileen heard herself declining, her attention wandering over thoughts of long ago. If Moira, who was so determined, could not bridge the distance between one class and another, how impossible her own dreams seemed. Even if she ever saw Jonathan Pemberley again she knew that she had no chance of winning his attention, let alone his love. Why then did thoughts of him persist in tormenting her, even here when she should have been enjoying herself?

She sipped her beer and looked across the dance floor where the gyrating couples spun under wildly flashing coloured spotlights in the ceiling. Everyone was having such a good time. Why couldn't she break this sudden mood of despair and forget him?

'Well, you certainly took your time,' one of her neighbours at the table suddenly announced, addressing a newcomer who was approaching. 'Did you manage to make your call after all that?'

'You nearly missed all the fun,' added another voice at her side, with a nod in Eileen's direction. 'We have guests.'

Eileen turned and looked at him sharply, feeling that he was making snide suggestions about them, but when she raised her eyes to gauge the reaction of their friend all such thoughts deserted her. For across the expanse of the table stood a figure in RAF uniform gazing down on her in equal astonishment.

Gareth James.

His father was ill. He had read the news in a letter from home which he had begun reading in the bumping, overcrowded Morris Oxford on their way out on the town. It was too late to turn back and, anyway, he felt little inclination to give up the night's entertainment for a letter which had clearly taken a week or ten days to reach him. But after they had arrived in Blackpool, he sat over his beer and felt guilty, so guilty that he just could not settle until he had done something about it. After all, it was his father.

Going in search of a telephone, he had mixed feelings about the old man. He had never gone out of his way to show him any affection over the years, although he was his only son. Work was his entire life and it was the ethic which he had tried to instil in Gareth for as long as he could remember. All through his lonely childhood after his mother's death, Gareth had been afraid of his father, afraid of drawing that cold eye upon him. Apparently incapable of affection, his father ruled with stern and unbending discipline. When he was about eight, Gareth had been beaten black and blue for talking in chapel. His father didn't have a cane to beat him with and so he went out into the garden and uprooted his runner beans to get one.

At nine he was sent away to Methodist college, but even at that distance his father never ceased to pile on the pressure. Gareth hated the place and longed to get away, but there was nowhere to get away to. So he had turned to his studies, unwittingly pleasing his father by working for the Cambridge scholarship which he himself had longed for and been denied.

And was he now dying? Even as he dialled the number his heart was racing with apprehension. He was an old man now, weak and frail. He even had to get a manager in to run his shops, although he went through all the accounts with a fine tooth comb.

When he heard that his son was abandoning his course at Cambridge to join the RAF, even before the war was declared, the fury of his resentment and caustic derision had depressed Gareth for days. He recalled that time at Charnwood, sunk in comfort and lethargy waiting for the posting to come through, when he had felt at odds with all the world, so out of place in the Pemberleys' grand house. Jonathan had shrugged when he tried to explain, telling him not to be so sensitive, to ignore the cold civility of his parents and the frosty disapproval of the servants, and to have a good time. He envied Jonathan's relatively uncomplicated attitude to his own father. The colonel had been furious when he learnt that they were joining the RAF, but

Jonathan knew how to handle him and there was none of that dark bitterness that hung in the air for weeks after Gareth and his father had clashed over something. Now Jonathan and his family were back on good terms and the colonel was apparently boasting to everyone who would listen about his son the fighter pilot. Gareth could never imagine his own father becoming reconciled to what he saw as his betrayal.

He let the number ring and ring but there was no reply. He knew that the telephone system had gone haywire because of the war, but he felt certain that there was some other explanation for getting no reply. Was he really ill? Rushed away to the cottage hospital for an emergency operation? Or was it already too late? Was the phone ringing in a silent house where his father was laid out in the unused front parlour waiting for the minister to come?

Damn, damn him. It was probably no more than wishful thinking. He slammed down the receiver and turned away. Why were relatives such a bloody bind? Why was it that he still felt something for the old man in spite of everything, in spite of all the ill will and downright cruelty of the past? Now he knew that he would probably brood all the evening, unable to get his father out of his mind until he knew for certain one way or the other. Damn him.

He wished that Jonathan was with him, not off somewhere in the south with his new squadron. At least Jon understood him. These other chaps were all decent enough, well meaning, but frankly he felt uneasy in their company, aware of the difference between them. They were all the same type: rich boys out for a lark, none of them taking the war seriously although they enjoyed their flying. Until the situation changed and they saw some action they would continue to play the fool and spend a small fortune running up mess bills which could have fed a family for a year back home in Wales.

When they had first joined up they were interviewed by a regular officer who beamed with delight when he learnt Jonathan's background. He was a keen foxhunting type and asked them questions about their schools and sports. Before the war opened the flood-gates to all manner of recruits, RAF officers enjoyed their hunting and riding. Some even stabled their horses on the station. It was all part of the same social round that

80

Jonathan, as a Pemberley, recognised all too well. The point was, however, that he had rejected all that kind of thing. He didn't give a damn for any of it, and that is what drew Gareth towards him. Jon would not have cared less. There was no side to him.

Gareth was in no hurry to get back to his group. Although the ballroom was rapidly filling up, he could still make out their table from the gallery where he came from the telephones. But looking down on the scene his attention was immediately caught by the sight of three young women in WAAF uniforms who had joined his companions: a vivacious redhead who held her glass for more whisky, another who kept her brown head bent low, and the third who turned her dark head away just as he caught sight of her face.

Her face. That face which had haunted his memory through a long bleak winter. He could never mistake it, not even when it was plain that she was in WAAF blue when he knew damn well she was safely back in Buckinghamshire in that bloody awful job of hers. He hurried on round the gallery, never taking his eyes off her, certain that he was not mistaken yet unable to understand what she could be doing here, in Blackpool, wearing that uniform. And as the music started up and the boys dragged two of the girls out on to the dance floor, he paused on the stairs and caught his breath as she stared straight ahead, as if lost in some kind of dark dream.

He could not have explained the way he felt but the sight of her brought back all the memories he had kept to himself since that first time at Charnwood when he had partnered her for a brief moment in the midst of the Paul Jones, holding her lightly in his arms, laughing about her hybrid family from the borders. She had made an immediate impression on him that he was loth to shake off. And when he caught sight of the housemaid in the library of Charnwood House with her heavy basket of firewood and coal, he felt it was fate that had brought them together again, as though to cock a snook at the Pemberleys and everything they stood for. Was that the reason he had found the courage to ask her out? No, she meant more to him than getting his own back, more than even proving something to Jonathan. That evening out they had spent together was memorable in more ways than one. Jonathan's discomfiture at discovering he had been dating one of the family servants only served to reinforce his desire to make a friend out of Eileen and to continue the friendship even while he was away at camp.

And so he had written to her. It was a great relief to have someone in whom he could confide and he found himself spilling out his thoughts on page after page. When she had replied he was over the moon, astonished at his own reaction, astonished even more by his desire to keep their correspondence private, even from Jon. He suddenly discovered that here was more than simple friendship. Her letters came to mean everything, giving him a sense of stability, a centre to his personal life outside and beyond his existence in the RAF and his camaraderie with Jon. But then it seemed that he must have embarrassed her, for before long her letters ceased as though through some unknown action he had alarmed or offended her. But now, seeing her there, he began to wonder if that really was so. Had he really frightened her off with his constant flow of letters, or was it simply that she had left Charnwood and joined the WAAF, and that in the confusion of wartime addresses their mail had missed one another? Why, that had to be it! There could be no other explanation; he was a fool not to think of it before.

He was filled with an overwhelming sense of excitement as he started on down the staircase into the ballroom. What a surprise she would get when she saw him there! Her last letter had been so warm and friendly, she would surely be pleased to see him again.

As he approached the table, Colin caught sight of him, roundly berating him for the delay in joining them again.

'Well, you certainly took your time. Did you manage to make your call after all that?'

'You nearly missed all the fun,' declared Peter, grinning all over his face and winking in Eileen's direction. 'We have guests.'

He said nothing. As he approached, the sight of Eileen's face rooted him to the spot and he just stood there, tongue-tied and nervous as a schoolboy. He saw fleeting expressions on her face: anger with Peter's light remarks, confusion and then open astonishment as finally she raised her head and her eyes met his. He saw the shock of recognition, a look of puzzled incredulity and something more, something less than welcome – or was he mistaken? Could it really be that she was not pleased to see him?

'Eileen, it is Eileen, isn't it?'

'Hello, Gareth.'

The flatness of her tone alarmed him. Such was his excitement at seeing her again that his thoughts tumbled round inside his brain, it was impossible to think straight. He could see Colin and Peter grinning at him like Cheshire cats, bloody fools.

'It's great to see you,' he blustered. 'You never said that you were joining up. You never wrote.'

'No, I'm sorry.'

He pulled out a chair, one of those abandoned by the dancing couples, and sat down dead opposite her, drinking in her troubled eyes and the hard mouth painted red. She looked very different from the quiet little borders girl he had taken out at Charnwood. She looked older, more sophisticated. The smartness of her uniform jacket and crisp shirt and collar gave her an air of authority and responsibility, as though she had learnt to look after herself. He was not sure he liked this change in her, but his senses acted independently of his brain. There was something exciting about her now; she was a woman and no longer a girl.

'I couldn't understand what happened to you. I wrote letter after letter, but you never answered. Not since last Christmas.'

He stared at her, the hurt visible in his dark eyes. Eileen felt acutely uncomfortable, highly aware of their audience, unable to control the sudden surge of fury and resentment which had swept over her at the first sight of him. How dared he re-enter her life like that! It was such a shock seeing him standing there, expecting her to welcome him with open arms after almost nine months as though nothing had happened.

Of course, it wasn't his fault. He wasn't to know that it was his letter which had caused her such trouble, which made her resent him so. But the way he sat there looking at her, with those dark languid eyes and little boy look.

'I never imagined for one moment that you had left. I mean, you didn't say a word about joining up in any of your letters,' he continued, talking so quickly that the words blurred to her ears. 'I thought a lot about you. Getting your letters meant a lot, you know.'

'Look, I'm sorry,' she cut in abruptly, 'but I don't want to talk about it.'

The frosty words cut a swathe through the talking at the table.

There was an edge to her voice which silenced them even though they had not heard her actual words. Gareth started back at the tone, his face lit by the lurid lighting from the dance floor, looking gaunt and shadowed. The sharp lines of his cheekbones gave him the look of a man far older than his years, as though suddenly aged by sorrow and hard decisions.

Eileen knew that she had wounded him. Her words were unforgivable without some explanation, but she felt only renewed anger at the sight of his despair. Seeing him again had dragged all her own grief out into the open and she had no desire to share it with anyone. He was too kind and considerate for his own good. She had no time to consider his feelings when her own had been torn apart, the old nightmares thrust again into her face. She just wanted him to go away, to get out of her life.

She took Colin by the sleeve pulling his face round to hers.

'About that dance. I'd like to dance with you now.'

Gareth watched in stunned amazement as he saw Eileen rise to take Colin by the arm and move out on to the dance-floor. He felt as though he had been struck in the face.

'Don't worry, old man,' Peter said glibly. 'You win some, you lose some.'

Gareth poured himself a stiff glass of whisky and tried to give a wan smile. He felt dropped down into deep despair, completely unable to understand how he had given offence, knowing only that he had lost her once again.

They arrived at Biggin Hill at the end of March. Their transfers had come through almost at once, suggesting that the war effort had been stepped up and drivers were in great demand. After their cold and disagreeable stay on the north-west coast, all three of them were grateful to be thrust into the heart of action. Biggin Hill was deservedly one of the foremost of fighter stations.

When they arrived the airbase was a hive of frenzied activity, bustling with aircrew and mechanics. Amid the gentle hills and clustered greenery of the Garden of England, the field was known to the RAF as 'the Bump', home of the famous Tigers of 74 Squadron under 'Sailor' Malan. Over the meadows and orchards of Kent the Spitfires went through training manoeuvres, giving beautiful displays of aerobatics in mock dogfights, in preparation for the day when the game could turn into reality.

The WAAFs were billeted out in villages round the base like Westerham and Ide Hill. They had considerable freedom and came and went, raising eyebrows among the more conservative locals who had never seen women in uniform, wearing make-up, and behaving with a radical abandon that went hand in hand with hard physical work. WAAFs at the base were assigned to all kinds of duties. They had struggled to show their worth, as though they had to prove something to the men, but they had found fulfilment in their demanding and often highly responsible posts.

Eileen soon found that new arrivals got the worst jobs. She was given the job of driving troops at the base to Sunday church parade in an old Dodge, little better than a glorified furniture van. The troops clung on to rope straps in the back, rocking and swaying as the old crock rumbled and protested its way along. It took all her effort to get the gears, and everyone at the back used to shout out encouragement. Once in church the fun was not over. The Forces had the back rows, behind their commanding officers and the local civilians. The old vicar used to ramble on and on, while the bored RAF used to play housey-housey on their knees or even read the News of the World to pass the time. Monday mornings usually began with a ticking-off by Sergeant Bayman after the vicar had rung up to complain.

In a few weeks between them, Eileen, Moira and Veronica drove everything from vans, long-loaders and Canadian jeeps to Vauxhall saloons when an officer needed a trip out. These were the jobs Eileen liked the best. Being out on the road gave her a sense of freedom and self-sufficiency, away from the confines and regulations of station life. She was popular with the officers, too. She was a good driver, she could change a wheel in record time, and she knew when to shut up when the atmosphere was tense or the officer was trying to grab a few hours of shut-eye. Some trips could mean she was out driving for fourteen hours or more, on other days there were only light duties around the camp. On the whole she averaged about 300 miles a day.

On their one day off a week they would go out together in gangs, smoking and ordering rounds of pints in quiet country pubs where unaccompanied women were normally shown the

85

door. They ran a kitty, everyone putting in sixpence or a shilling and drinking bitter or mild. Sometimes, on special occasions, they ran the bar, trying everything in shelf order, leaving a marker so they would know where they had got to for their next night out. It was a male world and there were very few women around. They knew that they were something special and got a kick out of shocking those locals who were slow to adapt to the new changes the war was bringing.

After the appalling winter, spring ushered in a period of warmth and brilliant sunshine. Only the news of the war destroyed the illusion that this was a year like any other.

The invasion of Denmark and Norway meant a new turning point in the war. After the stagnant months of waiting for something to happen, Hitler's advance took everyone by surprise. No one could fool themselves that Germany could be appeased any longer. Now that events were on the move they all knew it could not be stopped without a real fight.

In France the Allies had built up strong defensive lines. There were more British troops pouring into the country every day in preparation for the struggle that was sure to come. After the battles of the last war, it was certain that the German advance would be halted in France by the Maginot bunkers before any serious damage could be done. In frustration it was hoped that the enemy would then turn his back on the West and move against his erstwhile ally Russia, as Hitler himself had all too clearly outlined in 'Mein Kampf' years before. It was no secret that many in high circles believed that war could have been averted altogether had Britain only encouraged an early attack on the Soviets, but wily Stalin had seen through their tactics and entered into an unholy alliance with the Germans himself in order to delay the inevitable.

Back in Britain the local precautions against attack were seen as rather a joke. No one seriously believed that an invasion would come. The real battle would be fought on the Continent, with France as the final defensive line.

But the rapid German advance to the North Sea and the savagery of bombing raids made everyone nervous and jumpy. News of the loss of British shipping, the sinking of the *Glorious* by the *Scharnhorst*, belied the jaunty assurance of newsreel commentators with their cocksure arrogance: 'Apart from military secrets we have nothing to hide. We are fighting our war in the open. Our propaganda is all true.' Sitting in the dark watching the effect of German bombs on Rotterdam left a deathly chill of disbelief on audiences. Waiting and watching and yet being unable to do anything was having a growing effect on morale. They heard Chamberlain complain that Hitler desired 'the ruin of the British Empire' but they were more deeply affected by the bombs which killed and wounded 30,000 civilians in Rotterdam. The incompetence of their leaders was a main talking point, even in Parliament. Chamberlain was told in Cromwell's words, 'Depart, I say, and let us have done with you. In the name of God, go.'

When Holland and Belgium were invaded on May 10th, the country heaved a sigh of relief as Chamberlain resigned the premiership and the old war horse Winston Churchill stepped into his uncomfortable shoes at the head of a coalition Government.

Now the country began to move. Preparations began in earnest to face the realities of war. The news of history had pushed them to the brink, but was there still time to avert a disaster?

Weekend leaves were cancelled. A Local Defence Volunteer force was formed in order to provide home-guard defence if all else should fail. Churchill flew to France for urgent discussions with his French counterpart, Paul Reynaud, passing secret instructions back down the line using ex-Indian service officers speaking Urdu dialects.

As British forces marched north into Belgium to meet the threat, Rommel's Panzers crossed the River Neuse in fog. The German Army had arrived in France.

Attacking through the Ardennes forest, going round and by-passing the Maginot Line, the German tanks struck out for the English Channel. British and French leaders were out of touch with reality. They blindly ordered a counter-attack across all fronts although the Allied armies had been cut in two. At Arras the French Cavalry and the British attacked although they had only sixteen Mark II tanks, but there was no co-ordination in the south. Exhausted, short of ammunition, out of communication, the armies defending France collapsed.

On the evening of May 26th the British Expeditionary Force was ordered to evacuate from the sector around the French coastal town of Dunkirk.

Chapter Four

On the afternoon when Veronica was setting out on a night convoy through the country lanes of Kent villages her fiancé, Timothy Barton, Captain in the Territorials, found himself ushering his men out along the broken spine of the mole in Dunkirk harbour.

It was a scene of ordered chaos. The afternoon light was driven back by dark palls of smoke billowing from burning rubber and oil dumps which had been hit earlier by enemy fighters. It seemed as though the whole town had gone up in flames, a livid backdrop to the last act was being played out down at the wharfs.

There were still steamers tied up and waiting. Across the heads of his men, he could see the stretcher-cases being loaded on board the *Fenella* an old paddle-steamer, one of those pleasure boats more at home on a trip round the bay than stuck out here in the middle of a war. He was glad that their own wounded would not be risking their lives on that old tub. The *Crested Eagle* from Southend stood side by side with her neighbour, a fleet modern oil-burning passenger ship. As he shifted his arm in its sling to help the man behind him on board, he wondered how many more the ship could take. He saw the line of exhausted troops snaking out along the pier, their dark faces desperate, their patience and discipline a miracle in the midst of the horror and confusion of the disaster which had caught them up and deposited them in the trap between the advancing German army and the sea.

'Stuka! Stuka!'

The cry cut through the massed ranks of men and they fell on their faces like a house of cards as the heavy air was suddenly full of the sound of advancing aircraft. Face pressed to the wooden deck of the Eagle, Tim lay unmoving, listening for the bombs. The ear-piercing scream of the diving Stukas sent a ripple of terror among the men huddling for shelter. The German designers had fitted sirens to their planes to increase the panic and alarm among their victims. As the sickening wail grew louder, Tim turned his head and saw with one eye the image of death streaking out of the purple sky in an almost vertical dive towards its target. To the uninitiated it would seem that the Stuka must crash, but Tim knew that at the very last moment, the moment when its bombs were released, the Stuka would pull sharply out of its dive and climb away from danger.

The bright bird dropped its eggs and flew away, leaving the *Fenella* scarred and wounded, hit on deck and holed below the water-line. It was already going down.

A chorus of alarm went up as the Fenella slipped sideways and great gouts of water erupted over the wounded men who lay on stretchers balanced precariously on the tilting deck. There was an immediate move to save the helpless from the flames where the bombs had hit and from drowning in the turbulence of the narrow sea between the sinking ship and the edge of the stone-built mole. Screaming and shouting spread the panic. Wedged where he was between the wounded from his own unit and the hard metal side of the Crested Eagle, Tim could only watch as a few stretcher-cases were manhandled over the ever-increasing gap between the sinking paddle-steamer and the wharf, while others slipped helplessly into the swirling green-black waters and disappeared.

Those survivors brought back to the pier were given immediate precedence and taken on board the *Eagle* ahead of everyone else. There was no protest from the waiting line of men, crouching and standing along the fragile length of the wharf. As he made room for the newcomers, Tim thought that such men were worth more than this ignominious failure, betrayed and deserted by their field officers and by generals and politicians sitting safely back in England.

There was one poor devil bleeding profusely from a wood splinter in the chest, groaning and writhing in agony, another lying as still as death. Dragged from the sinking vessel barely in time, they lay among the screaming and the dying, wondering what more lay in wait for them in this hell hole.

Above the noise of shouting and the crackle of flames from the sinking *Fenella*, Tim was alerted to another sound above his head. He swung round, head tilted to the sky and saw the Stukas making their approach out of the bruised sky for another strike. He stared as though mesmerised as the pilot put his plane into the startling dive almost directly overhead. The speed of its flight and the growing pain of the siren's wail in his ears confirmed Tim in his belief that this was surely the end. This was death and there was no escaping.

Those who had heard the plane's approach and could still move among the press of bodies on deck and strung out along the pier began to run, pushing and pulling their neighbours as the first bombs rained down. On the *Crested Eagle* there was no room to move. All round him men buried their heads in their hands, unable to do more than cover their eyes from the terrifying spectacle overhead.

As the first bomb struck the ship the whole structure vibrated like a gong, trembling in the water with the force of the explosion. It was a direct hit. With a searing rush, the oil tanks that fuelled the modern ship burst into an obscene orange balloon of light, spraying red-hot metal across the decks. Heat and debris hit the men with equal force. A score of struggling figures were silhouetted in the raging firestorm, burning before their very eyes, their screams drowned by the roar of pressure as the *Crested Eagle's* wooden hull split asunder.

Tim was galvanised into action. All round him a wail of fear and pain soared in the air as it grew thick with the stench of oil and smoke. Tim knew he had to move before the whole ship was engulfed by flames. He tried to find his way over the side of the ship's rail to regain the safety of the wharf, but as his uninjured hand touched the metal he withdrew in horror, staring at the blistered paintwork burning his flesh. Suddenly he was capable of seeing everything about him in sharp relief. He was acutely aware of the trap they were all in. Flames had spread to the wooden pier-head, cutting off all escape to the shore along the mole. Bombs and strafing from the low-flying fighters had cut a swathe through the massed ranks of men queuing for a ship out of danger, and their corpses were already piled up along the wharf in grotesque huddles, men who only moments before had been living.

There was no alternative. Tim followed the example of other able-bodied survivors who were already plunging over the side of the ship to escape the flames and spraying metal fragments. Poised on the edge of the deck he looked out on the burning sea, awash with oil seeping from the ruptured fuel tanks. It was like a scene from Dante's *Inferno*. The sea moved with myriad colours of the night, a serpents' nest of coiled blue-black and brilliant green, shining and shifting in the light of the fires. Men jumped and were swallowed up by the inky vastness, lost beneath the waters. Poised for his life, Tim felt the lash of heat strike him in the back – and leapt out from the wooden deck.

The water was warm and sticky. As the sea closed round him, he felt an instinctive panic, an abhorrence of the sight, stench and cloying touch of the heavy liquid in which he was being sucked down under the waves washed from the half-sunken shell of the crippled paddle steamer *Fenella*.

He saw the hulk of the burning *Eagle* moving closer and knew that he would be crushed between the ship and the dock wall if he did not move away. The only thing was to try and swim for it, to make his way out through the open sea and hope he would be picked up by one of the smaller boats ferrying men from the densely packed beaches out to ships beyond the shallows.

Dense smoke obscured visibility but Tim was driven on by more than his usual determination. Those poor devils on the *Eagle* stood no chance at all. Help could not get near the blazing ship to rescue the wounded. They would die where they lay on their stretchers, out on the wooden deck, caught by the oil and the fires.

Figures were still leaping from the ship, clothes alight, skin seared by the intense heat. As Tim tried to swim in the thick waters, he was struck by a body falling from the side of the ship, raising a water spout that nearly drowned them both. Choking and gasping, face blotched and smothered in oil, Tim found himself face to face with the man who had fallen, but there was nothing he could do or say to him now. His charred face was blackened almost to the bone. As he lay in the water, his body floated, his burning clothes setting the oil on the surface of the sea aflame. Suddenly the whole area seemed to burst into life and a rising wall of fire threatened to trap him, blocking his exit to the open sea and the beaches.

Thrusting the body aside, Tim took a great gasp of the air, acrid and dark with smoke and burning oil, and dived down beneath the water, striking out under the blazing oil slick for as long as his breath would hold. The oil seemed to cling to his face like a spider web, thick and cloying and burning his skin raw. He surfaced, spluttering and coughing up salt water, only aware that he was now alone in a vast sea of debris and human corpses, with no sign of a boat or land. It was dark as deepest night, a dark conjured out of fire and destruction. He was aware of the rising tide and a sensation of drifting. It was suddenly very cold. The water seemed to burn his flesh and the pain in his arm and hand was intense. After days of forced marches and little food he knew that he was weak and could not last very long. In the rough sea it was all he could do to keep afloat. He felt weighed down with lack of sleep, with pain and lassitude, but inside he knew that such thoughts brought certain death.

You fucking fool, you'll get yourself killed. Get moving, you stupid sod, what the hell are you doing out here, get swimming, get to the shore. Move, damn it, what do you think – it can't happen to you? What makes you so special that you think you can't die. Get angry, get angry and stay alive. There's no one here to rescue you. It's all up to you, you alone.

It was slow and painful progress. He felt the water thick as treacle weighing him down. It was an effort to move at all, to keep his head above the rising waves, to keep his eyes open. He had no sense of time. The noises inside his head almost cut off the outside din, the screaming and the occasional explosions as the men in the water struck depth charges from the bombed ships. And then, looming up out of the smoke, he saw the outline of a rowing boat, a boat loaded with men in a portion of swelling sea filled with bobbing heads and outstretched arms appealing to be taken on board. Tim stopped swimming and stared at the sight of the little boat in the high sea swell. The men aboard were fighting off those in the water, striking their faces, fighting them off with oars and boat hooks. Already overloaded, the little boat was swamped in the effort to keep afloat. The sea heaved violently and a great wave of surf turned it over. The wind had changed. More men were being drowned than saved.

'You all right, mate?'

Tim felt a hand clutch at his jacket, threatening to pull him under. He fought and struggled to keep afloat, half aware of a face, pink and smooth with oil and water, close to his. There was an arm, apparently tattooed, holding him up. Once he realised that he was not being deliberately drowned, Tim succeeded in nodding his head, clutching at the other's broad and naked back. He felt the stronger man hauling him about in the water, taking hold of his neck and cradling him almost as they had taught him years ago in lifesaving classes. There was a moment of intense pain and he must have cried out because the man changed his grip. Tim felt himself borne backwards through the water, his chin cupped in a strong hand, the man's breathing short and desperate as he bore him back towards the shore. Drifting smoke and human flotsam in the water thinned as he staggered into the shallows, pausing to find his feet on the shelving sand and to pull Tim out of danger. They were quickly joined by men from the shore, men who had been waiting on the beaches for rescue themselves.

'Blimey, he looks bad,' someone said.

'Reckon he caught it when them ships went down. Oil burns.'

Tim felt the sand beneath his head and the odd sensation of firm ground cradling his aching body. It was no lighter now. There was no longer a sky overhead. His vision was swimming in and out of the daylight. He struggled to sit up, aware of a supporting arm.

'It's all right now, mate, don't you fret.' Tim recognised the voice of his rescuer close to his ear. 'The medics will soon have you right as rain.' The words were meant to calm and reassure him but there was something in that homely English voice which, although it meant well, alerted him to the fact that his troubles were only just beginning.

'Come on, come on, you can make it. Run!'

'I can't, you'll have to leave me. Go on!'

94

'For Christ's sake, you can't let him down now. Just move, will you?'

Their running feet echoed across the harsh stonework as they pushed through the barrier and saw that the guard had raised his flag. With their breath hammering in their ears they ran, waving their arms, calling on him to wait for them, their entrance shattering the silence of the deserted railway station. The guard had pulled open one of the carriage doors ready for them.

'Come on, girls. Want a hand up?'

'No, thanks, mate. You've done your bit for the war effort.' Moira hoisted herself up into the already crowded compartment. 'Sorry, folks, room for three more inside?' She grasped Eileen by the hand and pulled her up to join her balanced between the feet of the other passengers. 'Come on, Verc, I told you we'd make it.'

Veronica landed off balance and almost fell on to the lap of a burly matron in white gloves and straw hat as the carriage door slammed behind her and the train jerked forward.

'Blimey, that was close.' Moira had her cap in her hand and was carefully smoothing out the wrinkles in her skirt. 'We look as though we've been pulled through a hedge backwards.'

It was hot for June and far too warm a day for their best blue uniforms but regulations were regulations. The compartment was crowded and stuffy, full of eager passengers on their way up to town with baskets, briefcases and brown-paper parcels. There was a distinctive holiday atmosphere abroad in spite of the news.

They soon stopped staring at the newcomers and returned to their newspapers and comments. Italy had declared war.

'What I say is you can't trust an Eyetie.'

'Wops, that's what they are. Look what they did out in Abyssinia. Dead shifty, that's what.'

The conversation bounced back and forth around the three WAAFs as the train rocked its way north towards London.

'That blooming Mussolini. Reckon they must be mad putting up with a bloke like that. A right bloody pair, him and Hitler.'

'Beat the Frogs though, didn't he? Them Germans walked all over them, no trouble at all.'

'Never were any good as soldiers. I remember back in '16...'

'I simply couldn't believe it when I learnt they were bombing

Paris. I mean, it seems incredible. Paris! When I think of all the churches, the galleries.'

'Paris can't fall, old man. You shouldn't believe all you hear.'

Eileen shared a sceptical look with Veronica who had wedged herself comfortably between the door and the luggage rack. Her face was flushed from heat and exertion and with excitement at the thought of seeing Tim again.

Eileen was also excited. When Veronica got the telegram saying that her fiancé was back in England, safely out of France, she had begged them all to try and get a 48-hour pass and join her in London. It was more than a break from routine for Eileen, who had never been in London in her life. The thought of seeing all the places she had only heard about was thrilling, if not slightly alarming. In all his life her father had never been to London, and even with the war, it was a place of romance and wealth to her, a place where everyone who was anyone lived and worked, a mecca of opportunity.

Moira said that her grandmother would put them all up in her house in Finsbury and they would 'do' the sights. Moira knew all the places to see, and she wasn't just talking about Westminster Abbey.

'We'll see Veronica nicely fixed up with her feller and then we'll go and pick ourselves a couple. Won't we, Eileen?'

'You look pretty chirpy,' cut in a business-type in a three piece suit. 'Off somewhere special?'

'We've got ourselves a bit of leave,' Moira volunteered. Her bright voice cut through the conversation in the carriage and heads turned to look back at her. 'My friend's meeting her fiancé up in London.' She paused significantly. 'He's just back from Dunkirk.'

The word hung in the air as every head turned to Veronica, blushing profusely from the unexpected attention and glances of warm approval.

'Dunkirk? Bloody marvellous show. Well done!'

'Our boys certainly showed them.'

'Yes, it'll take more than blooming Hitler to get us down.'

'I saw our boys coming back. They had these special trains and people put up flags and banners, "Welcome Back", you know the sort of thing. They were hanging out of the train windows,

96

waving, and the WVS gave them tea and sandwiches. Worn out they were. Starving hungry and dead tired.'

'What, the WVS?'

'No, our boys!'

'Our Jack was there. Mr Billings took him over on that cabin cruiser of his. Took him as an extra hand.'

'What, in a boat, was he?'

'Right there, taking them off the beaches with the Stukas up above.'

'That was some rum show, I'll warrant.'

'Of course, we all knew that something was up when Mr Billings had to send in his details. Up to the Admiralty in London. They wanted to know all about his boat. And that was weeks before we even knew what was going on. Of course, later we put two and two together.'

'That was a pretty marvellous speech that Churchill made. "We shall fight them on the beaches, we shall never give in." Stirring stuff.'

'And the funny thing was, the sea stayed flat. Calm as a millpond, our Jack said. It was a blooming miracle.'

'More things in Heaven and earth, you know.'

'And your young man was over there? Damned good show.'

'You'll make a lovely bride, dear. Are you going to set the date soon?'

'War marriages? Don't hold with them. Marry in haste, repent at leisure, isn't that what they say?'

'What rubbish. My Bert and I got married in the last lot and we're still together. Four kids, two grandchildren and one on the way!'

'I expect you can't wait to see him, can you? All right is he? No injuries or anything like that?'

Veronica lifted her head sharply, suddenly frowning.

'No, no, nothing. At least, I ...' She turned to Eileen as though for reassurance, as if the thought had never once occurred to her in all the weeks of waiting. Once the trouble had started in France it had been a torment waiting for word from him, for some sign that he was still alive. The news that Tim was safe and back in England, not trapped in some German prison camp or the victim of their deadly *Blitzkrieg*, had so overwhelmed her that she had never even thought about the details of his escape from Dunkirk.

'Oh, he'll be just fine,' added the passenger swiftly, sensing her fear. 'I bet he got out just in time. You mark my words, dear, he'll be fit as a fiddle.'

Her words were meant kindly in reassurance, but Veronica looked away uneasily, her face turned to the window but unseeing the green landscape flashing by. It was too late for reassurance, for the seed of doubt had already been planted.

Crossing London was an awesome experience. There were more cars than Eileen had ever seen in her life before. There were vans and motorcycles and the huge red double-decker buses she had only seen in magazines. Everyone seemed in such a hurry. She was nearly knocked off her feet by a sudden rush of people getting off a bus, and her first thought was how rude these Londoners were, pushing her out of their path as though their own lives were so important.

'You can't wander off here, you know,' Moira told her sharply when she rejoined her friends on the other side of the Strand. 'We're going by tube. It's the quickest way.'

Eileen detected a change in the tone of Moira's voice as soon as they hit London. She appeared to be seized by the same sense of panic, almost a terror of standing still for a moment. Eileen would have liked to look round, to cross over into Trafalgar Square and see Nelson on his column, to do those things she had only heard about. But Moira was in charge. She stalked out along the street, leading them past piled sandbags into the Underground. It was a relief to get out of the intense sunshine but the smell of the tunnels soon hit her nostrils. She saw that the tiled walls were filthy and that the ground was covered in puddles. As they piled on to the slow, creaking escalator into the bowels of the capital Eileen's thoughts were in a turmoil, a mixture of fascination and repugnance.

'We go on the Northern and have one change.' Moira led the way down one of the tunnels and they had almost to run to keep up with her.

'I've never been on the Underground either,' Veronica confessed as they arrived on a narrow platform rocked by a warm wind from the looming tunnel entrance. 'Here comes the train.'

They found seats together and Eileen tried to trace their route on the map which was pasted right up near the roof so that she had to swivel her head around to try and see where she was. At every stop the doors opened and closed alarmingly, catching clothes and even legs between their vicious rubber jaws.

At Euston they had to change on to a different branch of the same line.

'We could have got a bus,' Moira said suddenly, 'but the tube is quicker.'

'We could have got a taxi,' suggested Veronica.

'What, made of money, are you? It's not worth it, just to the Angel.'

The Angel turned out to be a shabby rundown area to which they ascended in a creaking wooden cage. Eileen detected an immediate change in the kind of people she saw about her, their clothes and a look on their faces that spoke to her of ingrained poverty. Out in the busy road there were market people carrying wooden crates on their heads or pushing handcarts. Moira explained that Chapel Market was the cheapest place to buy food in the area, with people coming from all over Islington and North London.

'It's a very cosmopolitan area.' Veronica looked around at the dark faces and chattering children playing in the gutter. 'Italian aren't they?'

'Oh there's a lot of them around here. Some even grow vines up their front walls. But I expect they'll be keeping their heads down now Italy's sided with Hitler.'

As they walked away from the Angel they seemed to enter a completely different area. Behind the busy main streets they discovered a patchwork of tranquil little squares full of tall terraces of neat but shabby houses more than a hundred years old.

'They used to be owned by rich families, with servants out scrubbing the steps and all that kind of thing. But nowadays no one lives like that. Most are let out into rooms.'

Eileen bit her lip, thinking that she could have told her differently. She knew to her cost that there were still families who could live that well, with their servants and chauffeurs and nannies, even now in 1940.

They were passed by a horse-drawn milkcart making its rounds through the squares. On the corner of one street was a dairy with an outside hand-pump which Moira told them was a 'brass cow', penny in the slot, where you used to take your jug to be filled when the dairy was closed.

'Mr Jenkins kept cows in the back,' she added. 'We've got a lot of Welsh, too. They came out here when this was all just fields and a posh watering place.'

'Of course, Sadlers Wells,' said Veronica brightly. 'The theatre is just down the road, isn't it?'

'Our house is right at the back. You can hear the piano when they're practising. We get a lot of theatricals hereabouts. Lily even let a room to an opera singer once, but the singing got on everyone's nerves. Dancers are better, or vaudeville.'

In the centre of the squares were small gardens, extremely attractive and well-maintained. In one there was a church, in another a bowling green. Even though they were so close to the busy main roads there was no traffic at all in these peaceful backwaters. But there were signs of the war. At the entrance to Milton Square where Lily Cox kept her house there was a Wardens' station, sand-bagged against possible blast, with large signposts marking out the way to public air-raid shelters in a passage behind the houses.

'This is it,' Moira announced grandly, marching up the short flight of stairs to the green front door. There was an air of excitement about her, as though she could hardly conceal her pleasure at being home again.

It was a tall house in the middle of a terrace on one side of the square, its walls painted a pearly grey colour stretching up five or six storeys. While the small flight of stairs ran up to the front door, another longer flight ran down through the heavy black railings to a door in the basement which Eileen could see was a kitchen through the large open window.

The green door opened suddenly and Moira threw herself forward into the arms of a surprisingly tall woman who, but for her white hair, looked too young and active to be anyone's grandmother.

'Lily, these are my chums.' Moira was beaming proudly as she introduced them both by name. In the cramped hallway there was scarcely room to move and it was not until Lily Cox had shepherded them all down into the basement that they really had a chance to look one another over.

After all they had heard about her grandmother, Lily was even more than they had imagined. She was like her photograph, her features framed by silver white hair set into old-fashioned finger waves, the pale blue eyes steady with shrewd intelligence and not a little amusement. But nothing had prepared them for her strength and stamina. She was a good five foot nine and wore high-heeled shoes that had pretensions to style. She was dressed in a loose, flowered peignoir, as though she had just got up, but she wore long earrings that were faintly oriental in design and gave her an air of occasion.

'I have been so looking forward to meeting you both,' she announced in a voice that hardly wavered. 'I have heard so much about you from Moira.' It was an educated voice, a voice full of confidence and resonance, and Eileen remembered that she was used to public speaking. She looked from this surprising woman of nearly seventy across to her grand-daughter where she bustled putting on the kettle for tea and felt curious about the differences between them.

Veronica had responded to Lily's voice with an air of relief, relaxing immediately as she recognised and identified with her own background. Sitting at the large wooden table, she and Lily were discussing Tunbridge Wells as though they had known one another before. Eileen knew that Lily's life had been an unusual one, that she had been quite a rebel in her time, perhaps even from her family and its ties, but she still could not account for the gap between Lily's accent and sense of style and Moira's, and the discovery puzzled her.

'And what about you, Eileen? Moira tells me you come from Herefordshire. Not a part of the country I know, I'm afraid. Though I was once down that way at Ebbw Vale back in '26.' She saw the blank looks. 'The General Strike, dear.'

Eileen blinked. She saw that Veronica was staring at Lily, mouth open. They were both clearly picturing Moira's grandmother at the head of striking miners, out on the barricades.

'Don't get her started on politics, for God's sake,' Moira

intervened, fetching a huge pot of tea over to the table. But as she noisily began to set the table, Eileen saw that she was not really angry, that this was some kind of running skirmish between Moira and Lily. She caught them looking at one another and there was a good-humoured light in their eyes that spoke of a close and abiding friendship.

'You're looking well. Are you still getting around all right?' Lily poured the tea but left Moira to pass the cups around.

'You don't have to worry about me.'

'Who else is there?' She turned apologetically to her friends. 'She tries to do too much. Now the house is empty I keep wondering what would happen if she got sick.'

'You know I've never had a day's illness in my life! I don't have time to be ill.'

'You could fall downstairs and perhaps no one would find you for weeks.'

'Stuff and nonsense! There's Bert and Alice next door.' Lily gave a sudden laugh, a surprisingly girlish sound that was infectious, attractive. 'Did I tell you they were both working now? They have jobs in munitions. Alice put her foot down and told Bert it was time he practised what he preached and let her go out to work.'

Moira shook her head in disbelief and turned to her friends. 'You'll never believe this, but they're both nearly sixty.'

'With years ahead of them,' added Lily acidly.

'And Vi? Is Vi still here?'

Lily's face softened. 'Vi and George got married. Just the day before yesterday.' She turned to the others. 'Vi's a lovely girl. You'll meet them both later when we have supper.'

'I thought George was in France.'

'He got leave suddenly. They had a special licence at the Town Hall and I stood as witness for them.'

'Talking of supper, we've brought a little something.' Moira produced the packet of sugar and pack of bacon they had brought with them. The threat of rationing hung over all their heads, with many items in short supply.

'Well, that's really splendid,' said Lily. 'Things are very difficult here since we were invaded by hordes of society women from Mayfair. They simply descended on these districts and bought up the sugar by the carload. It just sent prices soaring.'

Moira was obviously not interested in her grandmother's unashamed radicalism and she seemed eager to change the subject.

'So we can take our pick of the rooms? I'll show Veronica and Eileen upstairs and we'll get settled in before supper.' Moira gave a sheepish grin. 'I don't suppose there'll be time to do anything very much tonight.'

Lily raised her eyes to the ceiling. 'That's my Moira. No sooner does she arrive home again than she's longing to get out on the town. That uniform hasn't changed you one bit, has it?'

Moira gave her a warm hug of appreciation.

'Sorry, Lily. I can't help wanting a bit of fun, now can I?'

George Tracey was in his late twenties, a short rather anonymous looking man with light brown hair and a pale, rather serious face. He looked dependable and rather dull, but Vi was clearly delighted with her new husband. She fretted and fussed around the kitchen, setting the table and pouring him tea while they waited for supper. Vi was making the most of her 'honeymoon' while George's leave lasted.

'How long have you got?' asked Moira, always blunt.

'Just one more day.' He glanced up to look at Vi with a mournful smile.

'It's not fair,' said Vi instantly. 'He only got back from France last week after a really terrible time. Half dead, he was and –'

'All right, Vi, that's enough.'

'You should hear what it was like. Honest to God, I never –'

'I said that's enough, Vi.' His voice was suddenly harsh. It was a warning, not to be ignored.

In the sudden silence Veronica said softly,

'My fiancé got out at Dunkirk. That's why I'm here. To meet him.'

George looked at her steadily but said nothing.

'Was it very bad?' she persisted, daring to presume on her right to know the worst.

'So-so.' For a moment they thought that would be all he would say, but after a long time he clearly felt a responsibility to take her seriously, perhaps to try and prepare her. 'It was a complete shambles, if you want to know. You can forget everything you've read in the newspapers. People here don't know the half of it. You ask your fiancé. You ask any man who was out there. A bloody shambles, a disgrace, that's what it was.'

The kitchen had grown very quiet. Vi stopped what she was doing, and Eileen moved to sit down, her glance meeting Lily's across the expanse of table.

'Go on,' prompted Veronica gravely. 'Go on, I want to know.'

'When the order first came through, none of us believed it. "We're pulling back," they said. We wanted to know what the hell for. We were up there and the French were backing us. We hadn't even seen a Jerry then. "Don't ask me," the feller said, "ask the bloody generals." So we began the retreat. And it wasn't long before we saw the Jerries, moving up in tanks, you never saw so many men move so fast. We ended up fighting by day and running by night. The bulk of our stuff got left behind. It was a right bloody shambles. We were told to wreck our trucks before we dumped them. There were burnt-out vehicles all over the place.

'Of course, no one knew what was really going on. The officers bluffed, trying to kid us they knew what was up, but really they hadn't a clue. It was every man for himself. Our unit stuck together, but we never saw our officer for dust. We didn't have so much as a map of the area. We had to work out which way the coast was because you couldn't trust the Froggies, even if you could get them to understand you. We lost ourselves straight away. And it was bloody hot. We were soaked with sweat what with running and hiding. It seemed like the whole world had gone crazy.

'I felt sorry for the people. Their own people. They knew no more of what was going on than we did. They just panicked. Got everything together in carts and waggons, even kids' prams. Running for their lives, just like they did in the last lot. They'd been through it all before. They knew the Jerries of old. But there weren't only the old and the poor. There were rich blighters, too, in their big fancy motors and their women in fur coats. Fur coats –

in May! Mind you, it didn't do them any good. They soon ran out of petrol and had to dump the motors on the side of the roads. The roads were blocked everywhere, crammed with abandoned cars and trucks. Easy targets for the Stukas.

'Do you know about the Stukas? That was real terror. You've never heard anything until you've heard a Stuka screaming down on you. They took a pleasure in it. I reckon it was a bit of a giggle to them, shooting up the women and kids on those roads. They'd come in low, guns blazing, aiming right at the poor buggers in the ditches and under the trees. You could see the line of machine-gun bullets marked out on the dust of the road. Horses, old folks, kids, they didn't care what they hit. It was just a bit of fun to them, on their way to drop their bombs down the coast.

'When we finally got to Dunkirk it was already too late. They'd dropped incendiaries and the oil tanks down at the harbour went up. The whole town was on fire. You could see the church tower, but the rest was a shambles. When we got in, the main square, Barts, was all in ruins, all burning. There were our boys and French troops just roaming round, wild. The Jerries dropped leaflets. "You are surrounded," that's what they said, in perfect English, too. And there was this little map – the first we'd seen for days – showing us how the Jerries had got us pinned in. "The match is ended. Throw down your arms." They said they took prisoners and we'd be well-treated. A lot of our wounded got left behind, you know.

'Me and my mates came across this hotel. We were starving, so we went looking for any food the others had missed. God Blimey, but you should have seen those blokes. They were in a cellar, blind drunk on the wine down there, singing their heads off as though there was no tomorrow. God knows if they ever got out. Some of them got violent, went out smashing and looting. Never saw an officer. Not until we found the beach.

'You never saw anything like it. It was a whole bleeding army out there. They were camping on the beach, miles of it. With their heads in the sand every time the Stukas came over. Up among the sand dunes was this hospital, what used to be a casino. We saw it hit with salvos. Christ knows how many wounded copped it there.

'We were all flayed out. Some of us had a bit of food or wine and were sharing it round. They were good mates on the whole. What we normally had was Machonochie Stew, this stuff in cans we called dogs' vomit. But we were so hungry that we'd have eaten anything. We used bayonets to open the cans. Those who had bayonets. There were plenty there without guns, I tell you. On our march there were just three rifles between fourteen of us. If one got hit, the next in line would grab his rifle. No joke.

'There were these vehicles what had been driven out into the sea to make piers. The officers had got men lined up, wading into the water up to their necks. I never saw any queue-jumping but I heard how some major was shot through the head for trying to get in one boat that was already full.

'The beachmaster at our place was a tough old bastard, but fair, I'll give him that. "You take your turn," he told us. "There's some has been here for days."

'Night was worse. Down on the beach it was a terrible place. There was this atmosphere. It was evil. I've never felt anything like it. Of course there were dead and dying all round, but it was more than that. More than the smell of blood, though the air was thick with it. What you felt was death. It was right there on the beach with you. You felt that it was there waiting, just waiting to snatch you up, that perhaps the next one would be you. That was the worst thing of all.

'They say they got most of us away. I don't know about that. I just know what I saw. Those who got drowned, those who were shot up among the dunes, the wounded. On the boat that took us off were mostly French.

'We were in bad shape. I only had my trousers and a vest. We were in a terrible state and we felt worse. There was no hiding this defeat. Half our blokes hadn't even got a gun out with them. I saw some throwing them away on the railway line when we got back. "The buggers will be here tomorrow," they said. Before they put us on the train at Dover I got reprimanded for not saluting some bloody little Hitler on the wharf. In his smart uniform, all clean shirt and polish. Never been further than Dover Castle, the shit.

'You couldn't disguise the size of our defeat. Anyone who saw us had to know what it meant. When we saw how they told it afterwards we just couldn't believe it. You could have knocked me down with a feather when I heard them lies. Those chirpy BBC voices on the newsreels. "Our chaps" and all that, saying that they'd got everyone out when we all knew damned well that there were still blokes trapped over there who we left behind. Trying to pull the wool over your eyes, that's what they're doing.

'And don't think it will stop there. The Jerries will be moving in on us in no time at all. And how can we stop them? We don't have the guns, we don't have tanks, nothing. That Kennedy, the American Ambassador, he knows the truth of it. He says we don't stand a chance, he says we're finished and that the Yanks should keep out of it. No one's going to come and help us out. They couldn't care less. We're all on our own and we're just not ready for it.

'I'll tell you, we've been betrayed.'

Veronica's rendezvous was set for eleven the following morning at Piccadilly Circus. Although the others thought she would want to go alone to meet Tim, this was clearly not what she wanted. She was so nervous at the thought of seeing Tim again that she was sure something would go wrong. She was bound to get herself lost if she went on her own, or miss him in the crowd. She had certainly seemed very nervous. Since the previous evening's revelations there had been an atmosphere of unease and apprehension. Veronica was even quieter than usual and decided to have an early night, retiring to the room she had been given on the third floor of the tall town house.

All night long she tossed and turned, unable to sleep. George's words had awakened old fears about what she would see the next day. She would not admit even to herself the fear of something being wrong, but she felt it with a dreadful intensity. Since childhood she had always been acutely sensitive to the ill-luck which seemed to haunt her. Even when she heard the news that Tim had come through Dunkirk alive, she could not rid herself of the feeling that something would go wrong. She knew that without Moira and Eileen there to support her and give her the moral courage to go through with it, she might well have chickened out at the last moment.

In the morning she did not appear until the others had already eaten their breakfast and cleared away. Lily offered to make her something but Veronica refused, looking noticeably pale.

'I really couldn't manage a thing. I suppose I'm too excited to eat.'

'That's only to be expected. Why don't you hurry Moira along and get there early? He'll probably be there waiting for you.'

They got a number 38 bus from opposite Sadlers Wells Theatre and travelled on the top deck because Moira said she wanted to point out the sights on the way, but tourism was the last thing on Veronica's mind.

She stared through the window in silence, her stomach knotted as they got nearer to the centre of town. It was another scorching day with temperatures already climbing into the eighties. She knew she was looking awful, her face strained and pale, sick with nerves.

'Chin up,' said Eileen suddenly, giving her hand a reassuring squeeze. 'You see, it will be all right, I know it will.'

Veronica gave her a weak smile and almost felt sorry for her. How could she be expected to understand the bad luck that had stalked her every move? Everything she did went wrong. Tim was the only good thing that had ever happened to her. She knew that she just did not deserve him. She didn't know what he saw in her in the first place. Eileen thought she was just clumsy and over nervous sometimes, while Moira seemed to think she was being deliberately difficult. The night before she had asked her why she was wearing such a hangdog expression.

'Why on earth are you so bloody miserable? It's going to be the happiest day of your life. You're going to meet a beautiful man, the man you adore, the man you're going to marry any day now. What have you got to complain about? Snap out of it, for God's sake. We're here to have a good time.'

This morning Moira was in tip-top form. She looked smart and fresh as a daisy, obviously looking forward to the day without a care in the world. Veronica envied her, wishing that it was all over and done with.

They took the bus as far as Green Park and, as they were early, strolled back along Piccadilly. There were barrage balloons on the skyline down towards Westminster and Buckingham Palace, and the spacious greenery of the park was disfigured by ugly slit trenches dug the year before. Outside the large hotels and department stores in Piccadilly were piles of sandbags. The war was everywhere.

As they approached Piccadilly Circus there were more crowds in the streets, many of them also in uniform. They had never seen so many different uniforms before: Aussies in large hats, Canadians and swish French officers or matelots with their red pom-poms. But there was more than just the sight of men from many nations. There were the wounded. Mostly British or French, these men bore the signs of defeat about them. They looked weary, dispirited, often wearing oddly ill-matched uniforms or with more obvious signs of conflict: bandages or limbs in plaster.

Veronica was full of an unspoken fear of what awaited her, of what she might see, knowing only the fact of Tim's survival.

Eros no longer stood in Piccadilly Circus. He had been taken off to Egham for the duration, and his plinth was surrounded by wooden boards forming a miniature pyramid smothered in official notices and posters demanding, Is Your Journey Really Necessary? and Careless Talk Costs Lives.

'What a crying shame.' Moira was more disappointed than the others at discovering things had changed. 'You ought to see this place on a Saturday night, with all the bright lights and the traffic. It's the heart of London – normally.'

Veronica stood in her smart uniform, twisting her hands and searching the faces of the ever-changing crowd which surged back and forth aimlessly at the Circus. She was half-longing, half-dreading to see Tim among the sea of strangers.

'Well, we are early,' said Eileen gently. She too was looking, trying to recognise the face of the young man she had seen only in a photograph, praying that all would be well.

'Veronica?'

The women all turned together and saw him. In one brief second Veronica was struck by the impact of it and a strange realisation that this was what she had expected all along. All the natural reactions were forced down as she met his appealing gaze. She was suddenly filled with an absurd desire to smile, mocking the fate that had cruelly betrayed her after all.

As she took a step forward she was quite unaware of the horror on her friends' faces but their pity reached her and she could not bear it. She put them behind her and found some inner strength which enabled her to show him a little of her old feelings, the love she had had for the man he had once been.

In his dull khaki the livid flesh of his face now appeared raw and cruel, small yellowing blisters all down one side of his cheek and neck. The contrast with his whole side, the left side, made it worse than it might have been, showing the world what he had been before.

'Darling, darling.' He held her tight in his arms but kept his head at a distance from her, as though fully aware of its effect. He released her but kept her hands in his, his dark eyes swimming with emotion as he read the struggle for control in her face. 'I should have told you. I should have written something but – I'm sorry, I suppose I'm a terrible coward.'

'No, no.' She was shaking her head violently, on the brink of tears.

'I simply didn't know how to put it into words. I don't know what you must think of me – I was too afraid that you wouldn't come if you knew the truth.'

'Don't, please don't. You know how I feel.'

He took her arm in his and they leant close together, scarcely aware of the others standing near them. 'I was lucky really,' he said. 'There's nothing wrong with me otherwise. I might have lost a leg or worse!'

'How – how did it happen?'

'The ship we were on got a direct hit. I managed to get overboard to make a swim for the shore. But the oil tanks exploded and the oil slicks floating on the sea caught light. When they pulled me ashore I could hardly see. The medics did their best for me, but it was rough and ready treatment because we were under fire.' He hesitated and then tried to give a crooked grin. 'The people here say I will be right as rain. There are things they can do.' He gripped her arm tightly, staring down intensely at her. 'I had to see you again, Veronica. Even if it was only to say goodbye.'

Veronica stared at her fiancé, uncomprehending. In a bare moment her fears had all been confirmed. Everything which had haunted her thoughts, conscious and unconscious, since Dunkirk surfaced now to jinx her future, to destroy her life.

Eileen flashed a look of alarm at Moira, but she stood there almost mesmerised by the sight of the blistered flesh, unable to disguise her loathing.

As though she suddenly sensed Eileen and Moira standing there, Veronica broke away from Tim's side and seized hold of Eileen by the arm, unaware that her nails had cut painfully into her flesh.

'Please. Please don't wait. I need some time. I...' Her eyes beseeched them both to leave her alone with him. 'I'll see you back at the house. Later.'

Eileen nodded wordlessly, taking Moira by the arm and steering her quickly away. She glanced back over her shoulder just once at the distraught couple huddled beneath the wooden plinth.

'My God, my God.' Moira was shaking, her steps almost tripping in her anxiety to get away from the scene. 'I just can't stand to see that kind of thing. Oh my God, poor Veronica. How could she bare to touch him? It's disgusting, horrible. He looks like a monster.'

Eileen pulled up with a jerk of her arm and turned Moira about to face her. 'Shut up, Moira, don't be so hard. It's not that bad.'

'Isn't it? He's grotesque, half of his face has been burnt off. She couldn't even look him straight in the eye. He'll never be any good to her now. She'll just have to realise it.' She shook Eileen off. 'It made me sick to look at him. Don't pretend you felt any differently.'

Eileen looked away, uncomfortably aware that it was true. Of course it was a terrible shock. His wounds were still new, the burns unhealed. It was just so unexpected. He should have said something – but said what? I'm horribly disfigured, you might not even recognise me?

'Come on, kid,' Moira added more gently. 'I think you and I could do with a drink.'

Eileen allowed herself to be pulled away and they crossed over the road. Moira found a bar which was just opening for the early lunchtime custom, and although the barmaid looked at them rather curiously, they were soon sitting with glasses in their hands in a corner of the red and gold decorated room.

'What is it?'

'Just get it down. You'll feel better.' Moira took a long drink and rested her head against the back of the seat. 'What lousy luck that girl has. I never met anyone so jinxed in all my life. And he was such a good looking bloke before.'

'He's still the same person.'

'That's no help to her though, is it?' She paused, looking suddenly angry. 'You don't think she would be that stupid, do you? Even Veronica wouldn't...'

'But she loves him.'

'There's love and love,' she shuddered in disgust. 'There's nothing to stop them being friends. But marriage – my God, can you imagine being in bed with – that?'

'For Christ's sake, Moira, shut up, will you? It's none of your business anyway. Veronica must do what she decides, and if she loves him, really loves him –'

'That's a lot of nonsense and you know it. You'd never do such a thing and neither would I. He's even half-expecting it himself. He knows that it's wrong. Veronica's a nice girl and she doesn't want to hurt him but there's a limit to every sacrifice.'

They fell into an uneasy silence and sipped at their drinks. Whatever it was it certainly seemed to calm them down, making Eileen feel much easier.

'That's what it's going to be like, isn't it? The war, I mean. It's what George was trying to tell us last night. All these months we've been fooling ourselves that it won't really happen, that everything will be all right. But it's not true any more, is it? We have to face up to it.'

Moira was staring at her, two deeply etched lines either side of her nose as anger mingled with alarm.

'Don't look at me like that,' said Eileen reproachfully. 'We've cried wolf long enough. The war is coming home to us now. We're not special, we're not exempt. What happened to Tim could happen to any one of us.'

'Is that right? Well, Miss Know-all, I don't want to know that! You can just keep your theories to yourself. If it happens, it happens, but I don't want to dwell on it. I don't even want to think about it.'

'Now look –'

'No, you look. We've only got 48 hours. This could be our last leave before the balloon goes up, and I'm damned well not going to waste it, any of it, thinking about death and destruction. It may never happen! And if it does –' she paused, nodding her head, '– if it does then I'd rather go down dancing and having a bloody good time than sitting around here moping and whining about it.' She stood up abruptly, picking up her cap from the seat. 'You can come or stay. I couldn't care less. But if you come, you shut up about the war. I've heard enough.'

Eileen wrestled hard to conceal her mixed feelings of anger and bitterness but the last thing she wanted now was to be left alone in the middle of the vast city among strangers. She got quickly to her feet and joined Moira at the door.

'That's better. Now let's see some life.' Moira was never one to bear grudges. She slipped her arm through Eileen's and breezily led the way out into Shaftesbury Avenue among the thronging crowds.

'Excuse me, miss.' They were stopped by a body planted firmly in their path. Under the wide brim of the kind of hat worn by Australian troops, a pair of bright eyes took in every detail of their appearance and seemed to dance with pleasure. 'Excuse me, miss, but you look as though you know your way round. My friends and I,' he jerked a thumb in the direction of two grinning faces behind him, 'we're interested in seeing a bit of London, you know? Would you perhaps like to join us for a spell? We could have a few drinks, a meal and a show.'

Eileen flashed Moira a look of suspicion but she appeared to take no notice. She was too interested in sizing up the Australian trio with their height and healthy tans, obviously won over by their flashing smiles.

'We only just arrived,' their spokesman added ingratiatingly, 'and it would sure be a privilege to have two such lovely ladies to guide us round.'

'We're on leave ourselves,' Moira announced, 'but I live in London normally. Before I joined up, I mean.'

'You do? Well isn't that lucky for us? What do you know, mates, this lady is a Londoner born and bred!'

'I tell you what,' said one of the mates, 'let's have a drink on it.' He took Moira and Eileen on either arm and turned with a grin to the others. 'Must be our lucky day, eh?'

'Too right!'

'That's some place they've got themselves,' said the one called Clive as he stood scratching his head outside Buckingham Palace. 'Just think of all that history, all that tradition. Did I tell you blokes our Ma came from here?'

'Yeah, Ol, you told us.'

'Just wait till I tell them back home. Fancy all that history going on right here.' Ollie had clearly established himself as the intellectual of the trio, eagerly bombarding Moira with a host of questions she soon tired of trying to answer. Like Clive and Wally she soon grew weary tramping round London in the heat and sighed with relief when someone suggested getting a drink.

The Australians showed a remarkable ability to put away pint after pint without any food to cushion the effect. Moira and Eileen soon gave up trying to keep up with them as what had been a tour of the sights soon turned into a tour of London's pubs.

'It's your round, Wally.'

'How's that? You owe me two bob, mate.'

'Struth, he's a mean bastard. Can't you see the ladies want a refill?'

'No, really.'

'I could do with something to eat, couldn't you, Eileen?'

'Why didn't you say so? Only got to say the word.' Clive nudged Moira in the ribs. 'Where's the best tucker in town then?'

'What about Soho?'

'Soho? Ho ho! Let's go!'

Eileen had no idea where she was and clung heavily on to Wally's arm as they trooped back across one of the parks in the afternoon light. Her head felt heavy and she kept bumping into the Australians but they didn't seem to mind. There was a lot of joking and laughter, and at one point Wally began to sing, but they even found the reproving stares of the passersby a real hoot.

'Sorry looking lot of poms.'

Moira had fetched them back to Soho and they found themselves in a sleazy back street full of shuttered bars and basement dives.

'Ease up, you blokes, take a look at this!'

'I reckon we're on to something here.' A shrill wolf-whistle cut the air. 'Who's game?'

'I don't know,' Moira said doubtfully, looking at the club entrance suspicously. 'I'm hungry.'

'Aw, go on, Moi, don't be a dill.'

'It'll be a good laugh.'

'Well –'

'Good-oh.'

Only once they were seated in the dimly-lit club where the Australians swore over the price of the beer, did Eileen realise that what she had thought were statues were really part of a nude floorshow. She looked round at Moira to see if she had realised too, but Clive was whispering in Moira's ear making her start to giggle loudly. He had his hand on her thigh but as he looked up he caught Eileen's eye and gave her a broad wink. She smartly shifted her attention back to the other show.

When they finally left, looking for a place to eat, they were in a street where Italian restaurants had notices asserting they were 100 per cent loyal to the King, but they passed them by patriotically and ended up in another pub instead. Eileen began to think she had had enough. Wally had taken a shine to her, starting to paw her while Ollie was at the bar buying more drinks. When he said something about getting a room upstairs, Eileen finally rebelled.

'I feel sick,' she announced, stumbling to her feet and dragging Moira from her tête-à-tête with Clive towards the powder-room. Inside the narrow, mirrored room, Eileen held her head and leant back against the flock wallpaper. 'You stay if you like, I've had enough.'

'You'll be all right, Eileen, don't spoil the fun.'

'I'm not having any fun, Moira. Wally's getting on my nerves.'

'Well, go back if you want, but I'm staying.' She shook off her hand and disappeared through to the bar to rejoin the others.

Eileen stayed leaning over the basin until her head stopped spinning. She shivered, wiped her mouth, looking at herself in the cracked mirror before she headed out into the bar. A wave of laughter and warmth flooded over her but in the corner where the Australians had been sitting the table was empty.

She stared around anxiously at the faces that filled the room.

Then she supposed they must have gone outside, but the dark street was deserted and silence closed round her. As she stared at the blacked out pub she realised that Moira had no intention of breaking up her night out and that she meant it when she said she would stay with Clive and his friends. If she wanted to go back to the house she would have to go alone.

Although it was very late when she finally reached Milton Square, Eileen, footsore and weary, was surprised to see a light shining up from the kitchen into the hallway. She opened the kitchen door and let herself in, astonished to discover Vi sitting at the table in a position of abject misery.

She raised her head at the sound of Eileen's entrance and it was plain to see that she had been crying for a long time. Her face was flushed and puffy with tears, her eyes red-rimmed. Eileen saw that she was embarrassed to be caught out by a virtual stranger. She shifted round, hastily drawing back a loose strand of her dark hair which hung limp across her damp face.

'I'm sorry,' both women apologised together and then smiled faintly, both ill at ease with one another.

'I got lost,' Eileen said by way of explanation. 'I don't know London, you see.' She glanced up at the clock. 'Is that the time? I must have been wandering round for hours.'

'What about the others?' Vi's question was polite rather than curious. Eileen could tell that she was eager to make everything appear quite normal.

'Oh, we split up earlier.' Eileen made a quick move towards the kettle. 'Do you fancy a cup of tea? If it's not too late.'

'That would be lovely.' Vi ran a hand across her eyes and gave a great sigh. 'I don't normally do this kind of thing, you know. It's just that George went back tonight and...'

'Oh yes, of course.' Eileen was quick to offer sympathy. 'How rotten for you. Such a short time together.' But she was thinking of Veronica and the pain on her face when she first saw her man.

'I'll be better when I get back to work. Not so much time to think.' She made herself busy wiping up some cups and saucers. 'The worst thing is not knowing where they'll send him.'

'Perhaps he'll stay here – now.'

'Yes, it looks bad, doesn't it? I hear they are going to evacuate more kids. They tried to get them all to go away last time, when war was declared, but so many came back as nothing was happening. That's what I do, you know, work with the kids.'

'You must have a lot of patience.' Eileen brought the teapot across to the table and they sat down. It was almost two in the morning. 'We had some evacuees in our village,' she said almost without realising what she was saying. It was the first time she had talked about Charnwood to anyone. 'It was quite a shock for the locals. I don't think they had seen anything like it. Some of the children had actually been sewn into clothes for the winter.'

'Or brown paper. Yes, I know. I get to see all sorts of things – scabies, headlice. They are so poor in Islington.'

'And the language! They'd never heard so many four-letter words!'

'In the country, was it? I could tell you some stories. No one could get to pick where they were sent and there were some right old mixups. Jews sent to Catholic areas, RCs sent to Methodists in Wales. Some who were used to inside lavatories ended up on farms where water came from a well while others hadn't a clue what a toilet was for! I suppose people just didn't realise how poor most people are.'

'In our village all the local bigwigs were the billeting officers. They made damned sure that none of the children were billeted on them. They sent them to cottagers who couldn't very well refuse. But the farmers were on to a good thing. You should have seen them, down there picking out the strongest so they could work on the farm. It was like a slave market!'

'A lot came back. Just couldn't take it. No cinemas, no boozers, no Woolworths! Bored stiff, they were, and so their Mums dragged them home again. It'll be a hard job trying to make them believe this time it's serious.'

'Vi, you've lived here for years. I was wondering about Moira.' She looked up sharply. 'I mean, she and Lily seem so different.'

'Well, they would be, wouldn't they? What with Moira's mother and everything.'

'Her mother?'

'Living in the back of beyond.' When she saw Eileen's frown she sat back, faintly amused. 'Didn't she tell you that? No, well,

117

Moira was always ashamed of her family. Her parents, I mean.'

'So they are still alive?'

'Of course they are. Did she tell you they were dead? Lily doesn't have anything to do with them though. When Marian married and went away, she didn't want to know. She married a farmer, you see. Some smallholding miles from anywhere. According to Lily he was completely wrong for her. Couldn't even write his name. And Lily had great hopes for Marian. Lily thought she might go to university. She thought she was throwing her life away, marrying someone like that, going to bury herself in the country.'

'And Moira?'

'When she got old enough she ran away. Found her own way to London and Lily took her in.'

Eileen thought she understood at last. She saw the reason for Moira's burning ambition to get on in life, to find security. She understood too the wide differences that existed between Moira and her grandmother.

She sat back in her chair, temporarily stunned by the amount of fresh information she had to take in.

'Didn't she tell you any of it? Dead secretive, Moira. She always wants people to think she's a Londoner by birth. Mind you, I don't know it all. Lily won't talk of it now. But if you ask me, I think mother and daughter had a hard time of it at home. I feel sorry for Moira.'

Veronica left Tim sleeping in the hotel room. They had said their goodbyes before and looking at his childlike calm now she knew it was better not to disturb him. At the reception desk she told them to wake him by ten. He was due at the hospital by noon, so he would have enough time.

She surprised herself by the way she went straight up to the desk, as though she had spent all her life in hotels. She didn't even feel nervous, she didn't give a damn what the hotel staff thought of her. When she had walked in on Tim's arm yesterday she knew they were looking at her. She knew what they were thinking, but she just didn't care. And, in the end, they had only talked after all.

'I know it's all changed,' he told her, his words tumbling out in

118

a rush. 'It's all different now and I want you to know that I understand how you feel. No, don't say anything. I don't want you to say anything you'll regret.'

She knew that he meant it. He seemed so sure of her reaction. He thought she could not love him now. But it was Tim; he hadn't changed. He was still the same man all the time. She knew what it cost him to say those things to her and yet he was asking her to give him up.

'I can't let you waste your life by marrying me.'

It took a lot just to persuade him to let things ride, at least until he got out of hospital. He didn't really believe her. He had convinced himself that she would leave him. He thought she pitied him, that she was only saying she still loved him out of pity. And perhaps it was partly true because she couldn't hurt him, not for all the world.

When she saw him standing there, having caught sight of himself in the mirror of the wardrobe, she knew that he felt a stranger to himself. She saw him hesitate, just staring at the glass as though he saw a shadow or a ghost. And tears, genuine angry tears ran down his cheeks, although in his shame he tried to hide them.

The memory now stirred her. In the streets of the city she felt the pain of being apart from him and knew that she had indeed made the right decision. She loved him. She loved him for what he was, not for his looks or any passing gifts. In all the years she had known him he had never once let her down. How could she now have let him down so cruelly? Their engagement would stand.

She had no idea how she would tell the others. But as it turned out only Eileen was there when she rang the doorbell.

Veronica had always felt closer to Eileen. From that very first meeting at the station in Gloucestershire, she felt that here was a friend in whom she could trust and confide. It was not that Moira was unfriendly; on the contrary, she had stood by her through thick and thin, often sticking her neck out to protect her from the wrath of brutal sergeants and parade-ground sadists. Moira was a rock, a source of strength, but Veronica felt she could no more have discussed Tim with her than she could have with her cold distant parents, though their worlds were as different as could be.

119

Moira always seemed to make light of her love affairs and if she had ever felt anything deep in her life she had never chosen to share it with either of them.

But in Eileen's company, Veronica soon found herself beginning to talk, settled in the soft cushions of flowery armchairs in a room washed with sunlight.

'He explained everything to me,' she said. 'He'll have to undergo treatment for several months. They want to move him to East Grinstead soon, to this special burns unit they have now. It's all rather experimental but Tim says they're doing some wonderful work there on pilots who were shot down over France. It's Sir Archibald McIndoe. He specialises in burns cases.'

Eileen seemed cautious about pressing her to continue.

'How much can they do for him?'

'He'll always have scars, of course.' She heard her own voice, cheerful but rather too bright for spontaneity. 'That's the result of the makeshift treatment they had to give him at Dunkirk. But with grafting – well, he could be quite normal.' Her voice died a little and it was hard to go on. 'Well, it's a chance we must take.'

Eileen got up and went over to her. She put a warm arm round her shoulders and Veronica could at last give way to her true feelings.

'Oh Lord, this bloody war,' she whispered. 'What's going to happen to us all?'

The news came just as they were preparing to leave for the station. Unlike Moira who had returned only to creep instantly into bed, Veronica looked fresh and alert and had insisted on cooking them lunch.

They heard Lily cry out and dropped their bags in the hallway, rushing upstairs into the front parlour where she always sat in the afternoons. The wireless set stood on a table occupying a central position in the busy room, befitting its new importance. Lily looked round as they hurried in, a copy of *Fame is the Spur* falling from her lap.

'Paris has fallen,' she told them.

★

London was quiet, as quiet as a city in shock. As they crossed town towards Charing Cross everyone they saw seemed to have their heads buried in special editions of the newspapers which blazed the news. France was expected to capitulate within the week. And everyone knew what that meant.

'We're next,' said Veronica.

'Vi told me that they will be evacuating more children next week. That means that London is sure to be bombed.'

'Don't talk about it,' said Moira picking up her case and moving away.

They entered the great arched station and looked for their train on the Kent lines indicator board. Moving among the unnaturally silent groups of passengers and staff, it seemed as though a paralysis had fallen over the population of the city. With France gone the cards were well and truly stacked against them. They knew there was no other line of defence. Everywhere dazed people stood together, newspapers in hand, their faces betraying their shock and apprehension over the future.

Britain was now the battlefield.

Chapter Five

Rationing came into full force with the tea ration in July. Tea was the nation's staple, tea was what kept the British going in times of trouble, without tea the whole fabric of society was threatened. More than the fear of Hitler's invasion, the British feared the loss of their daily cuppa.

'Thank God for the Forces,' said Moira in the NAAFI. 'They know we run the show on the stuff. They won't keep us short.'

'But they will keep us regular,' added Eileen with a grimace. 'I'd rather have prunes for breakfast than epsom salts in my tea.'

As the three women were on their way down to the MT section, one of the WAAFs just coming off duty from the graveyard shift cut across their path and singled Eileen out.

'I've got a bit of news for you.'

'What's up, Betty? Been listening in on the switchboard again?'

'One of the perks of the job, that is, love. Get to know all that goes on around here. And I mean all.' She gave Moira a knowing look.

'Come on, spill the beans.' Eileen was impatient, disturbed at anything that threatened the daily routine and security of her life on the station. 'I've not done anything wrong, have I?'

'Far from it. You're up for promotion, love. LACW.'

The others whooped with surprise and gave Eileen delighted thumps on the back. Leading Aircraft Woman. It was just one step up the ladder from zero, the lowest of the low.

'It goes with the job,' added Betty slyly, catching her audience by surprise. 'You're getting a new posting with an officer.'

'Who? Why? Does that mean I'm transferred?'

'Well, from what I overheard, you'll be staying here. He's some bod on special business. Fairweather's his name and he's a veteran flyer just back from France. A squadron leader, no less.'

'Perhaps he's a looker, Ei, perhaps your time has come!' Moira was having a good laugh at her expense. 'Trust you to get the jammy jobs. Just remember if they want you to be a sergeant you'll have to give up driving. What I wouldn't give to get myself a squadron leader.'

Betty gave her a quick look, adding slyly, 'From what I've heard, Pet, you've had more than your fair share already! You might leave some for us!'

'Some hopes she has!' said Moira after the PX Operator had gone off in search of her breakfast. 'Green around the gills, that Betty Wilson. She couldn't pull a brown job let alone an officer.'

'It might be fun, Eileen, a new job, getting out and about the country.' Veronica looked wistful. With her bad luck she always seemed to land up with the rotten tasks about camp, the work no one else wanted. Only when all hands were required for a long distance convoy did she get a chance of driving out on the open road.

'I'm going over to the office,' said Eileen. 'I want to get to the bottom of this. Perhaps Betty's got it all wrong.'

But she had not got it wrong at all. Eileen was duly promoted one rank and told to take the Standard down to the railway station the next Tuesday to meet Squadron Leader Patrick Fairweather off the London train. Knowing nothing other than his name, Eileen felt rather nervous. She spent a few minutes in the station forecourt tidying herself up so that she would create a good impression. No one gave a damn about petty regulations on camp; all the WAAFs wore make-up and a bit of jewellery from time to time. Perhaps a station not in the frontline would be more severe, but 11 Group was far too preoccupied with the threat of imminent invasion to worry about a few King's Regulations.

'You'll be waiting for me, I take it.'

Eileen swivelled round in the driving seat to find a face staring in at her through the open window. He was stooping, and therefore tall, his pale thin face emphasised by a high forehead and thinning hair. He was a lot older than she had expected. She quickly apologised and jumped out of the car, running round to salute and hold open the passenger door.

'All right, all right,' he said irritably. 'No need to go overboard.' He ducked and got into the car. 'Caught you out, did I? Are you going to be my permanent driver?'

'Yes, sir.'

'Well, what's your name then?'

'Howard, sir, LACW Howard.'

'No, your name.' He had an accent, a rather harsh northern accent that made everything he said sound flat and sarcastic, as though he was irritated by her. When she told him her name he nodded as if she had merely confirmed what he already knew. 'Very well, Eileen, let's get a few things straight. If you're going to get along with me, you had better not be one of those flibbertigibbet women always fussing about their looks. I can't abide a woman with nothing in her head but cottonwool.'

'But, sir –'

'But nothing. Look, what I need in my job is an assistant. You would need to be interested in what I'm trying to do down here. It will be hard work, a lot of driving, making notes. Think you're up to that? Because if you're not, then say so straight out and that's that. Nothing against you.'

Eileen stared at him, angered that he should have based his first opinion of her capabilities on an innocent glance in the mirror. His blunt manner had taken her by surprise. She was not used to officers speaking in that way to non-commissioned ranks. If they spoke to her at all, it was usually an order or some banal comment about the weather.

'If your work is interesting,' she told him, 'then I would like to continue with you, sir. Frankly, I'd appreciate something a bit out of the ordinary.'

He raised his eyebrows and a trace of a smile flickered over his wide, thin lips. 'Right then,' he said with a business-like flourish, 'let's see what kind of a driver you are, Eileen.'

Eileen wasn't sure whether he was deliberately baiting her or whether this was his normal manner. She decided that his accent was definitely Yorkshire, a species she knew only by hearsay and old wives' tales: brash, blunt, aggressive know-alls, farmers or steel hands, living in remote, windswept moors, Heathcliff and friends, or trouble up at mill all in all pretty difficult customers.

She gave him furtive glances as they pulled out of the station yard and set out through the bustling town. The little hair he had left was a nondescript brown colour, matched by dark eyes. If it had not been for his face he would hardly have merited a second glance, but his lean, sculptured features with high cheekbones had almost an Asiatic appearance that gave it strength and a strange dignity. His brown eyes were sharp and intelligent, not missing a thing. He caught sight of her looking at him and suddenly grinned. His whole face broke into the smile, becoming boyish and mischievous, with a wicked gleam in the eyes.

'Well, what is your opinion?'

She was horrified at being caught out and looked suitably abashed, but she was determined that his deliberate bluntness would not get the better of her. She had a feeling that he was testing her, trying to provoke her into revealing her own temperament.

'Well, sir, you're quite a lot older than I expected. They told me you had just come back from France.'

'And you don't think that an old man of forty could still be flying operational missions, is that it?' He ran a hand reflectively over his chin. 'Well, it seems that you and the top brass share the same opinion. It looks like I'm grounded now.'

She caught the wistful edge to his voice and said, 'I'm sorry, it must be rotten getting a desk job after you've had the chance to fly.'

'Have you ever flown? No? Well, it's a wonderful experience, Eileen. There's nothing like it.' He threw her a pensive glance frowning slightly. 'Absurd, isn't it, you being in the Air Force and never having a chance to fly?' He pursed his lips and nodded, as though making a mental note to himself. Then he added sharply, 'A desk job? God forbid! No, this is hardly a bloody desk job, Eileen. I'm here to smell out the ground, to gauge our potential. We're going to need every bit of luck we can get to pull through the next few weeks, but even if we survive we will still need to keep one step ahead of the Hun. They've got the scientific knowledge; we haven't. They are constantly devising new machinery, modernising their designs for greater range and efficiency. We should have learnt our lesson over Spain, but they buried their heads in the sand. They mistook their enemy. Spent all their time worrying about the Communist threat while they treated Hitler and Goering as something of a joke. Too many old men, old school tie, that kind of outdated nonsense. It's all got to change, Eileen, if we're going to win.'

Eileen frowned, concentrating on her driving, not quite knowing what to think about him. She had never heard an officer talking like him. She had hardly heard anyone talk so freely and with such confidence about politics. She suddenly thought of Gareth and the way he had shared his opinions with her so long ago. And now it seemed he had been right after all.

'What's the matter? Have I shocked you?'

'No, sir, it's not that at all. It's like a friend of mine says, it's still the old class system, isn't it? Those at the top, the same old faces. Just because they've got the titles, and the money, it doesn't mean that they've got the brains too. When you think about some of the daft mistakes they've made over the years, you wonder how the hell we're going to get out of this mess. Begging your pardon, sir.'

Far from taking offence, he appeared to be absolutely delighted with her little speech and they drove the rest of the way to the base in comradely ease.

At the station they reported at once, Eileen accompanying him to the wingco's office, waiting outside with the adjutant while the two officers conferred. She could hear their voices raised high with broad laughter in the other room and shared a speculative glance with the adjutant before the inner door opened. The wingco had an arm around his shoulders and their faces were flushed with good humour.

'Splendid, Pat, splendid.' The wingco caught sight of Eileen, who promptly stood rigidly to attention. 'Well now, is this your driver? Take care of the squadron leader, young woman, he's a very valuable addition to the base. And a bloody good flier. DSO and bar, with thirteen kills in France – it was thirteen, wasn't it, Pat?'

'Fourteen, actually, sir.'

'Don't take it so hard, old man. If things get too tight, you never know, we may have need of you up there again.'

'Dear God, I hope things never get that desperate!'

As Eileen followed him outside she was even more in awe of him than before. He was an ace! One of the top fighter pilots – and he'd never said a word.

'Let's take the car over to dispersal,' he told her, slamming the door and loosening his tie. 'Christ, I hate all this formality. I'll be glad to get out of these things.'

'Are you billeted in the village, sir?'

'So I'm told. We'll go over and have a recce later. But first –' He paused, catching sight of the first aircraft out on the grassy runway. 'Just the job! Take her over to that bird on the right. The trainer, that's it.'

It was a Tiger Moth, one of the old paper and string biplanes they used to take new recruits up in to run them through their paces. As Eileen drew alongside, wondering what he had in mind, Patrick Fairweather threw open the door of the car and rushed over to have a word with a mechanic in overalls. He came back with a self-satisfied grin all over his face and told Eileen to hurry and get out of the car. He seized her by the arm and hauled her over the turf towards the plane, where the mechanic was busy adjusting something.

'There we are, Eileen, don't ever say I'm not a man of my word.' He climbed on to the wing and produced an ancient flying helmet from the back seat, promptly exchanging it for her regulation headgear, pulling down the leather flaps on either side of her face, laughing at her terrified expression. 'You said that you wanted to fly!' he exclaimed and gave her a little push up and into the back seat of the twin trainer. With her heart in her mouth, Eileen found herself sitting in the cramped little seat, the helmet blocking out a range of sounds.

As he clambered into the front seat, he turned to her and shouted out,

'I thought you might as well start off at the deep end. No point in pussy-footing around.' He settled down comfortably in his seat and began a running check of the instruments. As Eileen sat there trembling with anticipation, she saw him testing his radio and talking into a mouth piece, presumably to the control tower. He suddenly dropped his hand and the engine spurted into life, rocking and shaking the machine as the mechanic pulled the wooden chocks away from the wheels and the Tiger Moth rolled forward, bumping over the grass.

As Eileen stared as if mesmerised at the green earth about her she could feel the power of the engine purring underneath, hopping and skipping over the field as though trying to leap into the air. All at once she was aware that there was some distance between them and the ground, a distance that was growing with every second. We're up, she thought incredulously, we're flying!

A surge of pure joy and wonder shot through her body and she was almost dizzy with a sense of accomplishment, as though she had been at the controls. Wide-eyed she stared at the now distant ground, watching as the buildings of the village shrank away, the hedgerows and the trees dotting the patchwork landscape. The wind whipped at her loose hair escaping from the helmet and she realised that she was gripping the edge of her seat with white-knuckled hands in what must have been absolute terror.

But now she could laugh at her foolish fears. It was wonderful, it was exhilarating. She felt herself grinning from ear to ear as she drank in all the sights of her first flight. It was as though she was seeing the world for the very first time. Just like a map, she saw the river and the roads laid out below her, the tiny dots of cars and even of people going about their daily lives. She recalled how many times she and her friends had stood on the ground watching the circling planes overhead, never realising the amazing experience that all pilots shared. No wonder it was so hard for them to give it up, to be grounded, as Pat was now. She felt overwhelmed with gratitude and admiration for him and his spontaneous generosity, to share this trip with her, to give her the experience of a lifetime.

In the days that followed Eileen soon learnt what a partnership could mean in her job with Pat. It was always 'Pat' as soon as they were outside the confines of the base and its regulations. She was told to cut all the formalities, the saluting, calling him 'sir', opening doors for him and all that business designed to separate and bracket them into classes.

'You do your work, I'll do mine. We're a partnership,' he told her.

His work was to inspect and evaluate aircrew and their offensive potential. In France, he said, he had learnt how ridiculous it was to use a modern Air Force for pamphlet dropping operations over enemy territory.

'It won't be pamphlets we'll be dropping soon. Bombing's the strategy for the future and not the featherweight hundred pounders which don't even dent the ground. I'm talking about 1,000 pounders, 1,500.'

Eileen flinched. It appalled her to hear anyone talk so casually of weapons which brought death and destruction on such a large scale, but Pat caught her reaction.

'No, we don't want to think about it now. I'm having a devil of a job making anyone take me seriously. That's what these interminable meetings are all about. You know the Air Minister stopped us bombing the German forests? He said, "Are you aware they are private property? You will be asking me for permission to bomb Esseb next!"'

'But the Germans bombed Rotterdam.'

'Yes, they learnt their lesson early at Guernica. Spain was their dress rehearsal but we're the main show.'

'I wouldn't live in London now for all the world,' she said thoughtfully, thinking of Lily and her household and their impending danger.

'My wife's there.'

'I didn't know you were married.'

'Ten years next month. We've got this little place up in Highgate. Just the two of us, you know.' The sadness in his voice suggested that if they had wanted children they had not been lucky. 'Grace wouldn't leave. I know, I've asked her, but she's got a mind of her own. Thank God,' he added as an afterthought with a wry smile.

She discovered that they were a very happy couple. She had wondered why he had never once tried to make a pass at her. After that, Pat often went out of his way to talk about Grace, not about their troubles as many men would, but to emphasise his contentment with his family life. Most weekends he would try to get back to London to be with her, and Eileen would drop him off at the station and collect him first thing on Monday mornings.

He was curious about her own relationships. She was amused by the way in which he broached the subject, quite unlike his normal blunt self. He knew the ratio of WAAFs to men on the station and rightly judged there was no shortage of offers, but when Eileen told him there was no one special in her life she thought he did not really believe her.

Each day they set out somewhere new. Eileen would file her route with the guardroom and get her 658 registered in their log book. But once they were out of the station and on the open road they felt free and able to relax. Pat and Eileen loosened their ties and rolled up their shirt sleeves. Pat took a pair of plimsolls to wear in the car and sitting back, enjoying the summer country smells, he would light up his old pipe, stuffing it with golden tobacco from a leather pouch, puffing away as they chatted about everything from the thatched country cottages they passed to history and politics.

As Eileen's uniform buttons grew green and tarnished, so their friendship grew. Eileen was intrigued by Pat's ideas, astonished at how much he had read, even though he had not been to university like Gareth. He was a blunt, practical man, honest in his opinions. Take me or leave me, that was his attitude. There was no side to him. Eileen could not help being shocked by some of his views but she was always fascinated. He seemed to offer her new opportunities to open up her narrow little world, forcing her to think for herself, to take in new ideas. And she tried to improve herself, took to reading the newspapers so that she could bring up some point when next she was out and about with Pat.

'You sound dotty about him,' Moira commented back at the billet.

'It's not like that at all.'

'I've heard that one before.' Moira could not seem to understand that there was nothing to their relationship other than friendship and respect. She always had to allude to something more, as though she had no more to offer anyone than her body. It made Eileen mad.

'He's too old for you anyway.' Moira had just washed her hair and now it shone like a Pre-Raphaelite halo about her face. 'You ought to go out with one of Alan's pals. I could fix you up, if you like.'

'Thanks for the offer,' Eileen laughed, exasperated, 'but I don't think I could keep up with your set. Where are you off to this time?'

'We're taking Dave's car to some hop over Brasted way. You should come. You're as bad as Veronica, always moping round here.'

'She got another letter from Tim this morning. You know what that means.'

'I don't know what she finds to write about. Nothing ever happens. If it wasn't for getting out and about a bit, I'd go spare.'

'I get out enough every day. It's another long run tomorrow.'

She helped Moira get into a slip of a dress that drew wolf-whistles of approval from the crowded car which roared up the cobbled lane and stood purring with impatience outside their door. Moira was off in a cloud of Chanel with one last pitying wave, squeezed in beside Dave, or was it Alan? It was hard to remember all their names.

'She's right. You ought to get out more.' Veronica was curled on the sofa with pad and envelopes on her lap. Eileen brought the supper tray and sat on the fireside rug and poured the tea. As she passed the cup and saucer she tried to explain how she felt.

'I'm happy, really I am. I didn't join the WAAF just to meet men. I know there are women out to get themselves a husband, but that's the last thing on my mind. I've been lucky getting this job and I suppose I don't want to make a mess of it.'

'You won't,' said Veronica with a grin. 'You've changed, you know. You seem more confident, sort of self-sufficient. I think that Moira feels you have drawn apart now you're working with Pat.'

'Is that what she thinks? I haven't done it deliberately.'

'I know. I suppose we were bound to change. I've got Tim back and you've got your work, but Moira – well, I think she's still looking for something in her life.'

On their runs, Pat would try to include Eileen in his business but this was not always possible. One day he attended a meeting of intelligence staff and Eileen found herself sitting for hours outside Arundel Castle while the rain lashed the car windows. When at last Pat came to the door with the Duke of Norfolk Eileen brought the car round and opened the door for him, saluting at attention. Pat gave her a wink as he got in but as soon as they were racing down the drive he was already taking off his jacket and relaxing.

'Thank God that's over. Sensible chap, though. For a duke.'

Further on he said, 'There's a little pub a hundred yards up on the left. Pull up there and we'll have a break.'

In the pub they both drank pints, ensconced on a wooden settle watching a handful of aircrew playing darts. Most pilots were little older than Eileen. The training schools were turning them out at twenty, which meant that by 25 a pilot was considered old, at 30 too old to fly. A couple of the boys recognised Pat and waved. Pat had no qualms about being seen with his driver, although it was strictly against regulations.

'The English summer,' groaned Eileen. 'This must be the wettest July for years.'

'It's cold, too. It reminds me of the way we used to sit huddled round an open fire over in France. I'd never been so cold in all my life. There was snow everywhere, even the ink in the wells froze solid. We were supposed to patrol the sector, but there was nothing going on then and it was just as well. The airfields were frozen and the planes grounded in blizzard conditions. Out in the sticks we had nothing but tents. It was no joke.'

'Did you see much action?' Eileen was tentative, aware that he had chosen not to talk of his experiences in France before.

'Not for a while. The occasional Jerry spotter plane would come over, taking photos, that sort of thing. We had some mock-ups of Hurricanes to deceive them. Make them think we had more planes than they thought. Then suddenly all hell broke loose. In about three weeks we saw enough action to last me a lifetime.' He cradled his pint glass between his pale hands and tilted his head round to glance at her. 'Do you know that one squadron out there shot down 114 enemy planes in ten days? We lost a lot of good fliers, but they lost more.'

'I didn't know that.'

'No, it's a forgotten war. The people I've met over here seem to think that the RAF let them down at Dunkirk. What they don't understand is that we were curtailed by orders from High Command. We were under orders to keep at 12,000 feet while the Stukas got below us and shot up the beaches. Our numbers were so low we were almost continuously in the air. The Government bods back here were so slow that they could not keep up with events. Old Dowding wanted to expand the Air Force, but he had to keep a reserve back here to defend England if and when France fell. His hands were tied. Out of about 250 planes sent to France only about 50 came back.' He paused, draining his glass. 'You know people rage at Chamberlain but he at least gave us an extra year to prepare for war. A year ago our Air Force wouldn't have stood a chance against the Hun. Today – well, we shall have to see, won't we? Another pint, Eileen?'

It was one Sunday early in August and Pat had not been able to get away. The rain was falling around them like stair-rods and Pat suggested that they find somewhere for lunch. There was little choice in the small towns and villages of the district, especially on a Sunday when the closeted conservative locals took their day of rest quite literally and every café and restaurant was firmly shuttered. The only place where food of any description was available seemed to be a small hotel in one of the market towns. It was a white Georgian structure, probably once a coaching inn, now ostentatiously pompous in its decoration, full of a Sunday clientele in their best suits and flowered hats. As soon as they entered the large dining-room Eileen knew they had made a mistake.

Pat strode out between the ranks of tables, leading the way to a vacant table for two already set with white linen and silver. As Eileen followed she was aware of turning heads, of uniforms brown and blue, of hostile glances everywhere. As she sat down, she felt acutely uncomfortable, aware that although she looked smart for once, her plain little uniform looked totally out of place among the top brass at neighbouring tables with their ladies.

Pat was seemingly oblivious of her discomfort, and already had his head buried in the huge menu and wine list. There might be rationing in the outside world but in the watering holes of the rich such restrictions meant nothing. Hotels, clubs and restaurants were all unaffected by the law so far, and as long as you could afford to eat outside the home, life could continue more or less as before. Eileen was astonished to see these well-to-do locals wining and dining when she knew from her own landlady at the billet how hard it was to get even the simplest of foods such as eggs and butter.

The waiter hovered over them, his pencil poised to take their order. Pat was just about to speak when suddenly the head waiter in his black coat and tails hurried anxiously across, glaring at his subordinate.

'Excuse me, sir,' he apologised, indicating that the waiter should leave this to him. 'I'm sorry, sir, but,' he gave a nervous cough and dropped his voice as though to discuss a delicate matter, 'but I'm afraid that, hum, non-commissioned ranks are not allowed here.' He straightened up, looking anxiously round, aware that every face was turned in their direction. He paused, but when Pat said nothing, he began to look acutely uncomfortable. Eventually he was forced to repeat himself. 'Officers are most welcome, sir, but I'm afraid your driver must leave.'

Eileen coloured with embarrassment, her face hot, her hands damp. She made a move to rise and her eyes suddenly met Pat's across the table. She had never seen him so furious. His Asiatic cheeks narrowed his eyes and they glinted menacingly in his pale face. She saw that he was struggling to control his anger. He replaced his unused napkin on the white tablecloth and slowly got to his feet. In a cold voice that carried right across the room he declared disdainfully.

'If she cannot be served here, then neither can I.'

And he left, allowing Eileen to lead the way ahead of him as any gentleman would escort his lady. His disdain effectively conveyed the impression that the service in the hotel restaurant was beneath contempt.

To Eileen the incident reeked unbearably of Charnwood and of how she had felt when confronted by Mrs Pemberley over the letters. An air of self-esteem had permeated the dining-room which even the threat of invasion and war could not apparently erase.

'Jesus Christ!' Pat clambered into the front seat of the Standard and ground his teeth. 'How can we hope to win the war while such ludicrous feudal attitudes persist?' He turned to Eileen. 'I'm really very sorry. That was a disgraceful exhibition.'

'But hardly your fault. It was good of you to walk out like that. I could have stayed here. I wouldn't have cared.'

'Then you should have. I cannot abide hypocrisy. Frankly, I'm surprised so many of that type are still around. When war was declared they were the kind to panic, trying to get the ships out of Southampton to the States, or making a dash for the Lake District and all points north. They must have been the only pin-striped refugees in history.' He sighed. 'Come on now, Eileen, cheer up.'

She pulled out of the town but she had only gone a mile or so out along the road when Pat suddenly turned to her, frowning.

'Park wants me to change sectors,' he announced. 'Things are hotting up and as we've more or less finished with assessment here, he wants me to move over to Kenley by the end of the week.'

Eileen digested this news, her mind racing ahead. She felt a certain panic at the thought that he was leaving, and yet there seemed to be something behind it. What was he proposing? Did he intend to take her with him?

'Well? Are you going to come with me?' He shifted in his seat. 'We get on well together. You've learnt to put up with my temper and you've been a great help, Eileen. But I don't want to make you leave if there's something to keep you here.'

Something, or someone.

'Look, it's up to you. I don't want to put any pressure on you. It's your decision – but I need to know tomorrow. All right?'

Eileen nodded but she felt caught in a dilemma. Working with Pat over the past weeks had opened her eyes to new opportunities she had only dreamt of. She had discovered her own ambition, her potential to do something with her life. The question that faced her was whether she was willing to give all that up, whether she would lose that chance in order to stay with her friends, safe in the security of their trio rather than braving new paths and new people.

Veronica hitched up her battledress trousers and wiped the sweat off her forehead. It was no use, whatever she seemed to do she alienated the flight sergeant and ended up with the worst jobs on camp. Perhaps it was something to do with her voice? She had caught one of the duty corporals mimicking her accent in the MT section and it upset her keenly. Jokes about her name she had learnt to take in her stride, but that time she had to fight to keep back the tears to save herself from further humiliation, feeling appallingly lonely.

She knew what was wrong with her. Ever since London she had been missing Tim dreadfully. It surprised her to discover how much he now meant to her. Her thoughts were constantly going back to him in hospital. She lived now for her brief visits to East Grinstead and for the letters that kept both of them going in between times. She lived every one of his examinations with him, dreading the time when he had to have a skin graft and was waiting for an operation.

Visiting times became life or death situations for her. She had to be on her best behaviour, trying to do every job she was allocated, however rotten, as quickly and completely as possible so that even the flight sergeant couldn't come back at her. The last thing she wanted now was a spell on jankers.

Not for her the jammy jobs that Moira sometimes landed: ferrying pilots to pick up new kites, picking up urgently needed supplies from outlying depots. She envied Moira her easy-going ability to get on with people from all kinds of backgrounds, even getting on to first-name terms with sergeants who terrified the life out of her. It was thanks to Moira that she had got away at all for her last visit when Moira swopped duties with her to stay on camp.

'If you really want to go, I'll fix it with Brian,' she promised.

They had been unloading supplies from the back of a lorry down at the transport depot and there was just the two of them, the packers having skived off to have a quiet smoke out the back. Moira suddenly humped her cardboard box to the floor and stood there looking at her.

'Are you sure you're doing the right thing, love?'

Veronica was almost relieved to hear her raise the subject. After weeks of silence she had begun to think she was too disgusted to mention Tim at all.

'I love him, Moira. Even more than before.' Her eyes held an appeal. She knew that she wasn't expressing herself the way she wanted, but she needed Moira to understand. 'He needs me, can't you see?'

'Of course I do, and I understand why you think you still ought to marry him, but...'

'But what?'

Moira shifted uncomfortably. 'Don't get me wrong, Veronica.

136

I'm sure he's just the same chap underneath, but have you really thought it all through?' She stopped short, angry with herself. 'Oh hell, I'm putting my foot in it, aren't I? Don't get all offended with me, but all I meant was – well, you're still young, you're not bad looking either and – well, just remember there are plenty more fish in the sea!'

But instead of being hurt or even angry, Moira's beating about the bush and unaccustomed delicacy struck her suddenly as funny. Moira's mouth opened in astonishment as she laughed, arms akimbo, standing there like an overgrown tomboy in her overalls.

'You're not upset with me?'

'You are a fool, Moira,' she laughed, flinging an arm around her. 'What are friends for if we can't be honest with one another?'

But looking back to that shared moment of warmth could now only bring a grim smile to her face. There was no escaping the fact that lately Moira had changed. At first she thought she was sickening for something, but as time passed and she still went on with her duties, Veronica began to worry. Recently Moira had begun to cut back on the amount of time she spent going out with her usual flock of male admirers and spending free evenings at the billet. When Moira was home she tended to keep herself to herself, often going to bed early complaining of a headache or exhaustion after a long day. She was paler too, and she seemed to make a lot less effort to look her best. The old routine of waking up at dawn to get her hair just so, and pressing her uniform into some kind of style was now pretty well abandoned. For the first time Moira had actually been pulled up by one of the WAAF officers for sloppy dressing.

After all they had been through together it hurt Veronica to think that perhaps something was badly wrong and yet Moira did not seem willing or able to confide in her friends.

She wiped the grease from her hands and climbed back into the Dodge, working hard to get the old crock going and then steadily ticking over. She was already late for tea and she knew that by the time she had taken the maintenance report back to the office she would be lucky to grab any hot water for a bath. There was no denying the fact that sometimes she thought she was plain crazy staying in a job like this.

When she finally made it back to the billet she thought she was alone. She had a wash and changed, looking forward to an evening with her feet up, but when she went into the lounge she discovered Eileen. She was sitting all hunched up in one of the armchairs, very quiet and still, staring out at the darkening sky. She did not hear her come into the room, she was so wrapped up in her own problems.

After a long silence, Veronica could stand it no more.

'Are you going to tell me what's wrong?'

Eileen turned sharply, amazed to find that Veronica had been in the room some time. Veronica sat curled on the sofa, a pile of knitting on her lap, the beginnings of a jersey she was making for Tim's birthday in September.

When Eileen told her what Pat had proposed, Veronica did not look in the least surprised.

'A job like that is a job in a million. You'd be a fool to turn him down now. You like him, you get on well together, and the job is stretching your capabilities. Look at the kind of people you get to meet! While I get stuck with the dull, routine jobs around camp,' she said without offence. 'We've been very lucky to stay together this long. Some girls lost friends to stations in the north of Scotland.'

'It's only Kenley.'

'Just down the road. See? It's silly to get so worked up about it. I'm sure that Pat will let you out to see us sometimes.'

'I'd hate to lose touch with you – after all we've been through. You're a real friend, Veronica.'

'What would you have done if I'd left the WAAF to marry Tim? I wouldn't have fretted and worried the way you have.'

'Is that what you have in mind?'

'When Tim gets out of hospital, yes, of course, but that won't be until he's had a number of skin grafts. Anyway, we were talking about you, not me. I think you have to go with him, for your own sake.'

'Yes, I want to, but what about Moira? What will she think?'

Veronica frowned, with a suggestion that she was more than a little irritated by Moira's behaviour. 'She's in her room now. Why don't you go and ask her?'

Eileen knocked at the bedroom door but it was a few moments before Moira released the lock and let her in. She looked terrible.

138

Her tawny hair hung in an unruly mess down to her shoulders and her pale face was wiped clean of all make-up. To Eileen she looked a good deal older.

'Are you feeling all right?' Her eyes glanced round the chaotic room, taking in the unmade bed and the scatter of cosmetics and bottles on the chest of drawers.

'Terrific.' Moira ran her fingers through her hair, catching them in the tangles. 'To what do I owe this pleasure?'

'That's hardly fair, Moira. I'm around just as much as you are.'

'Well, what is it?'

'I'm leaving.' The words came out with a rush, more cutting and abrupt than she had intended but Moira's irritability got to her. 'Pat's being transferred to Kenley and he's asked me to go with him.'

Moira flung down the hairbrush she had just picked up and stood, wide-eyed, glaring at her. A hot red stain flushed her cheeks and for a moment Eileen almost thought she was going to hit her.

'Oh well, that's just great, isn't it? If Pat asks you to go, then of course you must go – follow your lord and master.'

'What the hell's up with you? Why are you so damned bloody-minded all of a sudden?'

'Oh dry up, will you? You make me sick. Pandering up to that bloody man, trying to kid us that you're not having it off. God, I detest your bloody holier-than-thou attitudes! What makes you so special? Don't try and tell me that you don't get the plummy jobs for nothing.'

Eileen stood there, unmoving and silent. Her shock and horror must have shown because Moira's face twisted with anguish as she reacted to her own tirade falling into the heavy silence of the room.

'Oh hell, I'm sorry.' She came and took Eileen awkwardly by the shoulders, feeling her rigid and unmoving. 'I'm really sorry, Ei. I didn't mean any of it. It's just that I –' She broke away, and Eileen was alarmed to see tears start to her eyes. Moira's whole face erupted into a bleary red mist of tears and torment, awash with bitterness and fear that had been suppressed for too long.

Sitting on the edge of the crumpled bed, Eileen cradled her friend against her, stroking her hair as she might a child.

139

'What's wrong, love? Why won't you tell us?'

Moira pulled away a little, hugging her wrap around her as though the August night had grown cold.

'I'm overdue,' she said suddenly. 'Just a little bit pregnant, that's what.'

'Oh Lord. Have you checked?'

'Of course I've bloody checked. I've missed once and now I'm three days late again. Can't be more certain than that, can you?'

Eileen began to calculate back one month, no six weeks, even two months ago. And suddenly she knew. June, the London leave, and a trio of handsome Australians let loose on the West End. What were their names? Clive and –

'Don't look at me like that, Ei. It's bad enough.'

'But I thought you took – precautions.'

'Oh Christ, Eileen, I was drunk! I can't even remember – I don't know who . . .'

Eileen sat there, shaking her head, shocked. Moira who had always seemed so assured, so capable, had fallen into the oldest trap just like the most innocent green girl. She realised that if the WAAF officers found out they would throw Moira out of the service. It was a fairly regular occurrence, often followed by a speedy wedding. Such niceties, however, would not apply in Moira's case.

'What are you going to do?'

'Get rid of it.' She shuddered with disgust. 'I can't bear the thought of it. Something growing inside me. It makes me sick. I had to be sure.'

'Get rid of it? How?'

'God, you're so naïve sometimes. Lily will help me. She's always been in favour of legalising it. She makes a point of helping women out with money. It costs a packet.'

'But, Moira, isn't it dangerous?'

'I won't have a back-street job,' she said quickly, her face pale. 'Of course it's dangerous. Christ, I can't stand the thought of it! Why did it have to be me? And why now? I was waiting, you know, waiting, hoping that it would come right. I mean, it's not unusual to miss, is it? What about that time in Morecambe when you missed?'

'Yes, but I –'

Moira's mouth twisted. 'Ah yes, I was forgetting your halo, dear. But there's nothing very virtuous in not being tempted. You just wait until the right man comes along. I'd like to see if you're so bloody righteous then.'

Out in the kitchen of the cottage Eileen found Veronica making three mugs of cocoa.

'I thought we could all do with a cup.'

'Do you know, Veronica?'

She put down the jar and spoon and turned to face her.

'I guessed a long time ago.' She gave a deep sigh. 'She was so moody, so emotional. I caught her counting dates on the calendar. I just put two and two together.'

'It never crossed my mind.'

'No, it wouldn't. You were so wrapped up in your work, whereas I've been here night after night, writing letters, knitting – I had time to notice.' She smiled gently touching her on the arm. 'Don't take it to heart, Eileen. She'll have to sort things out for herself. Let's face it, she was always running the risk. You can't play around the way she has without facing that.'

'It seems so hard.'

'She was hard. She would pick up some poor chap and then throw him over, with never a thought for his feelings. Now she's learning her lesson the hard way.' She passed Eileen a mug of cocoa and stood stirring the others thoughtfully. 'The point is, I don't believe she's ever been in love. Not really. Not the way I am with Tim. I wouldn't care if he had lost an arm or leg, he would still be Tim. But she couldn't understand that. I feel sorry for her, I really do, but being sorry isn't much use to her now, is it?' She picked up the tray. 'I'll stay with her, Eileen, and see her through this mess. She'll need me now. She'll need all her friends.' And she went down the hall to knock on Moira's door and offer her the hot drink she had made for her.

It was August 12th when Eileen drove Pat over to Kenley. Her own case was in the boot, her mind made up, the tears she had shed over her farewell with Moira and Veronica dried on her cheeks. It was a new beginning.

It was a new stage in the war too. The weather cleared even as

141

Eileen manoeuvred the twisting country lanes away from Biggin Hill. As the grey rain clouds cleared away the patch of blue overhead beckoned the Luftwaffe raiders to make an attack across the Channel, the first serious bombing mission on an RAF station, at Manston.

Only later did Pat and Eileen hear the details. Perched on the cliffs overlooking the narrow stretch of water protecting Britain from invasion, Manston had virtually no warning of impending attack. 150 bombs hit the workshops and hangars, destroying a Blenheim on the ground. Strafing fighters swept in low. It was lunchtime and hundreds of personnel ran here and there seeking shelter. 65 Squadron had just taken off, the Spitfires missing destruction on the ground only by minutes. Men from 600 Squadron, who should have been sleeping after night sorties, worked under fire to get the Spitfires airborne while mechanics and men who should have done the work hid themselves in the deep shelters and refused to come out.

Officially there was silence on this crack in morale, but rumours went round aircrew between the stations. There was no hiding the truth. No one knew how they would react to being constantly under fire, under pressure day and night. Only to themselves did they admit to a secret, private fear that they would not be up to it, that they would break down in the face of danger.

Kenley airfield was a modern station spread between the railway line from Brighton to London and the town of Caterham. Only about thirteen miles south of the capital, it used London's old civilian airport at Croydon as a satellite field. The King himself had paid the station a visit in June, a sign of favour for the youngest service.

Pat knew the area well and was a friend of the station commander, Wingco Thomas Prickman. Pat already had his billet in the Officers' Mess in one of the larger houses in the village, and soon arranged for Eileen to take a room with a local family.

There were two squadrons at Kenley: 64 Squadron of Spitfires and 615 Squadron of Hurricanes. There were no aircraft to spare for the training of new pilots coming on to the base. On August

10th the training period for all new pilots had been cut from six months to just two weeks. It was a sensational measure, unheard of before, which shocked the service and showed just how desperate the situation had become. Don MacDonell, leading 64 Squadron, did his best to take the new boys up for a spin, trying to give them a vital bit of practice, to show them what air combat was all about. Some of them had never even flown a monoplane and their number of flying hours was lamentably low.

'It's the young ones who will die,' Pat commented grimly, looking over a new batch of pilots on their way for their very first session at target practice – without real bullets; there were none to spare. 'And it will get worse. The new boys will get the worst planes, the least reliable crews. It makes sense. The experienced fliers are the ones we need, so they'll have the most reliable back-up teams, the planes in best nick. Some of these kids won't last a fortnight.'

Among the experienced fliers the Auxiliary Airforce boys were the élite, ostentatiously waltzing around the station in their smart, tailored uniforms with the red silk lining that marked them out. They were the ones with the fast sports cars and tennis racquets, who spent their leaves riding with the hunt or in smart London nightclubs. Auxiliaries were said to be gentlemen trying to be officers, while the regular career pilots were officers trying to be gentlemen. The Volunteer Reserve were trying to be both.

Regular pilots took their careers seriously, building on peacetime contacts, wearing proper uniform, while VRs scoffed at the rules, only wore what they were comfortable in, flying in shirtsleeves and old cardigans, bringing their dogs along with them. The VRs were in a kind of pool, sent where they were needed. On the whole they were enthusiastic, often superb pilots with a madcap reputation. But not all pilots were officers. One quarter of all fliers were NCOs. On the ground in the mess they were segregated from their colleagues in the air, often cold-shouldered. This kind of meaningless discrimination made Pat furious. He knew many of these men, knew their worth.

'They share the same dangers in the air,' he pointed out. 'These attitudes will have to change if we are to win this war.'

*

One day Eileen met two of Pat's old friends from France. They were Poles who had escaped German occupation of their country to reach Britain for a chance to hit back. Eileen was busy washing her car, up to her elbows in suds when she suddenly became aware of the two young men grinning at her.

'Keep it up, you're doing a grand job. You can come and do mine after.'

Used to friendly ribbing, Eileen grinned and got on with her work, but they were not keen to leave her in peace.

'Pat not around?' It was the tall one who spoke again, the one with the golden labrador at his heels, his devoted slave. He came over and leant on the part of the car she had not yet reached. 'We were in France together,' he explained. 'But he got too trigger-happy, so they had to ground him. Now I hear the silly bugger wants to drop bombs instead.'

Eileen looked up into his amused eyes.

'He's with the wingco. Discussing playing silly buggers no doubt.'

'Let me introduce myself. Karol Rabowski.' He clicked his heels, holding out his hand.

Eileen looked at it and then at her own, covered in suds. He was very smart and dashing, his boots immaculately polished, the creases in his trousers sharp as a knife. She wiped her hand on the back of her overalls and shook hands.

'And this is my friend, Stefan Pniak, but we call him Pepper.' He lowered his attractively accented voice in a theatrical whisper. 'His English is, I'm afraid to say, execrable.'

Eileen cast the red-haired pilot a quick glance. He looked like a country boy, pink-cheeked and grinning, hands in pockets.

'And this is Lara, short for Larissa, a name from home.'

Hearing her name the labrador cocked her head to look up at him, panting in the heat, bright-eyed as her master.

'What a beauty.' Eileen bent and ran a friendly hand down her silky coat and stroked her chest. 'Are you on station? Shall I tell Pat you were looking for him?'

'Tell him he still owes me a fiver,' said the Pole, calling Lara to heel as they turned to leave. He cast Eileen a lingering look and then called out over his shoulder. 'You forgot to tell me your name?'

144

'It's Eileen.'

'I'll remember. We'll meet again, Eileen, count on it!'

The news that Alan had been shot down could not have come at a worse time for Moira. He had been flying patrol over the south coast and come down in the drink. The crash was witnessed by two of his pals from the squadron.

At the news Moira felt that she had to get away and be on her own. It wasn't the done thing to show too much emotion; death was becoming far too common for anyone to take it at all seriously. She had to hide herself away before she could give way to the tears of which she was ashamed, but then once the floodgates were open she found herself crying not just for Alan but for herself as well. It seemed that her whole world was crashing to pieces around her, that events were escalating out of all control.

It was not even as though she and Alan had been lovers. Of course everyone thought that they were, and he had wanted it at the beginning, but sex was the last thing on her mind since the whole nightmare had begun. And then Alan had been a real support. He never asked questions, never pushed her, but in some curious way she thought that he treated her with more respect than before. He was a real find, and in other circumstances she thought that she could have fallen quite heavily for him.

As it was, he was the only man she would allow anywhere near her. She could remember exactly when the first suspicion that she was pregnant dawned on her. She had checked her dates, kidding herself along that she had miscalculated. Then when she was proved correct after all, she decided that she was late this month because of all the recent turmoil following the trip to London. But all the time she knew it was a lie. And London was the cause of it. She chose not to remember. She pushed it to the back of her memory, blurred by too much drinking and a kind of self-loathing. To think of it at all was a sort of torture, a judgemental shadow over her whole future.

For days she went round trying to be cheerful. She kept on thinking that the next time she checked it would be all right. She found excuses to head for the lavatory twice as often as usual.

The dreadful fear and expectation marked out the hours of the day. Each night was a torment, leading to another day, another disappointment.

And then, when she could no longer lie to herself, an even worse nightmare began: the fear of what would happen to her if They found out – They, the WAAF authorities, her friends, the other women on station, Alan and all his gang. The appalling humiliation, the gossip, the speculation that would buzz around the camp – who and when? She had seen other WAAFs caught out, ignominiously summoned to Ma'am's office, leaving in a furtive rush of shamefaced activity while the station sang with the news.

How long before they found her out? Pride and bitter fury took over for a while, her moods swinging from one extreme to another. For a week she was savage to everyone, even to her best friends. She had almost come to blows with Eileen that night, at the end of her tether, hurt, bitter, disgusted with herself. And Eileen had come to her, so full of her own news that she was leaving, her life all nicely set out in a straight pattern, all worked out, while she – she had thrown everything away.

That was when she had decided. Two months gone. There could be no doubt now. The thought filled her with terror, but she knew there was no alternative. She had once heard of a woman who went to a back-street 'doctor' and died of blood-poisoning the day after. Everyone had found out. But on the other hand, she knew there were respectable places, posh clinics in the West End where they charged a bomb to keep it quiet. After all, it was illegal. It was not only the woman who was running a risk.

She knew she would be forced to go to her grandmother and tell her everything. Lily, who knew everything there was to know about women's problems and had helped countless women through this and worse. Lily would know what to do, who could help her, and where she could find the money. And yet it broke her heart to go to her grandmother with such news. She had never felt so close to anyone in her life as to Lily. Certainly not to her own mother, ever.

Lily had taken her in and protected her. She had nurtured her, wanting her to do something great and good with her life. That was the worst of it, the shame of having to tell Lily how she had failed her.

*

The Germans had launched a new wave of attacks, going for the industrial centres at night, scoring a hit on the Spitfire factory near Birmingham. As the break in the weather held, each day brought new attacks. Black Thursday brought an all-out effort with waves of bombers coming in from bases in France, Belgium, Denmark and Norway. Pat said it was clear that the Germans were testing the defences along the entire length of the country. The old aerodrome at Croydon, Kenley's satellite, became a target because of nearby factories, but the aim of the bombers was not too good: 200 houses were also hit, killing 62 people.

The next day Pat and Eileen were covering the southern-most edge of their sector, down at Beachy Head. Standing down on the cliff edge they had a ringside view of waves of bombers coming in over the coast. They had no idea of their prospective target. It could have been Kenley or any one of the stations inland in a direct line to London.

One of the enemy planes came in low, dropping a salvo over Eastbourne. He was having trouble with his engine, obviously dared not make the run and decided to get rid of his load in case he had to ditch. He was so low that Eileen and Pat could see the pilot in the cockpit.

'If I only had a rifle I could get the bugger,' said an exasperated Pat at her side, clenching and unclenching his fists.

But as the bomber made its turn back towards the sea the town's coastal defence battery opened up and he was caught in the ack-ack fire. Eileen watched in horror as flames engulfed the pilot as he struggled in vain to open his hatch. She could not believe what she was seeing right in front of her eyes, that a human being was there, dying. She had heard terrible stories of flamers, of pilots going up like torches. She knew the appalling effects, she knew what burns could look like, even fairly minor third-degree burns like Tim's. But to see it was quite another matter. She felt a constriction in her throat and wondered for a moment if she was going to be sick. She turned away as the burning plane fell out of the sky in a tail of brilliant flames.

'You all right?'

'Yes, of course.' She tried to give Pat a wan smile, but it turned sour. She was furious with herself for showing any emotion.

147

After all, there was a war going on and she was part of it. She could not expect to get through without seeing some of the realities.

They drove back through country lanes marked by the signs of conflict. Stray bombs had scattered across the land, pockmarking the fields, with craters becoming local curiosities, crashed aircraft becoming familiar landmarks. There was even a joke that people had begun to give directions not by signposts, which had long ago been removed to confuse German spies, but by the Messerschmitt down the lane, then first left at the Dornier and right by the Junkers 88!

People as they worked in the fields, picking or harvesting, would stop to take cover from the dogfights overhead, every face upturned in fascinated horror at the spiralling white vapour trails criss-crossing the summer skies.

Tangmere had been the target of the day's raid. It was in absolute shambles, so they heard, with people wandering round, dazed and confused. Caught on the edge of the South Downs, from the air it was clearly visible, an easy prey for enemy bombers.

Saturday August 17th dawned bright and clear, perfect weather for a major enemy offensive. Pat had not gone up to London for the weekend, having a lot of reports still to write, spending the day in and round the station. A full-scale alert was expected at any moment, the weather offering the Luftwaffe perfect flying conditions. The Kenley squadrons stood at readiness, the pilots dispersed round the field, stretched out on the grass in their shirtsleeves and Mae Wests reading and sunbathing, waiting for the alert to scramble.

As the day wore on and no attack alert came, everyone grew nervous. To Eileen it was like the oppressive heavy atmosphere that builds up before a thunder storm. As she crossed the field from Pat's billet to the NAAFI, she saw groups of people standing around, tense and irritable, scratching their heads as they gazed up at the empty sky.

'Not a sausage. Blooming amazing.'

'Can't understand it.'

As the afternoon crept on word went round that the silence had to mean something. There was no news of attacks on other sectors. It was peaceful everywhere and that could only mean one thing: the Germans were regrouping for a major offensive.

'The big one's on the way. Mark my words, it's the invasion.'

As Eileen went to join Pat that evening she saw the WAAFs going on the graveyard shift taking books and knitting on duty with them into the ops room. The NAAFI and mess were busy as there was no operational flying. There were aircrew everywhere, hanging around, waiting, uneasy.

The pub that Pat took her to was full of officers and fliers from the base. They hung round the bar with their drinks telling jokes and stories and trying to hide the atmosphere that had crept on during the day. The pilots took a pleasure in looking casual, even scruffy, off duty with their sleeves rolled up, each flier adding some individual touch to his getup.

Eileen went through the bar looking for Pat and, just as she saw him, collided with one of the pilots who had just entered the pub. Apologising, they broke apart, he stooping to retrieve his jacket with the thin stripe of pilot officer on the shoulder and wings on the breast. As he straightened up, his tawny shock of hair hung over his eyes and she saw his face.

Eileen stood there, rooted to the spot, unable to move. As their eyes met she felt a shock of recognition that was almost physical. He frowned, a little puzzled, a trace of a smile in his eyes as though he too was trying to remember. Then quite suddenly a brilliant grin broke over his face as he recognised her.

'Is it really you?' he asked incredulously.

There was a sudden weakness in her legs and she felt almost dizzy. For so long she had kept all thought of him at a safe distance and then, out of the blue, fate dealt her this surprise.

Dear God, she said to herself. Jonathan. Jonathan Pemberley.

Chapter Six

'Do come and join us, won't you?' Pat had stood up at their corner table, taking in the details of the unknown pilot through narrowed eyes. 'We haven't met before?'

'No, sir. Jonathan Pemberley. How do you do?'

They shook hands vigorously, looking each other over.

'Pat Fairweather.' They sat down. 'I used to cover Kenley before the French business, but you're new round here, aren't you?'

'Been here six weeks, sir.'

'Oh cut the "sirs" in here. What are you both drinking?'

'That's awfully nice of you, sir– ah, well, I'll have a pint of bitter.'

'Eileen? Your usual?'

Eileen smiled at him, agreeing, quite unable to speak. To Pat she looked convulsed with shyness, suddenly transformed from the assured and capable woman he knew her to be into a blushing schoolgirl. From the safe distance of the bar he watched them sitting together and knew instantly what was the matter with her.

He was a handsome chap, young, strong and healthy, but it was a puzzle how they could have known one another. He was so obviously out of her league. His name and his accent immediately told his story. But the war had thrown up all sorts of stranger pairings. Times were changing. When she had left Biggin Hill without any serious qualms he had supposed that Eileen had deliberately cut men out of her life because of some ill-fated romance in the past. Was this the chap who had made her so wary?

He decided that Pemberley didn't look like a rogue. He could usually spot the womanisers, the ones who made a sport out of scoring points, treating their women as goddesses when they met them, as tarts when they left them. That kind of man had utter contempt for any woman fool enough to fall for them. They really knew their own worth. But this one? He doubted it. Pemberley had obviously been shaken to find Eileen here. Perhaps he had not heard that she was now a WAAF. After all, it was not so long ago since she had joined up, she was only a kid really. And what did he know of her life before? She seemed to avoid all talk about it, and he was left with the impression that it was an area of her life she did not want to discuss.

As he brought the drinks over to the table, Eileen gave him a quick, startled look with her large green eyes, a look that was half-appeal, half-defensive.

'Cheers!' They all took a long drink and then seemed to relax a little. The noisy hubbub of the pub continued round them.

'Well then, Jonathan – I can call you Jonathan, can't I? – how did you meet my Eileen?' He saw that his use of the possessive struck home. If he had been in any doubt of the young man's interest in her it was now confirmed. He saw the quick glance he stole at Eileen as though to check her reaction. But Eileen would not let him answer.

'Oh, we've known one another a long time,' she said immediately. 'Through a mutual friend, actually.'

'Yes, how is Gareth?' Pat thought he detected an edge to the young man's words, and he wondered who this rival could be. It grew more interesting by the moment. But Eileen looked surprised.

'Don't you know? I haven't heard from him for a long time.'

'So you did write to him.' He made it sound like an admission of guilt.

'Well, yes, but then I joined up. And the letters just sort of died out.'

Pat saw at once that she was lying. Although she did not blush or look away, any of those clear signs of deceit, he now knew her well enough to detect when she was being deliberately evasive or telling an out and out lie.

'I hope he's all right,' she added hastily, trying to cover up for the awkward silence.

'Oh yes, I should think so,' said Jon. 'He did some special training after we got split up. He was a much better flier than me, you know. He came first in our group at Chester. I think they gave him some hush-hush job, testing or something of that sort. The last I heard was when a pal of mine ditched and came across him up at Duxford.'

Pat was instantly alert. He knew that Duxford was a centre for high-level experimentation of new air combat techniques.

'What does this friend of yours fly?'

'Oh, anything really. He's a born aviator. We trained for Spits, of course.'

Pat nodded, thinking that perhaps he could be at Duxford trying out the new cannon-armed planes. He had heard they were having teething problems.

'19 Squadron, is he? What's his name – in case we get up that way.'

'Gareth James.' Jonathan looked rather surprised and frowned. 'Do you move round a lot then, sir? I mean, are you only here temporarily?'

Pat knew that the young man didn't give a damn whether he stayed or went from Kenley tomorrow. What he wanted to know was how long Eileen would be around.

'Oh, I expect we'll stay around here a while longer,' he said pleasantly, amused by the relief on both of their faces. 'Especially if the action hots up.'

Jonathan tore his eyes away from Eileen and his broad, tanned face took on a rather grim and determined expression. Under that open, lighthearted façade Pat detected a serious, even deadly nature. Pat recognised it instantly. He had seen it every day of his life in France. He knew the killer instinct when he saw it.

'Oh it's certainly going to hot up,' said the pilot levelly. 'Today was an aberration. Something big is coming up, perhaps a full-scale invasion. They will try and knock out as many of our stations as they can. They'll try and take out our fighters on the ground before we can strike back. But it will never happen, sir. We're all ready and waiting for the chance to get back at them.'

'And how do you rate our chances?'

'You can't ask me that, sir. When I saw the first waves of Jerry planes coming over, I just stood there wide-eyed and disbelieving.

152

There were hundreds of them. It was pretty damned scary. And we don't really know how many planes they've got. All I know is that each bastard I knock out of the sky is one less. We'll just keep going with the men and planes we've got – until we run out.'

Pat saw that Eileen was staring at him, eyes shining. She was so obviously head over heels in love with him that Pat wondered what the problem could be between them.

'I admire your attitude,' Pat told him.

'Pat saw action in France,' Eileen cut in. 'He says it was really tough over there.'

'We owe you a lot then, sir,' Jon agreed. 'We would never stand a chance if you hadn't already wiped out so many Jerry planes.'

The correct and formal conversation hid a deeper, more tentative dialogue. Pat thought that if he had not been there quite the last thing they would have been discussing was the war. He could not take his eyes off her. There was no doubt they shared an immediate attraction. They sat there almost in a world of their own.

Was he glad for them or sad? It was no use getting too fond of anyone in this war. Who knew what tomorrow would bring? He was aware of a sense of isolation and regret that he had not managed to get away to London that weekend to be with Grace.

Outside, after Pat had diplomatically said goodnight, Eileen paused to look at the splendid sunset that had come at the end of the matchless summer day. The huge orb of fire slowly sank into a bank of pale mist, spreading flamingo and vermilion hues down into turquoise and deep purple. Without a word Jon joined her there, watching together until the sun had disappeared and they were plunged into growing darkness.

The night was still warm and there was the scent of fresh-mown hay on the rising breeze. Eileen and Jon stood side by side, untouching. And yet there was no disguising the force of attraction that flowed between them.

She jumped as if burnt when his arm accidentally brushed hers as they eventually turned away. Their eyes met and held. Nothing had been said between them, nothing to indicate that they would even meet again, but she knew and he knew that they would, they must. His eyes promised as much when he smiled straight into hers as they drew apart and took their separate paths.

Jonathan Pemberley stood and watched as Eileen hurried away from him into the night and he could smile at the wayward chance that had brought her back into his life. Perhaps if she had not stopped dead at the sight of him in the pub, as shaken as if she had seen a ghost, staring up at him with her astonished green eyes, he would not even have noticed her, let alone recognised her.

She had certainly changed! In that little blue suit she really cut a dash. Who would believe that just one year could make such a difference? When she sat beside him in the MG that night with Gareth he had thought her a mouse, wondering what on earth Gareth had seen in her to take such a chance under their own roof. But clearly he ought to have given old Gareth more credit for spotting a likely winner, a dark horse and no mistake.

Jon remembered that last summer at Charnwood with nostalgia. How young they had all been then, how untouched by the war and the threat of danger. He and Gareth had had the run of the old house, kicking their heels with impatience to get on with their training, sick of Cambridge and textbooks, eager for adventure and challenge in their lives. He remembered how they had gate-crashed the local hop out of boredom, but the village girls all seemed the same. Had she been there? Was that where Gareth had first met her?

Trust Gareth to get the best of it – and right under all their noses! What a shock it had been when he pulled that trick, but then Gareth had always been full of surprises. He seemed to take a delight in deliberately baiting people, coming out with highly contentious or controversial remarks that sent shock waves round the room.

Walking back to his billet on camp through the softly scented night, Jon realised that was how he had first met Gareth at Cambridge. He had admired this scholarship boy with his amusing accent and gift of the gab. He had been ragged for his radical views but he did not change them. He always had an opinion of his own, he appeared to know where he was headed.

That is what had appealed to Jon, that steadiness was what he needed in a friend.

When he took Gareth back to Charnwood as a Christmas house party guest he supposed he should have expected fireworks. Faced with the stuffy array of his father's friends, Gareth had been like a fish out of water. With Hayden Darcy his manner had verged on the offensive. Jon had had to make it clear to his family that Gareth was there as his guest, even if Gareth's unorthodox behaviour sometimes astonished him too.

Jon had always thought of himself as liberal, easy-going, but when he discovered that Gareth had gone behind his back in his own house he had been furious. Now he wondered why he had felt so angry. Was it just that Gareth had kept Eileen such a secret, or had he, even then, felt a twinge of jealousy?

When they had started their training up in Chester he became aware that Gareth was carrying on a secret correspondence with her. Secret from him. He had caught him one night writing back to her and forced him to come clean. Reluctantly, Gareth had admitted it was true, and only then had he learnt anything about her.

It wasn't just that she came from the same part of the country, or that she was nearer his own class. He seemed really stuck on the girl in a way that could only mean one thing in Jon's book. He was certain now that they had been sleeping together.

Gareth used to talk about her a lot after that, mooning round when no letters arrived. Although they both went out with the local Chester girls who came out to dances at the base, Jon saw that Gareth had not put Eileen out of his mind. He had felt rather sorry for him.

But how all their lives had changed in the past year! There was Gareth up at Duxford with his experimental fliers, and here he was walking straight into Eileen Howard without a word of warning.

He wondered if Gareth even knew that she had left Charnwood and joined up. He thought perhaps that she had followed him into the Air Force hoping that one day they would be posted to the same station.

It seemed rather ironic that now she should come face to face with him rather than Gareth. Had she been in love with Gareth?

155

She said they no longer wrote to each other, that they had lost touch. And certainly there was something in her attitude, in the way she looked at him that suggested that she could be available.

There was no denying that he was strongly attracted to her. She beat every other WAAF he had taken out on the station into a cocked hat. Was he thinking of taking her out then? Yes, why not? There was always a lot of competition for the girls. They were in such short supply that every woman, no matter what she looked like, had a busy time fending off the chaps. But Eileen seemed to have avoided the rugger scrum of Saturday night dating. She always seemed to have her officer in tow. For a while that worried him, but all in all he did not think that there was anything going on between her and Fairweather. He looked a serious type, some kind of specialist, hooked on his work and certainly old enough to be her father. Their relationship seemed casual, amiable rather than passionate.

He wondered what had made her leave Charnwood. Not much of a life, that. It was the first time he had thought about it. She seemed too bright for that kind of thing. She had a bit of go in her. Perhaps it was just patriotism that made her join up. He had to admire her spirit. He wanted to know everything about her, her background, what she thought, everything. He wondered who her people might be. Certainly they had to be badly off, or why else would she have been sent into service in the first place? Now she was clearly trying to make something of herself and good luck to her. He was more excited at the thought of seeing her again than he had been for months. They could have a bit of fun together. A few drinks away from the crowd, dinner somewhere quiet and cosy, leading up to a weekend away somewhere with style that would impress her.

As he entered his billet he gave one last thought to Gareth. It struck him as rather ironic that she should have found him rather than Gareth. He smiled wryly at the thought of picking up where his friend had left off. Perhaps that was what added the touch of extra excitement.

He wondered what Gareth would say when he heard?

At seven he was woken by the birds jumping up and down on the roof of his hut. He turned over in the narrow bed and heard the familiar sounds of Rogers his batman doing the morning rounds. Bright sunshine was already pouring through the gap in the blackout curtains, warning of a day ripe for an enemy attack.

Would they come over today? Yesterday the uncanny silence on the station had filled everyone with unspoken dread, as though they had a premonition that from then on things could only get worse.

Jon had seen his pals looking round at one another as they sat outside dispersal in the sunshine. Each man had the same thought. How many would survive the month, even the week? The general public had no idea what was involved. The newspapers could blare their phoney headlines all they liked, but no one except a flier could understand the feeling of being up at 25,000 feet in the still sky, all your nerves taut, all your reflexes keyed up for that vital two or three seconds that could mean the difference between life and death.

As he stood in the bathroom shaving Dutch came over and leant against the wall watching him.

'We've had word to shift our gear over to dispersal,' he announced in his leisurely growl. 'They must be expecting trouble. I doubt if we'll see this place for a while.'

'I always did fancy the outdoor life.'

'Shall I get Rogers to shift our odds and sods? Then we can grab a bite of breakfast before the Jerries make an appearance. I trust they're civilised enough to wait until after breakfast.'

11 Group had resolved to keep a standing patrol flying during daylight to give some advantage in case of enemy attack. It was a pretty dangerous job in Jon's opinion because of the over-whelming numbers of enemy planes that could suddenly appear out of the sun. Anyone who got bounced in that fashion had less than a cat's chance in hell of getting out of it in one piece. If they had time to pass the warning over the RT to HQ that was an achievement.

Over at dispersal their kites were in the blast pens. The hut that Jon shared with Dutch and others of their squadron had their names already scribbled in on the blackboard. They were among the top three at readiness, with another three in reserve, 'available' if they were needed. Against each pilot's name was the code letter of his aircraft. Since there had been no losses of late, Jon was still flying M for Mother and Dutch R for Robert. Both kites were, so far, in tip-top condition.

'Hello, you chaps,' they were greeted inside. It was a terrible shambles. Someone had been making a model plane and the pieces were still left all over the table. Others were already making themselves comfortable with paperback thrillers and the Daily Sketch.

'Did you hear about old Chips? His bloody RT packed up just as he was turning for home. Completely lost his way. Thought he'd bought it. He got caught in the clag at 20,000 and only found his way back by following a wave of Huns up the estuary to Gravesend.'

'You lousy lineshooter! I saw old Chips at the mess last night.'

'Well, if it wasn't Chips then it was someone else.'

'Why don't you keep your lip buttoned, old man? Some of us are trying to get a quick kip.'

Jon turned to Dutch and suggested they move outside. The atmosphere was still tense. No one could disguise the feeling that today was the day. Jon sprawled on the grass and flicked casually through Picture Post, but he really wasn't interested. Dutch had his head buried in a copy of For Men Only and seemed more engrossed. His curly head of carrot-red hair glistened in the bright sunshine like a Belisha beacon, product of mixed Scots and Irish ancestry. Since he had come to Kenley, Dutch had been his good friend and drinking companion, but he knew very little about him really. Friendships were easily made and broken, it was the nature of the times. Up in a dogfight it was enough to trust the fellow next to you to pull you out of trouble when you caught a Jerry on your tail. Tomorrow could take care of itself.

If things got too hot Jon knew that the controller could even order them to 'super-readiness', cutting down the five minutes to scramble to a bare fifteen seconds as the pilots sat in their kites ready to take off. Jon lay back and closed his eyes against the glare of the morning sun, when suddenly the calm was shattered by the urgent ring of the telephone in the hut. At once every man in the group started to his feet, staring as the Skipper got there first.

'False alarm, chaps. It's just admin. wanting to know our numbers.'

With a groan Jon sank back on to the grass, fiddling with the straps of his Mae West lifesaver. From where he sat he could see the roof of the small bungalow they used as the Ops Room. It was defended from possible blast by a six foot high wall, covered in a tent of camouflage netting. He thought it must already be boiling inside for the controller and his plotters. He wondered if old Fairweather was down there today. He had not disclosed the real nature of his work at the station, so it was obviously something pretty hush-hush. With his experience of combat he was clearly in a position to inject some common sense into the top brass's strategy. But even so, Jon thought it must be very hard to be grounded. He had come to love flying, even this terrible side of it. But it was undeniably a young man's game. You had to think faster and more clearly up there than in any sport he had ever tried. It wasn't so much a matter of brains or strength, though pulling out of a nose dive took one hell of a lot of muscle power. It was the sensation of being in command, of being the centre of the universe, able to control your own destiny. You were all on your own up there. One mistake and you died. It was that simple.

Jon had chosen the RAF because it was modern, adventurous and offered a challenge from the sedate and boring pattern of life laid out for him. He needed to demonstrate his independence, to break away from the ties of his family and their rigid expectations – just as Gareth had wanted to escape the expectations imposed by his much stricter father. Perhaps that was why Gareth always took risks. A superb pilot, he nevertheless dared more than anyone he had ever known, not in a mad, reckless way, but coldly, with calculation, as though breaking new territory. No wonder that the test pilots had taken him on. If Gareth's old man had only known what his son was doing now, he'd die of apoplexy!

The morning pressed on and Jon began to feel irritable and hot. He went and made Rogers get them some tea, but lunchtime drew on and there was still no sign of anything happening.

'Why don't they give us the low down?' he complained to Dutch. 'All this hanging about drives me insane. What the hell are the Jerries playing at?'

Perhaps he should have said nothing. For as soon as his words were out the telephone gave a persistent ring and he knew that this was it.

It was 12.45 exactly.

It was 12.45 and Eileen was eating her Sunday lunch when the order came over the loudspeakers to take shelter.

'Attack alarm! All personnel take cover! Attack alarm! Take cover immediately!' The tannoy crackled as there was a general scraping back of chairs as the crowded room got to their feet. 'Large enemy formation approaching. Take cover!'

'How large?' wondered the WAAF at Eileen's side, pale-faced.

'Let's shift, shall we, girls?' suggested a sergeant.

Some of the women calmly picked up their plates and moved towards the door. There was no panic. Emerging into the sunlight, Eileen saw the Spitfires of Jon's squadron scrambling, but she had no idea if he was with them. Looking up into the cloudless skies she could see nothing amiss. The Spits were climbing high, looking for the raiders, providing the first line of defence for the station at high altitude. Nothing seemed to be happening, there seemed no need for panic. Groups of men and women walked calmly towards the shelters in the sunshine.

Glancing up at the empty sky, Eileen followed them yet she could not believe this was yet another false alarm. The skin on the back of her neck prickled and the air seemed very still. She turned her head suddenly and looked across the field towards the spinney on the south side just as three planes appeared, skimming the tops of the trees.

For a moment she thought they must be British, they flew so low, dipping across the land together, bobbing up and down in the air current as they made their approach. Then she saw the giant black crosses under their wings and recognised the shape of the Dorniers as they came in for the attack.

'Run, run!' someone screamed. 'Hit the deck!'

The sound of firing filled the air round her as she began to run. There was a slit trench at the side of one of the huts, a zigzag affair, shallow but better than nothing. Eileen's mind was racing, full of sudden calculations about distance and range, aware of the whining scream of bombs hitting the field, all her senses on edge. Could she make it to shelter? Her legs suddenly felt heavy, unable to carry her. Her breath hammered in her ears. She could see

160

other people running, moving in distracted jerking movements within her shaken vision. They were all running in opposite directions. Plates of food went flying as they dived for safety into the holes in the earth.

Eileen buried her head in her hands as a bomb struck one of the houses on the perimeter, the blast spraying debris and splinters right across the field. When Eileen glanced up, the air was still full of dust and hot ashes and she felt her face and hair under her tin helmet caked in the stuff. The trench was full of cramped bodies, squashed in together at all angles, a tangle of arms and legs and astonished faces. The ground beneath them shook with the force of other explosions nearby and the whine of diving aircraft. She heard the boom of the Scots Guards' defence guns, for the most part old Lewis guns from the First War or Bofors guns. With her head cradled against the bank of sweet-smelling earth, Eileen heard the guns open up, only to be answered by the swish of German bullets spraying the ground all round them.

Eileen was astonished to hear under the din of battle a faint voice behind her. She shifted round and saw with amazement and wonder that one of her fellow WAAFs had begun to sing. As a bomb whistled down somewhere close Eileen could not hear what she was singing, only aware of her mouth opening and closing like a fish under water. But in a brief lull the tune was suddenly clear and she laughed out loud, and then joined in. While the barrage continued the trench was full of WAAFs all singing 'Ten Green Bottles' at the top of their voices in defiance of the bombs shaking the earth beneath their feet.

When she dared to look again she saw a Spitfire that had been hit on the ground by one of the bombs in its blast pen. Its warning horn must have been affected because it had started automatically, blaring across the airfield among the general hubbub. To the south of the field there was a thick pillar of dark smoke billowing up from the direction of the hangars.

Eileen wondered what had gone wrong. She had seen the Spitfires at readiness scrambled and airborne, climbing high to meet any attack, but these low-level Dorniers appeared to have crept in under their defensive cloak, taking everyone by surprise. Yet even as she looked up, she saw one of the Spits spiralling down at high speed to encounter the enemy planes, marking the blue sky with its clear-white vapour trail. Other heads turned upwards to watch as the Germans made a run for it, their mission already accomplished.

Escaping from the furious attack of the station's defenders, one of the Dorniers became entangled in the spider's web of defensive cables on the perimeter and was literally plucked out of the sky. They all stared in horror as the huge bird dropped like a stone, smashing into a small bungalow on the edge of the field in a fountain of flames.

When silence finally descended, the WAAFs clambered out of their trench, stiff-legged and covered in dirt and dust. Round them the wreckage was all too apparent. In dazed little groups people stood numb and staring at what, just 45 minutes before, had been a fully operational RAF station.

The bombs from the Dorniers had cut deep furrows straight across the field in an attempt to prevent future take-offs and landings. Enormous craters pitted the grass everywhere, littered with the flying debris from other explosions.

Whistles were being blown as station staff sprang into emergency routines. There were apparently unexploded bombs round the place and already a team of army experts were marking out the sites with 'UXB' signs. One bomb had fractured the station's water main and it was therefore impossible to try and put out the fires that were raging on every side. Not that water would have been enough to put out the thick oil fires from the hangars. The timber-framed buildings had been used for engineering work, for storing petrol and paint supplies, oxygen cylinders and transport. These had gone up in a volcano of flames and dangerous gases, belching out thick glutinous smoke and hurling heavy debris everywhere. One hangar had housed 50 private cars belonging to the top brass and pilots. Now it was just a burning shell amid a clutter of iron and glass, shredded rubber and wooden splinters. There were even dead birds which had been swept from the sky in the fury of the bombing.

Eileen had remembered Sunnycroft, the bungalow which had been flattened by the crashing Dornier. In a tangle of electricity lines she had to gasp and look away, her throat full, at the sight of a charred human torso suspended among the ruins.

'Come away from there!' said a voice roughly and she felt

162

herself steered away by one of the Scots Guards. 'Watch where you walk. There's Jerry everywhere round here.'

Over on the runway she saw a Hurricane which had been hit by flying debris. It stood there almost perfectly intact, except for its skin which had been completely peeled away, revealing its bare skeletal struts. She was passed by an improvised fire-engine blowing its horn. A converted London taxi, it sped across the field towing a trailer pump, swerving to avoid the bomb craters and warning UXB signs. They were heading straight for the station's sick quarters and hurrying after them Eileen saw that the large Red Cross which had been painted on the roof of the building had done nothing to prevent it being bombed by the German planes.

The sick quarters had received a direct hit. She saw that the roof had caved in on the patients, burying them under a mountain of smoking rubble. From all parts of the field people were rushing to help with the rescue work. Men were stripping off their jackets and getting to work with all available shovels and picks, but it looked like a long and daunting task. A fire was still burning in the ruins, while the crew of the fire-engine searched around frantically for a standpipe where they could find water.

She went to help with those being pulled out of the ruins alive. There was already one body on the grass, covered with a blanket. It was the local doctor, a very popular figure in and around the station, who had been caught on duty in the sick bay. There were a number of WAAFs also caught. One woman was in acute pain and asked for some morphia but all their supplies had been destroyed by the bombing. Eileen cradled her head until a stretcher-team arrived to take her to hospital in the town.

As she sat there Pat found her, wandering through the *mêlée* with his hard, anxious expression. He was bare-headed and caked in chalky-coloured dust, the sleeve of his shirt ripped and filthy. He gave Eileen a welcome hug. In their dirty faces, their teeth and eyes gleamed with pleasure and relief at finding they were both still alive and unharmed.

When the injured WAAF had been taken away in a Red Cross truck, Pat walked Eileen back across the field. He told her that he had been sitting in his billet catching up on his paperwork when the alert came. He had had no time to get out of the house before he heard the first scream of attack overhead. He hit the floor at once, an instinctive reaction, with only the table for cover as the whole house shook with the force of the bombing. The glass fell from the windows, in spite of the tape criss-crossed to prevent shattering. A tree in the garden had been completely uprooted, crashing into the greenhouse and demolishing the poor little Standard car which Eileen had parked there only the day before.

To Pat's astonishment Eileen suddenly burst into tears.

'Stupid, isn't it? I've been so calm – until now. Then just a little thing starts me off.' She sniffed. 'I'm sorry.'

'It's a natural reaction. Come on, let's get over to control and see what's happening about our boys in the air.'

Eileen stopped, halfway through wiping away the tears and dirt from her face. 'Will you ask about 64 Squadron? Who got up and...'

'Yes, I know.' His eyes smiled with compassion and indulgence, but he was thinking the same thought. Had Jon Pemberley taken off that morning? And if he had, had he got back safely?

The controller told Pat that damage was extensive. Three out of four hangars had been completely destroyed, the sick quarters had had a direct hit, HQ and the messes were damaged. There could be no doubt that the Luftwaffe objective was to wipe out the capability of the station to continue, but here they had failed. Although all airborne pilots had been ordered to land at Redhill, some of their pilots had either not heard the message or had brazenly decided to show that Kenley airfield was still operational. Even as they talked, one Hurricane from 615 circled and came in between the craters, landing with accomplishment on the burnt and battered grass.

Nine had died and at least the same number were injured. They had lost four Hurricanes on the ground, with two others and a Spit badly damaged. Other bombs had almost certainly fallen wide of the field, for smoke could be seen from the east, from civilian homes.

'No disguising this one,' said Pat. 'I wonder how the general public will react to coming under fire? Think they'll panic, sir?'

'Don't be such a pessimist, Pat. When their backs are up, the

British are pretty tough customers. It takes a lot to get us moving, but I don't doubt the courage and tenacity of ordinary people to pull through against the odds.'

What had caused more surprise was the way in which the women on the station had behaved. It was the first time that WAAFs had been in the front line and Eileen knew there had been a lot of talk about removing all women to safer postings, out of the danger zone. There was an entrenched idea that women were weak and would panic under attack, that they would go to pieces and hamper the station's operations. Eileen had never believed this was true, although she had not been in an attack until now. But she knew that women were quite capable of dealing with all kinds of other emergencies in their normal daily lives. They did not faint at the sight of blood or get hysterical and panic. In a hundred different ways women had to cope when faced with crisis situations, and did cope magnificently, often better than men. Now the men on the station were proud as punch that 'their girls' could stand up to anything that Hitler could throw at them. There was no doubt that spirits soared once it was shown that Kenley had come through the raid and was still operational. They felt they had won a great victory.

When Eileen left Pat with the controller and his staff to make an assessment of the damage, he watched her go with a wistful expression, knowing that she was looking for Jonathan Pemberley.

'Any reports on the squadrons?' he asked the controller in a matter-of-fact voice.

'615 had a few knocks. I'm afraid we lost one chap – crashed on Morden golf course. A couple of others crash-landed. Can't say if they were wounded or not.'

'And 64?'

'Just the one Spit hit on the ground. Though we still have a few chaps to get back. Ah! Isn't that one of them trying to get in now?'

Pat saw the Spit turning for a landing over the field. He was clearly making a recce of the damage, trying to find the best place to get down between the craters and the UXB areas.

Down on the field Eileen had also seen the Spitfire. She

watched as the little craft banked and swept in, bumping on to a short run of grass just feet away from one of the slit trenches. She saw the designation on its side, R for Robert, and wondered if it could be Jon. She began to walk quickly in the direction of the plane, hurrying as she followed her instinct that she would see him. The pilot was already climbing out of his cockpit, a helmet still covering his hair. At that distance she could not recognise him, and yet...

She felt herself almost running over the grass towards the plane, her heart hammering, an overwhelming feeling of relief and gratitude making her certain that this must be Jon. Thank God he was safe! When she saw the Spits scrambling to meet the attack alarm she had felt a presentiment that Jon would be up there with them, though nothing he had said the evening before had indicated that he was on call. She knew that he was flying, she knew he was in danger. All through the raid she had never seriously felt afraid for herself, but for him. The terrible sight of the enemy bombers had alarmed her for his sake. But at last he was down, safe and sound. And then, suddenly, the pilot whipped off his helmet and she saw the unexpected shock of ginger hair.

In her acute disappointment a fresh wave of fear took over. She stood there shaking, her heart in her mouth. She had been so certain, so sure that he was safe, that he was near. She felt sick and had to turn aside to hide her despair as the jubilant red-haired pilot strode past her. She heard him break into good-hearted laughter as he met up with one of his comrades, slapping one another on the back, delighted at their good fortune.

When Eileen finally turned round, her face once more composed to face the world, she saw standing before her, not the pilot of R for Robert but Jonathan Pemberley. He stood there watching her, unmoving, the figure of his friend departing across the field, leaving them alone.

For a moment neither of them made any move. It was enough to stand there drinking in the fact of their survival. In his eyes she read the same concern and wonder, the same compulsion to find her and be with her.

From the air he had seen the destruction of Kenley and marvelled that anyone could have survived the intensity of the German bombardment. Just as she had convinced herself that he was in greater danger than herself, so he had watched the assault from the air and feared the worst. He had imagined her trapped perhaps, crushed beneath rubble, wounded or dead. Once he landed, he had wandered the field in search of her, going straight away to the ruined sick quarters where there seemed to be the greatest concentration of people. But she was not there and no one seemed able to tell him anything. Yes, there were wounded WAAFs who had been trapped inside, but no one had the details. His fear had mounted as he walked away, conscious of a growing sense of desperation such as he had never known before. Even at the most intense moment in a dogfight, when everything was at stake, he could not remember ever fearing for his own survival. But this was quite a different matter. This fear for a woman he knew and yet did not know.

And now she stood before him, moving closer as though she had doubted her eyes. She stretched out a hand towards him and he caught it, suddenly pulling her straight into his arms. There was no hesitation, no doubt at all as they kissed.

Twenty-four hours meant nothing, the year that was past meant nothing. They were reckless of their situation, regardless of any convention, uncaring who saw them there or what might be thought of them.

The war had been brought home to everyone who lived in the vicinity of Kenley. They said that over 150 bombs had fallen on civilian targets outside the perimeter of the airfield, killing six and wounding a good many more.

The sight of parachuting pilots caused a panic. The police jumped to the conclusion that this was the invasion. With the local Home Guard detachment they immediately moved to the airfield, fancying themselves as the frontline defenders against a fullscale German advance. They set up road blocks, very proud of themselves. No one could approach without being challenged. Hoping for a Panzer Division, the Home Guard bristled with improvised weapons. How was the enemy to know that they only had one rifle among them with live bullets?

*

167

'Adams, Ma'am.'

Moira fell in behind the admin. corporal and drew herself stiffly to attention and saluted.

'At ease, Adams.' Ma'am sat poised on the edge of her chair, very precise and upright, every immaculate hair in place. Her thin elongated face set in a serious, rather pained expression as though Moira's request for an interview caused her considerable effort. 'Now, Adams, you have been told by the corporal that no 48s are being given. What reason do you have to go up to London?'

'It's my grandmother, Ma'am. She's seriously ill.'

The officer looked at her suspiciously.

'But is she really ill, Adams? With the present situation all leave is being cancelled. It's out of the question that I could grant you even compassionate leave unless your grandmother was actually on her deathbed. Is she on her deathbed, Adams?'

'She's very ill, Ma'am. She's asked me to come straight away.'

'Yes, but is she actually dying, Adams? You put me in a very difficult situation. We are on emergency alert. I cannot simply give permission for all and sundry to desert their duties.'

'But, Ma'am –'

'I think that is all, Adams. If you can bring me proof that your grandmother is in fact dying, I will reconsider the position. That will be all.'

'Ma'am.' Moira saluted, turned smartly on her heel and marched stiffly through the outer office.

Only once she was outside did she stop dead in her tracks, pulling her cap furiously from her hair in despair. All round her the station was alive and frantic with activity as they prepared for another day of raiding and danger.

For the first time in her life Moira looked up at the sky and wished she was dead. All those bloody German bombers and they couldn't even end her miseries.

The following day the weather broke and large scale raiding was hampered by the bad conditions. Churchill decided this was the time to make another speech in Parliament: 'Our bomber and fighter strengths now, after all this fighting, are larger than they have ever been. We believe that we should be able to continue the air struggle indefintely and as long as the enemy pleases...' – which was all very well, thought the men on the ground who actually had to do the fighting. There was no hiding the fact that Churchill's easy words angered and even embarrassed them, causing conflict and jealousy between the services, setting the fliers apart, the 'glamour boys' of the RAF.

To Eileen Jon seemed to typify the light, bantering pilots that the press had turned into heroes. War is a game, that kind of flippant approach to danger that at first appeared callous, unthinking. But the sporting analogy was false. They may have appeared to take everything lightly, but Eileen saw another side. She knew that no one talked of comrades who were lost or shot down, she knew that no one discussed their own feelings of doubt or fear. She learnt that no pilot in his right mind would take a drink before a mission. She knew that the weekend leaves and 48-hour jaunts were a necessary release of tension for men who faced death in a thousand terrifying faces.

She discovered that there were some pilots who carried mascots and odd souvenirs to testify to their survival. Pat's friend Karol carried a crumpled cigarette packet which he took on flight after flight. Others flew with revolvers in case they got caught in a burning aircraft.

Eileen and Jon saw each other only among a press of friends and comrades. It was becoming a tightly-knit unit as danger closed in. When Pat was issued with a roomy Ford V it was immediately commandeered by the whole group for off-duty trips. Jon, Dutch, Pat, Pepper and Karol would clamber in beside Eileen at the wheel, with Lara the labrador fitting in wherever she could find a paw's space.

Danger had made them all companions in arms and at play. When Jon was not flying and Eileen working with Pat, they were all together in some bar or pub with Lara settling down under the table between their feet, ears spread over her paws, black nose attentive, watching everything that was going on with interest.

'What happens to her when you fly?'

'Well, there's this WAAF,' began Karol but they all laughed, and Lara poked her head out from under the table to see what all the noise was about. No one was left out.

It was not a time for privacy.

Yet Jon soon made it plain that he wanted to be with Eileen whenever he could. He began to seek her out so that everyone on the station became aware of their new relationship. As Eileen had more freedom than most WAAFs she was lucky, but her off-base billet gave them no chance of being alone together. She knew they were very fortunate to have the chance to see each other so often. In less desperate times such a liaison between an officer and ordinary ranks would have been strictly prohibited, but Pat was indulgent towards them. He knew well enough that these pilots were facing death each and every day. Short affairs were now the norm. Although marriage was considered to be very unlucky in midstream, there were still some who took the chance. 'Come tomorrow and bring a hat' was an invitation to the bride for a wedding by special licence. One night's honeymoon in a hotel was a luxury.

For Eileen the whirlwind events of the past few days had swept her along, almost unthinking. It was a dream, beyond her wildest imaginings to be there with the man she had loved for so long at her side. It was with a sense of dread that she feared he would one day bring up the past. He had to be curious about the reason she had left Charnwood but he never said a word. It was as though he sensed her anxiety. Never once had either of them mentioned the past. It was as if everything that had gone before, their families, their differences, their former relationship, had never existed. Only the present now mattered, living for today, taking each moment as it came. The future was out of reach, it did not mean next year or even next month. Time was so very short.

In her billet Eileen would lie awake long hours of the night, prey to the sudden fears that darkness brought. The sight, sound and touch of him confirmed every feeling she had ever had for him. It was as though she had always known that this time would exist for them. And yet tomorrow he might be killed or injured beyond recognition. Her dreams were full of terror. She saw the German pilot who burned to death at the controls of his plane going down over Eastbourne. She saw the blisters on the face of Veronica's fiancé, a man with half a face. Would she have Veronica's strength to stand by him through such an experience? Would she still feel the same way about him?

Lying in the darkness she felt a constriction in her body. She ached with wanting him, wishing they could be together. But she could not shake off the echo of a small voice inside her warning that nothing lasted, nothing was forever.

You're a fool, she thought in despair. This love is doomed right from the start. You'll only get hurt.

As the weather cleared, serious raiding began again in force. Fate seemed to have turned against the British as wave after wave of enemy bombers swept in over the Channel. The sight of these bombers, 100 plus, 200 plus, with equal numbers of fighter support, was enough to put terror into the hearts of all who saw them.

On the night of August 24th to 25th a German raid on the oil tanks at Thameshaven in the river estuary went amiss. A number of bombs scattered over London, coinciding with the pubs turning out in Islington and the East End. Caught unawares, these were the first civilian casualties of the London *Blitzkrieg*. There was such an uproar in response that the RAF was ordered to attack Berlin in reprisal the very next night. Back in London ARP and military reservists were told to stand by.

On August 27th, incensed by the Berlin raid and the audacity of British bombers, raids were made on the London area, aiming for the docks which were the city's lifeline. The attack came in daylight. In the afternoon sunshine the Germans had no difficulty in finding their targets and aiming accurately. As the RAF fighters moved to intercept, bombs scattered across south London at random. It was the first battle to have been fought over British soil since Culloden.

A posse of press photographers and news men hung around the airfields looking for heroes. Put into uniform by the Ministry – all as officers – the journalists asked the pilots to scramble for the cameras, to give the public the kind of thing they expected from 'the Few'. Each day the newspapers headlined the numbers of aircraft shot down, like cricket scores: 'RAF versus Luftwaffe: Latest Score 146 to 20.'

The sight of pilots lying on the grass waiting for the alert to scramble was a thing of the past. As the attacks intensified there was less and less time between raids, sometimes only an hour to grab something to eat before they were up again.

The Luftwaffe threw everything in their arsenal against them. It was make or break. And as planes were lost and pilots forced to ditch or get medical attention, it looked as though it would be the pilots who broke first. There was simply not the manpower to cope with the crisis. More and more raw recruits were filling the vacancies left by the veteran fliers, shot down or wounded.

Pepper was the first of the group to go. He set off one morning in excellent spirits to meet a pack of bandits over 'Hellfire Corner' and was last spotted flying over the coastal strip. Karol spoke to him over the RT and he had replied cheerfully, 'Message received and understood.' The day went by without further news of him. Five days later his body was washed up near Dover riddled with bullets.

Whenever Eileen knew that Jon had gone up she would count the minutes until she heard that he was safely down. She knew that the German planes were at a distinct disadvantage, that they could not afford to stay in the air over Britain for more than a few minutes if they wanted fuel to get home again. A dogfight lasted a bare ten or fifteen minutes, a short deadly foray into the unknown. One second's carelessness could cost your life.

'There's nothing romantic or chivalric about it,' Jon told her. 'Basically it's a matter of assassination. Creeping up on your enemy while his back is turned. Lying in wait for him and hitting him before he's even aware that you are there.' He shrugged. 'Then it's all over for him. He's either dead or he bales out. He either makes it or he doesn't. Either way he's out of the game, whereas we have to get right back up there and go through it all over again.'

There was a strain of tiredness in his voice that made her turn to look anxiously up at him. They were walking in Selsdon Wood, a local beauty spot near the base, but even here there was little or no privacy. The wood with its abundance of wild flowers and lush grass was a popular place for courting couples from the district. It was hard to go a hundred yards without almost falling over some other pair of lovers looking for a moment's peace.

Eileen gripped Jon tightly by the hand, gripping his long, strong fingers in her own, sharing his weariness of spirit.

172

'What I don't understand,' she told him, trying to change the subject, 'is how you know where to find them once you're up there. Isn't it a bit like hide and seek?'

'It used to be, they say, but things have modernised. What happens is that Ops vectors us on to our targets. Sometimes we're even there ahead of them waiting.'

'But how do Ops know where they're heading? How do they know when the Jerries have crossed the Channel?'

'How? I can't really say,' he replied with a puzzled expression. It was obviously just something he took for granted. 'Sector gets its reports from HQ who know the whole picture. How they know I haven't a clue. It's all pretty hush-hush. Only the top bods know how it works.' He turned to look at her. 'Perhaps you should ask old Pat what it's all about. I bet he's got the right connections. All I know is that it works – and thank God for it!'

They walked on a little in silence and then found themselves a spot on the edge of the wood overlooking a field that was being harvested. The day was full of the colour and scents of summer, the aroma of corn, of dried grasses and flowers. It was all a lifetime away from the oil and dust of the base, the stench of burning metal and flesh. It was like another world.

When Jon suddenly announced that he was due for leave and thought they should try and spend it away somewhere together, she had not a moment's hesitation in agreeing.

'We'll go up to London and do the town,' he told her, laughing. 'We'll stay somewhere swish and paint the town red!'

'I don't care where we go – as long as we don't have half the squadron along with us.'

'Just us two. But mind you, I don't know when it will come. It's too hot just now to think of going. They were talking of pulling us out, putting us all out to grass for a while up in Scotland.'

'Scotland?'

'Don't look so alarmed! They couldn't do it. They can't afford to lose one man just now.'

'Well, we'll wait, won't we?' said Eileen with relief. 'It will all come right for us, I know it will!' The light of love shone in her eyes and he caught her to him, kissing her roughly, surprised at the vehemence of her response.

She leant against him, aware of the rarity of this moment

together, savouring its preciousness. The sense of living on borrowed time was always with them, throwing everything into sharp focus, heightening every experience. Life was for living, and there could be no turning back.

On Friday August 30th a layer of cloud and rain covered the approach of German raiders over Kent. By noon the RAF stations in 11 Group had all available fighters in the air to meet the threat. Everyone was stretched to the limit. The target of the bombers was the fighter stations themselves, the second time that Kenley, Tangmere and Biggin Hill were hit.

Three waves of enemy planes swept in over the Channel one after another, slipping in without prior warning. An earlier attack had successfully knocked out the south coast's electricity supply lines, effectively blocking the British top-secret network that had given the RAF such an advantage in the battle so far.

The raid on Biggin Hill was the first of six separate attacks over that dreadful weekend as the German bombers sought to obliterate the station from the face of the earth.

News of high casualties and widespread destruction reached Kenley that evening, and Eileen went straight round to Pat's billet.

'I heard there could be as many as forty dead,' she told him, pacing the cramped living room, her arms tightly folded against her chest. 'The WAAF quarters were hit. I'd just like to know that my friends are safe.'

'All right, Eileen, why don't we both take a drive over that way tomorrow?'

'You mean it? Oh Pat, that's marvellous. It's just that –'

'Yes, yes, I know. I have friends there, too, remember.'

It seemed incongruous the next morning to be driving through neat and peaceful country lanes when just miles away there were people dying. They passed haystacks in the fields where only down the road there were signs of another, more deadly harvest. Crashed aircraft scarred the land, their noses squashed into the earth, tails pointing to the sky that had refused them safety. The pilots were long gone, dead, wounded, or prisoners.

'How much longer can we last out, Pat?'

Pat sighed grimly, sinking down in the passenger seat, pushing his unlit pipe back into his pocket. Eileen thought she had not seen him so weary. The lines of fatigue and disillusionment were clearly etched on his sharp features, the pale skin stretched and drawn.

'I honestly don't know, Eileen. I don't think any of us have seriously ever had to face the thought of defeat before. Yes, we made preparations, but it was all somehow a cosmetic exercise, putting a phoney show on just to keep up morale. Perhaps the people who got the hell out of here had the right idea all along. The Government has made all kinds of bolt-holes for its treasures, they've moved everything that has the slightest importance out of London, even out of the country.'

'Will it come to that? A full-scale invasion?'

'I don't believe the Germans have ever wanted that. They thought they could do a deal with us – even after Dunkirk. Certainly there were plenty of people who gave them every encouragement to think that some kind of negotiated truce was on the cards. Who can say who was involved? Up to the highest levels? It's not fashionable to talk like that just now, but one sign of capitulation and they'll all come crawling back out of the woodwork.'

'Then we would be no better off than the French.' She shuddered. 'I can't imagine what it would be like – stormtroopers marching down Piccadilly, prisoners in the Tower.'

'If we can only hold them off for a few more weeks, then the weather may force them to switch their tactics. So far the fighting has been on more or less equal terms.'

'Equal?'

'Compared with what could follow. So far we have not given serious thought to our bombing strategy. Trenchard's old ideas are still hampering development. We have to do something about our night fighters. We have to pick out specific targets over there, industrial sites, dams, munitions.' He stopped dead and shifted round to look at her. His bright narrowed eyes fixed hers with an intense glare. 'Eileen, I'm going to tell you something now that is strictly between ourselves. I have been called up to London next week for a high-level meeting. And I do mean high-level.'

Eileen said nothing, though she was desperate to know more.

'I hope that I can persuade them to let me have a free hand. With the pick of the pilots and some of the new development models – well, I believe that within a few months we could train an integrated recce, bomber and fighter unit that would do more than these random strikes that achieve nothing. A kind of special operations unit. The day of the individualist is over now.'

Eileen trembled. She knew the dedication and resolute nature of the man she had worked with over the past two months. She had come to know and understand him as no other man in her life. She looked up to him and respected him for his integrity, for his unsentimental approach to the chilling growth of chaos that threatened to swamp others. He had no qualms about what action should be taken. Perhaps two months before she might have thought him harsh to the point of callousness, but no longer. She had seen for herself their desperate situation, discovered for herself the necessity for new measures, new attitudes, a new ideology. She had faith in his assessment of the situation, she knew that his recorded facts and figures were a damning indictment of Britain's ill-prepared state of defence. Given the chance to put his case, Eileen believed that Pat could turn the tide from defensive actions to offensive.

The problem was the question of time. Even next week was a long time off, time enough to destroy any hope for the future. How much longer could the weary pilots keep airborne? How much longer could the stations of 11 Group take the bombardment of wave after wave of enemy planes? Already the 1,000 pound bombs of Pat's earlier warnings were raining down on Biggin Hill. Britain was fighting this war alone.

Suddenly as they drove along the car began to swerve hard over to one side, almost as though they were in a skid. Eileen struggled with the steering wheel to bring the Ford back into the left-hand lane, but it seemed as though the car had developed a will of its own.

'For God's sake, stop,' snapped Pat irritably. 'Can't you see you've got a flat?'

She clambered out of her seat and went round to the back of the car. She saw that Pat had settled down and was intent on lighting his pipe. He obviously had no intention of helping her out, but then why should he? It was her job to drive and look after the car, that was what she had been trained for.

Nevertheless, Eileen could not refrain from a little grumbling as she sweated and strained to jack the car up. Pat had actually done her the favour of getting out, to make the load lighter, but he leant casually against a five-bar gate, smoking his pipe, and giving the odd encouraging words. He seemed to see something amusing in her efforts, a slow smile spreading over his face as he puffed away contentedly.

By the time she had finished she was red-faced and short of breath, her hands filthy. Pat found a rag in the boot for her to wipe her hands on and they were almost ready to set off again when they became aware of a storm on the horizon. Looking more closely, they realised that this was not a storm but a dark pall of smoke spilling out of the earth, bruising the untouched blue of the sky.

'Another raid. It must be Biggin Hill.'

'Look, aren't those our fighters?'

A wheel of birds, dark against the sun, continued on their deadly migration.

'They could be from Kenley,' said Pat. 'If they need our reinforcements then things must be really pretty awful. Get in the car, Eileen, let's get down there.'

Eileen felt more than a little trepidation about heading straight into a German raid. The billowing smoke told its own story. Yet she was also desperate to discover if her friends there were dead or alive. Nothing in the world would have made her turn back now. And anyway, who could say that Kenley was in any better shape itself.

Hardly had she got the engine started when Pat seized her by the arm. The air overhead was suddenly full of the scream of aircraft. For one terrifying moment Eileen thought they had been targeted for attack by the German raiders as she remembered George Tracey telling them of the Stukas mowing down civilians on French roads. But then she realised she could detect two distinctive engine tones.

'Get out, get into the ditch quickly!'

Lying beside Pat on the grass verge they saw two planes wheeling over the adjacent field in the deadly manoeuvres of a dogfight. It was a Hurricane and a Me109, a match of such inequality that Eileen felt she knew the conclusion even before Pat grimly shook his head and whispered,

'The poor bugger hasn't a chance.'

The Messerschmitt was a model of efficiency and manoeuvrability. It was capable of speed and a higher ceiling than the British planes, plus six 20mm cannon guns. Compared with it, the poor old Hurricane was a plodder, a large outmoded plane that had lost out to the Spitfire but still made up the majority of RAF squadrons. The Me109s used highly experienced pilots, often veterans of the Spanish Civil War, who had developed techniques of surprise attack on Spanish towns and raids out of the sun.

The yellow-nosed Messerschmitt weaved and danced its way into the perfect position for taking out the Hurricane. Eileen and Pat could only watch as the cannon shells struck the British plane, drawing immediate smoke trails as the Hurricane took a nose dive towards the field. The German wheeled once more and then moved off to rejoin its unit over Biggin Hill.

Pat leapt the wooden fence at the side of the road and Eileen followed as he sprinted over the stubble of the cornfield towards the downed aircraft. It was hard to run on the sharp stubble weaving between the stooks of corn waiting to be lifted by the farmer. The Hurricane had plunged beyond the ridge of the field with a pillar of dense smoke marking the spot. When Pat got there he could feel the heat from the flames already licking their way down the fuselage. But he hesitated only for a moment. When Eileen arrived she saw him struggling to get the hatch of the cockpit open, the perspex already buckling from the heat.

She hurried over, willing to help as much as she could, but Pat had forced the hatch and was now struggling to get the unconscious pilot out of his harness. The Hurricane stood normally at a height of about ten feet from the ground, but after its crash, its nose smashed against the hard-backed summer earth, it was easy for Eileen to get a foothold on the wing and help Pat to lift the injured man out of danger.

Together they pulled him clear of the wreckage, watching as the fire spread and caught hold of the fuel supply. The Hurricane burst into a fountain of flames, spraying sparks in every direction.

Kneeling on the sharp needles of the field Eileen could see that Pat's hands were skinned from his effort to release the pilot, and the back of his shirt was scorched from the heat.

It was impossible to try and lift the pilot back to the car, so Eileen ran back across the field alone, leaving Pat to improvise some first aid treatment for the pilot's bullet wound in the back. Clambering over the fence she got a good view of the aerial battle that was still going on not so many miles away.

There was no gate to the field on the main road but by cutting off down a rough-made lane on the left she soon came to a metal gate. Leaving the engine running she opened the gate, jumped back in and plunged out across the bumpy surface of the cornfield following the plume of smoke that marked the crashed Hurricane. There was little left of the aircraft when she arrived. She backed the Ford up to where Pat had the pilot stretched out on the corn. He was ashen-faced and had lost a lot of blood. He did not even groan as they lifted him into the back seat, although they must have caused him considerable pain. They laid him on his face, afraid that he might choke with the movement of the car over the uneven field.

Pat was scanning his military map of the district looking for the nearest hospital. As Eileen brought the car back on to the lane he gave her instructions towards the nearest town. Eileen had no scruples about putting her foot down and cornering without changing down. She knew that the life of the pilot could be at stake.

When they drew up in the courtyard of the small cottage hospital, a converted Victorian villa just outside the town, Eileen hit the horn with her fist, enough to wake everyone in the area. Yet it still took a few minutes before anyone came to discover what all the fuss was about. The town was on alert status because of the raid, and even at the hospital they had heeded the sirens and taken to the basement shelters. But when they saw the pilot bleeding on the back seat, their attitude changed to one of crisp efficiency. A stretcher was fetched and the injured man taken out of sight.

'You'd better let me take a look at your hands,' declared one of the nursing sisters and she looked so daunting in her starched white headdress that Pat agreed.

'Are you all right, Eileen?' he asked, turning his head away as the nurse disinfected the raw skin of his hands.

'Sure.' She shrugged off her awful appearance. Her stockings were ripped, her skirt and shoes covered in dirt and stains, her hands generally filthy. 'I could do with a wash, though.'

The nurse gave her a sympathetic smile and pointed the way to the toilet outside in the corridor.

When Eileen returned Pat was already bandaged and looking sheepish as the nurse gave him a lecture about what he should and shouldn't do over the next 24 hours.

'Stuff and nonsense,' he grumbled as they went back to the car. 'Doesn't she realise there's a war to fight?'

'I asked about the pilot. They're doing an emergency operation now to remove the bullets. They say his chances are 50-50.'

'Yes, he was lucky. But he won't be flying any more.'

Veronica did her best to be a good friend to Moira. When she was refused permission to take 48 hours off to go to London, her resentment had been all the stronger because the station seemed so quiet. Veronica determined to stay with her through thick and thin although she was suffering herself through her enforced separation from Tim. But Veronica was often required to bite back her frustration, feeling the sharp edge of Moira's tongue when things got beyond endurance. Veronica had to tell herself that Moira was not feeling herself, that she must be patient.

'I feel so desperate, Veronica, you just don't understand. The longer I wait, the more dangerous it is apparently.'

'I didn't realise. I've never known anyone who...'

'No, I'm sure you haven't.' She was chewing her nails, those nails she had so proudly painted for nights out. 'As though there isn't enough to worry about. It had to happen when there's a war on.'

'It happened because there's a war on.'

'I hope you're not just being kind to me, Veronica.' And she shrugged. 'Perhaps it will take care of itself.'

Veronica had been struck by the mournful quality in her voice and watched her very carefully after that. She observed the way in which Moira seemed to go out of her way to volunteer for the hardest jobs, always seeking out the most physical work as though she could cure her problems by sheer hard labour. Was she trying to make herself ill? Was she deliberately setting out to cause herself harm?

But the silence at the station was shortlived and ominous, a warning to them all of the danger to come. Before long Biggin Hill was strained to its limit to try and fight back against wholesale destruction.

As the sirens blared out their terrible warning across the field Veronica and Moira were caught out in the open.

'Attack alarm! Attack alarm! Enemy force advancing, take cover!'

The Dornier 17s were known as 'flying pencils' because of their distinctive long shape that was easy to recognise. As they swept in low over the field in shallow dives they approached their targets at under 100 feet, dropping their bombs on the principal buildings within the airfield perimeter. Behind them came the Heinkel 111s, fat cruisers, laying their deadly eggs at 12,000 feet.

They began to run as the first planes were heard droning overhead. Their main target were the aircraft out on the grass, many of which had only just landed after combat. As the first bombs fell, Moira and Veronica were running with a group of other women and mechanics from the nearby hangars. The noise of the explosion was tremendous, reverberating through the ground as though they were caught in an earthquake. The WAAFs were thrown off their feet, showered with mud and rocks in a cloud of thick dark smoke.

Veronica felt herself pushed face down on the scorched grass with one of the mechanics beside her. The earth seemed to rock and her ears were singing from the impact of the explosions. By tilting her head she tried to see Moira but the mechanic forced her head down again as another bomb landed not far away.

'Come on, run!' The voices came from behind, disembodied in the drifting smoke across the field. 'Run, I said! We're sitting ducks here!'

Veronica knew that there was a slit trench not more than 300 yards away, but that seemed an immeasurable distance to her now. She stumbled to her feet, noticing absurdly that her stockings were torn. She grabbed the mechanic's arm to keep her feet and they began to move like drunken revellers across the tilting landscape.

She was half expecting to find Moira in the trench. At one moment she had been at her side, at the next minute gone. But she was not there. As Veronica looked at the faces about her she saw that Moira was not one of those who had made it to safety and she felt a terrifying sinking feeling in her stomach as she stared out across the top of the trench at the smoke spiralling across the field.

She could see the Spits trying to scramble and take off in the face of the onslaught. She could see pilots sprinting towards their machines, braving the bullets erupting across the grass. But there was no sign of Moira.

Oh God, oh God, please let her be all right.

Two Spitfires sprang into the air with their engines faltering, just missing enemy bombs coming down. The earth beneath them exploded in a deluge of soil and grass, leaving a crater deep enough to bury a small car. Others were not so lucky. Veronica saw two of the planes shot down before they were scarcely airborne. A third tried vainly to hop into flight like a fledgling bird learning to fly but its wing dipped and scraped across the grass. The plane turned completely over, so that it cartwheeled across the field, landing on its broken back more than a hundred yards further on. The pilot was still inside, trapped in the wreckage. Scattered across the field in its wake was one engine and the wing which had been torn completely away.

It was over almost as suddenly as it had begun. The bombers had done their business, the damage was done. The sky was silent once more, only the afternoon sun masked by a screen of acrid smoke.

In stunned silence Veronica and her companions stood up in the slit trench, unaware of the dirt and mud that caked their clothing. They stared out over the terrible destruction, the wilderness before them. Deep craters pitted the grass and perimeter road. Black smoke poured from the damaged hangars and armoury. But out there, on the field, the bodies of two WAAFs lay still and unmoving, their legs and arms twisted in unnatural shapes.

'Moira!'

No one could stop Veronica hurling herself out of the ditch and breaking into a run across the burning grass, tears streaming down her face. As she reached the first corpse her whole body tensed and she stood there, rigid with shock and then relief as she saw it was not her friend at all.

Quickly she moved away, stumbling towards the second woman. She lay with her head twisted beneath her arms as though she could save herself from the full force of the explosion. But as Veronica moved towards her, they tried to prevent her from touching the body, seizing her arms and holding her back.

Desperate, furious, she tried to shake them off, swearing and crying, staring at Moira's body just yards away.

'No! Let me alone – I must go to her.'

'Veronica!'

She turned, eyes widening, disbelieving the voice she knew so well. She had to reach out and touch her face before comprehension sank in, before she could understand that Moira was alive and safe. In each other's arms, they cried with joy at being together again.

The WAAF deaths shook everyone on the station. Forty people had been killed altogether, the bodies spread out under groundsheets with just their legs showing. There was no time for mourning. All the station staff plunged themselves into work, as though to prove that their comrades had not died in vain. If the purpose of the raids was to shut down their station, then they were more determined than ever to keep it operational.

Fires burned on every side. People were rushing round with hoses and first-aid equipment. It was difficult to tell the sexes apart as everyone wore the same stained and filthy battledress, tin helmets pulled low over their begrimed and weary faces. As they moved between the tangle of metal girders and charred wood, they coughed from the heavy fumes of burning rubber.

The airfield was in a state of chaos. The Operations Room had to be moved temporarily to a village shop. The debris at the field had scarcely been cleared aside, the holes in the runways only roughly filled when the enemy struck again.

Power cables, water and gas mains had all been fractured and not yet repaired. It did not take a genius to understand that the object of these persistent raids was to cripple Biggin Hill once for all, wiping out planes and personnel. A dozen or more ᴊots had been killed. It was sure to be a similar story at every ᴊther base in 11 Group. Everyone wondered how much longer they could withstand such a merciless assault. Whole squadrons were being decimated. The new replacements often had only a handful of flying hours in their log books, untrained in combat, almost useless. A few more days of this and they would hardly be able to put up a single squadron.

Veronica was on duty near the wrecked WAAF quarters, helping to sift through the remains for any salvage. She had an old Bedford parked ready for loading, and bulldozers were picking up rubble to fill in the new craters on the runways.

When she suddenly saw Eileen standing there she ran forward and flung her arms about her neck.

'I was so worried when I heard.'

Eileen drew apart, laughing at her friend's appearance. In her battledress and with her long brown hair caught up under the tin hat, she looked like a slim boy, scarcely more than thirteen or fourteen. There was dirt and grease on her face and lines of exhaustion deeply etched on either side of her nose and shadowing her eyes. It was no young boy's face.

'How is Moira?' Eileen slipped her arm through hers as they walked.

'Nervous. We can't get leave, either of us, and won't while this lasts.'

'She said that Lily would help her.'

'What's that about Lily?' They turned sharply to see Moira standing there. She carried a shovel and looked red-faced and exhausted from digging. 'Have you quite done discussing my problems?'

'Oh don't look like that!' cried Eileen, going over to her. 'I've been so worried about you both. Don't spoil it.'

'Oh I'm sorry, Eileen. I'm just worn out and depressed, take no notice. Of course it's great to see you.'

'Moira, there's something I want to say. I feel so cut off from you now that we're apart. Distant, you know? But that doesn't mean I don't think of you both. And when you get time off to go to Lily's, well, I want to come with you if at all possible. You'll need a friend, Moira.'

184

'That's good of you, Eileen.'

'No, I mean it. Promise you'll let me know.'

Moira reluctantly nodded her head, as though giving way to something she could now only dream about it seemed so far away.

'Are you here with Pat?' she asked, changing the subject.

'Yes, he's OK except we saw this fighter shot down on our way here. We had to get the pilot to hospital immediately.'

'One of ours?'

'I honestly don't know if we'd have done the same for one of theirs. I've grown hard, I suppose.'

'We all have, Eileen. We won't recognise ourselves when we get through this – if we get through.'

The last week in August and the first week of September marked the 'critical period' for the airfields of 11 Group. Losses continued to mount heavily. In those two weeks over 200 pilots had been killed, wounded or gone missing, nearly 500 planes destroyed, 200 more than were replaced by new machines. Squadron after squadron was being withdrawn because of losses and battle fatigue. The loss of pilots was the main problem. Eighty per cent of all squadron commanders had been killed, wounded or withdrawn. Veterans were being replaced by green young boys, many with under ten hours' flying time.

Those who did survive were harder, more cynical than before. Gone were the gallantry and jokers of those early summer days. The new breed were deadly serious about their profession, uncompromising, ruthless, cold-minded killers in the air.

Around him Jon could see the strain taking its toll. Constantly on call, up in the air on sortie after sortie, exhaustion had made its mark on each and every one of them. His own friend Dutch was hardly recognisable as the flippant practical joker of their squadron. The Pole Karol whatever-his-name-was out-flew and out-lived more planes than they could supply him with. He was a top-scorer, the envy of the new boys on station, but they had not known the other Karol, the one who had laughed and sang on jaunts with Eileen and Pat, the one who could still shed real tears over the death of his friend Pepper. But that man was long dead, buried by the weight of bloodshed and bitterness that had turned him into a man who sought out the enemy and hunted him down

185

with such deadly, ice-cold accuracy and total lack of compassion. An assassin.

Jon knew that while he could still recognise the difference between Karol and himself then there was hope for him. Yet the constant pressure was getting to him, making him more nervous and irritable, more highly-charged than before. In the long rainless evenings he sought out Eileen's company almost with desperation. When he was with her he felt he could relax, be himself, pretend for a few hours that the war was a million miles away.

Only at those moments could he admit to feelings of growing insecurity. But he never talked about it, even to her. He knew that people always assumed he was full of self-confidence. Only Gareth had really understood him. He had seen through him, knowing that his mask of assurance hid an aching insecurity that was deeply rooted in his past. Perhaps Gareth understood because he could share that sense of loneliness, that need to prove oneself, the need to latch on to someone else for support. With Jon it had first of all been his sister, Honor: older and braver, flouting their parents' wishes, astonishing Jon with her audacity. But then she had married; he had lost her support and had been thrown, insecure and adrift, into the desperately competitive world of Cambridge. Finding Gareth had seemed like a miracle, boosting his confidence, making him dare all kinds of things, joining the RAF for example. And now it was Eileen. She gave him confidence, she gave him hope to go on, a reason to live.

The squadron was being withdrawn. With the prospect of leave coming through at last, he really felt there was something to live for. He and Eileen would paint the town red, they would forget all this, leave it all behind them. Eileen's officer had gone to London for talks at the Air Ministry, she was free to take her leave whenever he could get away. And today looked like being the last day.

He had already been up once. He had been terrified to find that his aim was unsteady, that his hands were actually shaking. Back in the mess, aching and almost too tired to eat, he had difficulty in holding a knife and fork.

'We're having to put you on alert again,' they told him.

'But we've only been down half an hour.'

'Sorry, Jon, there's no one left. You'll have to go up again.' They said that new replacements would be coming down from Yorkshire that afternoon. There would be nothing to hold up the transfer. Nothing to stop him getting away the next day. Just one more flight and he would be free.

If he survived.

Walking back to dispersal he had a word or two with the CRO crew. The 'plumbers' were amazing, they could turn a plane round in fifteen minutes, they could repair and patch up more than half the crippled kites that came down. They were the unsung heroes of this war.

Jon knew that his own crew was among the very best. With Jon's experience in the air, they gave him the best they had on the ground. He knew that this had vastly increased his chances of survival, and for that he was grateful. But the plumbers could do nothing to patch up his short temper, to erase the tension and sense of edgy depression that grew day after day. Some of his comrades were in a far worse state. They blew their tops at the slightest thing, so that it was really impossible to talk to them. You never knew how they were going to react. Others were less obvious. They covered themselves with icy politeness, withdrawing from the harsh realities, distancing themselves from the loss of their friends. When Jon looked round him he saw new faces, changed men. Each one graver, closer than before.

'What's the dope, Jon?'

'Pressure's still on. Looks like we'll be up again before long.'

'Christ.'

Barely ten minutes had gone by before the telephone rang. Dutch answered it and shouted, 'Scramble!'

As Jon ran for his plane, he saw that the mechanic had already got the engine going. His mate helped Jon into his parachute harness and gave him a hand up into the cockpit. Jon fastened the seat straps over his shoulders and pulled the safety harness round into position, clicking both straps into the metal clasp that secured them across the top of his legs. He settled himself in his seat, getting the parachute into a comfortable position behind him. When all that was done, he gave the thumbs up to the crew and reached over his head to pull the hatch down. But he did not secure it by turning the handles. He had seen too many pilots trying to fight their way out of a hatch that was jammed, plunging out of the sky still securely trapped inside their planes.

He quickly went through the routine of pre-flight checks. He had got this down to a fine art, cutting away the vital seconds. When this was done he was ready to give the 'chocks away' signal and plug in his RT lead. As the mechanic pulled away the wooden chocks under his wheels, he had opened the throttle with that harsh spitting noise so peculiar to Merlin engines and was moving out across the grass. Within a minute he would be up into the air.

Throttle gently, rapid acceleration, stick forward to lift the tail, and up. Wheels tucked at once. Pitch control back, throttle up to 200, gaining height as quickly as possible before the enemy came in. Get the advantage of height, get on to the sun side straight away.

'OK. Kenley Control here. Hello Red Leader, we copy. We have some customers. Vector 180.'

'Red Leader here.' Skipper's voice was loud and clear. 'How many bandits?'

'200 Plus.'

'Only 200? Too bad. OK, chaps, bandits due south.'

'I see something, Red Leader, down at 15 to 20.'

'OK, Dutch, let's take a look.'

Jon followed the lead, listening to the constant chatter over the RT. It was never silent. Even when they were not using it, sometimes it was possible to hear the Hun calling to one another even though they were some way away.

'Tally ho! Bandits at ten o'clock. Fighter support, looks like 109s.'

Jon settled into the engagement, with Round One to them. Finding the enemy before they found you was to be one step ahead in the game. From now on he would not fly in a straight line for more than thirty seconds at a time. As contact was made, a yellow-nosed Me109 shot past on his port wing and fastened itself on the tail of the Spit in front.

'Watch your tail, Kenny!' he warned over the RT, manoeuvring in until he sat neatly on the Jerry's tail. He was so close now that he had to be sure that he didn't ram him. He got him in his sights and let go a three second burst. The 109 seemed to buck, as though hit by freak winds. He had been struck in the weakest part of Messerschmitt design, the tail. He began to swerve out of control, breaking off into a spin.

'Thanks, Jon, I owe you one.'

'Make it a pint.'

'Behind you. Sharp right, Jon.'

Two 109s were closing fast out of the sun. Jon took rapid action, watching through the reflector sight as they closed in behind him, dancing up and down in the wake of his slipstream. He felt rather than heard the bullets in the moment that he broke away into a steep dive. It was one of the most dangerous manoeuvres in a Spitfire, throwing all the tension on to the weak wing structure. He dived and rolled, losing the pursuers. He broke the spiral and pulled himself out of the dive with his head pounding as the blood flooded back. The negative g forces of the dive could produce grey-outs, even black-outs. You felt that your heart was in your mouth, the plane barely in control. It was a dangerous line between safety and an unrestrained nose dive into the earth.

As he climbed back Jon was aware that he had lost ground, falling behind the rest of his squadron. He had a headache and his hands felt damp with tension. To be alone in the sky was to be vulnerable. He kept a watch in every direction, afraid of an ambush.

It was suddenly very cold indeed. He saw that he was at 28,000 feet, alone in the thin moist air. His Browning machine guns could freeze up if he was not careful. He could be jumped by a pack of 109s if the perspex hood of his cockpit misted over. Many pilots had died in just this way, alone and freezing at 30,000 feet.

He felt more nervous than he had ever felt before. He was acutely aware that this was his last fight, that tomorrow he and Eileen would be out of all this, and the longing that he felt for that security and release made him nervous. For the first time he was thinking about his own safety, worried about his chances of survival, and his former confidence took flight. Fear seized him like a cold hand, twisting like a knife. He no longer knew which way to turn or what to do. He was suddenly petrified.

The harsh crackle of the RT took him quite by surprise. He sat there staring at the leads, unable to answer.

189

'Jon, do you read me? Come in.'

He could see Red Leader now, riding ahead of him and below.

'I hear you, Red Leader. Trouble with the RT.'

'Good show, Jon. New wave of bandits coming in. Vector 90 and keep up.'

'Wilco.'

He hoped that his voice had not betrayed him. He took a few deep breaths, and tried to calm down. He could see the Jerries now, a number of slow 110s down at 15,000 feet in a tightly packed group. They were there to protect a new wave of bombers coming in, and possibly could have further 109 cover above. The 110s were slow, lumbering fighters, useful only in packs unlike the troublesome, highly active 109s. As the RAF moved in for the kill, Jon felt his spirits rise as he moved into the routine movements of attack.

It was a gift to pick off the slow-moving enemy fighters from above. They split the group and each selected a target. Soon the pack was scattered across the sky, with three already going down. All at once the RT crackled into life:

'Bandits on high. Watch your backs!'

A posse of 109s had found them. Jon took immediate evasive action, spotting his friend Dutch over on the right, wedged in between two turning 109s. Before Jon could react he saw that Dutch was already hit, a thread of smoke falling away behind him. It looked as though Dutch had carburettor trouble. He was falling back, losing height rapidly. The 109s swept in for the kill, confident of their own superior engines which had fuel injection. Dutch should have kept his head, but he obviously panicked and the attackers took advantage of his mistake.

They closed in, hammering the wounded Spitfire until flames were licking along the fuselage. Jon saw that there was no hope for his friend but to bale out. The 109s cut away, their work done, leaving their crippled victim behind. Jon was close enough now to see that Dutch still sat in his cockpit.

'Bale out, Dutch, bale out!'

'Can't – can't move my legs. They're jammed. Can't release the –' His words broke off, replaced by a shrill whisper of terror, 'Jesus, there's petrol leaking through! There's petrol everywhere!'

'Cut your fuel, open the throttle!' He wanted Dutch to empty the carburettor and try to prevent the fire spreading. He knew that the slightest spark in the cockpit could turn Dutch into a human torch.

'No use. Can't shift the sodding –' His half-bitten words were swallowed by a scream of such acute intensity that Jon's blood ran cold.

From his vantage point he could see the wave of flames completely covering the nose and cockpit of the plane, both inside and out. Before his very eyes he saw his friend engulfed, his clothes and gloves alight, his mouth open in a perpetual scream, as the plane fell forward into a terrifying spiral out of the sky.

Over the RT the echo of his scream ran in Jon's ears.

Dutch was dead. He was gone and there was nothing to be done about it. To dwell on his loss now was not only foolish, it was dangerous. He knew that he had to switch off the normal, human reactions to the death of a friend. It was impossible to care too much. He had to switch off all feelings of pity in order to survive.

But there was one thing he could do. He dived with the throttle wide open, moving in pursuit of the 109s, settling on their tail. He felt his eyes narrow with concentration as he got the plane in his sights, his body tense against his seat as he opened fire at just over 200 yards and kept his thumb on the gun button. Suddenly his brain was completely clear, suddenly he had no fears at all, no nerves. The first 109 went into a spin and plummeted out of sight. Without a moment's hesitation he automatically sat in on the tail of the survivor aircraft, experiencing a primitive rush of exultation as he hit the gun button and shot him down.

When he pulled out of the dive he was aware that the sky round him was empty. The silence struck him with renewed force, and only then did he become aware that his hands were shaking. He had scarcely been in the air thirty minutes, an average time for combat, but he was exhausted.

'Hello Red Leader, do you hear me?'

There was no response. He tried again but got nothing. He realised suddenly that his RT had packed up on him. He had no links now with the ground.

He knew there was nothing more vulnerable than a lone aircraft, lost and searching for its home field. With so many enemy fighters still in the air, he knew he could be easily sighted and hunted down.

Oh God, he thought, let me get down. Don't let them get me.

He knew that without help he was lost. He decided to drop his height and try to get a sighting of the field. He had little idea of his bearings and his mind was too full to give a cool-headed assessment of his position.

All in all, he did not give very much for his chances.

Eileen had been waiting for the return of the squadron down on the ground. When she had discovered that Jon had gone up again she felt afraid. She knew that he was almost at the end of his endurance, that he had flown sortie after sortie and come through them all unscathed, at least in body if not in mind. She only had to look round her at the other pilots to see what effect their persistent effort was having on the morale and character of young men who had been so carefree and optimistic only a few weeks before.

Tomorrow they were due to go on leave for a few days, and Eileen thanked God for it. One more delay and she could not be certain that Jon would not give way completely. He needed rest, good food and more than that, a total change in atmosphere, away from the tensions and pressures of the base.

She heard the first aircraft coming back and hurried down on to the runway in time to see the Spitfires dropping in over the field. Unable to see the markings on their sides, she had to wait, almost holding her breath, until the planes had taxied up and cut their engines. But on every count she was to be disappointed.

She turned her eyes skyward, searching the air for the next planes coming in. There were still three to come. She had not seen Dutch either. She stood where she was, prepared to wait until they all came in, a lonely poignant figure on the edge of the runway, drawing the sympathetic gaze of many.

The time went by and the sky was silent. She stood there like a statue, her hands clenched in her pockets, the nails biting into her palms as her patience deserted her. She had never been so attuned to the sounds of the sky, listening to every movement of the wind, waiting for that distinctive throb of aircraft engines.

Suddenly she heard one. The sound was fractured, perhaps a damaged plane struggling to get home. Then she saw it break free of the cover of the spinney to the south, limping across the tree

line. Others had also seen the plane. There was an emergency
ambulance standing by, ready to follow the crash waggons out to
meet the crippled Spitfire.

It came in low over the field, dipping one wing drunkenly,
seeming to touch down but then lifting off again, hesitant, barely
under control. It finally bumped on to the grass, swerving on its
right side. The emergency vehicles were racing to meet it, ready
to drag the pilot from the plane if there was any sign of fire
breaking out.

Only Eileen did not run to join them. She had seen the
markings on the side of the Spitfire and with a sickening lurch of
disappointment she knew it was not Jon.

There were still two planes out there, two which had not
returned from the afternoon's mission. Dutch – and Jon. As the
pilot of the damaged aircraft was helped into the ambulance,
limping, leaning on the shoulder of an RAF medic, he looked out
across the field and caught sight of her standing there. For a
moment their gaze met, and Eileen seemed to read a flicker of
pain there, a warning perhaps that Jon would not be coming back.

'Won't you come inside?' It was one of the WAAFs from the
Ops Room. She must have come down when she saw Eileen
standing there. 'They'll tell you the minute he gets in.'

'Haven't you heard from him? Hasn't he sent in a message?'

She shook her head, obviously feeling awkward, but Eileen
could not bear to see the pity and compassion on her face.

'Perhaps his radio's on the blink,' she added, trying to be
helpful, but every word she spoke seemed to confirm Jon's fate.

'I'll stay here, thanks all the same.'

She watched the other woman go back to her work and felt a
little ashamed that she had been so abrupt. People were trying to
be kind. They had given her a lot of leeway in her relationship
with Jon; it could have been a great deal worse. Everyone knew
the pilots were walking on a tightrope, desperate to hold out for
just a few more runs. Everyone was rooting together, working as
part of a team in order to pull through. They felt the loss of one
man as the loss of a limb. Common griefs and common joys were
shared together.

The light was fading. She knew that now there could not be
very much chance that he was still alive. If he had crashed or

landed at another field, word would have come through by now. If his radio was u.s. then he would be flying blind, but his fuel would not last for long. If he was wounded or out of control, he would have come down over the sea and be lost forever, sunk in a drowned aircraft on the seabed.

Despair ate away at her morale. If Jon was dead then there was no hope left for any of them. She wished desperately that Pat had been there, not still away in London. He was lucky, he had been grounded. His wife knew that he was sleeping safely at night, that he could come to her whenever he chose. He had done his bit on the front line.

She was so wrapped up in her own gloom that she did not hear the Merlin engine for a while. When she first became conscious of the noise the plane was already in sight, swooping in a low curve down towards the runway, rushing at the ground. She scarcely dared to look at the Spitfire, afraid to discover from its markings that it was not M for Mother but Dutch's plane. Dutch or Jon. It was a terrible thought to realise that her prayer for one must mean the certain destruction of the other. Lack of fuel alone would have forced him down. Dutch or Jon – who had survived?

The Spitfire seemed undamaged. It landed fairly smoothly, slewing slightly round to the left but coming to an abrupt stop. The emergency teams around the field had never seen a pilot get himself out of his plane so quickly; you would have thought that it was on fire. Down on the ground he stood there as though dazed, running a hand through his hair and shaking his head, as though astonished at his own survival. He shook off the attentions of the emergency people and began to walk back across the field when suddenly he saw her.

She felt unable to move. Her legs refused to carry her forward. She could only stand there waiting for him to come to her, oblivious of the movement all round them, seeing only each other.

He seemed almost to sway as he reached her, stretching out an arm to gather her in, holding her against his chest, rocking slightly. She held on to him, gripping his hand, her fingers tightly interlaced with his, her head on his shoulder.

The intelligence officer was there, trying to get information out of Jon, trying to debrief him from the mission as they walked

194

back across the grass. Jon was explaining about his radio trouble, saying something about getting lost after Dutch was shot down. As he talked, his hold on her tightened, as though he needed to feel her strength and warmth supporting him. He briefly sketched in the action that had wiped out his friend and brought down two, perhaps three of the enemy aircraft.

Unlike some intelligence people, F.L. Perry was no fool. He saw that Jon was still in shock, that his mind had temporarily blanked out the details as often happened for a few hours after combat. He saw also that his pilot was in good hands, and good luck to them both too!

'Come and see me later, Jon, and we'll fill out the report. I'll put you down for two and a half kills for the moment.' He slapped Jon on the back and walked away.

Suddenly alone on the empty field with the light fading fast all around them, Jon pulled her round to face him and drew her in to a long, desperate kiss that said more of his need for her than any words.

'Thank God, thank God, you're safe,' she whispered. 'Don't ever go away from me again.'

Chapter Seven

It was raining when they arrived. Heavy cloud hung low over the capital, trapping the silver barrage balloons, dull grey fish floating over Parliament. They caught a taxi and sat in the back holding hands, feeling secure, safe.

But as luck would have it, no sooner had they set out for London than word came through that the capital had suffered its first series of heavy bombing raids. This time it was no mistake, no accidental overspill of jettisoning spare bombs over civilian areas. From Saturday September 7 waves of deadly packed enemy bombers and fighters swept in over the Channel with London as a prime target.

For a week or more there had been warnings, with sirens wailing day and night as bombers sought out industrial sites on the outskirts of the city with varying degrees of success. On the 4th the Vickers-Armstrong factory had been hit with over 700 casualties. Stray bombs had scattered in the streets in nearby suburbs, but no one had felt seriously alarmed.

'When the sirens went we didn't take no notice. All week we'd been getting the sirens enough to drive you crazy. We were lucky to get three or four hours kip a night.' The taxi driver watched in his mirror for their reaction. 'Beautiful day it was, too. And then, blow me, I look up and there they are.'

'Quite a few, weren't there?'

'Reckon you'll know all about it, you being in the RAF. But for the likes of us it was a proper fight and no mistake. Christ, I says, there must be hundreds of the buggers. Begging your pardon, miss.'

Jon turned to Eileen. 'It was the East End docks they were after, you see.'

'Well, I live that way myself,' interposed the cabbie. 'Millwall. But I didn't see none of it, what with being down the blooming shelter. Stuck there for hours we was, thinking it would soon blow over. But by ten o'clock I was real browned off, I can tell you – well, it was closing time, wasn't it? Didn't get let out until next morning. Those wardens get a uniform on and they think they're another bloody Hitler. But then, blimey, what a sight!'

'Pretty bad, was it?'

'You don't know the half of it, gov. Thought the whole bloody world was on fire.' He half turned in his seat, manoeuvring almost without watching where he was driving. 'See, it was the stuff what they had in the warehouses what caught fire. And it spread. Spread like wildfire. They didn't have no control over it. Pepper and paint, stuff like that. And all stacked in old wooden buildings what had been there hundreds of years. Couldn't do a bloody thing about it.'

'But it all looks so calm here,' said Eileen, taken aback by the passion of the cab driver's account.

Apart from the piled sandbags and criss-crossed brown paper strips on the windows of the big stores, the city appeared virtually untouched. She and Jon were both relieved. After all the stories they had heard on the train they were expecting to see much more in the way of damage.

'Course it does. It looks all right here 'cause this is the West End,' said the driver with rather heavy-handed patience. 'But you ought to see it down East. Can't move for rubble and fire engines. I don't take no fares that way at all now. There's people moving out regular now. A right old tragedy and no mistake. And what's more they don't have any blooming ack-ack. Where are the bloody guns, that's what we want to know. How the hell they expect us to fight back, God only knows.'

'It must have been terrible,' Eileen said in appeasement.

'It takes a lot to get old London down,' Jon reassured her. He lowered his voice to a whisper. 'We'll still have a good time, I promise you.'

She believed him. In her state of almost dreamlike infatuation she was ready to go anywhere with him, to take up all his suggestions. It was so pleasant just to follow where he led, no need to think at all. The moment she had fantasised had come to pass. It was almost frightening, giving her a sense of awesome power, the kind of magic that willed dreams to come true. Jonathan Pemberley was here at her side, telling her he loved her with every look of his eyes, every touch of his hands, about to lavish all his time and attention completely on her for two whole glorious days.

They paid off the taxi driver with a generous tip and were made welcome by the doorman of the Green Park Hotel. The receptionist offered them special rates as they were members of HM Forces and told them there was a private air raid shelter for the hotel clientele in the basement.

As Jon signed the register with a self-assured flourish, Eileen stared down at the thick carpet of the lobby praying her panic would not show. She was certain that the hotel staff had only to look at them to know that they were not man and wife and to cast the most dreadful, shaming aspersions about the kind of woman she was. But when Jon turned and took her arm very firmly in his, she saw that the receptionist was not in the least interested in either of them, his face set in the most perfect mask of decorum and professional uninterest. They followed the porter with their bags and swept into a suite on the third floor with all the style of a well-married couple used to taking a few days away in town. Jon tipped the porter and then shut the door on the outside world.

'It's perfect,' she said.

'Yes, it's quite good here.' He joined her at the window overlooking the park, putting an arm around her waist.

For a moment she was startled, thinking that his remark meant he had been there before, that he had been there with some other woman. But as if he could read her thoughts he added quickly,

'It was recommended.'

She visibly relaxed. He reached up a hand and pushed back her hair, bending his head to kiss her throat. He felt her tremble and was surprised. There was almost a hint of amusement in his voice as he drew away. 'What's wrong? You're not nervous?'

She gave him a pale smile and smoothed her fingers over the flat lapels of his uniform jacket. She had never felt so uncertain in her life. The very dimensions of the bedroom in which they stood cut the ground away from beneath her feet. Now that the moment had come she felt a rising tide of panic.

'No, of course I'm not nervous,' she said weakly. 'It's just so strange to me. Being in a place like this – with you.'

'Well, there's nothing terribly grand about this place,' he said scornfully. 'Wait until you see the Savoy.'

'The Savoy?'

'Or the Dorchester – I thought we might go out on the town for a real splash-up dinner.'

The reprieve seemed like the answer to all her prayers.

'Oh that's wonderful!' She flung her arms round his neck and kissed him lightly on the mouth. 'I've never been anywhere like that before! Will I do, do you think, in my best blue?'

'There'll be a lot of uniforms around. Come on, are you going to change? I'll give you fifteen minutes.'

'Better make it twenty!' She picked up her bag and flounced into the bathroom astonished at her good fortune. She stood with the door closed and gazed at the grandness of her surroundings with a kind of awe. As hot water came belching out the taps and steam fogged up the expanse of mirrors, she laid out the skirt and jacket of her uniform, wishing she had something nicer to put on. She wanted tonight to be special, a night to remember.

She was so pleased that he had not tried to rush her into doing anything then and there. She needed to be wined and dined, to be wooed a little, to get into the right mood.

As she got into the water, she knew she would have to come to terms with the fear she had felt, the sense of panic at being alone with him in the bedroom. Of course, it was nonsense to compare him with his brother-in-law, with Hayden Darcy. That incident and the humiliation and fear of her experiences with Thomas had all been pushed into the recesses of her mind, not to be thought of. Jon could not have been more different from those brash and vulgar men, so why this nagging fear, why the flood of old memories like scars that would not heal?

With Jon she knew it was all going to be wonderful. He loved her; she knew it by the way he looked at her, by the way he had always sought her out as though he needed to spend every spare moment with her. She knew that he was different. He respected her, he had not tried to force her, and now he was spending all his money to make everything just right.

Even at the station he had been thoughtful. When he asked her if she was fixed up, she was shaken for a moment but she knew what he meant. He was amused rather than annoyed to find that she hadn't even thought about it and set off to the chemist's in the railway station forecourt, leaving her to watch their bags. Moira would have been prepared, she realised, but Jon had thought of it for himself, he was considerate of her welfare and would do the right thing by her. No fear of accidents here, no slip-ups or danger of finding herself suddenly in Moira's condition.

As she dressed she heard the handle rattle and Jon's voice, rather perplexed and loud reached her over the sound of running water.

'Why ever have you locked the door?'

'I'm just coming.' She picked up her things and turned the key in the lock. 'I'm sorry I've been so long.'

He caught a kiss in passing.

'You are a funny little thing. Now we'll be twice as long.'

While he used the bathroom she hurriedly finished dressing and unpacking. She held up her new nightdress which had cost her all her pay. She was a little afraid at her audacity yet admiring the sheen of the silk and the way it was cut so low across the breast.

'Hey, that's a stunner!' He stood in the doorway watching her, his eyes dancing. 'Is that all for my benefit? You're making me regret going out at all tonight.'

She dropped the silken garment on to the wide double bed a little self-consciously, confused by his remarks. For his benefit? Who else would she have bought it for? She would have died of shame if any man other than Jonathan had seen her wearing anything so fine and sheer, so revealing.

'But I've booked a table,' he continued with a regretful shrug of his shoulders, 'so we'll have to go.'

In the taxi she studied his face. He was still quite the most handsome man she had ever seen. His dark gold hair was slightly long, roughly brushed back from his wide brown forehead, mirroring his whole appearance which was casual to the point of deliberate disregard. If she had not known that pilots took a delight in setting out to shock people with their air of just having climbed out of a Spitfire after a particularly harrowing dogfight, she might have felt ashamed of his loosely fastened tie and half-unbuttoned jacket. But the way that he carried himself, the sardonic self-assurance of his walk all marked him out as a man to watch.

He was a powerful man, strong and athletic by nature. When he clasped her in his arms she had felt the strength that was in him, thrilled and not a little awed by the power of his body. She knew that she wanted him as she had never wanted anyone before. He had filled her thoughts for such a long time, she had never given any other man the slightest consideration.

She knew he was experienced and she was willing to be guided by him. If he was set on showing her the high life, she would try to live up to his expectations of her. She wanted to be the kind of woman he was proud to be seen with, at home at the Dorchester or the Savoy, wherever he wanted to be.

But faced with the imposing doorman who met their taxi at the entrance, all her courage deserted her. As Jon helped her from the taxi and turned away to pay off the driver, she stood there watching a procession of chauffeur-driven Daimlers and service cars disgorging a flow of brilliantly dressed diners into the hotel restaurant. For a moment she felt paralysed, staring at the uniforms, the women in furs, the glitter of diamonds, and she felt the clock had turned back nearly two years, to that Christmas houseparty at Charnwood and an awestruck housemaid in the midst of a world she scarcely knew existed.

She felt Jon's hand under her elbow and allowed herself to be guided up the front steps and into the busy hotel entrance hall. Around her everything intertwined into one dazzling circus of bright lights and thick scarlet carpets, of couples talking and walking, their images caught and reflected in dark mirrors. The women all wore long white gloves, flowers and jewels, their men in dark suits or uniforms with a touch of Ruritania about them; here a cavalry type with striped trousers, there one in green with silver buckles and black leather crossbelts. She was the only woman in uniform.

Jonathan led her into the restaurant, giving his name to the head waiter. As they paused on the steps, she felt she was safe with Jon, proud to be with him, their uniforms marking them out. She felt she was part of a commanding couple, aware of heads turning in their direction, of the interest in the women's eyes. On Jonathan's arm she was assured, she was accepted. He moved as though he owned the place, as though he ate here every day of the week, and his confidence cast an aura about him that encompassed her, attracting attention and making Eileen feel that she was someone special.

As they took their seats, Eileen felt that this was almost like acting. The sense of unreality, of dreamlike exaggeration cheered her. A dream was something she could handle, a dream had no repercussions. As she sipped an aperitif and felt the warmth relax her, she knew that she could handle it. Her heart stopped beating a hundred times a minute and she calmed down sufficiently to take a look around her. Being with Jon, in such a place, was a dream in itself.

At least she knew she would not make a fool of herself. Charnwood had taught her that much. She knew all the right cutlery; she could cast an eye over the French menu and nod appreciatively at Jon's choice of wine as though she actually knew what the stuff tasted like.

The curiosity of fate had thrown her into Jon's arms and an affair which plunged her into a society she knew she could never have joined before. The war had brought this about, an unimportant little side effect of the main show. Only in these exceptional times could she have entered this world on the arm of Jonathan Pemberley.

Around them at the other tables were faces as famous as their fortunes. War or no war, Lady Diana Cooper sat cheek by jowl with the Lloyd Georges, the Gwylyms, Bob Boothby and the Waughs. London society continued to dazzle as it munched and gnawed its way through a feast of unrationed delights, gorging themselves on oysters, grouse and caviar, with little regard for the bombs raining down on the East Enders.

The dance floor was crowded with swaying bodies, out for a good time, out to forget the real world. Watching the dancers, Eileen thought how much Moira and Veronica would have enjoyed the chance to see the bright lights! Very few had the chance to get away from the constant pressures of a frontline station and find a few hours of gaiety. She and Jon had come up to London for their long-awaited break, seeking some brightness and fun in an otherwise tense and dangerous existence. For this night they could pretend that there was no war, for this one special night.

Across the table they held hands with no need for words. It was wonderful to be there together, to be free from the strain and tension of the airfield. It was an illusion, but an acceptable one. For 48 hours they would try to put the past behind them and live only for the moment.

But the real world refused to be blocked out. Conversation from adjoining tables drifted in snatches their way, intervening to dispel their illusion.

'– simply heavenly! Of course, it's the Government's own fault if caviar is still imported –'

'More champagne? Another magnum over here!'

'That appalling little man Priestley on the BBC! Did you hear what he was saying about private property? You didn't? My dear! Something should be done. The man is clearly a Red –'

'I would rather listen to old Haw-Haw.'

'– quite quite dreadful. We had to wait a full twenty minutes for a cab.'

'Daddy says we should have gone to Canada while we had the chance –'

It was immediately plain that rationing and the servant problem were more important topics of conversation in such society than the Blitz or even the war situation in Northern Africa. To them the war seemed to have a singular dimension, limited to its immediate consequences on their own comfort, rising prices and complaints when their servants left them to join the Forces.

These butterflies were trapped in the dazzling amber of their own petrified world, a round of inconsequential talk and astonishing vulgarity.

'How are you liking it?'

She turned her face to Jon's and he was startled to see her expression. Was the steak tough? He couldn't understand the temper stamped on her pert little face. He thought she would have enjoyed being here, getting a taste of the high life for once.

'I love being with you,' she told him forcefully. 'But these people!'

'Yes, they are a bit much, aren't they?' He beckoned to the hovering waiter to refill her glass, apparently amused by what he saw. Even her bad humour seemed to amuse him. 'Don't frown so,' he rebuked her gently. 'You're giving the waiter a heart attack. The poor fellow thinks the food's off.'

'I'm sorry. I don't want to spoil the evening.'

'Good, then let's dance, shall we?'

Lost in the strong circle of his arms, Eileen was waltzed around the sparkling floor, wheeling in between couples as different from them as chalk and cheese. But she no longer felt awkward in her uniform, she felt proud.

Eileen could not help remembering that other dance in the village hall at Charnwood, when she had so very nearly claimed him as her partner and felt she would die when she had been disappointed. And now here he was, clasping her against him, his hands firm and possessive, their faces barely inches apart as the music mooched into a slow blues rhythm. Suddenly she wanted to go and leave this place. She wanted to be back in that hotel bedroom with their double bed turned down and waiting.

She began to laugh. It came from deep down in her throat, a warm chuckle that could not be denied. Jon caught her glance over his shoulder and turned to look at what had caught her eye. One of the dancers, extremely elegantly turned out in full dress suit complete with buttonhole carnation, was whirling his equally immaculate partner about completely oblivious of the fact that he still wore his table napkin tucked into the waist of his trousers, like a kilt, or a nappy, or a figleaf. To Eileen this only seemed to confirm her whole impression of the evening and her laughter was infectious. As Jon stopped dancing, caught up by the fun, other couples cascaded into them.

'Sorry, sorry – I apologise,' laughed Jon, shaking his head and taking Eileen by the elbow, about to lead her back through the dancers to their table when a hand descended on his shoulder.

'Jonathan, old chap! It is you, isn't it?'

The faint essence of violets should have warned her. As she turned, still in Jonathan's arms, she recognised him and her mind froze back in that moment which had been concealed in the darkest recess of her memory. She felt the colour drain from her face, all the warmth and laughter die, dropping instantly away as she looked up into the face of Hayden Darcy.

'Why, Hayden!' Jon was surprised rather than pleased. His eyes scanned the room avoiding his brother-in-law's eyes. 'Is Honor here with you?'

Hayden's face creased in a cynical smile.

'Of course, of course. I'd hardly be out on my own in a place like this, now would I?' His smooth voice conveyed the message, man to man, that perhaps on less conspicuous occasions he might very well be in such a place with a woman other than his wife.

Eileen felt humiliation standing there under his gaze. She was instantly back at Charnwood, his pleasant diversion, bait for an appetite that his wife could not, or would not satisfy. And she remembered how when she had run away his laughter mocked her all the way down the corridor.

Did he know her now? She forced herself to look up at him when he turned his head away. She saw at once that he could not know her. The incident which had marked her and brought her such debasement and humiliation when it was misinterpreted by the malicious Thomas had been no more than an amusing anecdote for him, something to toss into conversation with his banking friends.

'I haven't seen Honor for such a long time,' Jon was saying. 'Where are you sitting?'

Eileen was directed towards the edge of the dance floor where the remains of an ample dinner littered the table at which Honor Darcy sat looking bored and solitary. She wore white and her jewellery was all plain gold, catching the lights of the room and mirroring her perfectly set golden hair. She was like an ice goddess, carved for posterity, gilded but unmoved.

And then she caught sight of Jonathan. Her pale face and languorous eyes were suddenly aflame with such an intensity of passion and delight that Eileen felt jealous. She saw brother and sister clutch at one another, kiss and touch one another, as though each had been certain that the other was dead.

'So you're safe!' she cried, her eyes bright with unshed tears, still clutching at his jacket afraid to let him go. 'How could you do such a heartless thing?'

'Don't say that to him,' Hayden said abruptly. 'These flying boys are heroes out to steal all the glory –'

Jon broke away from his sister's embrace and gave her husband a cold stare. His full mouth was pinched with anger, a tight line of contempt and unveiled disgust.

'– while we,' continued Hayden as though he had not read the warning signals, 'are left with all the mundane business of running this bloody country and making money to keep it going. I envy you, old chap!'

Their enmity hung in the air between them like a challenge, like a gauntlet cast down over the fair hand of a lady, the sister who now stood with eyes eager for bloody combat and war for her pleasure.

'Jon, aren't you going to introduce me?' Eileen's calm voice cut through the burning silence and destroyed the spell that Honor had cast. She flashed Eileen a look of such virulent dislike that there could be no doubt that her intent had been serious. Eileen wondered how many of these little games she had played in the past.

As Jon made the intoductions, describing her only as a friend from the base, Eileen was alert for the slightest hint of recognition in their eyes. In Honor's icy stare she read hatred and suspicion and a warning to keep her distance. In Hayden's a cruel delight in baiting both brother and sister by an open invitation to the unknown stranger in their midst.

He had grown fat. The good life had taken its toll and the body that was once fluid and powerful now carried the weight of self-indulgence. His hair was greased and parted very precisely in the middle, baring an expanse of forehead red with drink and malice.

It was impossible to escape without at least one drink. Hayden had snapped his fingers to summon another pair of chairs, and Eileen found herself squashed in uncomfortably close between Hayden and Jon, with Honor comfortably on her brother's left, her arm entwined with his for full display on the tablecloth. While they talked about Mother and the wartime privations of life at Charnwood, Eileen contended with Hayden's duelling on her right.

For one moment she thought she had caught him out by talking about his work. She asked him why he was not in uniform too, and suggested that he was perhaps in a reserved occupation along with valets, chauffeurs, tea-tasters and funeral directors. But he chose to take her remark quite differently and visibly preened at being thought young enough to qualify for active service. When she expressed her anger at the way some men contrived to avoid service, he merely smiled expansively and said,

'What's a pretty girl like you worrying your little head about things like that?' She could have hit him.

Honor was telling her brother a long story about the Savoy Hotel. When she saw that Eileen was listening she lifted her voice, occasionally giving Eileen a quick glance from under hooded lids. She was clearly under the impression that her story was amusing and rather clever, but as Eileen listened she was awed by the utter callousness of this woman who was Jon's dear sister.

Apparently after the first heavy Blitz raid the previous Saturday, a group of East End residents had organised a march on the Savoy Hotel, haunt of politicians, journalists and foreign correspondents. Appalled by the destruction of vast areas of Stepney, led by their local MP, this 'horde of ranting, pregnant women' had descended on the hotel at lunchtime carrying banners, 'Our Children Are Starving' and 'Ration the Rich', waiting for the air-raid sirens to go so that they would be forced to use the private shelter in the Savoy. This shelter had, it seems, partitioned dormitories and cubicles for their customers, cosy double beds, and even a special room for snorers. Certain 'very well-known' people actually had their own private deep shelters reserved for them with their names on the door.

'I think it's disgusting,' Eileen said involuntarily.

Honor looked at her with interest. 'It most certainly is. They should never have been admitted to the hotel in the first place.' She turned on a sly smile aimed at Jon. 'But they didn't get away with it. The raid was only a false alarm, and as they couldn't afford to eat in the restaurant they had to go away. Apparently it was all rather thrilling – everyone cheered as they were thrown out.'

'I didn't hear anything about it,' said Jon doubtfully.

'Oh but you wouldn't, would you? It was all hushed-up, old chap. Bad for morale,' said Hayden.

'Don't they have shelters of their own?'

'Well, if their precious socialist councils don't spend their money on sensible precautions, that's their bad luck.'

'I had heard you were thinking of making a dash for it yourselves – frankly I'm surprised to find you both still here.'

'Someone's got to keep the old machinery ticking over,' said Hayden effusively. 'They wanted someone responsible to take the gold reserves over to Canada. Of course, I would have gone if they had asked me, but you know how it is. Couldn't get Honor a passage. All the liners booked out solid.'

'Mummy wanted me to go, but of course she couldn't leave Daddy behind.'

Jon cast Eileen a glance as though he had just remembered that she had her own memories of the Pemberleys. For one terrible moment she thought he was going to say something, but to her relief he got to his feet and said that they were going to make a move.

There were squeals of protest from Honor but Hayden sat back in his chair, not displeased to see them go. Jon kissed his sister and promised he would be in touch soon, but her sulky lips turned down and her cold eyes flashed at Eileen as though it was all her fault.

As they returned to their table, Eileen walked ahead of Jon, still shaking with emotion from the encounter. Jon caught her up and grasped her by the arm, turning her round brusquely to face him.

'What's the matter with you? What's wrong?' When he saw that she was white-faced with anger, he immediately released her. 'Look, I'm sorry, I didn't want to get involved with them.'

'I felt terrible. You ignored me completely. You sat there just lapping up everything they said without turning a hair. You never thought about me. You never once.'

She saw the dawning of understanding on his face and her anger intensified. He had only just remembered that she was not a total stranger to his sister and brother-in-law, that she too had her memories of Charnwood.

'It was humiliating. It never even occurred to you that they might recognise me, that your bloody sister might suddenly have exclaimed, "Oh Jon, darling! Whatever are you doing here with a housemaid?"'

'For Christ's sake, Eileen, shut up, will you?' He was aware that

208

people at adjoining tables were glancing in their direction.

'Oh yes, let's behave, shall we? Well I don't care very much for the way your kind of people behave. "Someone's got to keep the machine running, old chap" – it made me sick!'

'Is anything wrong, sir?' The head waiter had appeared, his pasty face strained with polite concern.

'No, no, get me the bill,' snapped Jon, irritably pulling out his wallet. 'We'll go now.'

'Thank God,' muttered Eileen, and sank into silence, eyes downcast.

Conversation from adjoining tables wafted over them, rippling her anger. Her nerves were jarred by the laughter and the bright buzz of scandal. She even heard one remark about the bombing that set her teeth on edge:

'I'm no snob,' said the man, 'but thank God there are plenty of common people to clear up the mess.'

It reminded her of those brash BBC broadcasters who talked about losses 'on a small scale' and 'slight casualties'. How slight was any death and injury? Now she knew that it was not so much a callous indifference to suffering as ignorance, a simple lack of imagination and understanding of what life was like for the vast majority of people. The 'common people' they despised so much. People like Eileen.

She knew now that it was ridiculous to try and bridge that gap. Between Jon's kind of life and her own there yawned a monstrous chasm that she could not hope to bridge, and now that she had seen it at first hand, she was certain she did not want to bridge that abyss.

She remembered the Pemberleys' New Year trips abroad, the spas and Switzerland. She remembered Honor Darcy's honeymoon in Germany. Now that she knew her she could almost imagine her dining and dancing with the Nazis, having Ribbentrop to weekend house parties. It was as Pat had said, there were many at the top who had never wanted this war, who would have been ready at any time to join the Axis Alliance.

Eileen felt ashamed for the way that the demonstrators at the Savoy had been treated. While some were safe in the West End, bombs were falling on the docks and houses of the East End. Whatever the newspapers said, they were not all in the same boat. The poor could not stay in hotels or clubs when their houses were bombed, they could not afford to eat out when their food was rationed or their gas cut off. You had to have money, it seems, to survive even in the Blitz.

Without speaking, Jon led the way out of the restaurant and they asked the doorman to get them a cab. There could be no greater contrast than the bright lights and luxury of the interior and the deep blackout and wailing sirens of the night. Eileen felt the cold air of reality wake her from the nightmare evening. She took Jon's hand and tried to give him a smile, determined that the ghosts of her past would not continue to haunt and blight her future.

The coldness which had descended to mar the evening remained to mar the night. The dream that had lived with Eileen for so long should now have become a reality, but the past had intervened. Alone in the hotel bedroom with her lover, Eileen was determined that everything should be perfect, that this first night should be a success, that he would continue to love her.

Tonight he would become hers completely. She had done her best to please him. She wore her new nightgown and wanted to look beautiful, only for him. Even with the moodiness and distance between then, he was disturbingly handsome. She watched him undress with a shiver of anticipation, taking in the broad back and slim hips, the powerful thighs and the chest covered with light curling hair. He was golden and beautiful in the soft lamplight of the room, but his eyes were shadowed and his expression petulant and unforgiving.

There were few preliminaries. He barely said a word before they were in bed. She welcomed him into her arms, feeling his weight, touching the smooth curves of his body and trying to disguise her own tense apprehension. He began to move against her, his kiss stifling her sharp cry of surprise and disappointment. His eyes were closed and he seemed quite untouched by her response, almost oblivious of her needs, completely absorbed by his own passion. She could only lie there observing the process of his fulfilment with a coldness, a sense of appalled detachment, as though it had been happening to someone else.

As he grunted and moved aside she was left with the overwhelming feeling, Is that all it is? Is that what they rave about, what poets go mad for, what Moira seeks time and time again? If she had not felt so let down, she might almost have laughed at the absurdity of the moment.

'Well, did you come?'

His question took her unawares. She had no idea what he was talking about. He lay there, half wrapped in the white sheet, looking pleased with himself. He had that handsome little boy smile that she had found so devastating. He stroked her with a leisurely hand, like brushing the fur of a pet cat.

'It's not the same for me, wearing these,' he told her, touching the place fondly. 'You really ought to get yourself fixed up now we're together. What did you use with Gareth?'

The matter-of-fact question touched her on the raw. She lay there rigid with shock and he must have felt it because he turned over, leaning down upon her, looking into her face.

'Don't tell me you took a chance? Well, if that doesn't take the cake! I'd have thought old Gareth had more sense. Can you imagine the rumpus there would have been if he had got you pregnant?'

She pushed him away abruptly, drawing a hand through her hair as she stared at nothing.

'Is that what you think?' she said at last, her voice barely audible. 'You think I slept with Gareth?'

'Oh come on! I know you did.'

'Did he tell you that? Did he go round boasting?'

'No, not boasting exactly, but...' he stopped dead, placing one strong brown hand on her white shoulder, twisting her round. 'What are you trying to say? Are you trying to kid me that there was nothing going on between you two? I saw you two together! He was besotted with you.'

'What, Gareth?' His words struck her dumb. She sat up in the bed half-naked, unaware of the cold, aware only of a shattered dream. Had Gareth been in love with her? She saw in Jon's eyes that it was true, every word of it, and that her denial had only made him angry. His tone was mocking, his reaction jealous.

'It's not true,' she said bluntly. 'I never slept with Gareth.'

He stared at her with narrowed eyes, his whole aspect clouded,

211

uncertain whether to believe her. He turned his head aside and frowned.

'But he loved you – I know, I saw him.'

'But we never slept together.'

His expression was quizzical, his smile crooked, sceptical.

'The poor sod. So you kept him dangling, hanging on, did you? He was crazy about you. He probably still is.'

'I didn't know he felt that way about me.'

'No?'

'No. I would never have dreamt –' She met his eyes. 'You're the only man I've ever loved.'

For one dreadful moment she really thought he was going to laugh. She understood suddenly the various remarks, the easy acceptance of her love for him. He took it all for granted. He treated it as nothing out of the ordinary for her as well as for him. But he did not laugh. There must have been a trace of something in her face that convinced him. He wrenched back the sheet with sudden violence and stared transfixed at the scarlet stain on the white bed.

'You little fool,' he muttered savagely under his breath, swinging his legs off the bed and flinging on his dressing-gown. 'For God's sake clear that mess up. Christ, what on earth are the hotel staff going to think?'

She woke in the morning, aware of the sunlight cutting sharp patterns across the balcony balustrade into the silent room. She lay on the very edge of the wide bed, aware that he was still there, that he had not left her after all. She turned over and saw that he lay with his broad back towards her, his brown arm curved across the blank pillow. She studied his sleeping face, all emotions in turmoil.

Last night she had thought that his love was an illusion. She had cried herself to sleep, cold and uncomfortable, still bleeding. She was hurt beyond belief by the casual remarks that had shattered the dream for her. All romance had fled when she learnt that he believed she had loved other men, including Gareth. But now she realised that he could not have known this was a further blow to her reputation, cruelly echoing her experience at Charnwood. He did not know that she carried this stigma with her, a wound that had been reopened last night. He could not have known that this was the reason for her resentment against his family, the reason why she had felt so uncomfortable and upset.

If he loved her at all it was not in a way she understood. She was more affected by the discovery that he actually did not mind, that he had accepted her affair with Gareth. He had gone into this relationship accepting that she was a woman of the world, that she knew all the rules. She had let him down, deceived him. She had ruined their break away and now it was up to her to make amends. That was how he must see it, but try as she might, Eileen could not forgive and forget.

She needed to get away, to be by herself for a while and think it through. She wished that there was someone else she could talk to, another woman, Veronica or even Moira. She suspected that neither of them would be able to help very much though. Veronica had not gone through this kind of experience and Moira probably would not understand what all the fuss was about. Who else could she turn to? She thought of the house in Milton Square with longing, remembering the midnight conversation there with Vi, remembering the sympathy and wisdom which Lily had shown Veronica.

She got out of bed, careful not to disturb Jon as he slept on. She cast one brief look at his childlike serenity and then picked up her clothes and departed for the bathroom.

She came to Milton Square on the Underground just as she had before in the company of Moira and Veronica. She felt proud of herself, tracing the multicoloured lines along, remembering to change at King's Cross to the Northern Line for the Angel. But somehow everywhere seemed more crowded than before. It was not yet nine o'clock and yet there were people in the tunnels walking round carrying bundles of bedding, rolled blankets and pillows. Pasty-faced and obviously exhausted, they almost looked as though they had been sleeping out of doors instead of at home in their own beds. Eileen could not understand what they were doing.

But when she came out of the tube in the cranking lift and saw what had become of the Angel in the brief weeks that had passed she at last began to understand the full meaning of the Blitz on London.

Where buildings had stood she now saw only mounds of rubble, some still smoking, barely dampened down. The street was full of fire fighting equipment, still strewn with debris from the previous night's raid. While she and Jon had been involved in their own personal struggle, outside in the black night bombs had rained down on these poor unprotected areas of the city, indiscriminately striking both public and private buildings. And while the wealthy clientele of West End hotels and restaurants had their own safe, private shelters to scurry into, it seemed that the people of North London had little choice but to sleep down in the Underground stations.

She felt that people were staring at her as she passed, trying to remember the way through the quiet squares to Lily's house. Here and there a block had been hit, whole walls sheered away, revealing the interiors like a doll's house. Peeling wallpaper fluttered, whole rooms still intact, the furniture barely touched. And yet the very next house might be quite perfect, not even a window shattered. It was like some grim lottery.

Passing the row of shops which included the old Welsh dairy Moira had told them about, one woman in a floral pinafore recognised her uniform and cried out angrily that the Air Force was not doing its job:

'Where were your lot when the Jerries were over last night?'

Eileen hurried away, feeling appallingly guilty although she knew the woman's remarks were unfair. The cynical contrast between these streets and the safe assurance of the society she had been part of in the West End only hours before made her sick with shame for the blindness of those with the power to change all this. Why had the Germans got through so easily? Why were there not enough shelters in the East End? Where were the anti-aircraft guns to protect London from attack? Undefended and defenceless, this was not war – it was murder.

As she crossed the square she saw with relief that the house was safe. It stood with perfect serenity in its block, protected by its neighbours on either side. Approaching the house, Eileen had a feeling of coming home, an eager anticipation to be safe inside and part of that easy community. She was certain that Lily would open the door to her without surprise. She hoped that Lily had liked her, even if only because she was Moira's friend. Had Moira got the chance to explain everything to Lily? Eileen hoped that she would not have to break the news to Lily or to lie to her.

She knocked on the door and stood there with absolute composure, eager to respond to Lily's cheerful greeting. But it was not to be. The green door opened and it was a very different face that stared out at her from the looming darkness of the hall. A bright fresh face crowned in short blonde curls, a strong face with high cheekbones and large bright eyes.

'Yes?'

'Is Lily there? Lily Cox? I'm a friend of her grand-daughter.'

The door opened further, revealing a blue siren suit and a pair of battered brown boots. Eileen could not make up her mind who this could be.

'Lily's out at a meeting,' said the surprising stranger. 'Can you come back later?'

'Well, not really. You see I'm up here on leave. I'm only here for a few hours.'

'How rotten for you. She'll be hours yet. She's having fire-watching lectures, you know.' She paused, looking her over. 'That's a WAAF uniform, isn't it? You look a bit washed out. Why don't you come in and have a cup of tea while I get ready?' She threw wide the door and ushered her inside.

Eileen had to admit that she felt terrible. In the mirror as they passed she noticed her pale face and the dark shadows under her eyes. It wasn't just that she had not slept much the night before, it was the shock of everything she had seen in London. She had built herself up to talk to Lily, perhaps even to ask her advice. It was another blow to discover that Lily was out, busy with a life of her own.

'Terrific, isn't she? Just keeps going. I wish I had a grandmother like her.' Down in the basement kitchen she bustled with the kettle and tea things, but then suddenly stopped stock still. 'I say, we'd better introduce ourselves, hadn't we? I'm Kitty Russell.'

'That's a nice name.'

'Yes, isn't it? I picked it out myself. I thought Kitty was rather dashing and Russell was my mother's maiden name. Better than what I was born with.' She grinned, looking more elfin than before. 'Do you want to guess what it was? The name I was born with, I mean – go on, you'll never guess!'

Eileen didn't think she could. She had no idea what the woman was talking about. She shook her head impatiently.

'Julie Poole. There you are, simply ghastly, isn't it? I have a job remembering it myself, so how on earth could you expect anyone else to remember it? Anyway, I feel like Kitty Russell now.'

Suddenly the penny dropped. Eileen remembered how Moira had boasted of the vaudeville types to whom Lily rented out rooms.

'Are you on the stage then?'

'You bet I am!' gushed the eager actress. 'You don't mean you've heard of me? You've seen me on tour?'

'No, I'm afraid not. What do you do?'

'Do? I act, of course, what else would I do?' She calmed down to pour hot water on to the tea. 'Well, not now, of course. There's not much call for actresses at the moment. The company I was with folded when half the cast got called up. Suddenly there were five women and no men – in the middle of an Edgar Wallace run, can you imagine? That finished us off.' She fetched the tea across to the kitchen table. 'So what's your name? Did you say? I think I missed it.'

'Eileen Howard.' She stirred her tea, a little uncomfortable. 'I just thought I'd drop in. See if Lily had heard anything from Moira.'

'Moira? Oh, that'll be her grand-daughter, of course. I don't know the layout very well yet. You see I only moved in here last week.'

'And Vi? Is she still here?'

'Oh yes. Nice woman, but not around much. Married, isn't she?' She took a quick sip of tea. 'Blow me, is that the time? I can't stop long, I'm on duty soon myself.'

'On duty?'

'I'm a warden. The first woman warden in the district. Don't you like my getup? They say we'll get uniforms eventually but by the time they get moving the whole damned war will be over!'

216

Eileen looked at her in a new light, with admiration.

'Isn't it very difficult to be a warden? You must be rushed off your feet just now.'

'And how! It's a bit like being head girl at school, you know? You need to be bossy, firm but friendly. Some of the old folks won't leave their homes even in the heaviest raid. You know what? I found one old girl sitting under the stairs with a saucepan on her head for protection!'

Eileen admired her briskness, her energy and ebullient commonsense. If she had known her better, this was the kind of woman she might have been able to talk to, the kind of friend she needed.

'It's a pity you're not around more,' she said. 'I wish I had more time to talk to you. I thought of joining the WAAF, you know.'

Eileen joined her as she began searching for her various bits and pieces of equipment. There was a satchel on the stairs, a first-aid kit in the bathroom and her torch was finally discovered in the chaos that swamped her back bedroom. She was due on duty at the local shelter.

'It was rotten last week. The sirens were blasting off day and night. People were going crazy, falling asleep all over the place. I bet I didn't get more than two hours a night. Everyone was really irritable, ready to pick a quarrel at the drop of a hat. And it was worse for me, being a warden. All the men had it in for me.'

'Oh yes, you said that you were the only woman.'

'When I first came here they nearly had heart failure. You should have heard the language! It was worse than the theatre and that's saying something! "Who's this bloody cow?" they said. Of course, most wardens aren't exactly what you might call saints. Around here they're bookies, street traders, bouncers, even a couple of scene-shifters from the Wells. They're OK, those boys. They knew I'd fit in because they knew you have to be tough in the theatre, but the others took a while to get used to me. Some of them were pretty old-fashioned, retired or too old to go to the front – well, forty seems old to me, doesn't it to you? We even have a couple of conchies – conscientious objectors, you know. But they've all come round now that we're getting the raids. They see that I know how to handle myself, and we all go down to the pub for a pint of bitter together when we get the chance.'

It sounded comradely and comfortable, the same kind of camaraderie that Eileen shared with Pat and Jon and the others at Kenley.

'Are you going to walk along with me a bit?' Kitty was finally ready to go, her tin hat with the 'W' for warden on the front sitting on her tight cap of blonde curls, the webbing satchel slung across her chest. When Eileen said that she would, an infectious smile broke out across her face and she slammed the green door behind them with satisfaction.

'Let's just hope it's still here when I get back!' she added sardonically. 'You need to be lucky in this job. I hear there's a black warden down in one area who's come to be regarded as lucky by the folks he looks after.'

Kitty explained that she was part of a team of five wardens in the area, operating out of a brick hut on the corner near the dairy. Some were full-time as she was, while others came on duty after shift work at the GPO at Mount Pleasant or on the railways at nearby King's Cross or St Pancras. She had got to know every street, every block of houses, all the flats and basements in the area under her control. She had to know all the residents too, know who were the awkward customers and who could be relied on for help. It was a good borough with a conscientious council before the war. As far back as the Munich Crisis they had been prepared.

'It wasn't their fault that they didn't understand the kinds of raids we'd get. We've had constant raiding going on for twelve or fourteen hours at a stretch – no one thought they would last that long. They supplied Anderson shelters for the back gardens, you know, but no one round here uses them. Since the rain they've found out that the damned things flood. No one wants to spend twelve hours up to their knees in mud and water.'

'Twelve hours? That's terrible!'

'You get used to anything after a while. People are more organised now. They take thermos flasks of hot soup and tea with them, and blankets to keep warm. In the large shelters they have a sing-song or do their knitting. They try and make the best of it.'

Eileen was astonished at her practical attitude to what seemed to be a truly terrifying experience. Trapped underground for twelve hours a day as bombs rained down above you, perhaps destroying your home and everything you held dear? Eileen thought she would go mad if she had to go through that.

'Of course I go out in the raids,' added Kitty nonchalantly. 'To check there are no lights showing, to try and get them all down to the shelters. You get to know the ones that won't go, and you have to leave them to it. Some make their beds under the kitchen table; they think that's safe. I saw thirteen packed into one room yesterday. Nothing would persuade them to get out.'

'But when the bombs are actually falling, what do you do then?'

'Then we get really busy. You have to round up the strays – people who are strangers to the district and have got stranded by the raid. We work with the fire-watchers, the job that Lily's going to do. They try and put out any incendaries and tip us off about any major fires and UXBs.'

'But you don't have to deal with unexploded bombs yourself, surely?'

Kitty gave a short laugh. 'Not if I can help it! I've got enough on my plate as it is.' They had come to the wardens' post. 'Well, it's been really nice to meet you.' She seemed uncertain whether to hold out her hand, but decided against it, obviously thinking that was too formal, that they were already better friends than that. 'I'm sorry that you didn't get to see Lily. Shall I give her a message?'

'Just say I called. I wanted to know about Moira.'

'Right, well, I'll tell her.' She smiled. 'I hope I'll see you again?'

'Oh I expect so. I'll probably be up here again sometime.' She turned to move away, a little reluctantly. 'Good luck – take care.'

'You too!'

As Eileen drifted off down the street she felt let down, sunk back in her earlier despair. She looked at her watch. It was barely ten, Jon would probably not even be up yet. What would he say when he discovered she had gone out and left him without a word? Would he be sorry, or relieved? Should she go back now, try to make it up with him or stay out awhile longer, go for a walk perhaps somewhere.

She had hardly reached the corner of the next square when the piercing scream of a siren riveted her to the spot. She just stood there as though she did not understand what the undulating wave of noise could mean, even though all round her the houses were gushing forth women and children with set faces and wide eyes. The sickening wail screamed up and down the scale, descending with a lurch into a growling throb before it started all over again. But Eileen could not bring herself to move. It was ridiculous; siren practice at this hour! It was barely ten in the morning. She was miles away from where she ought to be, miles between her and Jon...

'Eileen!' She was being shaken and as she focused her eyes she saw it was Kitty Russell, red-faced and panting, gripping her hard by the shoulders. 'Eileen, come on, it's a raid! You have to get to a shelter.'

'Oh but I can't. I mean, I have to get back – across town.'

'Yes, but not now,' said Kitty firmly.

Eileen found herself propelled back towards the square, towards the large 'S' that marked a public shelter.

'You stay in there.' She gave a quick glance towards the sky. 'I hope it won't last long. I'll try and drop in to see you later.'

Inside the shelter there were already twenty or thirty people. It was a large cavern, brick and cement, with hurricane lamps to give light. There were four bunk beds at the far end, already occupied by a number of small children. Their mothers were distracting them with toys and picture books, trying to disguise their own apprehension and strain. From their faces, Eileen thought they probably had not slept very much over the past days.

On the long wall there was a trestle table and two women in WVS overalls were busy setting an urn of tea on a small stove. When one of them saw Eileen staring she gave a cheery smile,

'Don't worry, love, we're just brewing up. A nice cup of tea will set you to rights.'

Looking round her at the faces of the local residents, Eileen felt that she alone was afraid, that only she had no idea of what was about to happen. She really did not believe it was serious. It could not really be happening to her.

She hovered near the steps leading up to the entrance, aware of running feet and whistles outside. The sense of panic in the street increased her fear. She felt that the brick shelter was closing in on her, and Kitty's talk of twelve or fourteen hour raids ran round inside her head. She wanted to get out, to get some air. She wanted to be with Jon, where it was safe, she wanted to get out before the whole world crashed, caving in upon her.

'Why don't you come and sit down, miss?'

She saw it was an older man who was speaking to her. His thin face was lined and drawn, yellowed in the light of the lamps. There was stubble where he had not shaved, and she suddenly realised that he was wearing his striped pyjamas under his trousers and braces.

'Just got to bed when the siren went,' he explained when he saw her looking. 'I work nights, you see. No bloody sleep around here.' He led her over to the bench against the far wall. 'What's that you're in? Army, is it?'

'Air Force.'

'Oh aye. Want a smoke?' He offered a pack of Woodbines. 'Soothes the nerves, they say.' He drew a long breath, blowing out smoke in an arc. 'Won't be long now, I daresay.'

Eileen sensed that everyone in the shelter was listening. The screaming sirens had died down and there was silence, a sense of growing unease as they waited. Eileen stared at them, accepting their greater experience, somewhat irritated by their calmness yet admiring their steady natures.

All at once her ears became attuned to a low droning rhythm overhead. It was a noise at once alarming and yet oddly familiar. The tone was changed by the depth of the shelter, by the shape of the city, but it was unmistakable.

She saw the reaction among her neighbours. She saw the bright fear in their eyes, the grim lines of their mouths, the tight jaws and pinched cheeks. She saw her own knuckles were white as she gripped the edge of her jacket, twisting the material, waiting, waiting.

Then she heard the sound. She knew it instantly. The high-pitched whistle rising louder and louder until...

She instinctively buried her head in her hands as the first bombs fell. The thunder in the cavern room was immense. It buffeted through the earth in waves, roaring round and through the brick and soil, repeated again and again. Somewhere behind her a baby cried and someone began to mumble under their breath. When the noise of the salvo died away, she realised that the woman at the tea urn was praying.

One, two, three – four: that was close! Five, six – a close shave

221

that time! A moment's break. The waiting was worse. For God's sake someone stop that child crying! Here we go again – one, two – getting nearer – three, four, five – Oh Jesus! – six – and away . . .

A growing silence. Faces began to lift, eyes began to ask questions. Is it over? Are we safe? Did we get away with it? But no, here's another. The low tone swelling, heavy, pregnant with bombs. A clear change of note as the bombs are released – one, two, three, four, five and six. Thin, rising screams, aching crashes, teeth on edge, nerves raw, ears ringing.

Her immediate neighbour had forgotten the cigarette drooping from the corner of his mouth. His long thin face drooped as he gave himself up completely to fate, to the savage roulette going on above.

Eileen was shocked at the way the children seemed half-excited, half-scared out of their wits. One toddler, swinging its legs on the top bunk, was grinning its head off, gurgling merrily as its mother shook with every crunch of the landing bombs.

There came a lull in the barrage and for ten complete minutes there was an uneasy silence. As the quiet spread, people began to shift about, getting up and stretching, showing some signs of life.

'Is that it?' Eileen asked her neighbour, relief breaking out all over her face. She was already planning how to make her way back to Green Park, thinking how she would tell Jon of her adventures.

'I doubt it,' said the man pessimistically. 'We should be so lucky.'

Eileen found herself looking at him with positive dislike. How could he dampen her hopes so casually? The noise had stopped, the raid was clearly over. She got to her feet.

'You can't leave yet,' he warned her. 'The All-Clear hasn't gone.'

He was right. They all sat round in the shelter waiting for that welcoming sound, but it did not come. There was a discernible tension, almost as bad as during the bombing.

All at once the shelter door was pushed open and three newcomers stumbled down the steps. Covered in dust and thick yellow dirt, they had obviously been caught in the raid until shepherded to the shelter by one of the wardens. Perhaps Kitty. It seemed unbelievable that people could still live outside in the bombing storm.

222

'Bloody hell, that was a close call.'

'Is that tea you've got there, love? My throat feels like I've swallowed half of London.'

The tea woman pushed two mugs into their hands.

'What, no sugar?'

'You must be joking!' she laughed. 'Don't they have rationing where you come from?' She watched them drinking the strong brew with indulgence. 'What's happening up there? Any sign of a break?'

'The warden said no. Pushed us down here and refused to take no for an answer. Tiny little thing she was, a real cracker.'

'That'll be our Kitty,' said the woman. 'Brave little thing, she is.' She turned round to the shelterers. 'Well, looks like we've got to sit tight for a bit,' she announced. 'Who wants tea?'

As they queued for their tea, Eileen felt at a loss. She had no idea what to do. Here she was, halfway across London from Jon, trapped in some air-raid shelter surrounded by strangers with no idea of how or when she would get back to join him.

'A bloody fine welcome home this is,' one of the newcomers was complaining. 'Just got back from the Front on leave.'

'The Front?' someone demanded sarcastically. 'What the bloody hell do you think this is then?' There was general laughter and agreement. 'You've had it soft, boy. Don't come here and tell us about the war!'

'I can remember the last lot,' said Eileen's neighbour, settling down comfortably with his tea. 'You're too young to know what I'm talking about but I remember it all. It's not the first time I've had German bombs dropped on me. We had Zeppelins, the lot, then. And no bloody shelters. It was worse than this lot, much worse. Everyone went bananas, rushing round, nicking and looting. You never saw anything like it.'

No, thought Eileen, and I don't want to. This was quite enough for her, enough to last her a lifetime – if she survived this experience.

'This time they gave us one of the Andersons,' the man continued. 'All in bits and pieces. Took us all day trying to put the bloody thing up in the ditch. Had to have a foundation, you see. Well, we got it all nice and comfy but blow me, it goes and rains and we're up to our necks in bleeding mud! Flaming useless! And when they went and dropped their bombs, the whole thing shook

223

like a jelly and we were tone deaf for hours after. The door was thumping away like there was some bloke outside trying to get in. Gave me quite a turn when I pulled open the door and there was no one there! We never used it again.'

Eileen let his voice drone on. It was somehow soothing, harmless enough and it took her mind off the droning of planes overhead once again. Oh God, would she never get out of here?

At three o'clock there was a twenty minute break in the raid. Kitty turned up, her face a mask of dust, her hands badly scratched from digging a dog out of a mound of debris.

'Poor little thing,' she told Eileen as her cuts were tended. 'The owners must have gone to work and left it there all alone. We couldn't see any bodies in the ruins.'

'What's it like out there?'

'Pretty bad. We had an HE in the Goswell Road. Brought down a whole block of flats. There were a number of incendiaries dropped over towards Rosebery Avenue. We've got a few fires still burning.'

'When is it going to stop?'

Kitty looked at her with the cold eye of experience.

'That's what we all want to know, isn't it?'

When Eileen thought of the comments she had heard the evening before, her anger swelled almost beyond endurance. She thought of the way the newspapers had boasted that London could take it, but now she saw for herself that they understood nothing. If she had not come to Islington and seen for herself what was happening there, she too might not have understood.

They were on the very brink of disaster. No gas, no water, no electricity. Shops ruined, houses demolished, fires burning everywhere. A glimpse of hell. Kitty said that there were thousands on the move, whole families forced to migrate from their homes, their ruined homes, searching for shelter and fresh housing. Thousands? Yes, it was true, a tidal wave of refugees, just like in France, families on the move with their bundles, the few things they had saved from the rubble, perhaps on a handcart or a child's pram.

224

Half the houses down East were already hit. The refugee centres just couldn't cope with all the homeless, couldn't feed them let alone house them. Nowhere to sleep, nowhere to wash. No change of clothes, no way of contacting friends and family. Absolute chaos.

There was a woman with two small children who had been caught in a raid. She was struggling to get them across town on a 38 bus via Piccadilly, but there was blast dust in their hair and clothes and they were generally pretty wretched. One of the other passengers strongly complained that they had been allowed on to the bus at all. She seemed to imply that their desperate situation was somehow their own fault. Was that how the West End diners saw the people of the East End? It was their own fault that they were poor, that they had no shelters, no ack-ack to defend them, their own damned fault that the bombs were falling on their part of town?

At four in the afternoon the raid was heavier than ever. Exhausted, drained of all emotion, beyond even the hunger which had tormented her earlier, Eileen listened as the bombs fell again. What else could be left for them to destroy? Surely the whole district must have been flattened by now?

Kitty was in and out of the shelter, her energy unflagging. She did her best to try and keep them informed. From the wardens' post she was in contact by telephone with her command HQ who had a better picture of what was going on. The only good news she could bring was that anti-aircraft guns had been brought into the area. At last they were fighting back.

It was about five when the All-Clear finally went. Eileen emerged from the shelter feeling giddy and uncertain on her feet. She followed the other men and women outside, listening to their excited happy chatter as though in a dream world. It was incredible to her to be out in the air and actually to hear birds singing in the trees. She just stood there, dumbstruck, listening to the birds in the square. It seemed like a miracle.

There was no sign of Kitty. She felt slightly at a loss without her new friend. She had been so completely in charge that Eileen felt she had come to lean upon her advice and now she floundered, alone in a devastated city.

She knew that she still had to cross London to try and get back to the hotel. She had no idea what Jon must be thinking. As far as he was concerned she had simply walked out on him, disappeared.

At first she considered walking to King's Cross to get the Underground, but the streets to the west of the square were in a tangle of twisted buildings. A heavy explosive bomb had hit Percy Circus and a resulting fire had brought emergency fire equipment and bomb disposal squads into the area, blocking the access roads.

Eileen began to make her way south and west, taking a path into Bloomsbury towards central London. It was impossible to walk in a straight line. The city was in chaos and she was obliged to bypass roads that were blocked or marked with warning UXB notices. Everywhere there were emergency vehicles dashing through the rubble-choked streets, bells clanging. Everywhere the dust floated in the swirling air, fires burned and buildings bore fresh signs of damage.

The walk had become a nightmare journey. Rubble and debris clogged the streets and footpaths, often there were shards of dagger-sharp glass inches deep. Eileen realised that she had before her a mammoth task in reaching the West End. But there seemed to be no buses running, although she saw one that had hit a crater in the roadway, sinking its front wheels up to the axles. Nor did she see a taxi or even a private car. The road was holed in several places, the tarmac cracked and uplifted as though from an earthquake. There were lines and cables down everywhere.

But she was not the only one on the streets. Now that the raid was over people emerged from their underground shelters and Andersons. She saw ashed-faced men and women stumbling among the ruins, or clutching pathetic bundles, staggering almost drunkenly down the road.

Eileen could not believe that less than twenty-four hours before she had been at the Dorchester surrounded by glamorous women and their escorts in smart dinner jackets, eating and drinking and making clever jokes about the East Enders gatecrashing the Savoy.

Now it seemed almost inconceivable that she had been part of such a carefree gathering the night before. She had fooled herself that Jonathan was different, that he somehow rejected the values of his society. Even though she loved him – and she did still love him, she decided – she knew that the gulf that separated them was not just of birth and background, but of personality and attitudes, matters that went much deeper than simple finance and breeding. Had she been serious? Was she out to really try and change him, to try and eradicate years of tradition? She would never be accepted as one of them even if she tried, even if she wanted to be one of them.

How much closer she felt to the people of the square than to the carefree diners of the night before. How much she had admired the bravery and sense of responsibility which Kitty Russell had shown, Kitty who laid her very life on the line for neighbours and strangers alike.

There was no point in deceiving either herself or Jonathan. She could not pretend to be comfortable in Jon's kind of society. It would not be fair to him or to herself. She felt she belonged with the women from the house on the square: Lily, Vi, Kitty and Moira, with friends like Veronica rather than Honor Darcy, with women who were doing something with their lives rather than walking out on it all.

They had warned her that darkness would bring further raids. It was after eight by the time she reached the hotel, filthy with grime and dust, exhausted from her struggle across the city. As she entered the lobby the sirens began their protracted wailing, shattering the exclusive silence and animating the hotel staff into action.

She took her key, aware of raised eyebrows at her appearance, quite uninterested in suggestions that she should go straight down to the hotel shelter. She smiled grimly to herself, confident that the German bombers would not dare to cast their load over Mayfair. After all that she had gone through that day, the wail of a siren held no further horror. She felt suddenly immortal.

As she turned the key in the lock she suddenly realised what it meant. It occurred to her that Jonathan could not be there waiting for her after all. He must have gone out, handing the key in to the desk clerk. But where had he gone? Her complacency turned sharply to fear. She had not been afraid of the raid until now, but the thought that Jon was out there, perhaps walking the streets in search of her, caused her terrible panic. She went to the window and stood there with all the lights out, looking across the park where the barrage balloons soared in the growing dusk light and the faint streaks of the searchlights making arcs in the sky.

About eight-thirty she heard the first crump of heavy artillery guns. Although far across the city the sound of ack-ack was unmistakable. She thought that in the East End the noise must be quite deafening, but somehow she thought that no one would mind. It was above all, a reassuring sound, a sign that something was at last happening to defend London. If the raid continued there would be little sleep for anyone that night, whether in their wet Anderson shelters or their comfortable beds in the West End.

It must have been almost midnight when she heard the pounding on the door. She had been sitting up in a chair near the window absorbed in the sky, watching the extraordinary *son-et-lumière* of the Blitz. She had felt no fear for herself, only apprehension for Jon who was out there somewhere looking for her.

She had to open the door for him. He already knew she was there. The key had gone from the reception and they told him that she had been back for some time. All the way up the stairs – the lift was out of action because of the raid – the pleasure he had felt on learning that she was still alive had evaporated, to be replaced by petulant anger, by wounded pride and a need to demonstrate that she had no right to walk out on him without so much as a word.

As she opened the door the look in his eyes was cold and challenging. He barged past her, arms akimbo, strutting around the suite as though he was lord and master of all he surveyed, including her.

'And where the hell have you been?' He did not wait for an answer. He began to pace the sitting-room, making exaggerated gestures. 'I was out of my mind with worry. You just walked out – vanished! What was I supposed to think? I've been walking the streets for hours.'

She shut the door to the corridor and just stood there, leaning her back against it, unmoving. She was watching him as though she did not recognise him, as though he was a stranger to her. Her face was pale but set. It looked like a mask to him, as though she saw straight through him, through all the bluster. But he was damned if he was going to tell her how sick with worry he had been all day, how when he woke and saw that she had gone he searched for her things, to be certain she had not gone back to Kenley without him. He felt shame and despair for his outburst and the way he had treated her the night before. But if she was waiting for him to apologise, if she thought he was going to crawl to her...

'Well, what's your explanation?' he demanded, turning away. 'You've been missing the whole damned day. I had no idea what had got into your head. I was going to the police.' He turned and saw that she was still there, still staring at him. 'Well, what have you go to say for yourself?'

She saw it then. She recognised the turn of the head, the tilt of the chin. She saw his mother in the hallway of the estate lodge at Charnwood demanding the letter, so sure, so certain that she was in the right, that she had the right to demand an explanation from her.

He had become Jonathan Pemberley. One of them. He was not talking to her, not to the woman he had courted, laughed and talked with, sought out in every moment of his free time at Kenley, brought to London so full of love. He had forgotten her. He was talking to one of his servants after all.

He stood there, arms blocking the room, like some golden god, full of himself, self-righteous, demanding an explanation.

She drew away from the door, turned and walked past him into the bedroom, so full of anger herself that she had to get away from him. But as she went to shut the door in his face he was there before her, his arm outstretched to keep it open. His face glared at her through the growing gap. She was no match for his strength and he was suddenly furious with her, disgusted by her calmness, by her withdrawal. He had worked himself up, his eyes wounded and hot with grievance. Knowing that he was in the wrong had only increased his sense of injury. Instead of falling into his arms with regret for the hours they had been separated, her coldness had poisoned his good intentions, and now it was all her fault again.

She was suddenly frightened of him. She read the warning in his eyes but could not move to avoid the blow. She found herself on the floor, her head spinning. She had struck the side of the bed as she fell and clutched at the bedspread. It lay draped around her now, like some Roman draperies in a piece of play-acting. Nothing seemed real. He was down on his knees, holding her head between his hands, and he was the one who was sobbing, murmuring something over and over again.

He laid her on the bed, but her throat ached so that she could hardly speak. It wasn't where he had hit her, it was because he had used violence upon her. She thought that nothing he could ever say would change that. She turned with her face in the pillow, unable to say a word, wishing that he would go and yet praying that he would stay.

She felt him sit on the opened bed beside her, felt his weight and his warmth as he leant towards her. She was still in a state of shock. From the joy she had felt at seeing him back safely, to the realisation that he could not forget his own anger, the pain of losing him had burnt behind her eyes. She had not felt the blow, but the anger and the humiliation of his rejection she had felt and still felt.

'Eileen, Eileen, my God, I'm sorry. Turn round and look at me.'

His voice was in her ear, leaning across her now to kiss her forehead. One hand stroked her back, but still she could say nothing. He drew her round, on to her back, gentle, but she lay with her head turned away from him, eyes closed, aware only of his warm caressing hands and his lips along the column of her bared neck. He was releasing her shirt, her skirt, soothing her through the material, gentling her, drawing her down into a spreading pool of relaxation.

When his mouth finally found hers, she was no unwilling partner. Her hands slid up into his hair and drew him towards her, welcoming. For a long time she did not bring herself to look at him, lost in the melting world round them. The sound of his breathing was enough for her, the slow exquisite movements of his hands. He was leading her and where he led she was learning, a willing pupil, but more than that. She felt that a whole world of

230

depth and experience lay just beyond their reach. To follow was not enough. She knew that she could answer if only he would ask her the questions she wanted.

He was leading her, hurrying now, barely waiting for her. A sense of urgency, almost of panic, made her suddenly open her eyes. The room was lit by lurid flashes from the sky beyond the window, plunging them into darkness, drawing them back to the light. She wanted to tell him how much she could love him, if only he would wait for her, but she saw from his face that he was already lost. His eyes were firmly shut against her, his face clouded. He was far beyond her and she was left with a terrible sense of loss.

As he moved aside he saw the tear on her cheek but misunderstood the reasons for it. Gently he brushed it aside, kissing her softly, his movements now all delightful consideration. But too late. She held him, cradling his head on her breast out of love, out of disappointment and despair that they would never be able to overcome the great divide that had always separated them.

When he said that he loved her she wanted to believe him. She told him she felt the same and while she spoke, she almost believed it was still true. But she knew that the sudden intimacy of the past two days had opened her eyes. She could no longer fool herself with dreams of a romantic future alone, she knew now that there had to be substance to her feelings, that there had to be something more.

On the train they sat together in silence, though they still held hands. She saw in his face a far away look, as though he had already put the London interlude aside, his thoughts turning once again to the sky and battles yet to come.

Had he ever been hers? She felt that she hardly knew him. There seemed an even greater distance between them now than when they had come away. The journey they had made together had merely served to show them what strangers they were.

She had forgiven him his sudden rush of anger, forgiven but not excused his behaviour. She would not have excused violence in herself or one of her friends. If Moira or anyone else had hit her, she did not believe they could have remained friends, but Jon had to be different. She knew it was a double standard, but for all she knew perhaps this too was part of love.

Eileen had not seen Pat since he went to London for his top-level conference. She knew that he had probably got back to Kenley just after she had left with Jon for their short leave. While she was away he had not been completely out of her thoughts. The air raid in Milton Square had made her realise how much she had come to depend on his company and support, and how much her job now meant to her.

Perhaps that was the reason why Pat's news came as such a shock to her. Coming on top of her time away, it felt like rejection.

'I'm being posted away,' he announced.

They were in the pub at Caversham, the first day back. She had been delighted to see him, eager to get down to some hard work, to fill her mind. Being away from the activity of the station was a deprivation. So much could happen in just 48 hours. At least the base was still operational. The sight of the first Spitfires had warmed her blood, filling her with a sudden rush of pride and a longing to be part of the team once again. She felt this was where she belonged.

Pat's words struck her at the heart of her new-found confidence.

'Going away?' she repeated, disconsolate.

'I'm being posted to head a new team working through the Ministry.'

'In London?'

'Yes, in London.' His thin mouth twisted wryly. 'Out of the frying pan into the fire, isn't that it? I hear you were caught in the Blitz.'

'I went to the Angel to see some friends,' she volunteered.

'Well, the Ministry's not exactly East London, but I couldn't promise that you would be safe.'

She stared at him, unable to say a word. She was still trying to condition her thoughts to accept that he was going away and leaving her.

'It's what I've wanted all along,' he was saying. 'Not quite a free hand, but it's a beginning. And it won't just be in London. There'll be quite a lot of running around to hush-hush establishments. Once you're cleared for security I'll be able to tell you exactly what I have in mind. It's up to you, Eileen, you only have to say the word.'

He must have seen the doubt in her face. It was as though he had read her thoughts.

'Yes, of course, there's Jon.' He sat back and tapped out his pipe against the edge of the table. 'Your private life is your own affair and I don't want to interfere. If you want to stay on here because of him, then I'll understand, but I think you should see that coming with me may be the better option. Have you thought what may happen if you stay? You could be reassigned to another officer. You could end up being posted even further away from Kenley than London.'

She was grateful that he put it so bluntly. He had evidently given the matter considerable thought and was ahead of her. It was very flattering to think that he wanted her to continue to drive him and she knew she would not find another boss quite so human, or so tolerant. All in all, she thought she would be a fool to turn down his offer after they had come through so much together.

'Look, don't make up your mind now,' he said swiftly. 'Think it through and let me have an answer tomorrow. I know you want to discuss it with Jon.'

But she knew suddenly that was the last thing she wanted to do. Jon would never understand the ties that bound her to Pat and his work. He would jump to conclusions, get a twisted impression of their relationship. She had learnt only the day before that he was jealous of her easy camaraderie with the rest of their little group, even of Karol who was so difficult to get to know.

But that was not the reason why she would not tell him about Pat's transfer. She wanted time to reappraise her own future and her new awareness of the limitations of her feelings for Jon. Was the love that she had for him to form the summit and boundaries of her life, or was there more for her, something still waiting to be found?

In the past months since she had worked with Pat she felt

233

herself stretched, pushing out the frontiers of her education and experience. She had discovered her own ambition. Now life was offering her one more opportunity to find out more about herself. Had she any right to turn it down?

'No, Pat, that's not necessary,' she told him suddenly confident. 'I don't need time to think about it. There's no doubt in my mind, no doubt at all, I want to stay with you.'

Sunday September 15th was cloudy with rain sweeping in across the south of England, hardly the best conditions for the most famous day of air combat. The main action seemed centred on the City of London itself as daylight and night bombing raids continued. The RAF strategy was to try and bring down as many enemy planes as possible en route to the capital, shooting them out of the air before they could cast their bombs over the most densely populated areas.

Only the night before Eileen had seen one of those jaunty cinema newsreels with the self-confident voice over that jarred the nerves because you knew the announcer was sitting safe and sound in some studio well away from the action.

'Hitler is getting a sound thrashing...'

And not only was he a non-combatant, secure in his reserved occupation... but his snide upper-class voice only alienated the majority of his audience.

'Wherever the foul sign of the swastika casts its evil shadow –'

It was really over the top. Why did they have to exaggerate with their propaganda? The reality was alarming enough. They still thought of the war in terms of sport; it was all a jolly game, with sporting victors and good-show losers, with scorecards. Perhaps that was how they saw it because they were not in the frontline. Like the social butterflies of the Savoy and Dorchester, so far they were immune from the effects of war, cushioned against its raw brutality.

When the BBC and the newsreels claimed exaggerated British victories it did nothing but harm to the morale of its frontline defenders. The propaganda claimed a five to one ratio of success in the air, but the pilots themselves knew that it was not true. Either they recognised the reports as lies or they came to believe

234

that their squadron, their own section was lagging behind their comrades, that they were not up to scratch. False propaganda blighted morale.

But now that the whole of London had become a target they would surely have to change their tune. On the day that Eileen and Jon had returned to Kenley, one lone bomber had hit a corner of Buckingham Palace. Although no one was injured and the damage was relatively slight in comparison with the destruction in the East End, this single incident had served to demonstrate that even the Royal Family were not totally immune to the risks of modern warfare.

Back on standby, Jon could not settle into the routine of the station. He had lost the impetus, the driving power that had fired him. Now that his leave was over the future stretched out before him, one continuous round of conflict and tension ahead, a constant battle of will to stay alert and therefore alive.

The squadron was full of new faces. To Jon they all seemed like schoolboys. The sight of their rosy cheeks and nonchalant arrogance set his teeth on edge. He knew that their life expectancy was down to a matter of days, weeks if they were lucky. He felt a million years older than them, alone and isolated. He knew that they regarded him with something like awe, not only for his status as squadron veteran but because he had survived for so long without injury. They put up with his moods out of admiration. They thought him a grump, perhaps a little combat-happy: 'they all go nuts after a while.'

He knew he had thought the same about Karol. After Pepper's death, he saw Karol struggling through a period of readjustment, but Karol had survived more than the German bullets, he had survived his own neurosis. Now that those same fears and morbid obsessions had come to haunt him, Jon discovered that Karol was getting married.

Jon knew the girl. He had seen her round often enough, the young WAAF officer who looked after his dog, Lara, whenever he was flying. She had an admin. job on the base where they were indulgent enough to allow her to take Lara to lie under her desk while Karol was away. He thought that her name was Ruth. He remembered Karol stooping to pat Lara on the head as he left, then turning to pat his WAAF officer on the head, knowing he had them both to come back to.

That day, Karol flew with his squadron of Hurricanes. He was nearing the end of his tour of duty. There was talk of a transfer to another unit behind the lines, up-country somewhere. Karol had apparently been seeing a lot of Eileen's officer, Pat Fairweather. Whatever it was seemed rather hush-hush, and Jon rather resented the way Eileen had said nothing about it to him. He felt increasingly isolated.

Karol landed back at the field about lunchtime. He was full of complaints about the filthy weather that had settled in. He said that conditions were becoming impossible and that the fighting was spreading over the London suburbs. He himself had been involved in a dogfight somewhere near Hammersmith on the river, but some of his squadron had flown over the Houses of Parliament and Big Ben. One enemy plane had been shot down and crashed into Oxford Circus. The battle had really come home to the heart of the capital.

In the afternoon Jon was scrambled to intercept a second wave of German bombers and fighters heading up the Thames. Everything the RAF Command had that was air-worthy was thrown into the battle to meet this force of 400 enemy fighters protecting 100 Dornier bombers. The situation was grave.

'What reserves have we?'

'There are none.'

Eileen was aware of the desperate atmosphere that had been building at the station throughout the day. She read the tension on the faces all round her, but there was no discussion. It had gone beyond talking now.

Looking out at the rainclouds, Eileen was ill at ease, aware of something threatening in the atmosphere. In the back of her mind she recognised the sensation, although she could not put a name to it. No one openly talked about the power of evil and yet that was what it was. A sense of evil in the air. A brooding atmosphere that could not be defined, insubstantial, like mist on the land, like smoke before wind.

Out there beyond the horizon, death laid its hand across the land, over town and countryside alike, there was no safety. And somewhere out there Jon was at odds with an enemy force of enormous proportions, with more than his own life at stake.

Perhaps she knew already. He was not overdue, the planes of his squadron had not yet returned, but when she saw Pat walking over the grass towards her she knew.

She met his eyes but said nothing. It was Pat who made the first move, taking her by the hand. She read the message on his face before he could find the words to tell her.

'It's Jon, isn't it? He's been shot down.'

'We've just got word.' He hung on to her hand. 'He came in over the City. They've taken him to hospital. There's still hope, Eileen, there's still a chance he will live.'

Chapter Eight

It was a white wheel or a saucer hovering almost directly overhead. He had never seen a craft like it. It emerged out of the clouds, the only object within his range of vision, descending then rising as though bounced on air currents in the sky. There came a persistent ringing in his ears, a harsh metallic droning like water down a drain, a ringing in some metal container, grating, mounting panic like wanting to be sick, a mixture of heat and ice. Struggling for the surface, fighting your way up, aware of voices now, aware of moving faces and hands passing back and forth before the white wheel.

'Hello, old man, back with us?' The echo of the words that were recognisable through the mist of noises and movement bounced back at him, one moment full of startling clarity that was almost painful and then drifting away again.

'No, don't try to sit up. You're doing fine, just fine.'

He felt weak as a baby. The world was still spinning but the face of the man who spoke had now settled into focus, a pair of bright dark eyes meeting his across a white mask. It all seemed to be white, but what he had thought was a wheel appeared suddenly to be an overhead light, huge, flat and round as a dish.

He realised that he was lying flat on his back staring up at the ceiling, but a ceiling where? It was not his billet that was certain, and for some inexplicable reason his mind started to play tricks on him and he thought it was his old room, the nursery back at Charnwood. He was almost about to say something but it was as though his mind was operating on two quite separate and distinctive plains. As one half of his memory dipped and swooped back into his childhood throwing up the scene with almost frightening clarity, the other more rational half of his brain told him it was nonsense, that these were events of almost twenty years before, even though they appeared as vivid as what he had done only yesterday. Yesterday...

He remembered the billet, he knew suddenly that he was a flier, but – ah, he had it now! It was the hotel, the strange room at the hotel just off Green Park and he was still on leave, with no need to panic. But who?

'Eileen?'

'What's that, old man? What did he say, nurse?'

'I think he called for someone, sir.' It was a woman's voice, drawing close now, a woman's presence close to him.

'Eileen? Is that you, Eileen?'

'Married, is he? Better check it out, nurse. Well then, old man, can you hear me? Don't worry about a thing. You'll be right as rain.'

He was suddenly aware that he was alone. The walls of whiteness closed in upon him once again and he was full of an appalling terror...

'Eileen!'

He saw them now. They were diving out of the cloud, thick white cloud after the rain. Below him was the river, but it had no colour except fire. The whole world was on fire, burning up, burning up before his eyes just like Dutch. Fire in the fuselage, spreading fire...

He screamed. He felt the shock waves pass out of his body and through the air, buffeting the plane as it fell, twisting, burning, falling, dropping like a stone...

They gave him an injection as they held him down. It took three of them to hold him, but after a few minutes the drug began to take effect and he quietened. At last they released him, pulling up the sheets, white against his white face, his pallor broken only by colourless beads of sweat on his forehead. The doctor wrote a sentence or two on the clipboard notes and hung them back at the foot of the bed.

'Keep an eye on him, nurse. If he doesn't settle we'll have to double the dose. The next 48 hours will be critical.'

*

239

'Well?' Veronica sat on the edge of the driving seat with the window wound down as Moira emerged from the admin. office.

'I've got it! A 48 at last! I can't believe it.'

She got into the van beside her still stunned by her good fortune. After weeks of waiting she had really given up all hope of getting away in time. Veronica reached over and gave her a quick hug before starting up the engine and pushing the old van into gear.

'It's marvellous news,' she said as they rumbled along the pitted perimeter road of the camp towards the gate. 'You must let Lily know as soon as possible.'

'I'll try and get a telephone call through tonight. Or send a telegram.'

'And Eileen. Don't forget that she promised she would go with you.'

'Oh, I know she offered, but I . . .'

'Don't you think that she meant it? You're wrong, Moira. She's been very worried. I know she wants to go with you.'

Moira looked uncertain but she wanted to be reassured. As her excitement at getting the pass evaporated, she began to consider the real purpose behind her journey and she began to be afraid. The thought of making that train journey up to London alone filled her with dread. The experience was bad enough. She needed someone who knew and cared enough to go along with her.

But as it happened it was Eileen who managed to get through first on the telephone that night, breaking her news about Jon's crash and announcing her plans to move to London.

'Lily will put you up,' Moira told her over the whistling telephone line. 'She'll be glad to have you there. And it will be dead handy for Bart's Hospital.' She paused, feeling her way warily. 'When were you thinking of going up?'

'As soon as I can. I'm more or less a free agent just now, shifting some of Pat's papers up and down. Obviously I want to get to see Jon as quickly as I can.' She reacted to a note in Moira's voice. 'Why? Moira – you haven't heard anything, have you?'

'Yes, I've got it at last. A 48 hour, that's all, but it's enough.'

'Oh Moira, love, I'm so pleased. When can we go?'

'We? You mean you still want to come?'

'I promised, didn't I? Anyway, now it all works in fine. When does your pass run?'

'From tomorrow afternoon's duty.'
'Right then, let's get down to plans.'

After an emotional farewell with Veronica, Moira met Eileen at the station in the nearby town ready to catch the first train up to London. She had just brought a small holdall and stood at the ticket barrier looking pale and very frightened. Eileen's heart went out to her as she hurried over to her and they walked to the train. Eileen talked lightly, trying to take Moira's mind off the next 24 hours, complaining that she had not been able to borrow a car to move her suitcases up to London.

It was a relief to both of them not to be alone. The shadow of the medical profession had fallen across their otherwise healthy lives, tainting both their futures. To be alone with their thoughts, prey to fears and prophecies, was a torture which neither of them could endure. Having a friend close at hand was a real comfort.

Moira had said there would be no trouble in arranging a room for Eileen in her grandmother's house. It was the ideal position, situated halfway between her new post at the Ministry and Pat's house in Highgate. But more important than either of these, it was barely fifteen minutes away from St Bartholomew's Hospital.

Lily was ready and waiting to welcome them. She and Moira fell into each other's embrace and Eileen was deeply affected to see the tears bright on their cheeks. There was no need to say anything at all about Moira's dilemma, understanding was plain in Lily's face.

'I'm sorry I missed you before, Eileen,' Lily said, drawing apart from her grand-daughter to give her some attention. 'But I always knew that you would be coming back.'

Eileen had felt it too. There was always something welcoming and familiar about the house in the square. There was an aura of comfort and safety about it, even in the threat of continual air raid warnings.

'Kitty's on duty, and Vi's at work, but they'll both be back for supper tonight. We eat early these days – so we can get a hot meal before the nightly show begins.'

'Is it still as bad as before?' asked Eileen, following Lily up the narrow little stairs with her suitcase.

'An incendiary landed on the church only last night. I spotted it coming down – you get a marvellous view from the roof, you know, you must come up and see it – and it didn't do much damage.' She stopped abruptly on the upper landing. 'But you'll have heard the worst, I suppose? About the bomb on Marble Arch tube?'

They had not heard a thing. Completely absorbed by their own worries they had not heard how the Underground station received a direct hit while hundreds huddled on the platforms for shelter.

'Everyone thought it was one of the safest in London,' said Lily. 'It was heavily reinforced with girders but it seems that the bomb fell between them. Eighteen were killed, caught by the blast, all naked. The force of the explosion ripped the tiles from the walls and killed another two, like arrows, they said.'

'Where can people go now then if even the deepest shelters aren't safe?'

'You know how it is, Eileen,' said Lily with an air of resignation. 'They say that we always prepare to fight the last war and not the next. There we were, all issued with our gasmasks, with trenches dug in the parks, and all because the generals got it into their heads that this war would be another 1914.' She gave a sour little smile. 'Mark my words, the next war won't be anything like this one either.'

'The next war? Blimey, you're an optimist, Lily!' exclaimed Moira grimly, 'we'll all be bloody lucky to survive this one!'

'Kitty told me she was lucky to grab a bath between alerts.'

'Well, I warn you both, the sirens are apt to go from six to eight times a day,' Lily told them. 'Usually it starts about six, often with a lull around nine, but then it gets going and we have to grin and bear it until dawn. Every night on the trot. And now the nights are drawing in for the winter it won't help matters.'

They had arrived outside Moira's old room and Lily opened the door.

'You should get some rest, darling,' she told Moira. 'I'll call you when supper is ready. I hope you're hungry because you mustn't eat any breakfast tomorrow.'

The colour died in Moira's face and Lily slipped an arm round her waist. 'Don't you worry about a thing. I'll be there with you all the time.'

242

'What – what time do we have to be there?'

'At ten. Don't worry, darling, this time tomorrow it will all be over and done with.'

Moira gave them both a wan smile and retreated to the door of her room. 'I think I'll try and take a nap,' she said evasively. 'Shut it all out. Don't forget to call me later, will you?'

After Moira had gone inside, Lily met Eileen's gaze and they moved on up the next flight of stairs to the floor above.

'This will be your room if you like it,' said Lily, opening the door on the left. 'Otherwise there is an attic bedroom, but it's very large and difficult to heat now that winter's coming.'

'No, this is lovely.' Eileen took in the high bed, the thick pink and white rug, the black lead hearth and polished wooden shutters. There was a large imposing Victorian wardrobe with round feet and mirrored doors, and a low armchair that matched the deep blue curtains. 'I'm really very grateful to you for taking me in like this,' she said spontaneously. 'The Air Force pay quite a handsome allowance.'

Lily waved her hands as though casting out devils.

'I'm not concerned about money, my dear. Why, we may wake up tomorrow and find that the house has gone! If there's one thing we've learnt it's that money doesn't count for much any more. There are more important questions just now.'

Eileen watched her as she went and firmly closed the door. There was a conspiratorial gleam in the blue eyes as they looked at her.

'Tell me honestly, Eileen, how long have you known about Moira's condition?' She saw Eileen's hesitation and frowned. 'Look, Moira has told me that she is no more than six or seven weeks. I don't believe her. Something has been troubling her for a long time now. I'm right, aren't I? She is more than that?' She paused, expecting some response but when Eileen said nothing she added quickly, 'I have to know, dear, because if she's more than twelve weeks...'

'Is it really dangerous?'

'It's always dangerous. I won't pretend otherwise, Eileen, I've seen many women go through it. Things can go wrong. But if she's more than three months pregnant it makes it doubly difficult.' She sighed. 'I'm not asking you to betray a confidence. Moira doesn't want me worried, but she doesn't understand what's involved.' She sat down on the edge of the bed, prepared to press home her case. 'You know, in my younger days it was thought rather radical to bear a child out of marriage. There was even a vogue for it in the last war. Women claimed what they called "the privilege of motherhood" and saw it as their duty to have children for the country. But now that seems very nationalistic, doesn't it? A bit like Hitler's *Küche, Kirche, Kinder* – but this war is quite different. It seems irresponsible to bring any child into a world like this with so much death and destruction.'

'Then you're not opposed to what Moira wants.'

'No, certainly not. Anyway, it would be her decision. It's her life, her body, and she must make her own decisions – in everything.' She caught the look in Eileen's eyes. 'I want the best for her, Eileen, as you do.'

'Yes, I do. You're right, Lily, she is more than twelve weeks. It happened the last time she was here in London.'

Lily got up and put a reassuring hand on her shoulder.

'Thank you, my dear. I knew that you and I would get on well together. Now we will both see to it that Moira can start again.'

The eggs which Eileen had packed were very welcome as there were hardly any to be seen in London these days. Lily immediately incorporated them into the ingredients for their supper which was timed for five-thirty.

Vi arrived back just after five, looking tired and drawn. She was in her nursing overalls and carried a heavy bag of first-aid things which she had taken round all the school shelters in the district. When she saw Moira and Eileen the mask of tiredness fell away and she greeted them both warmly, delighted to learn that Eileen would be staying now she had been posted to work in London.

When Kitty turned up, filthy from yellow blast dust and dying for a bath before the nightly raid, Eileen really felt that she was welcome. She saw that Kitty was as pleased as she was that they had met again and could pursue their instinctive friendship. She felt that Kitty would have hugged her if she had not been so caked in dirt.

'What's wrong, Eileen?' she asked, guessing that something

was wrong, and Eileen was obliged to tell them about Jon, about his crash and how he had been taken to Bart's Hospital.

It was difficult for her to talk about him before them. She was eager to tell her news as simply and briefly as possible, just giving the facts of the crash as she knew them, afraid of their pity. She saw that they were appalled, even Moira who had heard the essential details before.

Tomorrow when there was a chance she would go to Bart's and find out the worst for herself. Until then there was nothing she could do. The reports from the hospital had all been the same: yes, he was still on the critical list but he was as comfortable as could be expected. What did that mean? What was the extent of his injuries? No one would tell her over the telephone, but when she went there she was determined to find out everything.

'We'll go together in the morning,' Kitty said unexpectedly. 'Bart's is very close by, you'll see.'

Eileen gave her a smile of thanks and turned back to help with the supper as though to close the subject for that night. They all went their separate ways until the meal was ready. Kitty announced she was taking over the bathroom and soon the old pipes were loudly complaining at the rush of water upstairs.

It was less than ten minutes later when the lights suddenly went out. Eileen was plunged into darkness in the kitchen, knocking a dish from the dresser, the crash echoed by sharp little exclamations throughout the house.

'Terrific!' Her eyes searched for Lily's in the gloom. 'Are you all right, Lily? The electricity must have failed.' Her voice died away as the sinister note of an air-raid siren filled the square outside.

'Come on, Eileen, give me your hand.'

Together, she and Lily found their way to the foot of the flight of stairs that led up to the ground floor of the house and the front door into the street.

'Lily, are you there?' It was Vi's voice calling out from the landing above. 'Are you alone? Do you want some help?'

'No, it's all right. Eileen's here with me. Where are the others?'

Kitty was still in the bath, cursing and muttering under her breath as she struggled to get herself out and dry and find her clothes again.

'Where's Moira?'

'I haven't seen her,' answered Vi's voice. 'She must still be up in her room.' They heard her stumbling up another flight and then calling out Moira's name, but there was no reply.

'She can't have gone out. We would have heard her.'

'Perhaps she went back to sleep.'

'With all this racket going on? I don't like it.' Eileen went and knocked on the bathroom door. 'Kitty, where's your torch? Is it in your bag?'

She heard a lot of movement behind the door and a curse as what were obviously the contents of Kitty's satchel emptied themselves out across the bathroom floor. After a few more muttered comments, the lock was slid back and a naked arm appeared waving a torch.

'Bloody thing. I forgot I had it! I'll be right there,' she promised, 'as soon as I fish my shirt out of the bath!'

Eileen found the switch and a beam of yellow light cast a powerful swathe through the black landing. She hurried on up the stairs towards Moira's room, hearing Vi moving round in the darkness up above her.

'Vi – what's wrong?'

Vi's sharp cry had alerted her, but the silence that followed was ominous. As Eileen ran up the final flight of stairs to the landing and turned the corner, the light from the torch caught Vi and Moira in a spotlight.

Vi turned from leaning across Moira's crumpled body, her face a ghastly yellow in the torch beam. Moira lay with her knees under her chin and her head thrown back in the deep shadows.

'My God! What happened?'

'She must have slipped in the dark – Look, Eileen, I left my medical bag downstairs in the kitchen.'

'I'll get it for you.'

'No! Let's try and get her on to the bed first.' She moved to Moira's head and indicated that Eileen should take her feet.

'Should we move her?' She was suddenly tense and afraid. Moira was so still, lying at such an awkward angle.

'We have to,' Vi snapped back. 'Look!' She thrust forward her hand, palm forward, into the glare of the light. It was bright with blood. 'She's haemorrhaging.'

Eileen saw that the carpet around Moira's legs was dark, wet

246

and sticky to the touch. She barely refrained from crying out, and her eyes met Vi's wide stare.

'Take her legs,' Vi told her.

At the first movement there was a soft moaning and Moira began to stir. She rolled her head from side to side, clearly in pain.

'Moira, Moira, can you hear me? We're going to move you into the bedroom, all right? Just be brave, love.' She nodded to Eileen who took the weight of her legs and, balancing the torch in one hand so that some light was cast ahead, they lifted her. She screamed with pain, a sound that cut the silence of the house and seemed to echo down all the flights of stairs and earthed in the ground. But they did not stop to put her down. Vi determinedly backed in through the bedroom door, manoeuvring to carry her round the corner. While Vi held her, propped against the side of the bed, Eileen used the torch to pull the covers off and find extra sheets to lay beneath her.

'Get some towels,' Vi suggested, watching as Eileen ransacked the wardrobe and chest of drawers, moving with the single torch beam like a burglar round the room.

As they were lifting Moira on to the bed, they could hear Lily calling out from below, anxious to know what had happened.

Eileen discovered a candle in her progress around the room and lit it near the head of the bed.

'I'll take the torch and fetch your bag,' she suggested. 'I'll be twice as quick if I can see my way down to the basement.'

On the stairs she met Lily slowly climbing her way up.

'What's wrong? What's happened to Moira?'

'She slipped when the lights went out.'

'I heard a scream.'

'I have to fetch Vi's bag quickly.' Eileen hurried on down the stairs, unwilling to try and explain to Lily the thoughts and fears that were now burning in her own brain. There was so much blood! Would Moira be all right? Should she go to hospital?

By the time she had raced down to the basement and discovered Vi's medical bag propped up under a chair beneath the kitchen table, the first unmistakable drone of bombers overhead could be heard.

Kitty appeared in the doorway dressed in a very curious combination of clothes, having thrown on the first things that came to hand. Eileen told her what had happened, without stopping in her search among the kitchen cupboards for anything else that might prove useful to Vi upstairs. Kitty joined her, revealing a shelf of old oil lamps under the sink.

As they started back up the stairs the local ack-ack guns opened up with a loud roar. Eileen knew that Kitty thought they should all get out of the house as quickly as possible, but then Kitty had not seen Moira. There seemed no alternative but to keep Moira where she was, although the thought of being trapped on the fourth floor during an air raid scared her to death.

Panting, Eileen redoubled her efforts, pulling herself up by the banister rails, aware of the flashing lights streaking through the high windows on every landing.

In Moira's bedroom they found Vi and Lily crouched over Moira trying to staunch the flow of blood. Kitty quickly lit an oil lamp while Eileen opened Vi's bag and emptied the contents onto the discarded bed cover on the floor.

Moira was rolling from side to side on the bed with the pain, her knees drawn up and down in spasm. Her face was white even in the glow of the lamps and her hair clung to her forehead limp with sweat. She did not seem to be really aware of their presence, although she clutched Lily's hand as the spiral of pain increased. The pain seemed trapped inside her, struggling to escape, swelling, tearing across her body and round her back. Blood flowed, thick, dark, alarming. There was more blood than Eileen had ever seen in her life. Even in the strange light from the lamps it glowed rich and dark, the life force ebbing from her body.

She's going to die, thought Eileen. No one can lose that much blood and live. She stared at Vi's set face, despairing, distrustful, almost ready to blame her and yet at the same time astonished by her calm authority and the efficiency with which she gave Moira a pain-killing injection.

Even with the shutters closed firmly against the raid outside, the room had an unearthly quality. The women knelt and stood round the bedside as though in some extraordinary tableau, almost a parody of the Bethlehem story. While outside the night raged with sound and thunder, the whole sky over London was rent apart with the fireworks of war.

As the drug took effect, Moira seemed to quieten and her breathing eased. She was still bleeding and felt very cold to the touch although the room was rather warm, but the pain had eased. She turned her head and seemed to catch sight of them for the first time, acknowledging their presence with her eyes although she did not say a word.

Vi told her that she was going to be all right with a kind of certainty in her voice that did a great deal to reassure her friends. She also gave her the news that she was losing blood, that she was sure to miscarry.

'I'll stay with you,' she promised, 'all the time.'

Kitty offered to fetch a doctor but then realised what the rest of them had been thinking. Moira would miscarry and there was nothing that a doctor could do for her, but they alone knew that the accident was in its way providential, that it had usurped a more deliberate action by less than 24 hours. With no questions asked.

Although Kitty had to report for duty, none of the others would be moved from the house to leave Vi and Moira alone. But up there among the crashes and tracers of the guns, they felt as though they were all tempting fate. The drone of the aircraft was even more intense, the whistle of every bomb as it fell all the more hideous, the tremble of relief when it had passed all the greater.

One, two, three – this is it! No, over – and here's another . . .

There was something about the dark which made the night raids all the more terrifying. Faced with that random evil falling from the skies, all the old primitive fears of childhood returned to haunt you. Crouched low near the foot of the bed, Eileen felt herself once more a frightened child, scared of the dark, of the shadows that lurked so menacingly in the corners. That same fear of the unknown, of the great terror outside just waiting to get you was what she felt now, cast out to take her chance.

It put into question all thoughts of eternity and predestination. Did she believe in God or fate, or did she just accept that death on a night like this was simply a matter of lottery, the random finger on the trigger who signed her death warrant?

Suddenly it all seemed pointless: the struggle to get ahead, to make something of your life when in one brief second a falling bomb could wipe it all away, as though you had never existed. What did any of it mean?

One, two, three, four – there came a crash so close that the old

249

house shook violently. The oil lamp on the chair slid forward and would have fallen had Vi not caught it. Outside there was the sound of crashing masonry and smashing glass as the windows fell from their framés somewhere along the road.

Eileen went to the window, looking through a gap in the shutters down on to the tiny pockets of garden at the back of the houses. Lit up in the flashes of the lurid overhead lights, she saw the family next door scurry away from their Anderson shelter and disappear into the darkness.

A gasp of pain brought her back into the other struggle going on within the room behind her. Moira gasped for air, clutching at Lily's hand with white knuckled fingers as her body arched and contracted. She groaned as the pain swelled, brushing off Lily's soft words, her face white then grey as she pushed the pain out of her. Vi was ready with cloths to take the rubbery tissue from her body, vanishing from the room with the torch, as Lily and Eileen soothed and covered the exhausted woman on the bed. It was over at last.

Eileen herself felt weak and stunned as she drew a blanket close around Moira's shivering body, stroking the damp hair back from her face. She felt a surge of relief and pity for her, and anger for the pain and suffering she had endured. In days past countless women had suffered and died with this. It seemed so wrong that they should have to pay so dear a price while men seemed to get away scot-free.

The anger she felt must have shown in her face because as she looked up she met Lily's blue gaze and knew she understood.

The next morning Eileen popped her head round the door of Moira's room to see how she was. Vi was still sitting by the bed and she looked up as Eileen appeared, quickly moving towards the door so as not to disturb Moira who was sleeping soundly.

'How is she?'

'Much better. She fell into a deep sleep about five o'clock and her temperature is getting back to normal.'

'She lost so much blood.'

'She will be weak for a while yet. When did you say she had to be back in camp?'

'The day after tomorrow.'

'She should be able to manage that, but she'll have to avoid all heavy duties for a while.'

'I'll let Veronica know. She'll try and cover for her, perhaps even get the MO to do something.'

But Vi looked alarmed. 'She mustn't tell anyone.'

'Of course not! Don't worry, Vi, we'll put our heads together and think of something. I'm just grateful that you were here to help. I don't know what might have happened to Moira otherwise.'

Just then Kitty's voice called out from below and Eileen realised she was wanted.

'I have to go, Vi. Kitty's promised to show me the way to Bart's. I'm going to see Jon.'

'Keep your fingers crossed. I'm sure he'll be all right.'

'Yes, I do hope so.'

It was her only chance to go to the hospital before she was required to report for duty at the Ministry later in the afternoon. Kitty walked her part of the way along St John Street, pointing her in the right direction as she entered the City of London. Kitty's bright chatter helped to take her mind off what lay ahead, staving off the moment she had dreaded.

In the past few days she had moved like an automaton, going through the motions of everyday living, even through the move to London and the nightmare with Moira the evening before. She had not allowed herself the leisure to think about all that had happened. She had barely reconciled herself to the new relationship between them which demanded so much more from her than she had anticipated, when everything changed. She could scarcely come to terms with the thought of losing him.

She was left with the overwhelming sensation that somehow she was to blame. Either through her own selfishness, her decision to go with Pat, or through not loving Jon enough, expecting more than he could give.

She could not get the memory of that day in Piccadilly out of her mind. It returned again and again to torment her. She remembered the excitement and apprehension on Veronica's face turning to sudden horror at the sight of the man she loved.

Eileen resolved that whatever opposition she met at the

251

hospital she would make them let her in to see him. However ill he was. She wanted to know the worst at once.

Round her the very ruins seemed to shout at her, casting their shadow over her unhappy walk. She looked around her at the destruction, thinking that the few brief weeks had taken their toll on old London. The proximity of the docklands meant that the most historic parts of the city had come under attack. The dome of St Paul's Cathedral rose majestically on the southern skyline, rising up from the ruins of the surrounding buildings, stark and defiant, a miraculous symbol of survival and hope to them all.

As she approached the entrance to St Bartholomew's she saw that even the hospitals were not immune from attack. There was evidence of a fire and shrapnel holes pitted the walls as she crossed to the porter's lodge and asked for directions to Jon's ward. There was a notice hanging just inside the door reminding staff that it was forbidden to cross the yard at night in their white gowns.

Up the bare steps and corridors, her shoes ringing on the spartan linoleum, Eileen felt a chill about the place, a sense of clinical detachment from the tragedies that faced them on every side. Eileen passed several men on crutches, their worn faces marked with the pallor of long weeks in hospital, and her heart sank. Now that the moment had come at last, she was horrified at what she might find. Was he dying or disfigured, scarred or without sight? The vivid memory of Tim's face flashed into her mind, echoed by the story of Dutch going down, his plane still on fire, trapped inside the burning wreckage.

She found a nurse at last. A gleam of recognition came into the woman's face, replacing irritation at being interrupted, and she promptly led Eileen through a ward of neat metal beds which were all occupied.

'You must be very busy,' Eileen said politely, apologising for taking up her time. 'Are these all service men?'

'Blitz victims,' replied the nurse curtly. 'Mostly splinters. Glass, that's the worst thing, can cut you to pieces. We have the theatres working 24 hours a day down in the basements.'

'And Jon?'

The nurse stared at her with suspicion and decided against saying anything. 'You must speak to the doctor. Doctor Walters, that is.'

252

'Is he on duty now?'

'*She* will do her rounds a little later. You ought to be able to get a few words then.' She paused outside another doorway. 'He's in the bed just on the right. He'll be pleased to see you, but don't stay too long.'

Jon lay in a narrow iron bed in a sea of white linen. Behind his head was a stack of hard hospital pillows, wedging him into a semi-upright position. The bedcovers were raised by some form of cradle as though to avoid friction with his body, but there were no bandages visible, no signs to indicate what could be wrong with him.

In fact, his face seemed remarkably the same. Yes, he was somewhat paler than usual but that was only to be expected. He had a cut on his chin but it was superficial and could as easily have come from a slip while shaving as from the death plunge of an aircraft from the skies.

For a moment Eileen's heart skipped and she thought that someone somewhere had made a mistake. All those gloomy reports, the hesitant replies over the telephone when she had tried to force some kind of forecast from unwilling nurses, all that had led her to believe the very worst. Jon was at death's door, or his injuries were so extensive, so appalling that no one dared to tell her the truth.

But looking at him now, and looking around at the others in the ward who all seemed to bear obvious signs of their injuries, Eileen felt a surge of optimism that life might not be so very different for them after all. He was going to be all right.

He suddenly caught the movement near his bed and turned his head in the nest of pillows to face her. The look that came into his face as he recognised her was beautiful. His eyes filled with light and joy so that no one who saw him could have doubted how much he loved her.

'Eileen.'

It was only when he raised a hand towards her that she realised how weak he was. His forehead creased with the effort required to raise the arm from the white bed and stretch it out towards her. She plunged forward, seizing his hand with both of hers and holding on to it for dear life, deeply moved.

'My darling, darling, are you all right?'

He smiled at the absurdity of the question, the fact that he was

253

lying there, trapped in the bed unable to move, with the threat of the Blitz bombing outside.

'Fit as a fiddle,' he assured her. 'Come here. Let me take a look at you.' He drew her nearer and she went willingly, feeling the lack of strength in his hands, stunned by his new frailty.

She sat on the hard chair next to his bed, moving it round so that he could look at her without having to strain his head round. They held hands, gazing at each other, perfectly content.

'I wanted to come before,' she said, 'as soon as I heard, but they wouldn't let me.'

'I wanted to see you so much.'

'And now you will be able to see me every day! Yes, it's true, I've been posted here to London. I'm living just ten minutes up the road. I'll be able to spend all my free time here with you.'

'But that's wonderful! You're so clever, Eileen, getting a move up here just to be with me.'

Eileen looked away, trying to hide the guilt she felt. How was he to know that she had intended moving to London even before his accident? She wondered now how she could have been so callous, glibly going ahead with her own plans and not even discussing it with him at all. What was the matter with her? Didn't she know how lucky she was to have someone like Jon in love with her? And he did love her. As though he sensed her sudden mood he said gently,

'You're a marvellous woman, Eileen. I don't deserve you.'

'Oh nonsense.' She felt the heat burning her cheeks. 'I've been so worried about you.'

'Silly girl. Bloody stupid thing I did, that's all. I didn't see it coming.'

She didn't want him to talk about the crash. Already he was grasping her hand tighter, getting himself all worked up. Far better to ignore it.

'When I get out of here, we'll have to make up for lost time,' he told her with a playful gleam in his eyes. 'Though, mind you, some of the nurses in here are smashers – isn't that right, nurse?'

Eileen looked round to find the nurse who had conducted her into the ward standing behind her chair.

'Come on now, Mr Pemberley, don't show me up in front of your young lady.'

254

Eileen was not sure how she felt about that description. The nurse took her presence there for granted, and seemed to know her name in advance. She wondered if Jon had been talking about her. She watched as the nurse fussed with Jon's pillows, all her stiff actions rebuking him for moving in the neatly ordered bed.

'I think that's enough excitement for one day,' she announced briskly. 'Miss Howard will come back and see you another day.'

'Every day,' said Eileen emphatically, resenting the way in which she was being hurried away from him. She clung on to his hand, unwilling to let him go, but the nurse was waiting, giving her a hard stare across Jon's back. Eileen knew that she wanted her to go so that she could have a word with the doctor before her rounds. Giving in to the inevitable, Eileen bent to kiss Jon awkwardly on the mouth, aware of his cold, dry lips.

That and the look in his eyes made her suddenly afraid. She saw that he was really quite ill and alarm flickered between them like an electric current, as though they were afraid that they might never see one another again.

Eileen followed the nurse down the aisle of beds, looking back towards his bed where he sat against the wall of pillows watching her. As she reached the door of the ward he raised his hand weakly in farewell, and she had to turn sharply away as tears started into her eyes.

'The doctor will see you now.' The nurse had guided her towards a bench in the echoing corridor, leaving her there while she fetched Doctor Walters.

'Miss Howard?'

Eileen looked up into the face of a woman perhaps ten years her senior. She had a pale face with a rash of freckles across the cheekbones and a mop of unruly chestnut hair that gave her an air of the country. The white coat she wore hung open over a plain olive green dress and had clearly seen better days. A stethoscope hung half-heartedly out of one of her large patch pockets.

'I understand that you are Mr Pemberley's fiancée. I just wanted to have a word with you about his condition.' She sat down on the bench, unaware of Eileen's attempt to correct her first observation. 'You were lucky that you came today. He's been semi-conscious most of the rest of the time. He was very lucky, you know.' When there was no response she leant forward to offer encouragement and what she obviously thought was sympathy. 'You mustn't upset yourself unduly. He'll get over it in time; they all do. Once he's well enough we'll arrange a transfer to the prosthesis unit at Roehampton.'

'The what?'

'Prosthesis: false limb unit. They can do some pretty marvellous things these days – mind you, they're getting a lot of practice.' As though she had just realised the reaction her cheerful words had evoked in her companion she lapsed into silence, the dawning of awareness creeping slowly over her face. 'But you have just seen him,' she protested, rather angry. 'You must have known.'

Eileen dumbly shook her head, still reeling from the shock and unable to concentrate. The doctor's voice picked up again, full of that brisk professional optimism.

'It's not really the end of the world, you know. It could have been a great deal worse. He only lost the tibia and fibula – the lower part of his leg – while some of the others ...'

'Which leg?'

'I beg your pardon?'

'I asked which leg he has lost,' repeated Eileen coldly.

'Well, the left, actually,' said the doctor rather too blandly, as though she could not see what difference it made which leg he had lost. The point surely was that he had one leg left and was not a total write-off. 'He's come out of it extremely well,' she pointed out, rather annoyed that her enthusiasm was having little effect on her audience. 'Life must go on. It won't do him any good at all to see you upset. It's up to you to keep up his morale.' She paused significantly. 'Sometimes it takes a while before we know what effect it has on the mind.'

Eileen stared at her. Was she saying that Jon could go crazy, that when he realised the extent of his accident he would sink into a deep depression – or worse?

'Just take it steadily,' the doctor was saying. 'Give him a few days before you mention it.'

'Mention it?' The last thing Eileen could imagine would be sitting at Jon's bedside discussing his amputated leg. She thought back to the white bed with its cradle that lifted the covers clear – of what? The leg that was no longer there?

256

'I'm glad you came, Miss Howard,' added the doctor finally, now on her feet. 'He was asking for you all the time. Eileen is your name, isn't it?'

'Yes, yes, that's right.' Eileen stared at her incredulously.

'Well, no doubt I'll see you again.'

Eileen watched her retreating figure and could not remember if she had thanked her or even said goodbye. Doubtless she meant to be kind but her words had cut Eileen to the bone. She stared at the closed door to Jon's ward and then dumbly turned aside, walking with slow, heavy steps back down the corridor, hardly aware of her surroundings.

Outside in the street she felt the faint sunshine of a late soft September and shivered. She had to sit down, her head was throbbing and suddenly she was very cold indeed. She needed a few quiet moments to try and collect her thoughts, to try and come to terms with what she had just learnt.

Off Aldersgate Street she found a Lyons teashop and went inside. The nippy brought her a pot of tea and she sat there at the table by the window, cradling her hands around the cup, dry-eyed.

Only Vi was at home when she arrived. She was busy boiling water to sterilise her medical instruments before setting off on duty again. Her overalls were wet and muddy.

'I was called out when a water main fractured,' she explained with a wry smile. 'This kid was trapped and everyone was up to their eyes in mud.' She stopped suddenly, aware of Eileen's own appearance. 'What's wrong, love?'

Eileen told her everything. There was something infinitely comforting about Vi Tracey. She had a natural aptitude for compassion and caring, drawing people in trouble to her like some homely earth mother. Even as she rested in the circle of Vi's reassuring arms, Eileen gave a thought to Vi herself and wondered who there was to listen to her problems.

'Don't worry, love, there's lots of things they can do these days. They have specialists who can fit them up with...'

'Yes, that's what the doctor said.'

'Well, there you are then. He's luckier than some of them. At least he's alive.'

257

'But he was so active. He played sport and...'

'Yes, love, I know, but you mustn't think about that now. We've all been hit by the war one way or another. Look at your friend with the boy who was at Dunkirk.'

'Veronica.'

'That's right. She put a brave face on it, didn't she? She still loves him. And I know that if anything happened to George...'

'Oh Vi!' Eileen clasped her hand. 'You're so kind, thinking about us all the time while poor George is out there somewhere. It must be awful for you. Have you heard anything?'

Vi shook her head, betraying something of the despair she had tried so hard to hide. 'It would be easier if I just knew where he was. I don't know if he's even embarked yet. He seemed to think it would be North Africa.'

'I'm sure he'll be all right, Vi. Perhaps he hasn't even gone yet. Perhaps he'll turn up here one day and surprise you! I thought they gave them leave before sailing.'

'I don't know, Eileen. Sometimes I just get this feeling...' She shook her head. 'Silly, isn't it? I mean, I know it's daft, but I just get this feeling that I won't ever see him again.'

'Oh Vi! You mustn't ever say such a thing! It's nonsense. George will come through all right. He's a born survivor. Look at him in France – tough as they come.'

'Yes, yes, of course you're right.' A ghost of a smile flickered on her face and she made a visible effort to try and cheer up. 'We're a right pair, aren't we? And upstairs there's Moira.'

'Is she still sleeping?'

'Yes, and the best thing for her. Lily's with her. She'll be feeling a bit better tomorrow.' She began to scrub her hands at the sink. 'Just goes to show you, doesn't it? It doesn't take a Jerry to ruin a life – some of us seem hell bent on trying to do it all by ourselves.'

Eileen found it almost impossible to concentrate at work that afternoon. The staff sergeant in charge of the motor pool for the Ministry must have thought her pretty slow-witted, having to repeat himself more than once as he explained how she was to log her mileage and sign for petrol. When Eileen left to meet Pat with the Vauxhall saloon she had been issued, he leant through the driver's window and made some crack about smart little WAAFs who knew a good job when they got it. Eileen woke up to the insult and promptly wound the window up on him, knowing she had made herself an enemy.

Pat was waiting for her on the steps of the Ministry on a corner of Whitehall. She was so pleased to see him that she could almost have hugged him if it had not been for the passersby. It felt more like five weeks since she had said goodbye to him at Kenley than the five days in which they had been separated.

'Have you seen Jon yet?' he asked her before they had even entered Trafalgar Square.

'I went this morning.'

'And?'

Eileen flashed him a quick glance. 'You knew, didn't you? Why on earth didn't you tell me what was wrong with him?'

'No,' he said calmly, watching her carefully through narrowed eyes, 'I don't know what's wrong with him. I see that you're pretty upset, Eileen. Let's pull over and discuss it.'

'No, I don't want to discuss anything. Just tell me where I'm supposed to be driving.'

'Highgate. You take –'

'I'll find it.' She drove north in silence, constantly diverted by the road signs warning of bomb craters and UXBs.

'Aren't you going to tell me?'

'Oh, I'm sorry, Pat. You must think I'm an ungrateful sod. And if it hadn't been for you offering me this posting I'd never have been so close to him.'

'Forget all that. Just tell me what's Jon's problem.'

'Problem? They don't call it that at the hospital. Condition, that's the word they use there. Nice word, isn't it, for someone with an amputated leg.'

'Oh Christ.'

'Yes, lousy luck, isn't it? But it could have been a lot worse. We do have to keep his spirits up – or that's what they keep telling me.' All her bitterness suddenly came pouring out. 'And when he's up to it they're going to fit him with a false limb, one of those tin cans we saw at Kenley.' She blinked angry tears away. 'I just can't imagine Jon, of all people...'

Pat placed a steady hand on her arm, telling her to pull over.

259

Meekly she obeyed him, her eyes clouded now, and he sat quietly while she finished the sudden storm.

'Well, there's Bader,' he said when she had quietened. 'He's still flying, you know. He wouldn't let anything keep him out of action.'

She thought of Douglas Bader's bravery and of Duxford. Duxford, the station where Gareth was.

'I know that it seems terribly unfair just now, Eileen, but he really was lucky. Look what happened to Dutch and Pepper.'

'Yes, I know, but...'

'He's got a strong personality. He won't let this get him down, you'll see. And I hear they can do wonderful things now.'

'Oh not you, too! Everyone has been falling over themselves to reassure me what wonderful advances modern medicine has made thanks to the war. Good, isn't it? War brings advances in medicine, machines – even in slum clearance! All the things no one had any time or money for in peace.'

'Yes, you have a point,' Pat agreed mournfully. 'I suppose war brings out the innovator in us all. Even me. Here I am devising new ways of dropping bigger and better bombs.'

'Yes, but that's different.'

'I like to think so. But if you feel that now you want to drop out.'

'Drop out?' Eileen was astonished. 'That's the last thing I need now. The job is the only thing that will keep me going! I'm sorry I went on so much, Pat, I didn't want you to think...'

'Enough said,' he assured her. 'I know you're right, Eileen. Jon wouldn't thank you for giving up now.'

Next day Eileen spent most of her time with Moira. She had slept the clock round and was looking more human, with some colour back in her cheeks. Eileen had taken over from Lily and Vi at her bedside and they kept one another·company, very conscious that after today they did not know for certain when they would see each other again.

'You must write and let me know what's going on.'

'Oh, I expect it will be very dull down there now,' said Moira. 'I certainly won't feel much like doing anything exciting.'

'Not yet.'

'Perhaps not at all. I mean it, Eileen. I'm never going to get caught out again. I kept thinking all the while how different things would have been if I had gone home with you that night – that night it happened, you know.'

Eileen didn't know what to say to her. It had been her thought too, but she was too sensitive and too fond of her friend to say anything of the sort to her face.

After a late lunch with Lily, Moira began to get ready for the trip to the station. Eileen had the car from the motor pool although it had got her into trouble with the sergeant there. She had it all worked out. She would take Moira to the railway station before going on to pick Pat up from Hendon later.

Moira was reluctant to leave her grandmother and Lily was moved by the sight of her gaunt appearance in her uniform.

'You take good care of yourself, darling,' she told her, holding her tight. 'Please let me know you have arrived safely.'

'I'll be OK, Lily, really I will.' She looked at Eileen and grinned. 'I'm not an invalid, you know.'

'But you take things easy. Don't try doing too much.'

'Please don't worry!' She hugged Lily and picked up her small holdall. She reached over and gave her one last kiss and then they were off across the square to where Eileen had parked the Air Force car.

'I feel a bit wobbly,' Moira confessed. 'I hope it goes off soon.'

'Make sure you get plenty to eat.'

'Don't you start, Ei! I've only got myself to blame.'

'You're too hard on yourself.'

'No. I'm just trying to be realistic that's all.' She gave a mocking little laugh. 'If you like I'm turning over a new leaf.'

At the station they had only a few minutes before Moira's train was due to pull out. Eileen walked down the platform with her, carrying her case despite her protests. They had trouble trying to find a seat in the crowded train and had to walk right to the end before there was any space. They put Moira's holdall to reserve a seat and then she stood at the open carriage window to say goodbye.

All too soon the whistle sounded and belching black smoke from the engine billowed out across the platform. Eileen reached up and gave her a final hug.

261

'Don't be a stranger – promise!'

'I promise. Thanks for everything, Eileen, you've been a real friend.'

The train moved forward with a great hiss of steam as their hands stretched out across the widening gap. At last they lost hold and Eileen stood back, hand raised in a forlorn wave as Moira's white face was lost in a cloud of smoke and soot.

Pat's new project seemed to confirm her very worst fears. Once she had been cleared by security Eileen was soon privy to all aspects of his plan to build up the greatest, most specialised bomber group ever seen. From the men he had personally selected over the past months, to the latest machines, he was set on providing Britain with a force capable of striking at the heart of the enemy's resources.

Eileen soon found that her duties were expected to cover note-taking at various meetings Pat set up in and around London. She was soon driving him to many of the Government's most secret establishments situated in lonely country houses in the Home Counties. They were most frequently at Bentley Priory, the HQ for Fighter Command, the gothic house high on a hill in North London, once a girls' school, and Bomber Command at High Wycombe. But most fascinating was Bletchley Park, an old red house with its grounds full of long wooden huts and donnish looking types in ancient tweed jackets and spectacles. Eileen could never quite understand what went on there. It was obviously something secret, and her security clearing did not go far enough to even allow her a peep inside the place.

'What goes on here, Pat?' she asked him once she got the opportunity.

'Intelligence work.'

'But half the staff are civilians.'

'Yes, they brought them out of the universities especially. Mathematical brains. I suppose it's for decoding German signals, that kind of thing.'

'Can they do that? Jon once told me that HQ could warn the fighters when the Jerries were coming in. He said they knew in advance and were vectored into position, ready and waiting for them.'

'Yes, that's true.' Pat chewed on the end of his pipe. 'I suppose you can be told now that security have cleared you, but strictly speaking it's still hush-hush. Very few people know about this. We pick up advance warning of approaching aircraft through a series of towers along the south coast. We can tell more or less as soon as they set off across the Channel.'

'Good God!'

'Yes, amazing, isn't it? We're years ahead of the field. The Germans and the Americans are way behind us. The "pips" are monitored by cathode-ray tubes on the ground in special stations – manned by WAAFs, incidentally. The reports are sent to Bentley Priory from these Chain Home Stations and then sector controllers are warned.'

'It sounds incredible.'

'Yes, but it works.' He puffed away contentedly on his pipe. 'Mind you, the Jerries have tried to take out some of the towers in the chain. They are far more advanced in their bomber capacity. We ought to beware. The whole nature of war is changing.'

'So the bombs just go on getting bigger, is that it?' She shuddered. 'I wonder what kind of world will be left when we're finished with it? Will there even be such a thing as a winner? Will winning mean anything when all that's left is a heap of rubble to crawl out from under?'

Life soon fell into a remorseless pattern of work, air raids and hospital visits. Pat's business, whether in town or country, set the timetable, each day being different from the one before. Eileen would hurry straight to Bart's whenever her duty was over.

She soon discovered that it was easier to get round on foot in the damaged streets of the capital than in the car. Every time she entered the City boundaries she faced new traffic obstacles where new roads were blocked with rubble, offices which had been whole the day before having come crashing down in night time raids. Sometimes she borrowed Kitty's bicycle if it was getting late. It made it easier for her to give other wardens, who did not understand, the slip whenever a siren sounded and she was expected to take cover in the nearest shelter.

Eileen amazed herself with her growing nonchalance regarding her own safety. Whenever a siren split the air round her, she would redouble her efforts to get to Bart's or to get back home, in spite of the shouts and whistles of the wardens who thought they were doing her a good turn. She knew differently. Her day was full enough without having to waste hours sitting in some shelter. If a bomb was going to get her, then at least she would go with Jon or her friends rather than a crowd of strangers.

But this routine certainly took its toll. Within days she was almost dead on her feet after rushing from one end of London to another. And the worst of it was that Jon expected so much of her visits. It was the highlight of his day. She could tell that he had been waiting for her, counting the hours until she came again. He was petulant when she was late, never seeming to notice her exhaustion. Perhaps he did not realise that she got little sleep at night because of the raids. She told him about the house, about Lily and Kitty, Vi and Moira and Veronica, but he was not greatly interested. His thoughts seemed very far away. He said nothing to her about his condition, never once mentioned his crash or anything about his leg, and so neither could she. The future was never discussed.

It was not only that she was tired. Conversation itself was very limited. He had nothing new to tell her:

'Lying here on my back day after day,' he declared bitterly with the martyred air of a knight at rest. She thought he had never looked so handsome, his blond head nestled in the pillows, gaining strength and colour day by day.

But when she tried to tell him about Pat and her work he seemed irritated, and she felt immediately guilty for reminding him about the Air Force life that he could no longer be part of. So she talked about her new friends at the house while he looked at her with narrowed eyes full of suspicion. He could not believe that she really enjoyed the company of women as much as she said. He seemed to think that friendship could only really exist between men, having the idea that women were in competition with one another, that they were bitchy, always ready to stab one another in the back. Neither could he see what a woman would need in another woman when she could have a man. Only those who were past it would waste their time with a bunch of females. He somehow implied that Eileen was lying when she said she was with them. Eileen began to think that he was jealous of all her friends.

She told herself that it was not his fault. He had little else to do except conjure fantasies out of thin air as he lay here hour after hour. Sometimes the pain seemed to trouble him again. And oddly enough it was his left leg which hurt the most. When Eileen asked the doctor about it, she merely shrugged, declaring that it was a common enough phenomenon. He would get over it, she said. They gave him morphine for the pain.

A weary scepticism began to grow among Londoners as the Blitz continued. Casualty figures were high, but the official data was not believed.

'Add a nought to it,' they said cynically. The evidence before their eyes was enough to convince them that the figures were being doctored to try and keep up morale.

There were clearly more homeless and refugees than anyone had anticipated. Lily said that they had calculated on Spanish Civil War estimates, and that the East Enders ought to have been dead under the rubble of their houses not choking up the emergency relief channels that were only designed to cope with one or two hundred not thousands.

'It's the women and kids who suffer the most,' Lily pointed out. 'Two wars I've seen and still they don't learn. Of course, men enjoy war. Don't laugh, dear; it makes them feel important, they get to give everyone orders. Women are far more sensible. Women plan ahead. What fool in his right mind would indiscriminately drop bombs on the most historic centres of culture in the name of civilisation?'

Talking with Lily, Eileen thought that perhaps it was true that women had far more potential than men gave them credit for. Everywhere she met women who had new responsibilities. In the past months they seemed to have taken a leap forward. They were involved in projects and discussing matters they would have thought a purely male preserve a year before.

It was the war that had opened their horizons, pushing them into thinking for themselves, making decisions, taking on jobs from engineering to heavy construction work. There were women shipyard workers now, women foresters and tractor drivers, women bus conductors and drivers. Eileen was reminded of pictures she had seen in one of Lily's books about the Soviet

Union. Now she saw the very same thing happening over here, and all because the war had made women important.

'If we come through this,' said Eileen, 'we will never be satisfied with going back to where we were before.'

At night Eileen either sat in the shelter in the square with Vi or, when she was on duty, she would seek out Lily who was firewatching on the roof.

After the first visit, Eileen lost her fear and thought it rather exhilarating to be up so high above the City. To the south between the chimney stacks rose the splendid dome of St Paul's Cathedral silhouetted among the flames and smoke of the burning buildings. It was as though some deity protected the structure from harm. The cathedral had become a symbol of their will to survive.

As evening came, Lily would take up her position on the roof, checking first that the water buckets on every landing were full and that the stirrup pump was at hand. Incendiaries were the least of their problems.

'They are not a very intelligent device,' she told Eileen firmly. 'All you need to do to extinguish them is to shovel them outside, or cover them with a sandbag as soon as you spot the green flame. Never, never throw water over them. The core is magnesium, you see, and you don't want it exploding, throwing molten shrapnel in every direction.'

Eileen worked out that there were 36 IBs in each container and five containers to each plane, making 180 incendiaries dropped from each German plane over London. Looking out at the sky when waves of enemy bombers rumbled overhead it was an awesome thought.

At first the evenings were quiet, almost ominously so. Looking out across the rooftops the City brooded, waiting for the bombardment to begin. Often there was a beautiful sunset.

'I never really noticed the sky before, did you?' she said to Lily.

The blackout made the stars hang heavy over London, almost awesome in their perfection, indestructible, unapproachable. An infinity of silence separated them from the gaudy show of lights that would soon dare to rival their brightness as the searchlights scored through the blackest night.

'On such a night anything seems possible,' Lily replied, staring out over the tranquil square below, queen of her domain. 'One might even believe there was no war at all.'

As if to mock her words, at that very instant the callous call of the sirens destroyed the calm of the night. The criss-cross beams of the searchlights flashed into action and they put on their tin hats in readiness.

Amid the drone of approaching aircraft the loud report of London's barrage made all talk impossible. Scarlet shooting stars marked the aim of tracers, their deadly fragments scattering wide over the streets below. It was said that shrapnel from their own ack-ack killed more people than the German bombs.

Over near the GPO at Mount Pleasant there was a burst of chandelier flares. Amber-red they glowed, then green like some pantomime Demon King. The night sky reeked of high explosive and bitter smoke. The memory of Guy Fawkes Night bonfires on the green, and of thick pea-souper fogs or delicious aroma of woodsmoke, more than all of these was the odour of war in the city.

Lily was indomitable. She stood her ground among the rooftop sandbags like an admiral on the poop deck. She showed no fear. She was far too busy to show signs of any nerves at all. Even the sight of her beloved London burning could not induce tears to break her strong resolve to carry on. She gave Eileen courage and a renewed sense of purpose, for how could she be weak when Lily set her such an example?

South of the river a gasholder took a direct hit. The sky was suddenly rent apart by the flash of a giant explosion. There was a great uprush of seering white light as thousands of cubic feet of gas blazed in a vast mushroom cloud high above the city in apocalyptic intensity.

For a moment Eileen felt she was watching the end of the world. Is this how it will be, that very last moment? One brilliant light turning night into day and then unending darkness?

It was not that Moira did not understand. Veronica had a right to go away if she got the chance. After all, she hadn't seen Tim for weeks. But in the time since she had got back from London Moira had somehow come to rely on her friend always being there, good dependable Veronica.

She had been really terrific helping her to get back on her feet.

She had covered for her, swopped duties, even brought more trouble on her own head for her sake. Frankly, she wouldn't have known what to do with herself if she hadn't had Veronica there to keep her company. They had become real stay-at-homes, curling up after supper listening to the radio, reading or knitting. But watching Veronica covering sheet after sheet of paper in letters to her fiancé eventually made Moira realise the sacrifice that her friend was making.

'Couldn't you get yourself a 48 now?' she asked her one morning over breakfast.

The flame of hope lit up Veronica's eyes.

'Well, I could, I suppose.'

'Don't you want to go and spend some time with Tim? The heat's off here now. Surely Ma'am would give you a weekend. Or don't they let him out of that place?'

'But I wouldn't want you to be alone here.'

'Don't be daft, love. I'm a big girl now.'

And so it was her own fault. She had encouraged her to go. She had forced her to make all the arrangements. But seeing her excitement as the weekend approached, Moira felt the first pangs of discontent gnawing away. Resentment and even jealousy were there too. After weeks and weeks of restraint, of wanting to hide herself away from company, she now felt totally unsettled. She thought of Veronica with Tim and even Eileen with Jon and her discontent grew.

Eileen got to meet some of the other wardens who worked with Kitty in the district of Milton Square. There were some pretty rough diamonds but they were good lads on the whole. Kitty was the only woman.

Only Mr Sykes was a pain in the neck. He was a Salvation Army bandsman who had avoided active service. There was nothing wrong with the Sally Ann, but Jim Sykes was a hypocrite. Although he was always moralising, Kitty soon found out that underneath his holier-than-thou mask he was a determined womaniser. Only a part-time warden, he continued with a job as a clerk, creeping his way up the promotion ladder at work by stepping into the shoes of absent colleagues who had volunteered for the Forces. Kitty loathed the way he would leer at her, his eyes flicking up her body while his thin voice whined on about duty and moral responsibility.

'He gives me the creeps,' Eileen agreed on their way home one night.

'What gets on my nerves is his bloody self-righteous attitude. If he makes a mistake then it's just bad luck, but if anyone else slips up we never hear the end of it. And he's such a bloody pessimist. Sometimes I just want to scream.'

The main sewerage outfall had been destroyed in the bombing. The Thames stank appallingly for days, first of sewage and then of the harsh chemicals they poured in to disperse it. London was full of evil odours and drifting coloured smoke.

'I'll never be the same again after some of the things I've seen,' said Kitty, and told Eileen how the day before she had discovered an old man in a house who refused to go to the shelters. 'He said he couldn't go and leave his wife who was sick. I went in to see her and there she was, all wrapped up in blankets in front of the fire. "I have to keep her warm," said the old boy, but when I got close – well, she'd been dead for weeks! The stench – you can't imagine it.'

Kitty surprised herself as much as Eileen with her new-found nonchalance. She said it just showed the breadth of her capabilities which the war had brought out.

She used the stub of her cigarette to light another.

'God, my last fag! I've never smoked so much in my life. You know, I used to laze around in bed until eleven if we didn't have rehearsals. Now I always wake up immediately alert, ready for anything. I enjoy my work, I enjoy my responsibility. I feel really useful for the first time in my life. I feel indestructible!' She cast Eileen a look as though she expected her to laugh. 'You don't think I'm crazy, do you? You feel something of the same.'

'I do. It's been on my mind a lot lately. I thought I was getting a split personality because when I'm with Jon he always seems to minimise my work. He's just not interested.'

'A lot of men are like that. They can't seem to accept that any job a woman does could be important. I suppose it's only to be expected. Jon's there in hospital feeling useless and you're out and about doing exciting things at work.'

'Some days he's so irritable, as though he blames me for everything. Talking just turns into point scoring contests. He makes me feel stupid, inadequate – and yet he needs me. He goes mad if I'm late getting there to see him. You know, I often wonder what would happen if I was caught in an air raid. He seems so vulnerable.'

She didn't tell Kitty what Jon had said to her on her last visit: 'A man alone hasn't the strength to overcome all the trials of life. He needs some support. You're my support, Eileen. Don't let me down.'

She knew that she could never allow herself to be weak enough to share her problems with him. He said she was his support and comfort. He wanted her to be there bright and cheerful, full of hope, bolstering him when he was depressed. He never seemed to notice when she felt low or exhausted. It put appalling pressure on her.

The thought of his injury was repellent when she remembered his physical strength and health before. She would have liked to talk to Kitty or Vi about it, but it was too personal and seemed like a kind of betrayal. Many women would have given him up. Moira had felt sick when she looked at Tim's injuries. Would she have continued with someone like Jon simply because of who he was, for the hope of a secure future? These things which had not meant anything to Eileen before the crash now appeared to be her only comfort. Now she began to wonder how much Jon would care for her if he had not had the accident. If he did not need her so much, would he still care?

It was odd being at the pub in the village again, and stranger still to be there alone. There were some raised eyebrows as she walked in and it took a lot of nerve to walk straight up to the bar and order a drink for herself.

'Hello, Moira. Haven't seen you in here for some time.'

'No, Ted, been a bit busy. Make it a gin, will you?'

'Meeting someone, are you?'

She thought he looked at her disapprovingly. She shifted uncomfortably. 'I'm a bit early,' she answered evasively.

Sitting in the corner, away from Ted's suspicious eye, Moira felt quite out of place. The pub was too quiet and all the other customers were couples, huddled together around the small knee-high tables, blocking her out. There was no one she recognised.

The population of the station was changing all the time now. Dave and others from Alan's old gang had long since moved on. As the pilots came up for rest periods they were transferred as a unit to a quieter part of the country to rest and recuperate before being sent back into action, often at another station.

Moira finished her drink, feeling really sorry for herself and thinking there was no point in sitting there just to make a fool of herself. The whole weekend stretched before her, surprisingly empty without Veronica there to keep her company. It was a bleak prospect.

She was just about to get up and leave when the pub door swung back and a large group of aircrew piled in, laughing and talking loudly as they plunged towards the bar. Soon Ted was rushed off his feet and the pub was buzzing with life.

Moira caught several of the young men examining her, giving her the old wink and a nod, while she pretended not to notice.

'Your glass is empty.'

She looked up into deep brown eyes. It was a face she did not know, smiling and self-assured, older than the others.

'Won't you let me get you another?'

'I was just about to leave.'

'Why? Didn't he turn up?'

She flashed him an angry glance, but he was smiling at her and she could only smile back.

'A gin?'

'That would be lovely.'

She watched him at the bar. The others made room for him, out of respect for his age and rank and – yes, she saw it then, a limp, a very plainly discernible limp as he fetched the drinks back to her. He was nice looking, not dazzling but smartly turned out as though he took a certain pride in his appearance. She guessed that he was pretty well-heeled and wondered if he was married. As he set the glasses on the table she saw that it was his right leg that was the trouble and wondered what his story might be. Did his leg wound mean that he was grounded? That perhaps he had a nice safe desk job? That only made him more attractive. No risk

271

involved there, no chance of heartbreak.

He sat down beside her, rather close.

'Cheers.'

They clinked glasses, watching each other closely with undisguised interest.

'It would be nice to know your name,' he said.

That week in October was one of the worst for a long time. Four Underground stations were hit within three nights. The worst was at Balham where the bomb tore through the surface of the road outside and left a crater large enough for a doubledecker bus following behind to drop into. The bomb fell through to the platforms below, bringing down masonry and rubble, ripping out cables and pipes, smashing the water conduits and bringing the whole lot down on the densely packed platforms. Those who were not killed outright by falling rubble faced a hell of gas and rising water all in pitch darkness. They said that screams could be heard from the road above but hundreds were lost in the stinking blackness as water rose up the emergency stairs.

'There were 600 killed,' Kitty told them at the house.

Deeply depressed, Eileen arranged to meet Vi later that afternoon and go to help her at one of the local shelters. She had to be busy these days, to take her mind off the agony on every side. Only the day before incendiaries had landed on the Angel and across at Percy Circus. The peace and beauty of the early Victorian squares she had so admired had been destroyed forever. Even those houses that had not been hit began to look like slums.

Arriving at Bart's Eileen trudged up the stairs towards Jon's ward feeling very low spirited. Nurses and ward orderlies were already beginning to put up the blackout shutters and turn on the lights. Eileen felt half dead on her feet after a particularly exhausting week. She knew that her battledress was grubby, but she had no time even to change into a skirt or a clean shirt before coming out. Jon would just have to put up with it and be grateful that she had come nevertheless.

Doctor Walters had said that he was making fine progress, and that he might be able to get up into a chair for a few hours a day very soon. She knew that the staff were eager to get him transferred out of London to an RAF hospital where he could convalesce before going to the false limb unit at Roehampton. The City was too dangerous with the heavy raids, and anyway, his bed was needed for emergency Blitz victims.

She pushed open the door to the ward and stopped dead. At Jon's bedside she saw a middle-aged woman sitting on the visitor's chair, a rich dark brown fur thrown back from her shoulders as she leant forward to hold her son's hand. Mrs Pemberley.

Eileen stepped back from the threshold, suddenly cold with shock. The door swung back and shut off the scene of maternal comfort, but although Eileen had not even seen her face she could picture it in her mind's eye, replaying the scene in the lodge at Charnwood over again.

'Oh hello, Miss Howard.' It was one of the regular nurses on the ward approaching the door with a tray of pills and bottles.

'Nurse, I see that Mr Pemberley already has a visitor.'

'Oh yes, that will be his mother. Don't you know her?' She gave her a curious stare, obviously finding some mystery behind the inquiry. 'It's strange you haven't bumped into her before, what with her being down here so often.'

'She comes down often?' asked Eileen in stony horror.

'Once a week regular. Drives down apparently. Though where she gets her petrol from, God only knows.' She snorted disparagingly. 'Mind you, that sort always manage to find a way round the regulations, don't they? Think they're a cut above us ordinary mortals.' She cut off abruptly, as though she had just remembered Eileen's connection with the family. 'No offence, dear.'

'No, of course not.'

'Aren't you going in to see him then?'

Eileen felt like turning right round and going home. She had promised Vi she would help her on duty that evening and could always use that as an excuse. But the nurse's words had made her angry. Apparently Mrs Pemberley had been visiting Jon every week, travelling down from Charnwood in spite of the petrol rationing. And all the time Jon had never said a word to her. He had made her think that she was his only visitor. She doubted that he had even mentioned her to his mother.

For this reason Eileen refused to simply vanish into the night. Much as she loathed the idea she felt she had to show herself. If Jon was ashamed of his association with her, then it was better by far that she knew it now.

She followed the nurse into the ward, her eyes on the bed where Mrs Pemberley sat with her elegant back to the door. It was Jon who saw her first but his face betrayed nothing, neither welcome nor displeasure.

Eileen crossed behind Mrs Pemberley's chair and leant across the bed in front of her. She kissed Jon very demonstratively, leaving no doubt of her claim on him. She could almost feel the shock wave, the indrawn breath, the dry snap of disapproving lips. As she drew back, forced to stand because the only chair was occupied, her eyes met those of her former employer for one brief second before they both turned away towards Jonathan.

Eileen was certain that Mrs Pemberley had recognised her. She had seen the colour rise in her cheeks, and the bright light in her eyes. She knew very well who she was, and Eileen had deliberately left her in little doubt of her relationship to Jon. But if Eileen had expected a scene or raised voices, then she had forgotten the code by which Mrs Pemberley conducted her life. She was far too well bred to make a scene in such a public place. Instead she directed herself to her son alone, cutting Eileen out, as though she had never walked through the door, as though she simply did not exist.

'So tiresome not being able to get away to Switzerland this year. One feels so exhausted.'

'You're looking so much better, Jon darling!'

'I simply have to do everything myself.'

'Pat sends his best wishes, darling.'

'Wiltshire – you remember Wiltshire the gamekeeper, Jon – well, he fetched in a lovely brace of pheasants for hanging.'

Eileen could not bear to look at her. The sound of her strident voice was enough to aggravate her.

'Work keeps me so busy just now, racing around from the Ministry to Command HQ.'

But Mrs Pemberley was not to be outdone.

'The Vicar came to tea last week to discuss the Harvest Festival. Such a charming gal, his daughter . . .'

274

'How I wish we could be back together.'

'You must remember Emily. Such a sweet child. Fine bones. She rides with the Mowbray Hunt. None of the gadding about you expect from fast gals.'

Jon's silence and Mrs Pemberley's snide remarks were more than she could bear. She leant forward and touched his hand.

'I have to go now, Jon darling. I'm expected on shelter duty before the raids start.'

'Of course, the Red Cross keeps me so busy – but I always put you first, Jon.'

'Take care of yourself.' Eileen was on her feet. 'I'll be in to see you tomorrow – and everyday as usual.'

Mrs Pemberley suddenly leant back in her chair, raising one imperious finger. Her voice was arch and cold:

'One moment. Wait for me outside. I wish to talk to you.'

Eileen stared at her for a cool minute and then said levelly,

'You're not talking to one of your servants now.'

As she turned on her heel the silence echoed behind her, and then she heard quite distinctively the composed drone of her voice.

'Oh yes, and Sir John asked to be remembered to you.'

Outside in the corridor Eileen's face burned with anger and humiliation. How dare she behave as though nothing had changed! As though she was right back there in the hallway of the lodge, wearing another uniform, confronted with a guilty letter, still a servant. And how dare Jon sit there so complacently, saying not a word in her support, in her defence. No introductions, no fond word to set her at ease, to demonstrate her new status. He sat there mute, his very passivity seeming to say he took his mother's side against her.

Outside, she seized Kitty's bicycle in fury and turned into the street towards home, eager to get away. She became aware of the sounds of the night round her and realised that the raid had begun.

Overhead the searchlights played on the vast canopy of the sky, rivalling the moon riding high above. That moon which beckoned the German planes towards their targets. To enemy bombers looking down on the heart of the City of London Eileen thought the streets must have appeared as plain as the lines on the palm of her hand. And all the barrage from the ack-ack emplacements could do little to prevent another night of destruction.

Eileen pedalled away from the hospital as though the very devil was after her. That dreadful woman! Going on and on about the Red Cross while she was using up all their petrol ration. Driving Jon crazy with her trivial gossip. The vicar and his bloody daughter! And how dare she insinuate that she was fast, that she was gadding around while bloody Emily was doing really useful things like riding with the Hunt.

Across the city bombs began to drop. Eileen looked behind her, very conscious of the deserted street. She heard wardens' whistles in the short intervals between explosions. The air was growing thick with the stench of smoke and high explosive and Eileen realised she ought to take shelter, but she was loth to be trapped in this district. She wanted to get back to an area she knew, where the local shelters were all known to her, where she had learnt which buildings were safer than others.

In the glare of the raid she saw that it was already eight o'clock and that she was as late for her meeting with Vi as if she had stayed all the time with Jon. She redoubled her efforts, turning into St John Street, still with the long uphill haul towards Rosebery Avenue and the Angel. Her breath came in searing gasps burning her throat as the air thickened. The light was lurid and theatrical. She could imagine the panorama at her back with the City on fire, but she felt little fear. Even when she was finally forced to take shelter, huddling in a doorway, her mind was still absorbed with the confrontation with Jon's mother rather than her own danger.

She remembered how she had been instructed by Schofield the butler never to talk to Mrs Pemberley unless asked a direct question. No matter how urgent, a servant had no place speaking to her employer. She was there to be seen and not heard. Just like the hospital. Mrs Pemberley had looked through her, acting as though she did not exist. Until the final moment when Eileen was about to leave. Then she had snapped her fingers, telling her to wait outside with all the calm authority of the lady of the house to her housemaid.

What had she planned? To warn her off, to pay her to leave her precious son alone? Jon had not even the courage to speak out or even try to explain to his mother all that had happened to bring them together.

That hurt her more than anything that Mrs Pemberley could have said to her.

The noise about her was deafening with bombs falling very close now. She had to wait for a break before she could attempt to get back to the square. Mingled in the sounds of the night were emergency bells clanging as fire engines and ambulances rushed to the scene of some tragedy. Over to the south a barrage balloon burned with a blue flame and flashing sparks. It sank rapidly behind the rooftops.

Huddled, lonely in the doorway, Eileen felt hurt and humiliated. She was bitter about what she saw as Jon's betrayal. She hoped that he would realise how much he had hurt her by hiding his mother's visits from her. Did he feel so little for her then? She thought that she was his only visitor, the only one who cared, the one who gave him the will to survive. He had seemed to depend on her visits so much. And yet all the time his bloody mother had been turning up, bearing gifts from the country no doubt, things that were unobtainable in the city.

So, it seemed that he could do without her. Well, let him! Let him go and stay with his mother, let him become another version of his own father, cocooned, despised . . . Would she go back to see him? Would he want her there now that his mother had a chance to turn him against her? Her thoughts were in a turmoil, she no longer knew what she felt about him.

When at last she emerged from the shelter of the doorway and got back on to her bicycle, she thought it would be quicker to cut up through the side streets towards the square, avoiding what seemed to be a large fire over on the Goswell Road. She pedalled uphill near Sadlers Wells, watching the tower of the church in the square draw closer and closer. She was very thankful to reach home at last.

But she had hardly reached the front door when she saw Lily emerge into the square with Alice Armstrong, their neighbour. They were both looking extremely agitated. Suddenly all her own problems were forgotten as she hurried forward, leaving her bicycle on the pavement.

'Lily! Are you all right? What's happened?'

'It's the school. Dame Alice's. It got a direct hit. Kitty's gone over there now to try and help.'

'But that's where...'

'Yes, that's where Vi was working in the shelter.'

Chapter Nine

Dame Alice's School was well known in the district. People came long distances to use the deep shelter under the school buildings in the knowledge that the basement had been especially reinforced for emergency use. But Eileen doubted whether even such a shelter could withstand a direct hit. Look what had happened at Balham tube. Hundreds of women and children could be dead or trapped down there. And Vi was among them.

As she hurried out of the square and down towards St John Street, she could already see the scene of the tragedy marked out by a high dark pall of smoke. The street all around her was lined with fires from flying debris. Black smuts and stinging ash whirled down the street and the air was choked with strange smells. Men and women had appeared from nowhere and were running in every direction, fear on their faces, some screaming and crying.

In St John Street the smoke hung about in sinister layers. One building burned with vivid green flames and the heat was so intense that she had to skirt round it. Dust spirals floated in the unearthly glow of the moonlight.

The volume of noise from the continuing barrage made her ears sing. The flashes of ack-ack seemed colourless, washed out by the vicious moonlight which lost all its beauty in its bitter betrayal. As she neared Rosebery Avenue the dense black smoke made it hard to breathe. It swirled out across the street, masking her view of the school which occupied a whole block between the street she stood in and Goswell Road. She guessed the fire from nearby buildings would mean a four or five pump job. But it was high explosive which had struck the school, and HE killed more people through blast or terrible injuries, leaving them crippled, buried under tons of rubble.

As she approached the corner the drifting smoke lifted abruptly to reveal the full horror of the tragedy. The sight which met her eyes was unbelievable. The whole block which had been the school site had quite simply disappeared.

Dame Alice's had received the full force of the bomb but a number of neighbouring houses in Owen's Row had also gone. The school appeared to have collapsed in on itself, to have imploded rather than exploded, like a house of cards, destroyed in a few terrible minutes.

The houses in Owen's Row had caught fire and looked in a state of collapse. Darting black figures were silhouetted against the light. Tongues of flame flicked out from the empty windows and doorways while belching black smoke shot skywards. There were glass and splinters underfoot, the wood blistered, glittering with sparks. A bright scarlet light shone over everything.

Eileen saw the urgent movement as an ATS fire engine and a grey truck pulled up to deal with the fires. They would try to stop the flames from spreading towards the pub on the corner of the street. Firemen in thigh boots and tin helmets moved quickly and efficiently to link up the hoses that lay in the street like serpents, coiled and black in the gutter.

The full horror of modern warfare was plain to see all round her. Survivors of the bombing stood round in aimless clusters, ochre from head to foot with the thick blast dust and plaster, marked with streaks of blood from flying glass. Behind them came the rumble and hiss of falling walls and ceilings as the firemen played water jets on to the ruins of their houses.

A man stood near the entrance to one of the houses which stood virtually intact. He appeared distracted but otherwise unhurt. Until he turned round. Then Eileen saw that the back of his jacket had been completely ripped away by the blast.

He was lucky to be alive. Bodies were often left unmarked although they had suffered massive internal injuries. He stumbled forward, holding his hands to his head, and a WVS woman went to him, guiding him away from the fire. From the way she shouted Eileen guessed that he could be suffering from pierced eardrums after the force of the blast. He was led away to the pub on the corner which seemed to have been turned into an emergency post. The landlord of the pub was a well known local warden.

Outside the pub stood other survivors with WVS women and neighbours. An old woman, wrapped in a blanket, swayed to and fro, crying convulsively. Her white hair was singed and she wore only one slipper. Kitty had always said there were too many old people left in London but they refused to be evacuated. Either they could not imagine living anywhere but their two-up, two-down, or they were too proud to accept what they saw as charity. The remaining houses in Owen's Row now appeared stark and skeletal against the heavy smoke pall rising from the far end of the little street. Further along the school had stood just an hour before. The houses in the row had crumpled sideways like a fallen pack of playing cards. Rooms were exposed. A stairway leading away into darkness, into thin air. Like a doll's house or a set in the theatre when the curtain rises, Eileen was privileged with an insight into the lives of the occupants: a supper table laid with crockery, a loaf of bread on a platter, all untouched; a pair of men's trousers and braces neatly folded over the back of a bedroom chair; a child's toy dog on wheels parked in a narrow hallway. Rose-patterned wallpaper danced in the glare of the dying fires. A white antimacassar gleamed, reflecting in the cracked distorted image of a full-length mirror. Eileen turned briskly aside, ashamed at the exposure of these private things, angry at the destruction which marked the ruin of so many lives.

Although it was not yet nine o'clock the damage was as bad as anything she had seen after a night of continuous bombing. Ahead of her were mountains of rubble twenty to thirty feet high. She could see the shattered ribs of the building silhouetted in the mocking moonlight, showing how the school had caved in upon itself.

Although the night was horribly bright, those rescue workers already on the spot worked with screened hand torches because of the blackout regulations. The air was full of the choking smell Londoners came to know so well, a deadly mixture of high explosive and thick coating brick dust and plaster which hung over bomb sites for hours.

A group of men and women were shifting the surface of the bricks and fallen masonry with their bare hands, cursing as the stones were lifted only to find that the trapped body beneath was already dead. Eileen saw the corpse hauled out of its hole and laid to one side. She saw it was a woman, once middle-aged, her dress stuck to her lifeless limbs with thick wet yellow mud. All her humanity had gone. There was nothing in the sight of this clay figure to suggest that only an hour before she had been moving, breathing, thinking. Perhaps preparing tea for her family, perhaps on her way to the shelter. A life wiped out in one rapid gust of air. Life was so fragile after all.

Eileen followed the rescue workers over the rubble, stumbling after them towards the heart of the tragedy. Scarcely breathing, she disciplined herself to step over the bodies beneath her feet. There were seven or eight bodies within a few yards of one another. All were horribly mutilated. Shards of glass lay all round, like jewels of ice in the unfeeling moonlight.

'Bastards.'

She turned to find a young man, little more than a boy really, standing at her side. His face was coated in that dreadful yellow dust and his dark eyes appeared strange and alarmingly bright in the bland colouring.

'I'd kill them all, every bleeding one.' He was clearly expecting an answer but when she remained silent he turned on her violently, demanding, 'Well? Wouldn't you? That's all they deserve, the lousy bastards.' His hate carved deep furrows at the corners of his mouth and he suddenly looked much older. He seized her by the sleeve of her battledress, dragging her over the bricks. 'Look at that,' he told her bitterly. 'Now see if you don't think they should be wiped off the face of the earth.'

There were two bodies, one decapitated, thick black blood in a pool. A man and a child.

Eileen pulled back sharply, the taste of bile in her mouth. She turned to look at the boy but his gaze was fixed on the carnage and the look in his eyes alarmed her. She moved quickly away, tripping and stumbling her way across the rubble away from him, hating the excitement she had witnessed in one so young.

It was impossible to tell where the perimeters of the school had been. The gardens of the ruined houses and the grounds of the

282

school had merged under a tidal wave of bricks and mortar. If anyone had survived in the underground shelter then they must surely be buried fifteen or twenty feet beneath the ruins.

The moonlight cast fierce shadows across the bomb site. Ghostly figures drifted in and out of the whirling smoke rising in patches over the ruins. It reminded Eileen of a thick pea-souper fog full of the smell of woodsmoke and chemicals. Just then, one of the figures detached itself and picked a way over the fallen brickwork towards her. It was not until she was a yard away that Eileen recognised Kitty Russell in her overalls and tin hat.

'Blimey, your face!' Kitty's teeth shone in the dark cloud of her face and Eileen felt her hand touch her cheek, coming away caked in the sallow dust.

'You're no picture yourself,' she said wryly.

She cast a long look over the little groups of people moving amid the rubble. Faint lights like candles flickered across the uneven ground.

'I had to come when I heard. Is there anything we can do?'

'God only knows. It's sheer chaos at the moment.' She tipped back her tin hat and pushed aside her dusty hair. 'We're waiting for the demolition boys to get here. We can't do a thing until they lift some of this stuff.' She kicked at a piece of timber with her boot. 'It could cave in at any minute. There's nothing holding it up.' She gnawed her lip. 'There were hundreds in the shelter, they say. Charlie's got the figures of the regulars.' She glanced back over her shoulder. 'They think they heard a noise back there.'

'Then there's some hope?'

'It will be a long business. Perhaps all night.'

'Here, Kit!' The sharp cry summoned her back to join the main group and Kitty set off at a run, moving expertly over the uneven ground, with Eileen flagging behind, slipping into the tight circle of anxious faces.

'Could be several down there,' Charlie was saying, his shadowed face lean and gaunt as parchment with its covering of dust. He crouched near an opening in the wreckage where two timbers and a steel girder formed a kind of archway over a gaping black hole. He had his torch and flashed it about near the entrance. There were bricks and rubble all over the place and thick caking mud. Worst of all was the sour damp smell seeping up from below, like rotting vegetables pervading the whole area.

'Anybody there?'

In the sharp silence the atmosphere was electric. Tension gripped every figure in the circle as they willed anyone trapped below to answer. Charlie was down on his knees in the dust, straining to catch the faintest moan or muffled cry from the earth. After a few moments he raised his head and looked round the ring of despairing faces above him.

'Call again,' someone encouraged him.

'Hello! Can you hear me?'

The silence was intimidating. Desperation showed in Charlie's knotted muscles as he seized the timber joists in his bare hands as though it was possible for one man to pull them clear. He called again, his voice cracking.

'I know I heard something,' he told them lamely, sitting back on his heels, forlorn.

He was just getting to his feet when a sound like a low moan came from behind him. It came again before he could return to the hole, his wrinkled face pressed into the darkness.

'Can you hear me? Call again!'

Almost at once there came a faint affirmation, a human voice calling up through the tangle of broken girders and timber into the night.

'It's a woman,' said Charlie, his face breaking into a wide grin that stretched the yellow skin into a thousand cracks. 'Can you call again, love? Tell us, are you hurt bad?'

Kitty seized Eileen by the arm.

'I'm off to fetch the demo boys. Hang around till I get back, OK?'

She nodded, feeling numb, feeling useless, unable to do anything except gnaw her fingers and watch as Charlie tried to keep contact with the victim underground.

She had not said anything about Vi to Kitty. She did not want to alarm her until she knew for certain that Vi had gone to the school that evening, that she had been in the shelter when the bomb struck. But although she had said nothing, the thought of Vi trapped beneath her feet, Vi perhaps lying crushed and dying, haunted her mind. And the worst of it was the feeling of guilt. Guilt that she had not been home in time to catch Vi up, to keep her promise to go with her to the shelter. If only she had been there perhaps it would all have been different. Or perhaps she too would have been trapped under tons of rubble.

When Kitty returned she had with her a gang of heavy rescue men from the City of London squad. In their clean overalls and tin hats marked with a white 'R' they looked fresh and confident. They soon set to work round the opening in the ground with efficiency and amazing speed. Charlie and Kitty drew back with the others and let them get on with the business of shifting away some of the rubble. It was a job for professionals. Any hasty movement could have brought the whole works crashing down on those trapped beneath. In the past month these men had learnt a trade in life and death that could only come from active experience out on the bomb sites. And they learnt quickly. Guided by expert knowledge from local wardens they traced their way between a maze of tangled gas and water pipes to search for survivors. If there were any left alive under the ruins of the school, then these were the men who could find them.

Charlie produced a crumpled paper with a list of names. He told them that these were the regular shelter users, the ones who held registered shelter cards. They were the people most likely to be in the basement shelter of the school when the bomb fell.

'Jesus,' said Kitty softly as she glanced at the length of the list.

'Yeah, that's a lot of people,' Charlie commented. 'Whole families, mothers and kids.'

'Not all,' said Eileen. She glanced across at Kitty, her eyes betraying her distress. 'There's Vi. Vi's down there, too.'

They began to tunnel towards the trapped survivors. One of the demo men went first, timbering as he went. His men worked in silence, smoothly and efficiently. They saw that he was testing for gas every few minutes.

The full moon which had brought the bombers now aided the rescuers. But progress was painfully slow. Haste could result in the whole mountain of rubble caving in. They feared that the debris that was moved would bury any survivors deeper still. They put in timber supports to take the weight but as they moved down into the earth the wooden struts began to creak ominously.

285

'Don't worry, love,' Charlie told Eileen. 'He knows what he's doing. Engineer, he is.'

A whistle shrilled for silence and immediately all work ceased. 'Quiet, quiet!'

They were listening for sounds from the tunnel, only too aware that the rubble and wreckage could distort direction. When the silence had continued for a full minute, they went back to work, their faces grim. They changed places in the tunnel every twenty minutes. The demo leader emerged, wet and caked in slimy ochre mud. He was taken off for a hot cup of tea down at the pub and a chance to dry off. Water was seeping into the tunnel from a burst water main and there was no time to be lost. The next man prepared to lower himself into the pit.

About ten minutes later he called up to his mates on the surface, saying that he could hear the woman calling again. Everyone immediately became animated. The thought that someone was still alive seemed to give them renewed strength.

The woman was apparently wedged in by a fallen timber beam. She had not been in the basement itself but on her way down one of the staircases when the bomb hit. Rubble and plaster had showered down upon her but the ceiling beam had formed a tiny air pocket allowing her to breathe.

The news was discouraging. They had hoped she was one of many survivors and that they had discovered the main shelter under the school. But now it seemed that this woman was alone and quite a distance from the main body of people in the shelter.

'It's all right, love, we'll get you out.'

As the tunneller emerged from the expanding hole, her reply was quite audible to the rescuers on the surface. She was no more than six or ten feet below.

'Don't leave me!'

'It's all right, love,' Charlie called out as the next man in the team started down.

Then all at once there came a terrible low rumbling noise. The earth under their feet began to tremble and the surface area around the mouth of the tunnel was sucked in before their eyes.

Charlie grabbed the man in the hole round the shoulders before he was dragged under in the landslide. Kitty let out a sharp little cry, but he had him securely under the arms and with help from the others got him clear as the opening slid together and all evidence of a hole vanished.

'Oh Jesus, Jesus.'

Kitty and Eileen moved away, unable to do anything more. They knew that the woman they had found was now surely dead. The rescue team would seek another entrance into the hell below, looking for the main basement shelter with over 150 women, children and old people still missing.

Down at the pub there were frantic people searching for friends and relatives who had gone to the school shelter for the night. As soon as Kitty appeared she became the focus of attention for those who were desperate for news. She was known to everyone in the area as a warden and they expected her to have detailed information, but she had to disappoint them. She told the inquirers that it could be hours yet before they knew if anyone would be brought out alive.

These people were desperate for confirmation one way or another. It was the dreadful uncertainty which tortured them. The strength of the women astonished Eileen. Here they were, living in the frontline of battle themselves, yet few showed signs of giving way to fear.

She saw Mrs Leyland searching for her daughter. It turned out that she had been caught out by the raid when coming home from work, and by the time she reached her house the child had been taken into the shelter by a kindly neighbour. Now that kindness had tragically backfired and the Leyland girl was among those trapped.

The WVS women volunteers were ladling out hot tea to all comers. The pub was still open and crowded with first-aid people and walking wounded. Tea helped to keep down the dust, but it was a precious item these days. Rationing meant that tea-leaves were never thrown away. Whenever a new pot was brewed, they simply added another spoonful to the sodden mass in the bottom of the urn.

Kitty caught sight of one young boy, an eleven year old she knew from nearby Hadwell Street.

'Sam, what you doing here?'

From his face she saw at once that he, too, had lost someone in the school bomb. Eileen watched as Kitty skilfully extracted the whole story from him. The concern in her face as she listened to his story made her want to cry at the injustice of it all.

He had been out playing with some young tearaways from a local street gang when the sirens went. Old Jim Sykes the warden had caught him running home and stopped to give him a lecture on being out on his own. By the time Sam escaped the dreadful Sykes it was gone eight and his mother and sisters had already set off to the shelter. Knowing that he'd cop a hiding when he finally caught up with them, he was in no hurry to reach the school. And that had saved his life.

Those last few minutes made all the difference between life and death. At nine minutes past eight the Germans dropped their high explosive and Sam lost all his family in one appalling blow. Now it appeared likely that he was the sole survivor.

The tunnelling went on all night. Once they had found the position of the basement shelter, the rescue team set to work, making more than one entrance down towards the victims. The basement had covered a large area, but it soon became apparent that when the school had collapsed the rubble from floors above had poured into the shelter, dividing it off into sections.

The depth of the wreckage varied in each case. Where gas and water pipes had been ripped from the walls, there was a danger of flooding or of finding people who had drowned when water poured into their confined space.

Kitty had found a priest wandering in the ruins and brought him up to the scene of the rescue attempt. He was a local Roman Catholic leader and many of the Italian families in the area had known him. According to the shelter list there were many of his parishioners among them. With his soft Irish brogue and practical common sense, he was not an unwelcome participant in the scene. He moved from one tunnel to another, ready to give comfort to any survivors or absolution to the dead and dying.

Charlie was anxious to do his share of the tunnelling. Whenever he got close to finding someone trapped, he redoubled his efforts using dreadful curses as he heaved the debris aside.

'Come on, you fucking...' Sometimes he would remember that the priest was right there beside him and abruptly apologise. But

288

minutes later, in the tension and struggle to reach his goal, he would forget himself again. Soon it became a kind of habit:

'Christ, fuck it, sorry, Father, bleeding hell, sorry...'

The woman he found was buried up to her neck in plaster and caked in ochre. The rescue team got enough of the rubble away so that a nurse could get in to give her a shot of morphine to ease the pain. Until she was free to the waist no one took any chances; they were too afraid that the tunnel might cave in on her. Her legs were pinned by a girder and bricks and only when these were cleared and propped up, could they pull her out and see the extent of her injuries. The nurse told Kitty later that she would almost certainly have to have both legs amputated below the knee.

Kitty gave Eileen a concerned look at this news, thinking of Jon, but this was no time for private grief. Eileen was soon busy fetching more stretcher crews forward to pick up the wounded.

Out on the Goswell Road a line of ambulances stood waiting, their women drivers smoking as they waited. Sporadic gunfire could be heard in the distance but the focus of the raid seemed to have shifted away from their part of London.

There had been 400 bombers over or so they said. The biggest raid to date with heavy fighter support, and all because of the full moon. How could they go on night after night, taking such remorseless punishment? Eileen thought she had never seen such bravery. The Londoners seemed to take it all so calmly, trying to make light of it, trying to carry on with their lives as best as they could. There were no civilians in London now. Every man, woman and child was in the frontline. She thought the whole city deserved a bloody medal.

Charlie emerged from the night for a break in the pub. Most of the wounded had now been taken away to rest centres or back to their homes and there was an uneasy lull. As Eileen fetched mug after mug of strong tea out to the rescue squads, she had seen the strain on their faces. Now she saw Charlie collapse, an old man after his exertions. Kitty found a cigarette and divided it with him, getting him to relax.

He told them how he had heard screams from beneath the rubble, perhaps four or five feet further down, no more. Screams that were silenced by another more terrifying noise: the sound of gushing water. Somehow, somewhere, the rescuers had disturbed a water main or perhaps it was some earlier disturbance, but the water was rising in the shelter and the terror of trapped women and children plainly reached the rescuers above.

The Fire Brigade went to bring in pumps to try and stop the water level from rising, but it was bitterly cold down below ground and by the time they broke through they could see into some sections of the basement, but it was already too late for some of those trapped.

'They had no chance,' he told them wearily. 'Copped it, just like that.'

Just six were brought out of that hole alive.

Nothing could dissuade Charlie from going back to his work. The men in the tunnels now changed places every half an hour, but they were all very tired as the night drew on. Charlie's face was etched with filth and exhaustion. One of his comrades was weeping from sheer tension as they found more pockets of bodies among the ruins.

You could tell from their voices when the people they came across were already dead. It was heart-breaking when the digging stopped as the bodies were pulled out along the tunnel. A nurse and the priest stood by but the rescue team would shake their heads.

'No chance, mate. She's a goner.'

As the first faint light of morning broke through the drifting dust, Kitty and Eileen seemed to find new strength. The sunrise when it came was ironically beautiful, casting pale pink and golden rays across the tortured ruins while high above the late moon still hung in the cold air.

They had broken the exhaustion barrier and now felt that they could stay all day until they knew the worst. Not until their friend's body was fetched from the rubble would either woman leave the site.

Thirteen hours they toiled, tunnelling deep under the shifting rubble, almost careless of danger now. As each new victim was brought up to the surface they were laid out, covered with a blanket, until the stretcher crews could take them away.

160 had been trapped. The majority had died from the initial fall of masonry as the school buildings collapsed in on them. Whole families had died together: here a mother with two sons, just eight and ten; there an Italian group: mother, three daughters and two sons, aged from six to twenty; another comprising grandfather, mother, father and three daughters. Old men and women in their seventies and babies of just a few months, they all died together. Scarcely a street in the area had escaped without loss.

Eileen was full of admiration for the courage of everyone she saw about her. There was nothing special about the rescuers. They were just ordinary local people who, for the most part, had never held any responsible posts before, many of whom were unemployed.

She had heard J.B. Priestley talk on the radio about a People's War and now she understood what he had meant. The whole country was involved in the struggle, not just the Forces but women, children and old folk. The frontline was everywhere; it was right here, in every street, in every home. It was the 'common' people who had been despised for so long who, by their strength and determination, would pull them through the worst of this war and show that they were the real strength of the country.

Individual loss and private grief had little place when all the old barriers between families and neighbours were falling away, to be replaced by a growing sense of community. They gave each other support and comfort. Together they would find the strength to win through.

As Eileen and Kitty watched and waited they had little to say to one another that would ease the blow. As the hours passed the realisation that Vi was dead became fact. They stood in silence as the rescue squad brought out the bodies one by one.

Violet Tracey's was the third from last.

The day after Violet Tracey's funeral a woman turned up at the house to take her room. She said she had heard about Lily through the local rest centre for refugees and was told there could be a good safe place for her.

Safe? Yes, it seemed that Iris Kennedy was in need of some

protection. Since leaving her violent husband almost ten months before she had been on the move, earning her way as a barmaid, but somehow he always seemed to catch up with her.

'I can't seem to shift him,' she told Kitty and Eileen over a cup of tea at the kitchen table. 'The bugger turns up out of the blue, roaring drunk and ready to beat the hell out of me. Look!' She rolled back the sleeve of her heavy woollen cardigan to display a mass of yellowing bruises the length of her arm.

Kitty exchanged a glance with Eileen, sharing the same immediate thought. Iris Kennedy was no lightweight herself. At 45 or perhaps it was 50 she had an ample figure, large but not running to fat. She looked as though she knew very well how to look after herself. Her husband Bill must surely be a mountain of a man to take his belt to her in the way she had described.

'When you think of all the poor folks who've copped it in the Blitz, it makes you sick,' said Iris. 'Bloody Jerries can't even drop one on him! And he never did a decent thing in his life. When I think how I've worked my fingers to the bone and then rushed home to get him his tea on time – well, I'll go to our house!' She took a long draught of tea, shaking with emotion.

'Perhaps you've shaken him this time.'

'Perhaps he's dead. It's what he deserves. Do you know he once tried to throttle me? Drunk he was and red with rage. He'd drunk the rent and more, and thought he'd take it out on me first. He put his hands round me, pressing hard here' – she demonstrated on her own neck – 'until I almost blacked out. But then someone came by, lucky for me, and he had to stop. He never said nothing to me, not a word. Just took my wage packet and went off again to drink the bloody lot.'

'Didn't you go to the police?'

'Don't make me laugh. They wouldn't give a toss. Family matters, dear, that's what. Anyway, my throat was killing me. I couldn't say a word for days. It hurt like hell.'

'So then you left him?' asked Eileen, wondering how she had put up with him that far. But Iris shook her head.

'I had to get some cash together first. He had this job but I never knew how much he earned. He used to give me something for food, you know, but he never had any idea about prices or rationing. He said I was conning him, the lousy bastard.'

Just then they heard the front door slam and Lily's footsteps on the stairs. Kitty welcomed her, taking her basket from her, and then rapidly filled her in on Iris and her situation.

'Well, that's no problem,' said Lily, gratefully accepting a cup of stewed tea. 'As it happens we have a room for you.' She said nothing about the circumstances by which the room was now vacant, although Iris might have guessed. 'I just hope that brute of a husband of yours doesn't suddenly turn up here one night.'

'I think I've really given him a run for his money this time. I want to make a fresh start, if I can. I want to be my own woman, earning my own money, do you see?'

'Oh yes, dear,' said Lily, 'I think we all understand that.'

All Moira knew was that this was the new contingent of pilots for the base. They were Canadians, already tried and tested in battle but now returning to active duty after a rest period. She had met a Canadian flier before, one of Alan's friends, and he had been outgoing, a bit of a lad, boastful.

When she finally heard the train shunt into the station she got out and went to meet the aircrew as they turned out into the yard. Her initial opinion of Canadians was confirmed by a cheerful round of wolf-whistles and bright comments which Moira shrugged off with tolerant good humour. She directed them into the back of the covered truck and was preparing to leave when one of the fliers called out,

'Hey, don't forget our skipper!'

Moira hustled herself out of the cab and went in search of the missing Canadian, relieved that she had not turned up at camp minus the leader of the little group. It was bad enough to get sent out on extra duty at a few minutes' notice without blotting your copybook by leaving a – what was he? – a flight lieutenant behind.

'You haven't seen a stray flier, have you, Fred?' she asked the local station master as he was packing up for the night.

'I think you're looking for me.'

As she turned Moira saw a moving pile of fishing tackle and rods carried by the missing Canadian. He was wearing a leather bomber jacket and a peaked cap that totally shadowed his face. His voice came from behind a forest of rods.

293

'Flt Lt Rangel, is it?' She pronounced his name in a hard, almost Germanic way which, to her surprise, had him hooting with laughter.

'Ran*gel*, Ran*gel*,' he corrected her, 'in the French way. Geoffrey Rangel, from Quebec, you see?' He shifted the rods in his arms. 'I'll shake hands when we've dumped these little items.'

'I see you intend to go fishing,' Moira commented scathingly as they crossed the forecourt towards the truck.

'My passion,' he told her enthusiastically. 'We've just been up in Scotland. Fantastic! I've never seen such salmon like that since – well, since back home.'

At the back of the truck he loaded his precious tackle on to his men who bore it with good humoured jibes and then, as he pulled down the canvas flaps, Moira caught sight of his face for the first time.

She felt suddenly rooted to the spot, unable to move. Her eyes were centred on the action of his hands as he secured the canvas, on the shape of his nose, the line from jaw to throat that set her pulse racing. When he had finished he pulled the cap from his head and ran a hand through his thick dark hair. Yes, more than a touch of French inheritance there. And knowing it somehow made him all the more attractive.

'Well? Shall we go?'

She had to pull herself together before he noticed something. She became all efficiency, hurrying forward and opening the front door for him.

'Don't bother with all that stuff,' he told her, swinging himself up into the cab in one fluid very physical move.

She hurried round and climbed up into the driver's seat, very conscious of his closeness, aware of his attention as she started up the old truck with solid professionalism.

As the truck rumbled up the road in the darkness only the cats' eyes flashed, picked up by the masked headlights in the blackout conditions. She tried to avoid looking round at him, but it was pretty difficult to restrain herself. He had unzipped his leather jacket and sat with a foot balanced against the dashboard, half turned in her direction. He was really quite something.

'Is it far to the camp?'

His question took her out of her daydreaming, but she was

294

delighted. 'About half an hour, sir.' She flashed him a sideways glance. 'Did you come down from Scotland today?'

'No, from York Shire.' But he still made it sound like the ends of the earth. She rather liked the new pronunciation. 'We left before dawn and we've had to sleep in the corridor of the train.'

'You must all be jolly tired.'

'Well, I guess we're pretty tough.' She knew that he was looking directly at her and a surge of excitement shot through her. 'Tell me your name.'

She told him, meeting his eyes as he searched her face, aware of a sudden sense of recognition.

'I guess you're a local girl, hey Moira? You know this area pretty well.'

She didn't deny a word of it.

'I just love the countryside.'

'I knew it. There's something special about a woman who's country born and bred. I just can't take those flighty city types, all paint and powder, you know? I like the natural sort.'

Moira kept a tight check on herself as she concentrated on the road ahead. She was only glad that in her haste to get down to the station she hadn't had time to get properly made-up that night.

'Seeing as how I'm a total stranger round here,' he added plaintively, 'how would you take the suggestion that maybe you could show me around? I'd really appreciate your company, Moira, and maybe you'd know some of the best rivers hereabouts? I guess a country girl like you would enjoy a spot of fishing?'

Fishing had suddenly become the most attractive of pastimes. She saw it now – a weekend away, a secluded riverside hotel complete with swans and candlelight.

'Perfect,' she said.

He produced a pack of cigarettes, a foreign brand, and helped himself before offering them over to her. Their hands touched as he lit one for her.

She knew it was crazy and irrational. She had not gone out with a flier for months – not since Alan had bought it. She had stuck with Peter Martlesham, safe in the knowledge that because of his leg he had a good ground job. That meant a certain security, that he was always going to be there whenever she wanted him. Peter had money and he was good fun. He had a certain polish that beat other contenders – and there were many – by a mile. They had some good times together, going round in his car, putting up once or twice at a classy country hotel. He treated her right. She thought she saw distinct possibilities for the future with him. Hadn't she always said that she was looking for a nice, safe, and rich husband?

Why then was she putting all that at risk now – and just because of a flier! Because even though she knew it was crazy, she simply couldn't help herself. Absurd, irrational, even irresponsible – but the moment she saw him she knew. Perhaps for the first time in her life she had fallen head over heels in love, and she knew that she could not lose that chance now.

In the evening as they were clearing away the supper things there came a ring at the front door bell. Eileen and Lily looked up apprehensively; callers were rare after blackout.

Eileen went upstairs to see who it was and was rather alarmed to find a soldier in khaki on the doorstep. His cap was pulled low across his brow, shading his face, and in the darkness of the street and hallway, Eileen had no way of recognising him.

'Sorry to give you a fright,' he said, and his voice was vaguely familiar. He seemed to be trying to place her too, shifting his feet on the steps. Eileen noticed that he had a kitbag beside him on the ground. 'Is Vi in?'

She realised at once who he was. George Tracey, Vi's husband, returned for embarkation leave.

The full irony of the situation hit her with a wave of bitterness. She leant forward and pulled him inside the hallway.

'Oh, George.'

'I'm sorry, I don't think I know ...'

'It's Eileen, Eileen Howard, you know, Moira's friend. I live here now.'

She shut the front door and switched on the dim blue light in the hall. It did not do a great deal to help illuminate the scene, but she saw that he was looking at her rather oddly, perhaps remembering their brief meeting and the Dunkirk story.

'Who is it, Eileen?'

Lily's voice called up from below, but rather than answer her

Eileen insisted that George come on down to the kitchen.

'Oh, it's you, George.' Lily stared at him, her face blanching, her eyes straying beyond him to Eileen.

'Hello, Lily love.' He went straight over and gave her a kiss. 'Where's Vi? She's not working tonight, is she?'

'You better come and sit down, George.'

'Only I've got my bit of leave before we embark. Only 36 hours, mind, but I don't want to waste a minute of it. I said to my mates...' He fell silent, turning from one to the other, suddenly disturbed by their faces. 'What's wrong? What are you looking at me like that for?' His face grew rigid and his shoulders tensed. 'Where's Vi?' His eyes widened. 'Oh Lord, not Vi!'

Lily went and laid a hand on his shoulder.

'George, love...'

'Not Vi! Oh God, God, what's happened? Tell me, for Christ's sake. What's happened to her?'

Lily sat down beside him at the table, holding his hand. She put into words the tragedy of the school Blitz, explaining how Vi had gone into the shelter to help with the children, and how she had died with them.

George was suddenly choked, his chest heaving with the surge of emotion as tears flooded his eyes. His body seemed to sag, crumpling forward across the table, still holding Lily's hand.

Eileen went and stood out in the garden, frost on her face in the raw night air. The paving stones were damp under her feet. The night was cold and clear and the moon shone with an icy glare, silvering the ragged plants and grasses of the borders, frosting the brickwork of the walled garden.

She was weeping with anger and bitterness at the cruelty and injustice of it all. They had been married for such a brief time. It was senseless. There was no reason or pattern. Fate was wicked, playing games heartlessly with people's lives.

She little realised that fate was about to play her another trick.

That afternoon it was a very subdued woman who arrived at Bart's Hospital. Her heart was not in her visit to Jon – the first since her unexpected meeting with Mrs Pemberley on the night of the school raid. Since then she had been completely absorbed

297

by the raw brutalities of war, first with Vi's death, then the funeral, and finally George Tracey's pitiful appearance at the house. As she climbed the stairs to the ward she had no idea how she would be received, and at this moment she cared even less. Personal problems had paled into insignificance.

And yet it was a time for surprise meetings. As she pushed open the door to the ward she halted abruptly in her tracks. At Jon's bedside there sat another unexpected visitor: Gareth James.

He got to his feet, as astonished to see her as she was to see him. There was something different about him. It was not just the uniform. He looked older, more assured, almost another man from the hesitant young pilot she had met at Blackpool or the moody student of Charnwood days.

'Eileen!' exclaimed Jon, sitting up against his armchair of pillows. She went to his side immediately.

'Jon, I'm sorry I haven't had a chance to get away.'

'Don't be silly, darling. Come and give me a kiss.'

As they kissed Eileen could feel Gareth's eyes upon them. She drew away, watching Jon's face, now so full of life and colour. There was none of his usual mood of irritation today. He had not looked so well in weeks. She thought perhaps it was just that he was pleased to see his old friend again, or that he was really glad that she had come back. Did he regret what had happened on her last visit?

'Don't you remember Gareth, darling?' he was saying, and there was something in his voice, a faint undertone to the friendliness that made her wary. 'Someone up at Duxford heard that I'd pranged and so Gareth thought he'd come and polish me off!' There was a trace of his old cynicism back again.

'Of course I remember. How are you, Gareth?'

She tried to keep her voice completely neutral, but all the time she was remembering Jon's accusations their first night together in London. Was that what was wrong? He had told her that Gareth had always been in love with her, infatuated, that was the word he had used. And she remembered her shock and the way it had tainted their time together, making her seem cheap, then naïve, making a fool of her.

As she met Gareth's eyes it was hard to keep back the resentment she felt towards him. Not only for destroying her

298

happiness with Jon but the old score over the letters which had brought her disgrace at Charnwood. Disgrace and shame, that was what he had brought her. It was little wonder that she should look less than delighted to see him there.

'I'm very well,' he replied, his deep voice full of the musical Welsh lilt which she had forgotten. He stared directly back at her with the eyes of her childhood, a face so familiar to her that she felt her alienation in the white hospital ward all the more. 'And you're looking very well yourself, Eileen,' he added, his voice even and without emotion. There was nothing in his face or attitude to confirm or deny Jon's old assertion, yet Eileen felt acutely uncomfortable in his presence.

'I'll say she is, a real cracker!' Jon kept an arm about her waist possessively, as though to demonstrate ownership in front of his friend. 'I don't know what I'd have done without Eileen. She's been the only one to keep me going, coming here everyday even though she's rushed off her feet with work.'

Eileen could hardly disguise the way she felt about Jon's sudden burst of spontaneous support for her. In all the weeks she had been coming there to visit him, he had never once praised her. In fact, until he spoke, she had no idea that he had ever considered her efforts, her problems, let alone understood them.

'Eileen's engaged in some very high-powered stuff these days,' he was telling his friend. 'Hush-hush, you know. That's right, isn't it, darling? She works with Patrick Fairweather who used to be down at Kenley with us. Don't suppose you ever came across him? Blunt, no-nonsense Yorkshire type.'

'As a matter of fact, yes, I know him quite well,' said Gareth, taking them both by surprise. 'That's the reason that I'm down here, actually. Pat's forming this new group and –'

'– he's asked *you* to join it?'

'Yes. You see I came down to meet him about six weeks back and he explained what was going on. He thought I might do a bit of good and invited me along. He seems to have his head screwed on all right.' He paused and looked at Eileen. 'He mentioned that you were working with him, Eileen.'

'Well, you've got me to thank, old man,' Jon declared with a spreading grin. 'It was yours truly who told Pat what a bloody good flier you were. Fly anything, I told him. You remember that evening in the pub, don't you, Eileen?'

She did indeed. It was the evening they had met each other again. But she felt betrayed. Pat had said nothing to her about signing Gareth for his special operations group, nothing at all to even indicate that he had met him. She supposed that he must have noted down Gareth's name that very evening after Jon had praised his natural abilities as a pilot, and later checked out his record and called him for interview. And all without even mentioning his name to her.

'So it looks as though I'll be working with you and Pat in the team,' Gareth concluded, and he cast her a look that did not go unmarked by Jon in the bed.

'Then everything works out just fine,' said Jon. 'You can be the best man at our wedding. Eileen and I are getting married just as soon as they let me out of here.'

It was obviously a day for bolts from the blue. Eileen and Gareth both stared at him with round eyes of astonishment, struck dumb by his confident announcement. Gareth saw her reaction and frowned, but when she did not deny it, he took a deep breath and said quietly,

'Then I must congratulate you. Both of you.'

As though his words had somehow set the seal on the event, Jon gave a hearty laugh, pulling her closer. She turned her head from one to the other, alarmed at the way in which the decision seemed to have been taken over her head, all cut and dried.

'Now just hold on,' she protested.

'What's wrong, darling? Don't be coy in front of Gareth. He's a man of the world. I'm sure he understands the situation very well.' He raised a hand to caress her face while noticing the reaction on Gareth's face. 'It's not that we have to get married – unless Eileen's been keeping it to herself.'

'Jon!'

'Aren't women the end? You tell them how much you love them and need them and all they think about is appearances!'

She saw then that he meant it, meant every word about loving her, needing her. In his eyes she saw an appeal behind the gaiety, an echo of his former desperation. She saw that he really did need her and wanted to be committed to her and she to him. Until the meeting with his mother she had half been expecting that he would ask her. His depression, his sense of insecurity had all convinced her that he looked to her as the mainstay of his future once he got out of hospital. He depended upon her. The thought of a future alone seemed intolerable, but then his mother had turned up. Or rather, she had discovered that Mrs Pemberley had been coming in all the time, that she was not the only one he had to depend upon.

What had convinced him that there was a future in their relationship? Had his mother's undoubted hostility been beneficial after all? She wondered if the thought of being isolated in the countryside with his family had forced him to make a decision, without even asking her. She supposed it was flattering that he wanted her to be his wife in spite of his family's opposition, but there was still something that did not feel quite right about the whole thing.

She left the ward with Gareth as visiting time came to an end. Jon kissed her and then waved them off, looking his old self, apparently quite assured and happy that the future had been settled.

Outside in the corridor Eileen was more than ready to say goodbye and leave Gareth there and then. But he had other ideas.

'I hope to God you know what you're doing,' he told her bluntly, catching her off guard.

She looked at him and saw that he was furious, his lips drawn in a tight line of disapproval, eyes hard and unforgiving.

'It's no picnic looking after a cripple, you know. He'll be totally dependent upon you, and when he gets out of here he'll need you more than ever. You can't realise the pressure there will be. You'll have to pack in your job, for a start, you'll have no life of your own. It would be much better for all concerned if you were to back out now – before it's too late.'

'Back out? But I don't want to back out.'

He glared at her, his face shadowed with undisguised disgust.

'Then more fool you,' he declared savagely.

'How dare you! How dare you come here with all your bitterness and take it out on us. We were happy – we don't need you to come along.'

'Happy? Oh yes, and I suppose you thought that he would marry you even before the crash.' He shook his head. 'Jon doesn't

301

think you'd be sacrificing anything by marrying him. He thinks he's doing you a favour offering to marry you at all!'

'You bastard.'

He saw her face and the passion he had aroused and for a moment she thought he regretted going so far, but he did not apologise or make any move towards her. He simply turned abruptly on his heel and left her standing there.

The next day when she visited Jon she deliberately arrived at the hospital later than before, hoping to avoid any chance of meeting Gareth again. She knew it was going to be hard enough working with him as part of Pat's team but that was at least in the future and she thought she would not have to be alone with him.

But she need not have worried. There was no sign of Gareth and Jon was sitting up in a wheelchair, absolutely delighted with his own progress. He talked for the first time of going to the special unit at Roehampton and of trying out the new technical devices that could help him to walk again. He painted a bright picture of the future, including her in everything. He was like his old self. He looked better, he felt better, he was warm and considerate. She began to wonder how she had doubted his love for her or her own feelings for him. Everything was going to be all right after all.

But when she came out of the ward, her spirits high and with never a thought in her head about yesterday's scene, she found Gareth sitting on the bench against the far wall.

He got to his feet when he saw her, and she automatically assumed that he was waiting to go in to see Jon and hadn't wanted to meet her. But to her surprise he did not cross over to the door but came across to her, blocking her exit to the stairs down.

'You must let me talk to you. You must let me apologise.'

'All right, you've apologised. Now let me pass.'

'No, look...' He took her by the arm, then seeing her expression let go of it again. 'We can't talk here. Isn't there somewhere we could go and have a drink?'

'I don't want to talk to you at all. I just want to go home.'

'Yes, you must think me a real bastard for what I said yesterday.'

'I don't think of you at all,' she said sharply. 'You've already caused quite enough trouble in my life, thank you very much. I'd prefer to see you as little as possible in the future.'

He was frowning, genuinely puzzled and offended by her remarks.

'How have I caused you trouble? I've never consciously done anything that would hurt you.'

It was the softening in his voice, that edge of vulnerability that made her believe him. She could not keep up her cold act of repudiation. She sighed wearily.

'Look, I've accepted your apology. Let's leave it at that, shall we?'

'Come and have a cup of tea at least and I'll know that you've forgiven me.'

She thought that this was nothing less than blackmail but he seemed determined. If she didn't give in she suspected it was likely they could be standing there arguing all night.

'All right, just one cup, and then I must go.'

She took him to the Lyons café, which was the nearest place she could think of and with the idea that the occasion would be as brief as possible. Also, it was rather noisy, drawing many customers from the neighbouring business areas, and therefore provided good cover for conversation and any unfortunate outbursts that might occur.

They said nothing to one another as they were served with tea. Gareth insisted on ordering buns, perhaps remembering as she did that other distant occasion when they had gone out together.

But they were very different people now. The war had aged them, matured their outlook, destroyed many of their youthful dreams and fulfilled others. Gareth did not look 23 any more than she looked or felt her own age. Responsibility and suffering had left its mark on them both, and if she thought that he looked more assured for the change, then perhaps she did too.

'I –'

'I'd –' He stopped, apologised, and let her go on.

'I was just going to say that Jon's announcement yesterday came as much as a shock to me as it did to you.' She stirred her tea vigorously although there was no sugar in it. 'He sprang it on both of us out of the blue.'

303

'Then you haven't made up your mind to marry?'

'Oh yes,' she said sharply. 'There's no doubt of that. It was just that he hadn't brought the idea out into the open.'

'Well, I wish you would think twice about it. I've seen a lot of pretty awful injuries in this war, a lot of pilots whose lives have been destroyed. It affects them psychologically as well as physically, you know. The crash is really just the beginning of their troubles. You don't realise what can be involved. The whole thing could turn into a nightmare.'

'Look, I don't know where you've got the idea that I've had a nice, safe war so far. I've probably seen things just as terrible as you have. I was posted first to Biggin Hill and then to Kenley. I was there all during August and September when the bombing raids were at their height. And since September I've been here, in the heart of London, facing the Blitz night after night – so don't you try and tell me what it's all about because I've had my full share.'

'I'm sorry.'

'And I don't need your advice. Jon and I have something special. It's going to take more than this to break us.'

'What do his family say?'

'What do you think his family say? You can be certain they are not wild about having their former housemaid become their daughter-in-law.'

'Then you're a lot braver than I gave you credit for, you and Jon.' He sighed, opening his hands in a gesture of surrender. 'What more can I say? You've clearly made up your minds. I wish you well.'

Eileen sat back, watching his face.

'Do you? I wish you would, Gareth. I wish we could all three forget the past and be good friends.'

She saw a shadow cross his face, some natural reaction which he fought to keep down. But before he could answer her there came a low wail of an air-raid siren from the street outside.

'We must find a shelter.'

'No, it's all right, I must go home.'

But out on the street they were immediately caught by a warden and forced to join the growing crowd of people hurrying down into the nearby Underground station.

*

The tube station was already filling up with its usual clientele of regular shelterers, people who queued every afternoon to get places down on the platforms for the night. It was normal for the best places to be taken by the time the shelters opened at four pm. By seven the only places left would be on the emergency stairs.

It was the first time that either of them had used the tube for a long time. They had heard or read stories about the popularity of the tube as public shelters but neither of them had seen the real state of things for themselves. In September the Government had appealed to people not to use them and there was a lot of talk about 'Blitz moles' and the danger of developing a 'deep shelter mentality'.

'All that means,' Kitty had explained, 'is that the Government are afraid people will sit out the bombing rather than try to carry on as normal.'

Eileen had suspected they were really worried that production would fall if people took too much care of themselves. She couldn't see much difference between the 'moles' in the tube stations and the 'moles' who hid themselves away in luxury hotels in the Lake District. Except that the latter had never lifted a finger to help with war production.

Hustled down into the Underground tunnels, Gareth caught hold of Eileen by the arm so that they would not be separated in the crush of people. As they moved deeper into the earth the noise of the wailing sirens gradually disappeared. Down on the platforms there were fights for space.

'Here, give over. That spot's already bagged.'

'Get lost! Ground's free, mate.'

'Not where I come from. Shove off!'

There was a racket selling space in the best places. People would put down bundles to save a space supposedly for a friend and then auction it off later on, often for as much as half a crown which could have paid for a decent hotel room.

'Will we have to stay here all night, do you think?'

'I expect they'll tell us if the All-Clear goes,' Gareth told her. 'Look, let's spread my raincoat out and we'll be more comfortable.'

Even though the platforms were filling up, the trains were continuing to run. People were not allowed to put down bedding beyond a white line painted eight feet from the edge until after the trains stopped running when they could move forward another few feet. Passengers alighting from trains which stopped at the station were obliged to pick their way over the bodies as they tried to make their way to the exit, but often the shelter warden would refuse to let them out in the raid.

As time passed and the platforms filled up the air became stale. The hot wind that blew through the tunnels carried foetid smells and swarming mosquitoes. They were shocked by the conditions they found themselves in, by the people packed in close together, huddled and pitiful.

By the wall, wrapped in a shawl and an eiderdown, a mother tried to feed her baby. Next to her was a woman in a bright red coat and flowered headscarf struggling to control her rebellious ten year old. The boy was terribly thin and his shoulders were sharp and hunched under his pullover. His mother clearly found him a handful, trying to get him to sit down and behave. He kept asking her the time, apparently because the longer a raid lasted the more likely school was to start late next morning or be cancelled altogether.

Several of the children had their heads shaven and painted blue against lice. The warm, foetid atmosphere was a breeding ground for dirt and disease. Another woman, thin-faced and sweating, was six or seven months pregnant and looked feverish perhaps with 'shelter cough', the euphemism for a 'flu epidemic hitting the whole town.

Where Gareth and Eileen sat propped against the wall near the exit tunnel there was at least some ventilation from the trains, but the smell became unbearable as the night wore on. Of course it was much worse at the other end of the platform where, behind a flimsy hessian screen, a bucket provided the only toilet for all these people. As they were below the sewerage mains it was quite insanitary and stank to high heaven after only a short time.

'It's terrible,' Eileen whispered, hunched up and ill at ease in the midst of such misery. Round her some were sleeping, although with the crying of the babies and arguments that were still going on, there was a good deal of noise. 'I can't bear to think of these people coming here night after night.' She stopped, aware that everything she said was clearly audible to those near them. 'How do you put up with it?' she asked her immediate neighbours, a family of grandmother, mother and two children.

'Oh it's not so bad,' said the mother, busily changing the nappy of the youngest child. 'We've tried all different shelters and this is the best of the lot.'

They had trouble believing this, but the woman told them about Tilbury shelter under the railway arches at Stepney down in the East End. It was used as a store for margarine which had long ago gone rancid.

'It was no place for the kids,' said the woman. 'A load of spivs and card-sharps and – well – that kind of woman.'

'Whores,' said the grandmother helpfully, 'that's what they were.'

'All right, mum, that's enough.' Her pained expression flashed towards the children. 'It wasn't right, not with the kids. But it's not safe where we live. Top flat, you see.'

'I got bombed out last week,' chipped in an old man sitting just beyond the little group. 'We were on the second floor. Bomb went straight through.' He moved closer, getting friendly. 'My old woman's still in hospital. 'Course, I reckon as how we were lucky.'

Eileen looked on as the conversation settled into a pattern that had come to be routine all over London, a kind of competition to outdo the others about the size of bomb they had had, the amount of damage their bomb caused, and whose was the worst. After hearing half a dozen bomb stories you became blasé. Even the children went round these days talking of 'stiffs'.

Eileen noticed that Gareth was grinning at her and in spite of herself she smiled back. She found it hard to keep up her anger and old resentment in such surroundings. The conditions forced everyone into an unavoidable intimacy.

She found herself suddenly looking at him in a new light, and what she saw surprised her. He was certainly better looking than she remembered. Or perhaps it was just that his face showed more of the character of the man. His strong, sculptured face had lost a lot of his moody indecision. The hotheaded diatribes of youth which had so alarmed her had gone. He still had a temper – she had seen that for herself – but there was a sense of power about him which spoke of new confidence and assurance. He impressed her.

It was impossible to go on thinking of Gareth in the same way down here. She found that she had to forgive him, even for those things in the past which he had inadvertently brought about. Perhaps, after all, she had been unfair to him.

The night wore on and her head drooped. She did not remember falling asleep, head on his shoulder, or the amused glances of their neighbours imagining they were sweethearts with no place to be alone.

It had not stopped raining all day. Water was everywhere, dripping from the trees down her neck, dripping down her sleeves into her filthy gumboots, splashing off the bare branches and spreading circles in the river. But somehow Geoff just did not seem to notice. He sat on the river bank, his hat pulled low over his face, perfectly contented as his bait was taken and he brought in a new catch.

'Just great, isn't it?' His white teeth flashed a grin in her direction, completely oblivious of her misery.

Moira watched as he unhooked the wriggling fish and placed it in the net in the water.

'I just don't get it, Geoff,' she complained. 'What's the point if all you're going to do at the end of the day is just put the damn fish back where they came from?'

He looked up, surprised. 'What else would I do with them?'

'Why, eat them, of course.'

'Why, Moira, you've got a real sense of humour! You almost had me fooled there!' Still chuckling to himself, he turned back to the river and more serious business.

Oh God, thought Moira, why did I ever agree to come? She sat there huddled and miserable, sure she would get double pneumonia, her hands wrinkled and blue with cold. Why did it have to be fishing? She could have put up with anything else, even rugby or mind-stultifying cricket. At least then there were ways round the fanaticism; you could sit it out in the clubroom or bar, but here there was no escaping the mud, the wet and the sheer physical discomforts just for the sake of being with him. Was he worth it? She stared at his face, as blissful and contented

308

as a child's although it ran with water, and her heart turned over.

God, she must have it bad if she was willing to put up with all this.

'Well, the light's going,' he announced, turning and giving her that remarkable smile. 'I suppose we'd better call it a day.'

She moved to help him with his tackle, squelching in her boots which had let in the water. She knew she must look a mess, but he didn't seem to notice. As he swung his rods over his shoulder, he laid a weighty arm round her and planted a long kiss on her lips.

'Had fun?' he asked.

'Terrific.' She held her face up to his, expecting another kiss.

'We'll try that pool down the weir tomorrow then.' He pushed the pannier into her hands. 'Carry that, will you?'

It was astonishing to realise that it was a month since the school tragedy and Vi's death. Life had to go on even though the Blitz continued with its remorseless terror. 'We can take it,' said Churchill but many people wanted to know who 'we' were. After visiting bombed out streets in Battersea, Churchill had told the press that it was not too bad. But then, he didn't have to live there.

The November raids brought mud in their wake. As winter seized the country and coal rationing began to bite, morale flagged. Rescue squads worked in filthy conditions, gas and electricity cuts made everything much worse. Bombed houses had to be patched up, with tarpaulins over damaged roofs to try to stop the damp seeping through.

But on the 13th only 25 bombers came over London, the lightest raid since they had started. The next day was even more strange. Londoners could not understand the uncanny silence and an evening without the wail of sirens. People found it hard to sleep in the unaccustomed stillness of the night and spent the following morning grumbling about it.

Then the news broke that the Germans had switched their target from London to the Midlands. Coventry had been almost obliterated because of the aero-engine factories. Birmingham was hit on three successive nights, killing and wounding thousands. If London would not break, they would test their strength on the rest of the country.

Pat heard that thousands of civilians in Coventry had tried to get out of the city in fear. The situation was so serious that the authorities wanted to declare martial law to prevent the panic from spreading. Civilian casualties were high.

Pat was privy to much of what came through Bletchley Park these days. He was often there with members of the aircrew he had selected for his new team. Eileen still had not entirely forgiven him for what seemed to be his secretive recruitment of Gareth behind her back. The two men seemed to get on like a house on fire. Gareth's practicality matched Pat's no-nonsense approach to tactics and planning and he always seemed to be around these days so that it was difficult to avoid him.

A new way was needed of carrying the war to the enemy and Pat was especially interested in Gareth's familiarity with new techniques of instrument flying. Night-flying on instruments required a very different temperament from the more individual often reckless bravery of battles earlier that summer. The RAF were using twin-engined Bristol Blenheims, painted black for night patrols. Their pilots needed to be able to pick out barrage balloons, to avoid searchlights and ack-ack, to develop night vision. Both Gareth and Karol had been selected because of their ability as fliers but also because they had proved themselves, coming through the wicked days of August and September unscathed in body but harder, more efficient mentally.

Karol turned up one day at Bletchley Park. As Eileen drove past the sentry who checked her papers and ticked her name off his security list, she found Pat on the steps of the red brick mansion talking to their old friend.

Karol, strong-chinned, with his wry clever face, seemed more relaxed and easy-going since his marriage to Ruth, the WAAF he had met at Kenley. Eileen was keen to see her again and they soon arranged to have a night out somewhere all together.

'We'll have to get a dog-sitter in for Lara,' said Karol with his smart grin. 'She hates being left alone.'

The night out was nothing special in the end. London was comparatively quiet, with provincial cities taking the full force of German bombing. Each time the sirens went now fewer and fewer people ran for the shelters. Conversation might stop for a moment but then everyone continued as normal. Even the wardens had given up trying to force people to take cover. In cinemas they merely flashed a notice on the screen announcing an air raid and asked people to leave their seats quietly so as not to disturb those who stayed to watch the film.

But sitting in the pub between Karol and Pat, with Ruth and Gareth, Eileen felt relaxed for the first time in months. It was wonderful just to be able to sit and chat and have a drink, forgetting her everyday routine. Now that Gareth was in town he had helped to take some of the burden of hospital visits off her. Jon quite enjoyed having his friend there to talk of the old days at Cambridge and Chester, but on the days she went alone, Eileen detected a new mood in him. She wondered whether Jon resented Gareth's good fortune in coming through so far without injury.

'What's all this stuff he's involved in?' he asked her. 'He doesn't seem to fly any more. What's he become? Another glorious pen-pusher?'

Eileen thought he resented not being part of the war any longer. He made sarcastic and patronising remarks about her own work, telling her not to get carried away.

'When we're married,' he told her, 'you'll have to give up all this nonsense.'

She looked round at her friends in the pub and wondered what it would be like to be stuck away in the country – if the worst came to the worst at Charnwood – isolated, trapped. Sitting here, the idea suddenly struck her as absurd. Eileen Howard – the new Mrs Pemberley?

'What's so funny, Eileen?'

She looked up to find the others waiting to share in the joke and she had to lie to cover her confusion. But as she gave a self-deprecating laugh her eyes met Gareth's and for an instant she felt he had guessed her mood.

He made her unsettled, uneasy. The way his shrewd eyes took everything in made her feel increasingly insecure, as though she ought to be re-examining her life. She began to wonder what he expected of her.

The next night, December 8th, the Germans returned to bomb London in force. 350 to 400 bombers, they said. Even the BBC at Langham was hit. But the following day the edge was taken off the Blitz by news that the British forces in North Africa were beating back the Italians.

'It's about time we had a bit of good news,' said Eileen as she walked with Gareth out of the Ministry motor-pool.

'Won't you come and have a drink to celebrate?'

'Oh, I don't think so,' she answered automatically, very aware that there were only the two of them. And then she looked up, thinking she might have offended him. 'I can't tonight,' she added quickly. 'I've so much to do. Perhaps another time.' And she leant over and kissed him lightly on the cheek, just missing the corner of his mouth, then disappeared down the road. He stood there, dazed and unable to move, feeling suddenly very lonely and unhappy.

He couldn't get her out of his mind. Not that she had been absent for any real length of time in all these long months. It helped when he was busy. It would be even better when he was back flying again and did not have to see her every day, knowing that she was Jon's, knowing that she had never given a thought to any other man.

She had never for one moment taken him seriously. She seemed obsessed with Jon to the point of sacrificing the rest of her life as some kind of glorified nurse and companion, subjugated to his moods and tempers and probably under the thumb of that cold bitch who was going to be her mother-in-law. What kind of life was that? Sometimes he half suspected that she could see what faced her, but it was as though she deliberately pushed the truth aside. He had done his best to try and dissuade her. If she preferred to throw her life away then why could he not let her get on with it and let her alone?

At work he found himself gravitating towards her. She was usually there at Pat's side, taking notes, organising his schedules, driving him from place to place. Even when she was not admitted to high-level conferences she would sit in his office catching up on paperwork, always conscientious, always so serious-minded. He would saunter into the office on the pretext of hoping to catch a word with Pat, hanging round while all the time watching her at work.

312

On such an occasion he knew she was working on the Mannheim project. He had volunteered to go on the night raid but Pat was saying he must wait, that he needed him for more experimental work planned in the New Year. The Mannheim raid was important, though, and he thought Pat had probably asked Karol to go.

'Have they decided on a date yet?' he asked her, leaning over her shoulder to read the papers on her desk. He placed a hand on her back as he leant forward.

To Eileen his touch seemed to burn through the material and she tensed under his hand, finding it difficult to concentrate.

'It – it will certainly be before Christmas. Next week –' She glanced back at him, frowning as she briefly met his gaze. She didn't know what to say. He was looking at her in a way that left her little doubt in her mind about him. She knew she ought to say something, or do something, but the spell held her and lasted until they heard the sound of movement from the inner room and Pat appeared with a bevy of officers and Ministry officials to bring her back down to earth.

The doctors at the hospital maintained a strictly professional attitude to pain and suffering, rather as farmers do. Jon was reminded of the way the gamekeepers at Charnwood brought up their pheasant chicks, always prepared for sacrifice.

During the long hours of solitude, suffering and delirium there was all the time in the world for thinking of the future. He slept badly, thinking too much. It was his mother's fault. She made him feel like an invalid. He saw the distaste thinly disguised on her face every time she visited him. She brought him flowers from some bed at Charnwood not turned over to growing vegetables. Mournful, heavy-headed blooms, they drooped at his bedside, withering. Looking at them he remembered his childhood with growing resentment and was afraid for the future.

The pain in the leg that was not there had one advantage. It kept alive the memory of his independence, of the life he had led that had taken him away from the suffocating embrace of his family. He had made it on his own. He had done something with his life that did not owe a thing to influence or family

313

connections. For a brief moment he had been his own man.

And he thought about Eileen. He remembered her face when she entered the ward and saw his mother there, and the guilt he had felt, not being able to tell her the truth. Did she love him? It was the first time he had thought of it. Women always seemed to see him differently, and those he had met and loved in the past were those already in his path. He had never had to pursue any woman. Not once had he been in love, needing love. Until now. He began to realise that there was no one more important to him than this woman, this ordinary pretty unremarkable woman who exasperated him, and yet supported him.

He wanted to talk about her. As he listened to the chatter in the ward, learning that men were born gossips, he saw that no one would understand. They talked lightly; no one wanted to share a private grief. There was no one left he could talk to.

I've suffered too much, he thought with resentment. I'll go off my head alone. Why isn't Eileen here?

The sea was rough, the weather, as always, unkind. Even in the close circle of his arms, Moira felt the wind like a knife through her coat and tears pricked the corners of her eyes.

He seemed so comfortable, at home with the elements, a strong man of nature taking storms and blizzards in his stride.

'Don't you just love the sea?' His enthusiasm shot through his whole body, wrapping her up in a fierce embrace, wanting to share everything with her. 'I wish you could see it back home. Wild, with icebergs coming down from the North.'

She shivered, pressing closer, wanting him to keep on talking. They passed the concrete blocks and stood on the deserted sand watching the grey, glassy waves pounding the barbed wire at the water's edge. 'Danger,' said the sign, 'Mines. It is forbidden and dangerous to proceed beyond this line.' She stood with her hands deep in the pockets of his greatcoat for warmth as they kissed. She didn't give a damn about the cold or the grinning Home Guard sentry up on the prom above. Being with him was enough.

'Guess it's time we turned back.'

'Oh no, Geoff, I . . .' She searched his face, wishing that for once he would actually tell her what he felt. His big handsome face was so open, so honest. Why couldn't he see how much she cared?

'It's a long drive, honey. I don't want to get you into trouble at camp.'

'It's OK. I'll go straight on duty. Geoff, I –'

'What is it?' His wide innocent eyes betrayed nothing.

'Oh forget it. You're right, it's getting late. Let's go.'

She had never felt so inadequate. Days together but never a night. Never so much as a suggestion. They had the opportunity to be together once or twice but it seemed that he was holding back, not wanting to get involved. She knew that he wanted her, and for a desperate week she thought he must be married, that he was that rare creature a faithful husband. But it was not true. One of his squadron had told her. She had to come up with another solution if she could.

In the car going back she marvelled at the change he had brought about in her. She had always gone out of her way to follow London styles and fashions, to be thought sophisticated and wise to the ways of city life. But, for him she had altered her appearance to try and be everything he expected her to be: the simple country-loving girl he wanted. Only she knew how ironic it was. She had told no one of her farm background, of the home she had walked out of ten years before. It was her secret, and now it had strangely reverberated to play tricks with her life. If she hadn't felt so desperate, it might almost have been funny.

As they drew up outside her billet she was reluctant to leave him. She leant across his open window and they kissed with more passion than she could remember. But as she straightened up, she was seized suddenly from behind and thrown back against the side of the car with the strength of anger. Jarred, bruised, she felt stunned as she recognised his voice with a deadly sinking sensation in the pit of her stomach.

'Think you can two-time me, do you? Come here, you bitch!'

'Hey, what the hell is this, pal? No one touches my girl.'

'So you're the new fancy man? Come here, you bastard and I'll knock your block off.'

Moira staggered up from the bonnet of the car, aware of pain in her back. She saw Peter Martlesham lunge at Geoff as he opened the car door to meet the attack. But he was too quick for him, slamming the door back and catching Geoff's hand. His grunt of

315

pain seemed to fire Martlesham on. He tried to grab Geoff's throat through the open window of the car. Moira screamed and flew at him. She grabbed his back, hearing the door of the house open behind her, aware of Veronica's voice full of fear. Martlesham slammed his elbow brutally into her breasts and she doubled up with agony on the damp grass.

'You slut! That's what you get for dropping me.'

Geoff kicked open the car door and plunged out of the driving seat.

'Keep your hands off her, I said! I don't know who you are, buster, but you've sure got it coming.'

The big Canadian seemed almost to dwarf his rival, swinging his fist in a manner that seemed totally professional. The blow caught Martlesham solidly on the jaw and he staggered and lost his balance. Moira saw him collapse on his bad leg and topple backwards.

Geoff moved in to seize him by the lapels of his jacket, almost lifting him off the ground. His face was contorted with anger but Martlesham was beyond sense. His eyes blazing, he turned to glare at Moira, blood on his mouth.

'OK, OK, tell your tame ape to get his hands off me.' He shook himself free, landing awkwardly in the mud. 'Big man, are you? Well, you can have her and welcome.' He brushed himself off, still unsteady on his feet. 'She's nothing but a whore.'

Geoff hit him, and hit him again as he went down for the second time. Who knew where it might have ended had a military police vehicle not screamed up in response to a call and two MPs broke up the fight.

'He would have killed me,' protested Martlesham, white-faced and bloody.

'Sure would!' Geoff looked ready to have another go at him if he got the chance.

'He was waiting for us. He started it,' Moira told the police.

'We'll have to run him in,' said the senior officer looking at Martlesham. 'Take the names of the other two.' He turned to Moira. 'There'll have to be an inquiry.'

'Have you been drinking?'

'He reeks of it,' Geoff put in sarcastically. 'Dutch courage, eh, pal?'

316

Martlesham ignored him, giving his name and rank to the MP. But as the policeman turned towards the others, he spoke up.

'You all know Moira Adams, don't you, chaps? The whole bloody camp knows her.'

'That's enough.'

'Let me get at him.'

The fight threatened to break out all over again but the MPs were tough customers and held them apart. One took Martlesham off for first aid treatment at the camp while the other took particulars of Moira and Geoff's ranks and their addresses.

'I'll come with you in your car,' he told Geoff when they had finished.

Veronica had come out and took Moira by the shoulders. As the MP and Geoff moved towards the car, Moira looked imploringly towards him. He cast her one look, fingering his throat, and then turned with the MP and drove off.

'Oh my God.'

'It's all right, Moira, come on in now.' Veronica steered her away towards the house.

'He didn't say a word. Did you see? He just went without a word.'

'Don't worry. I'm sure he'll be in touch again in the morning.'

'No!' Moira freed herself. 'No! Didn't you hear what he said about me? Didn't you hear what he called me?'

'Geoff?'

'No, that – that –' She shuddered with almost physical disgust. 'I wish he'd killed him. I wish –' She seized Veronica by the arm. 'What's going to happen? He'll never come back to me! What will the police do? How did they ever get here?'

'I rang for them.'

'You – what?' Moira was staring at her, her face draining of colour.

'I thought they were going to kill each other.' Veronica looked startled. 'Come in, now.'

But Moira stood stock still, shaking with temper.

'You thought! You thought! You stupid, interfering fool! Why don't you keep your nose out of my affairs?' Veronica's silence seemed to enrage her even more. 'What the hell did you have to do that for? Of all the bloody idiotic...'

'But, Moira –'

'Oh dry up, will you? You've done enough harm.' She pushed past her into the house, scrambling to get her things for her duty shift. Seeing that Veronica had followed her into the bedroom, she became very cold and brutal. 'You make me sick, d'you know? Always hanging around, telling me what to do. Why don't you just clear off and leave me alone?'

Veronica drew apart a little, looking at her with a sudden calmness.

'As a matter of fact, that's exactly what I will do.' She saw that she had caught Moira's attention. 'I was going to wait before I told you. I was going to pick the right time. But now it seems you've picked it for me.' She stood back in the doorway and drew a deep breath. 'I suppose I've taken just about as much as I can stand. We've been through a lot together, but you don't seem to have learnt a thing. I've seen you go from man to man without a thought, just throwing your life away. You hadn't got the courage to tell Peter it was all over, and this is what happens. You've only got yourself to blame if you lose Geoff now.' She saw that Moira was going to speak but she put up a hand to silence her. 'No, I'm going to say it all now. I've had enough of you, of everything. I'm leaving the WAAF. I'm pregnant, you see, and I'm getting married.'

Moira stood staring at her in absolute astonishment. She said nothing, could say nothing. Veronica had never seen her so shocked.

'I have my own life now,' she added more softly. 'I can't go on the way things are. I wanted to leave as friends, but if you can't accept some criticism from those who love you then I'm sorry. Geoff's a nice man. He cared a lot about you – look at the way he defended you out there. You'll be a fool if you let him go – but it's your own affair, Moira, and I won't interfere ever again.'

She turned and walked out of the room, sad but unrepentant. She did not see Moira gnaw her lip, biting back the fierce emotions that threatened to boil over out of control.

Eileen had the whole of Saturday off and had spent the afternoon at the hospital visiting Jon and talking to his doctor. Jon was making such good progress that he was due to transfer to Roehampton in the New Year. But the news had not cheered him. On the contrary he seemed particularly depressed, sunk deep in a gloom that Eileen could not dispel. He resented the fact that Christmas was coming and she could get out and about with her friends.

'You think more of them than you do of me,' he complained. 'If you really loved me you would spend more time here.'

'If you really loved me' was a common beginning to rebukes about the length and frequency of her visits.

When she returned to the house she was deeply depressed herself and went to have a bath before it grew dark and the air-raid sirens went. She had just got out and was about to change in her room when Iris knocked on her door.

'There's a friend of yours downstairs,' she said. 'Gareth James.'

Eileen was startled. She had tried to give Gareth a wide berth, eager not to repeat what had been an unsettling experience for both of them. The knowledge that once he might have loved her had a profound effect upon the way she looked on him now.

'Oh God, Iris. Say I'm out, will you?' She did not think that he even knew her address.

'Can't, love. I've already said you're in.' She gave a lopsided grin. 'What's wrong with him, then?'

'Nothing, Iris, that's the trouble.' She sighed. 'OK, I'll go down now. Thanks for letting me know.'

She went to the top of the stairs with her dressing-gown tightly belted, nervous as a kitten.

'Hello, Eileen.'

He stood in the hallway, hands thrust deep into the pockets of his trench coat with the collar turned up.

'You'd better hurry up. We're late.'

'Late?'

'Don't say you've forgotten – it's Ruth's birthday. We're supposed to be meeting the others at Covent Garden.'

She had forgotten. All thought of the date that had been arranged for a week or more before had gone out of her head. She stood at the top of the stairs trying to think of an excuse not to go.

'What's up? Don't you want to go?'

'Of course not,' she said hastily. 'It's just that I'm not nearly ready.'

'I'll wait, it's all right.'

She changed behind the open door of her wardrobe while he sat uneasily on the edge of her bed, looking at the photographs she had on the side table.

'Who's that?'

'It's my father.' She peered around the wardrobe door as she struggled into a slip. 'It was taken a long time ago.'

'And this?'

'That's me with a couple of friends. You met them that time at Blackpool, don't you remember?'

He did remember. He sat there staring at the photograph in his hand in silence, lips parted. He seemed completely absorbed in thought when she finally emerged, fully dressed, to brush her hair. She felt troubled as she looked at him, sitting there on her bed, and hurried to get ready and get him out of there. She was sure it would all be all right when they were with Karol and Ruth.

But when they finally turned up on the steps of the Opera House at Covent Garden they were already 40 minutes late. The Opera House had been taken over by Mecca as a ballroom with the band on the stage, the seats removed for dancing and the galleries used as refreshment areas. It was a favourite spot for dancing and already music drifted out on to the street where Gareth and Eileen stood uncertainly, wondering what they should do.

'They're probably inside looking for us. It's too cold to hang about outside. We might as well go in now we're here.' He was afraid that she would suddenly call the whole evening off, not wanting to be with him alone.

But as a new wave of arrivals washed up the steps of the old Opera House they were both borne inside without further discussion and although they both kept up the pretence of looking for Karol and Ruth, they both knew it was impossible to find them in such a crush.

After depositing their coats they emerged on to one of the circular galleries which had once held balcony seats for the ballet or opera and now had little tables and chairs so that you could drink and watch the dancers down in the bowl of the theatre. The music was from one of the popular all-women bands that had made their mark since the war began. They were playing 'You're the Cream in my Coffee' when Gareth suggested they should go down to dance and Eileen found herself agreeing.

The dance floor was packed. They were only two among many couples wearing uniform. Gareth held her lightly as they danced in and out of the crush of dancers, sharing the warmth of the atmosphere among couples out to enjoy themselves for at least one night of the Blitz. Even when the music was interrupted in the middle of 'Red Sails in the Sunset' to announce an air raid, the spirit of the evening refused to be dampened. There were even some impatient catcalls and whistles until the band struck up again and everyone ignored what might be happening outside.

But the mood of the evening had subtly changed. The lights were dimmed and coloured spotlights played over the dance floor trying to catch out the more tenderly entwined to general laughter. In the tightly packed crowd the shifting lights created a more intimate atmosphere and couples drew closer. 'Begin the Beguine' and 'I'll Pray for You' and the mood had dipped into romance. The lights were lower, revealing a myriad of stars in the roof. It was just as though they were dancing in some exotic garden, waltzing together in the shadows with soft, yearning music drifting out on the warm night air.

The laughter had stopped. The band played 'Goodnight Sweetheart'. They were dancing very close together, the look in their eyes that had been light-hearted only moments before had now grown suddenly serious. The smiles died as their eyes caught and held. He was looking at her, lips parted as though he would say something. But he had no need of words for his gaze was full of all the deep unspoken things that had lain between them. They stood together, swaying slightly in their cradle of arms, only aware that from this moment on everything had to be different.

Chapter Ten

Rationing bit deep as people began to think about Christmas, the second of the war. But how different from that Christmas during the Phoney War. Now people really understood what it was all about. Bombed out, rationed, working long hours and sleeping where and when they could, it was little wonder that everyone intended to have the best Christmas they could – in spite of Hitler.

One day Veronica suddenly descended on Eileen at the house in the square. She appeared as surprised as Eileen to discover that her letter had not arrived to warn of her visit.

'It doesn't matter, it's wonderful to see you!' And it was. Eileen found herself staring at her friend, astonished by the visible difference in her face and figure. Not only was she out of uniform, wearing an extremely smart grey suit with a white silk blouse, but she carried herself with new style and self-assurance.

'You look – so different!'

'I feel marvellous. Oh Eileen, I'm so happy! Tim and I are getting married and I want to tell you all about it.'

'That's great news.'

'Please say you're free. Can we go out and celebrate?'

'I have to be at the Ministry by three, but I'm all yours until then.'

'Then let's go Christmas shopping!'

Eileen could not get over her friend's confidence. She watched her in admiration as she turned heads in the street, the Free French matelots with their red pom-poms bobbing in a sea of uniforms as she passed.

Queuing was the new thing. Before the war it had always been a free-for-all getting a bus, but what with rationing and increased bureaucracy at every level people accepted a policy of 'fair's fair' which they would not have stood for before.

Since the centre of London had been hit the large stores like John Lewis or Bourne and Hollingsworth were casualties of the bombing. It was a strange sight to see bowler-hatted men in city suits with measuring tapes checking out the gutted ruins along Oxford Street among splintered glass and sinister shop window dummies. Armed police stood on guard to prevent looting, waving away any press photographers who forgot the censorship rules. Eileen and Veronica soon found that if you had the money the flourishing black market offered a variety of luxury items which could no longer be found even in Knightsbridge or Bond Street.

Exhausted by their shopping they settled into a restaurant just off Leicester Square within sight of the bomb damage on the south side.

'I'm leaving the WAAF,' Veronica announced out of the blue, waiting for Eileen's reaction. 'I'm pregnant.'

'No!' Eileen's exclamation attracted the attention of faces at the neighbouring tables and she grinned at Veronica shame-faced. 'No? Really? Was it planned?'

'You bet it was!' laughed Veronica. 'I wanted to leave, to get married and this was my guarantee! No, really, it's all just marvellous. I've never felt so well in my life. I've never been so happy. Oh Eileen, isn't it just terrific to be in love?'

'I suppose so.'

Veronica saw that she had touched a sore spot. 'Oh Ei, I'm sorry. I forgot about Jon for the moment. He is all right, isn't he? I mean, he is adapting to it all?'

'Yes, yes, he's really doing quite well.'

'But?'

'But nothing. Everything is just fine. Really.'

'Remember, I've been through all that. I understand how difficult it is to adapt.'

'But you love Tim.' She stopped, appalled. It was out before she had even realised what she was saying. She stared at Veronica in horror and immediately denied it. 'I didn't mean...'

'Didn't you? Oh Eileen, you can talk to me.'

'I don't want to talk,' she snapped back, pushing the subject aside. 'Let's forget it, shall we?' She took a long drink, aware of the uncomfortable silence. 'I'm so pleased about you and Tim. Have you set the date yet?'

'It will be sometime in the New Year,' said Veronica, not pressing her further. 'I'll be a free woman by Christmas and we hope to go to Tim's parents for a few days. Then he has one last operation.'

'Another one?'

'They've been very successful. You won't recognise him when you see him.'

'So I'm invited to the wedding, am I?'

'Idiot!'

'We'll have to have a night out together, you, me and Moira.'

Veronica looked away, tracing a pattern on the tablecloth with her finger. 'There have been some problems with Moira.' She seemed to summon up her courage before continuing. 'To be quite frank, Eileen, I've had one hell of a row with Moira.'

'But, why?'

'Oh, she was fine for a while when she got back from London. We spent more time together and she seemed to have settled down. She was steadier, more sensible, you know.'

'Then – let me guess – she met someone?'

'Peter Martlesham, yes. He was a lot older than her, a bit of a rake honestly. But he showed her a good time – until Geoff came along.'

'Geoff?'

'He's a flier, a Canadian. Amazingly good-looking. He just seemed to sweep her off her feet. She threw caution to the wind and hurt Peter pretty badly. I think he wasn't used to being thrown over. As I said, he had a bit of a reputation, bags of money. He was the one who gave girls the push, not the other way round. Well, one night he waited for her to come back from a date with Geoff and a fight broke out. It was dreadful.'

'My God, Veronica, what happened?'

'The MPs broke it up. Geoff got suspended by his CO and Peter asked for a transfer.'

'Oh Lord.'

324

'That's when we had our row. Perhaps I overdid it. But I was so angry! I'd seen it all for all those months. She was treading on everyone round her – and that's when I told her. "I'm leaving," I said. "I'm pregnant and I'm getting married." She just stood there, dumbfounded. She didn't seem able to grasp that I could walk out on her.'

'She took you for granted.'

'I think the baby was the last straw,' Veronica said. 'She saw how happy I was to be pregnant and it hurt her.'

Eileen sat back, upset by the rift between her two friends but able to understand the reasons why it had come about. Perhaps she half suspected this would happen. There had been something in Veronica's earlier letters to suggest it.

'I suppose you think I've grown hard,' Veronica added sadly, 'but I've had enough. I really don't want to know any more. She must get on with her own life.'

She seemed to have lost all the gauche timidity that raw recruit had had that freezing cold night in Gloucestershire when they had met. She seemed another person from the clumsy WAAF always on jankers.

'No, I don't think you're hard at all,' Eileen reassured her. 'I admire you. I envy you, in fact. You seem to have really found yourself. You know what you want to do and you go out and do it. You're very lucky. I've never seen you happier or looking better.' She stretched out a hand across the table and firmly clasped her friend's. 'I wish you every happiness, you and Tim.'

Eileen felt her envy bite deep. She saw that Veronica was a truly happy woman while she and Moira somehow just didn't seem able to do the right thing. Oh, to be that certain, that sure! She could not help wondering why she could not feel the same way about caring for Jon for the rest of her life.

The news of a truce over Christmas was greeted with elation by Londoners. Arranged via the British and German embassies in Washington in the neutral United States of America, it agreed to a break in the bombing from Christmas Eve to December 27th.

The last heavy raid before the truce came on the 22nd and although most people were working long hours, twelve-hour shifts to boost war production, they began to turn their attention to the coming festivities. Simpsons in the Strand showed that it was still possible to serve sirloin to much comment in the press. Turkeys might be scarce and expensive, toy shops might be empty, but holly and paperchains were still hung up in houses and shelters across the land.

Eileen received separate Christmas cards from Moira and Veronica on the same day. However rudimentary the cards were this year, it was still a pleasure to get them. What was strange, however, was another card, postmarked in Hereford, from her father and new step-mother Rose. After months of frosty silence, the card seemed like a gesture of reconciliation. The card had been sent on from Kenley, which served to illustrate the sad distance which had grown up between Eileen and her family. She had to go out to buy a card especially, feeling contrite, perhaps over-doing her love and greetings in return. She wrote her new address, although in all honesty she did not know if she really wanted a reply.

She had long since outgrown her family ties. She wondered what they would have in common if she went back now. She thought that perhaps only children learnt independence earlier than others, that they came to see their parents as individuals with a more equal eye. There was no family hierarchy to keep her in her place. It seemed of far more importance to her to have about her people with whom she felt at ease, people she liked for themselves not because they were family. The warm and supportive atmosphere of the house in the square seemed more like a real family than any she had ever had before.

Eileen invited Gareth to the house at Christmas as he seemed to have nowhere else to go. Pat was with Grace, Karol with Ruth. She knew that Gareth would be on his own if she did not take pity on him.

She planned to visit Jon on Christmas morning, taking along the small present she had for him, returning to the house in time to help preparing the lunch for friends and neighbours. Besides Gareth there would be Lily, Kitty, Iris and Herbert and Alice Armstrong their neighbours. It would be quite a party.

Things started to go awry when Jon gave her the small silver-wrapped box containing her Christmas gift. He had clearly got one of the nurses to do the wrapping, and as Eileen untied the silk ribbon she wondered what the other woman must have thought of the diamond pendant that nestled inside.

326

'I knew a ring would be no good,' he told her, carefully watching her reaction. 'The WAAF won't let you, but I thought you could wear this all the time.'

'Oh, it's lovely, but...'

'You can't refuse. It's my engagement gift to you.'

As Eileen bent over the bed to kiss him she felt a terrible sense of guilt. She was in such a turmoil of passion that she could not think straight about Jon or Gareth. There was intolerable pressure upon her, pushing her from one to the other with no time for reflection or honesty. She had to shelve all her problems, unable to deal with them, unwilling to face them.

Back at the house she did not show the pendant to anyone. She took it out of the box in her room and held it up to the light of the window. It seemed an unearthly, spiritual thing, ice rather than fire, purity not passion. She pushed it to the back of her drawer, to forget it. She could not see herself now or ever decked out in jewels like the women she had seen at the Dorchester. Why did he not see that? Why couldn't he accept that she was different? It was a gift for someone who would be impressed by the trappings of marriage to someone like him. But it was the essential heart of the matter which troubled her.

In the kitchen Lily was in charge of operations, apron-clad, like a general commanding her scullery minions. Eileen thought of the huge kitchen at Charnwood and smiled to herself. Kitty was there, bustling round with crockery and tureens, efficient as ever but looking remarkably out of place in a dress. It was the first time Eileen had ever seen her out of trousers or her warden's overalls. And Iris had done herself up to the nines. She was a really handsome woman in a warm ruby colour and a lipstick that matched. Somehow she managed to get them some gin to help things along, and Herbert and Alice from next door had brought some beer. When Gareth arrived with a bottle of whisky, they knew this was really going to be a Christmas to remember.

'I bought this for you,' he added, producing a flat package that set them all agog.

'Well, go on, open it!' Kitty encouraged her, supported by a chorus of curious approval.

'If she doesn't open it soon, I'll open it for her!' Iris chipped in cheerfully.

So Eileen unwrapped the parcel, worried by Gareth's

motivation, ashamed that she had not thought to buy anything for him. When the last layer of wrapping paper fell away, she found she was holding in her hands a green silk blouse of a cut and style that drew admiring comments from the others.

'Oh Eileen, it's wonderful!'

'It matches the colour of your eyes.'

'You must go and put it on straight away.'

She held the precious object up against her, slightly overwhelmed. 'Shall I?'

There was an immediate chorus of assent and she took her cue to leave.

Up in her room she changed into a plain black skirt and then lifted the silk blouse from its wrappings. She wondered if Gareth had bought it on the black market. They were talking of bringing in clothes rationing even for ordinary everyday things. She thought it must have cost him a small fortune. It seemed such a luxury when she had not given nice clothes a thought for so long. She wondered if he guessed that she had never owned anything so stylish and so simple. When she put it on she saw what a difference it made. She stood back looking at herself in the mirror, aware of a new light in her eyes, feeling somehow special.

There was a gasp of admiration in the kitchen as she walked in. The women cooed, Herbert uncharacteristically gave a wolf-whistle and Gareth just stood and stared at her.

'It's really lovely. Thank you so much.'

'You deserve it,' he told her, his eyes full of other words.

Eileen saw that Kitty and Lily had exchanged a curious glance and to break the spell she immediately set to, laying the table, bustling round and getting Gareth to help her.

'You shouldn't have,' she whispered as they set out the cutlery together. 'I feel terrible. I haven't bought you anything.'

'I don't care. Being here is enough.'

'What are you two whispering about?' Iris piped up gaily. 'Plenty of time to bill and coo later on.'

Eileen's flash of appeal went unnoticed and she wondered if for one awful moment Iris had misunderstood about her fiancé, confusing Gareth with Jon. But Lily came to the rescue, crying for assistance to lift the turkey from the oven. After that things really went with a swing. Lily carved, Kitty served potatoes and vegetables and Iris refilled their glasses. The meal went incredibly well and by the time Lily set the Christmas pudding alight – the contents of which were a miraculous combination of the traditional and the inspirational – everyone was extremely merry and comfortable with one another.

Eileen relaxed, admiring the way in which Gareth settled into the strange though informal atmosphere as though he had known the others for years. Herbert played up to him as the only other male in the gathering, trying to score points off his wife, but Alice was too sharp for him. They were both looking tired. Their factory was now working day and night to boost production, where only the year before there had hardly been enough work for one shift.

'I wouldn't work in a factory for all the tea in China,' said Iris emptying the gin.

'It's not so bad. The pay's good.'

'She earns more than I do,' complained Herbert. 'We've lots of women taking over work now. I have to show them what's what, of course.'

'Of course,' added his wife sarcastically.

'But they're a good bunch, I'll say that for them. We have a few laughs. Not yesterday, mind you – we were just coming off shift when one girl got a call over the intercom. We all knew what that meant. She'd got this telegram, see, about her old man. The whole shop fell silent. A kind of respect, you know.'

'Come on now, let's not get gloomy,' Iris put in breezily, shaking off the mood. 'Any more to drink?'

'We've got cake to follow.'

'Carrot cake, is it, Lil?'

'No, it is not,' said Lily firmly. 'It may not be quite the traditional recipe, but I daresay you'll not refuse a slice!'

The late afternoon sun was already sinking across the square before they had finished, washing the basement in warm amber colours that added to their sense of well being. But just as the shadows of dusk were lengthening, Iris gave a shriek of horror and stared white-faced at the window. Everyone turned to see what had frightened her and found an uninvited guest out on the basement steps peering in through the steamy glass at their celebration.

329

'Christ save us?' screamed Iris, throwing back her chair and retreating the length of the kitchen. 'It's that bastard, my husband!'

Kitty went over and tried to calm her while Gareth and Herbert were also on their feet, trying to find their way through the scullery door outside. They had no knowledge of Iris's stormy history but her face betrayed her fear of the burly figure outside.

'Don't you worry, love,' said Alice encouragingly. 'My Bert will sort him out.'

When Gareth and Herbert appeared out of the side door, Bill Kennedy turned to stake his ground on the basement steps. He was truly a bull of a man, short and thick-muscled, minus a neck. In the dying light his rolling face glowed red with drink, the only advantage to the opposition. From inside the kitchen they could not hear what Gareth said to him but they saw Kennedy take a lunging swing at him and Iris screamed.

'Oh Lord save us! He'll kill us all!'

But Gareth had caught Kennedy by the arm and Bert moved up to seize the other, pinioning the furious drunk against the wall.

'Shall I get the police?' Kitty suggested, hovering at the door. She didn't wait for a reply as Bill Kennedy kicked and swung at his captors. 'I think I'd better bring a couple,' she told the women in the kitchen as she ran up through the house to the front door.

It seemed an age before she returned with two local bobbies, PCs Fowler and Norman. When he saw them Bill Kennedy swore and lashed out, knocking the helmet off Sid Norman and almost catching Ted Fowler in the groin. Their good humour died and a charge of drunk and disorderly turned into a more serious charge of assaulting a police officer. Out came the handcuffs and Kennedy was formally subdued.

'He won't be troubling you no more,' they reassured the party. 'A Merry Christmas to you all!'

Back in the kitchen Lily had tea for the rescuers. But Iris was still quaking in the corner, sobbing and shivering, all her confidence shattered.

'How did he find me? How did he find out? Lord, can't I ever be free of the swine?'

The Christmas mood was decisively broken and the party began to peter out. Herbert and Alice started to make a move and

330

Eileen saw that Gareth looked uncertain about whether he would outstay his welcome.

'That was good of you, plunging in like that,' she went over to tell him. 'He looked a dangerous customer. You could have been hurt.'

'I doubt it. He was pretty drunk really.' He hesitated, giving a backward glance at the scene round Iris. 'I don't suppose you fancy a walk? It seems a pity to waste a night like this. No bombs, no sirens.'

'I'll just get my coat.'

Eileen was struck by the way in which Gareth had joined in the erratic and down-to-earth atmosphere of the house. She could not have imagined Jon in such a situation. He would have felt awkward there, embarrassed, perhaps even condescending. She had never invited Jon to meet her friends, or taken them to visit him. The two worlds were separate, two parts of her own life which she did not attempt to marry together.

Only Gareth seemed able to cross that gap, able to adapt as she did between the two worlds. It struck her suddenly that they were very alike in many ways. In all the time she had known him she had not seen that before, and now the realisation struck her with the blinding force that often comes when something really very simple and obvious is unwittingly revealed. She laughed at her own blindness, and was still laughing as she appeared in the hallway to meet him.

Gareth took her hand as they walked and his fingers began to stroke hers. In friendship, she told herself, only in friendship. But as though he had read her thoughts he turned suddenly and whispered, 'You know that friendship's not what I want.'

They walked on a little more slowly, unspeaking. At the corner of the square, where the oaks spread a homely bough out across the path, he stopped still. They stood hand in hand, eyes meeting. She knew that she had only to move to break the spell the evening had cast, but move she could not. It was as though her very stillness and silence gave him permission to speak for them both. There could be no doubt of it when she looked at him.

'I love you, Eileen. I've always loved you.'

He put his hand behind her head and kissed her, and then she kissed him, her lips moving on his, her arms round his neck, they

331

kissed together. There was no contest in it, no leader, no teacher, it was not something he imposed upon her, did to her, something she took from him as a gift. It was a shared moment, mutual joy, an instinctive coming together, a coming home.

They drew apart only a little, enough to see one another's faces, hands touching, torn between pain and pleasure. Pain for the guilt she could still not override, pleasure for the discovery she ought to have made before. Pleasure for his knowledge that he too was loved, pain for the time that had come too late.

'I love you,' he repeated, the words exquisitely painful in his accent. 'But, don't you see? It's too late for us. There's no future for us now.'

She looked into his thin, shadowed face, full of misgivings. How easy it would be to delude themselves. The peace of this night, its mystical quality and serenity at the end of a bloody year had woven a spell over them. But in the fresh raw New Year who knew what was to come? How could they promise anything to one another with that threat hanging over their heads, that threat to all their futures? The truce would soon be over and he would be back flying missions again while she ran the gauntlet of bombing.

Gareth was very different from Jon. War was not a game to him but bloody slaughter, an evil necessity to be over and done with as soon as possible. He had entered into the conflict only for this, not for adventure or gallantry or false patriotism. If lives were sacrificed there had to be reason and purpose for it, there had to be progress.

Taking her face between his hands he told her coldly that if he had not loved her it would all have been much simpler. If he didn't care so much they might go to bed together and it would all be over. But it was no use, he loved her and it was not enough for either of them. They both knew it would not end at a light affair.

'Don't you see? We have no choice.' He saw the appeal in her eyes but before she could speak he bent quickly and kissed her. A hungry kiss for what might have been.

When at last they separated, he kept hold of her hand until the last, reluctant to lose the moment.

'Perhaps you should marry Jon,' he said gently. 'He at least has a future. Even if it is only in a wheelchair.'

332

*

The truce ended with the worst bombing raid over the beleaguered City of London on the night of December 29th. It was the weekend. The city was silent as a graveyard. The offices and banks which had kept going even in the heaviest raids were now deserted, the wardens and fire-watchers in their own homes across London. It was a clear moonlit night.

In two waves they came. Their target was the commercial heart of the capital, stretching along the twisting ribbon of the silver Thames in the moonlight.

From the rooftops above Finsbury, Lily saw the first incendiaries drop about six-thirty in the evening. The sky from the river to the rising ground of Highgate and Parliament Hill Fields was alive with the hum of bombers.

Eileen joined Lily on the roof. They stood in awed silence at the terrible spectacle of London burning.

The flashes of ack-ack like forks of lightning lit up the majestic dome of St Pauls to the south. It seemed that the sun had set unnaturally in the east, spreading its scarlet rays out across the city from the Barbican to Fleet Street.

Baskets of incendiaries tumbled from the skies hitting the buildings with shooting sparklers. Flames of lime-green and orange flared in the gathering smoke. The sky became lurid with sickly colours. Arson had become a prime weapon of war. The incendiaries cascaded with an unreal white light, spreading fires with alarming speed. Pumps and hoses were of little use when the water mains cracked from the heat. On hundred-foot turntable ladders black against the raging fires, exhausted firemen vainly attempted to control this second great fire of London.

At Surrey Docks pepper caught fire in the warehouses and spread waves of liquid fire through acres of old wooden buildings. Solid timbers fell cascading into the street and shooting sparks spread the fires. Like ants in this terrifying world, the tiny figures of firemen struggled with lengths of hosepipe in a vain attempt to control the conflagration. Fireboats out on the scarlet waters of the Thames sprayed river water over the warehouse fronts. In the raging heat of white-hot flames the paint on the sides of the boats began to blister.

There were more than 1,500 fires in the square mile of the City, igniting one from another, spreading like wildfire. Windows shattered in the heat, ambulances struggled to get past collapsing walls. Dray-horses had to be led away from stables already ablaze. The heat-engendered winds, driving the fire before them, became a tornado of swirling embers and scalding ash, whirling death and destruction. A firestorm. Ripping and burning, a searing gale of fire at a temperature of 1,000 degrees Fahrenheit.

Up on the rooftops a mile or more from the centre of the holocaust, the women stood in silence to see St Pauls rising out of the destruction, and the tears rolled down their faces.

A welcome to 1941 and a war that seemed without end. Eileen discovered that Bart's hospital had been damaged but survived the fire, continuing its work unabated, but six Wren churches had been consumed, lost forever. She saw the Union Jack still flying from the ruins of the Guildhall and felt a catch in her throat. In spite of heavy losses of shipping in the Atlantic, in spite of drastic food rationing and bombing the length and breadth of the country, the spirit still survived, to struggle on another day.

Yet depression hung like a heavy mist seeping into the bones and try as she might, Eileen could not shake it off. At home they took to playing card games in spare moments; solo or rummy could block out reality for an hour or two. Everyone had to struggle through each bleak day and Eileen kept her own problems to herself. The days dragged, hope dying when Gareth did not appear. Everytime she heard 'I'll Pray For You' played on the radio, every time she sat with friends in a pub, it all came back to her. When she was with others she tried to hide her despair behind a mask of cheerfulness and efficiency, but she grieved that Gareth found it so easy to keep to his word.

It was on January 11th as she returned to the square as the haunting red disc of the setting sun hung beyond the rooftops that it happened.

He stood in the shade of an oak tree watching the direction in which she must come. She knew at once from his face that he had finally discovered his resolution was impossible to keep. He caught sight of her and moved directly to meet her, his dead-set stare indicative of the determination which had driven him there to see her. She raised a hand to touch his face, needing to say nothing, knowing that they had to be together – even if only for this single night.

She linked her arm in his and walked him across the square towards the brooding house in the dusk-light. And as they approached, and the air-raid sirens began to sing, they climbed the stairs together.

In the empty house the bedroom became a sanctuary, safe from the raid, safe from all intrusion from the cold world outside. If anything, it seemed that the raid kept them company in the night, growing apace from a gentle distant droning, and building, building into a staccato explosion again and again.

The bombing seemed to intensify their need for one another. She slid her fingers into his dark curling hair drawing him down to dissolve in melting intolerable sweetness. So close to the edge, they no longer cared if the next bomb fell on them then and there. It was a gamble they willingly accepted for the joy of sharing this night together.

Apart, abandoned, tender and together again, he raised his head from her bare shoulder as the tears ran back into her hair. He knew and understood that moment of sadness that follows fierce joy. She knew herself now and was not willing to lose a moment of such lilting beauty. She clung to him with a desperate happiness, appalled that she could have deceived herself for so long.

'I don't ever want to let you go.'

His touch was tender, loving, but he did not know how to answer her. There was nothing he could say that would reassure her.

Perhaps the night raiders took pity on him. Suddenly the sky was heavy with the throb of their aircraft engines, loaded with thousands of pounds of explosive. There came a shrill whistling noise as a stick of bombs hurtled down across the square. The foundations of the old house shook with the brutal force of the explosion, the windows rattled and the very bed seemed to sway as from an earth tremor. The percussion of noise reverberated round their room as a savage orange light invaded the house and the air filled with the acrid smell of burning.

335

Whistles and clanging bells were already to be heard in the square as Gareth and Eileen hurried to the window. The bombs had struck the adjoining side of the square, smashing into the tall terrace of neat houses, tearing a bite from the block and filling it with fire and billowing black smoke.

He stood just behind her at the window, arms on her arms, taking her weight against him as tiny figures scurried in the square below. People appeared from every side. There was a fire engine, wardens in blue overalls and neighbours all agog. The spell of silence was broken.

'Are we jinxed?'

He looked at her closely without understanding her new melancholy.

'Are we being punished, do you think?'

'I don't know why you say that,' he told her.

'Don't you feel guilty? Don't you think that we might have to pay one day for being so happy?'

He held her tighter, but was choked with horror at the suggestion that had been lurking in his mind ever since that day he had found her again.

A jinx? A premonition perhaps? He had no gift to see into the future. He did not know what would be the end of all this business. He only thought he should never have come back to her to bring such short-lived happiness, without knowing the end.

The next time they visited Jon together at the hospital Eileen was afraid that he would know what happened between them. She was very careful to behave towards Gareth in a detached manner, concentrating on Jon.

'How are you feeling today?' Gareth asked cheerfully.

'I could do with a Scotch.'

'When you get out of your hospital blues we'll have to make up for lost time.'

'Then you'd better leave some for me,' Jon warned him.

Although he was smiling he thought he had almost overdone the sarcasm. He had been struggling very hard to control the depression that had fallen over the New Year. He just wished they would realise that the sight of Gareth did nothing to help.

The way he sauntered into the ward, so fit, so full of life, so helpful, had come to nauseate him. Sunk in his chair, with the bandaged stump propped up before him, he was constantly reminded of his new incapacity. Perhaps it was true that a man comes to hate those who have seen his weakness. He had little to do all day except dwell on his own misfortune. And now he had suspicion to contend with.

He saw that she was looking newer, finer. She was happier than she had been the week before. And they thought he did not know. They thought they were so clever, hiding what was going on behind smiles and chatter. Did they think he was so stupid?

He knew from the moment that Gareth appeared what would happen. He saw from his eyes that he had never really got over her. Gareth had been jealous, hurt by her attachment to his best friend, but for weeks Jon was certain that nothing had happened between them. Now he was just as certain that everything had happened. It was there in their eyes, in the soft secret little glances that they thought went undetected.

He said nothing. He bottled up his anger and fierce aching resentment because the fear of what might happen if he lost control was too terrible. He could not bear to lose her.

He was repelled by his mother's suggestion that he should abandon Eileen and return to Charnwood. It came as no surprise to him. He knew that his mother hated her, although she was careful not to give him any specific reason. There was an element of truth in what she said. If he had been well he was not sure how long their affair could have lasted. But he was not well. He was no better than his father, trapped in his bloody wheelchair, confined to the ministrations of a wife who ignored him and hired help who despised him. Was that to be the future that awaited him at Charnwood?

With Eileen the future was uncertain, but he had felt her love for him, aware of her innocence, of her loyalty. When he offered her marriage he knew that he was breaking all the rules. She might not have been the kind of girl he would have chosen as a wife in other circumstances, but she was the one he wanted now. He felt her gratitude and loyalty would support him as he came to terms with his new life. A quiet life somewhere in the country, not at Charnwood, not with his family. A fresh start together. It seemed to offer them both a chance.

From his hospital ward the future stretched bleakly before him, war or no war. Unlike Gareth he had a very firm belief in the future – and was terrified of facing it alone.

Eileen went to work full of misgivings. Guilt and rebellion fought to have the upper hand. She had never imagined that she could fall in love with Gareth. She had never marked him out at all. She found him interesting only because he was Jon's friend, and her obsession with Jon made her blind to his interest in her. But it was her affair with Jon which had opened her eyes, not only because he had thrown Gareth's love for her in her face, but because, inexperienced as she was, she had recognised the shortcomings in her relationship with Jon.

She knew even then that there had to be more. She had woken up to the possibilities of a more passionate, more mature love. In Gareth she had suddenly discovered the care she had been denied. Closing her eyes, she saw him as clearly as if he was there in the room with her. She remembered the night together in the crowded tube station, Christmas under the still trees in the square, the night in the house while the Blitz raged.

And yet – the thought of Jonathan hung over her head. She had loved him, still cared for him, but could she now desert him? He had shown he needed her. In spite of the enormous differences between them he wanted to marry her. Marriage would mean new security, a chance to enter a society she could never have attained. Marriage to Jon would mean a life spent looking after an invalid husband. It would be a life of ease and security – even if the war was lost, the Pemberleys had connections. But was that what she really wanted? A year before the thought of marrying into the Pemberley family would have been absurd, unthinkable, a fantasy. But in that year the whole world had turned upside down.

Where were all her dreams? She had had such hopes when she had gone to Charnwood, hopes to improve herself through her own potential. But an appalling disillusionment had awaited her there, and only the WAAF and the companionship of other women had prevented that experience from damaging her life.

For the first time in her life she felt stretched, able to look after herself, capable, respected. Then love had come along and she was diverted. She had never thought of marriage as the be-all and end-all of her existence. But where was that happy woman now? Her life had become full of strain and tension, guilt and doubt. The moments of joy were few and far between. Was it enough?

She had learnt to stand on her own two feet the hard way. Now it seemed that all the decisions had been taken out of her hands. Surely she should attempt to resolve her own life before she committed herself to anyone? She felt less willing to change and reshape her life to fit into anyone else's. But Jon clearly did not see it that way.

When she went to visit him alone she noticed a marked difference in his attitude. Bitterness crept into his voice and he seemed to have lost all his optimism about the future. The slightest thing would upset him. He was full of unwarranted criticisms. For a time she put up with his moods purely out of guilt about Gareth, but when his attitude persisted she began to despair.

'The doctor says you're not progressing as well as they expected,' she told him firmly. 'Getting depressed won't help.'

'I just want to get out of here.'

'Of course you do, but...'

'You don't understand.'

'I'm trying to.'

'You don't care any more. You spend all your time with other people, with Pat, with Gareth.'

'Gareth's away and Pat and I are out of town most days. I rush back here to see you every day. Why would I do that if I didn't care about you?'

Why indeed? She felt tired and run-down. Her period was due and she was drained and irritable. The pressure of work was quite enough without her visits to the hospital, and even though the raids were lighter now she was still exhausted.

And she was missing Gareth. He and Karol had been sent on some sort of course for a week. He was due back tomorrow and only the thought of seeing him again kept her going. Even if she had to share him with other people, even if she had to hide her feelings. But in the back of her mind there was a nagging worry about something Pat had said about a big operation that would soon get under way.

Eileen felt certain Pat knew there was something between the two of them. He knew her so well that he could surely assess her moods from day to day. He had begun to be circumspect in his enquiries about Jon. He never mentioned them as a couple any more.

She knew that Pat would listen if she wanted to talk about it, but before she could even decide to bring it out into the open, Gareth took the matter out of her hands.

He joined her on his first day back on duty on her visit to the hospital.

'My own darling.' He looked at her unsmiling, suddenly pulling her into his arms and kissing her mouth.

Eileen was so happy to be with him that it was difficult to disguise her elation in front of Jon. She found herself treating Gareth with unusual brusqueness to cover the pleasure she felt everytime she looked at him. But her play-acting soon turned into harsh reality as Gareth stunned them both with his news:

'I'm being posted away. I'll be flying reconnaissance in future.'

Jon looked at Eileen and saw the unfeigned shock in her eyes. She knew that in spite of the bland way Gareth described his move that this was no routine job. Reconnaissance was a euphemism for a variety of operations linked to the planning of bombing missions. Jon was not fooled either.

'Isn't that rather risking your neck, old man? I thought you were safely battened down in a desk job.'

'Hardly that.'

'Well, a damned sight safer than scouting round in the dark over enemy territory. What's wrong with you? Have you got a death wish or something?' His eyes shone with more life than Eileen had seen in them for days.

'Someone has to do it,' Gareth responded with a shrug.

'But why does it have to be you?'

'The other chaps are all married. I have no ties, no responsibilities.'

'The Jerries are in a bit of a jam now, if you ask me. No need for sudden heroics surely? You ought to think about the future.'

Gareth laughed bitterly as though to dismiss his future, but Jon seemed sincerely troubled, as though somehow he had got things confused in his own head. Perhaps he had been wrong about Gareth and Eileen after all?

Outside in the hospital corridor Eileen seized Gareth and tried to make him tell her why he had done this.

'This job – it's the Hanover mission, isn't it?'

'Don't blame Pat. I elected to go. I'm the best flier he's got.'

'And Karol?'

'Karol's just got married.'

She bit her lip. 'I see.'

'No, you don't. Look, you must try to understand. I can't hide away. There's no point in anyone getting hurt.'

'A bit late, aren't you, Gareth?'

'Look,' he said with his accent more pronounced, 'look, you must see that it's the best thing for all of us.'

'I see you're obviously looking for a way out. Couldn't you think of any other way of doing it without deliberately trying to get yourself killed? What will that solve?'

'Don't be ridiculous.'

'*I'm* being ridiculous? How could you do such a thing to me – to Jon – to yourself? What are you trying to be – a hero or a martyr?'

He took both her arms and tried to hold her still, aware of curious glances from a nurse and a couple of patients nearby. In the crowded corridor they couldn't even talk properly.

'Why can't you try to understand?' he whispered savagely. 'I've always known that there was no future for us. We should never have got into this. It's just caused a lot of pain.' He looked at her, fierce conflict in his face. He was remembering her slender arching neck against the pillow, her softness, her sighs. He let her go, deeply moved. 'Is this what you want? Are you honestly happier now that we both know...'

'Don't! Don't! I don't know any more what I should do. I only want what you want.'

He shook his head, his face dark and sunken-cheeked, growing gaunt in despair.

'What do I want? I want to stop needing you.'

With one last look he turned abruptly and walked away from her.

Out on the street there was no sign of him. Eileen was jostled by busy office workers anxiously making their way home, standing and blocking the pathway, eyes blinded by the tears which ran unhindered down her face. He was gone, he had not waited.

She felt totally let down, dropped into despair – bitter, aggressive, hurt. She ached, hugging herself for comfort in the fading light, setting her face against the raw wind. The weather was sharp and desolate. She couldn't stop crying. Wrapped in her coat, with the collar turned up, she groped for a handkerchief, unable to stop the tears streaming down her cheeks, wetting her hair. She began to walk blindly, only realising after two blocks that she was going in the wrong direction. She turned, moving through the rush-hour crowds, oblivious of the outside world, her thoughts all of him.

She stared at the faces of the passers by, not knowing who they were, where they were going, thinking of him. In the streets and through the steamy windows of cafés, shops and buses, anonymous faces, different lives, different futures...

When she got home there was no one there. Dusk had fallen long ago and when she tried the switches she found there was no electricity. She went to put a kettle on the stove but the tap merely dripped sluggishly. She came to the conclusion that the supply had been cut somewhere in the area through bomb damage. It could be hours, perhaps even days before it was on again.

She stumbled up the stairs in tears again. On every side she saw only despair. Her mind was in a turmoil and her head ached. She could not bear to think because all her thoughts were haunted by emptiness. She had never felt so alone as now.

In the lounge upstairs she lit a fire and sat pouring over some of Lily's books from Boots Library, but even the 'A' class novels straight off the best seller lists could not distract her. She stayed huddled in the firelight, and that was where Lily found her.

Before long Eileen found herself telling Lily everything. Out it all came in one long torrent of passion and tears until she could add nothing more, she was repeating herself, going round and round in circles.

'You must think me a dreadful fool,' she concluded, looking up into the steady blue eyes.

'Not for a moment. You have to take what you want in this world. I always thought that caution in love was most destructive.'

'Were you very much in love with Moira's grandfather?'

'Very. It was my choice, the baby, you know. I thought if I could not marry him then at least –' She caught sight of Eileen's face and smiled. 'Didn't you know? I never wanted to get married. Even before I met him. Which was just as well, because he was very married and already had three sons.'

'Oh Lily, weren't you unhappy?'

'Whoever said there wouldn't be pain as well as pleasure? Of course, it was very hard at times. But it was worth it. I had Marian, you see, and later, when she went away, I had my work.'

'I never realised.'

'Why should you? It didn't matter to me, about Marian's illegitimacy, I mean. It was my decision to have her, not an accident, and I had very precise ideas about her upbringing. But it hurt her – more than I realised at the time. In the end she turned her back on everything I had tried to teach her. She left me and married a farmer.'

'Yes, Vi told me.'

'Ah, poor Vi.' She stared into the flames, stirring the coals with a poker. 'She took her chance, too. They were happy for the brief time they were together.' She stopped and looked at Eileen. 'You know what I'm saying, don't you?'

Eileen nodded, and smiled for the first time that evening.

'You're telling me to put myself first. To take the chance.'

'I'm saying that unless you know yourself and know what you really want life will pass you by. Can you really imagine playing the housewife in some country village? No, of course not.' She took her hand and concluded, 'If you marry Jon and see it only as a sacrifice, then there's no hope at all for the marriage.'

At work she did not see him and began to live with a rising panic that he had already left town without telling her.

But on the Friday, as she was about to leave, one of the clerks came racing after her to say there was an urgent call. She took up the receiver with certainty that it was him, relief and delight in her voice as she answered.

'I'm leaving tonight, I just got word,' he told her. 'My train leaves from Euston in an hour. Can you come?'

'Of course, of course. Wait for me at the entrance.'

It meant rearranging her schedule. The motor pool sergeant was not delighted. He eyed her suspiciously, unwilling to issue her further petrol when the week's allocation had already been used. It took a good fifteen minutes before all the red tape had been completed and she was driving down Whitehall. The rainclouds had burst and the little car swished through puddles, but she stepped on the gas, unwilling to delay, to lose even a few precious minutes. Nothing else mattered, she was going to meet him.

The traffic at the intersection of Tottenham Court Road and the Euston Road was held up by a water main which had burst, blocking her path. She could not afford the time to wait in a traffic jam and decided to park the Ministry car and walk the rest of the distance to the station.

She fastened her raincoat as she ran, dodging the cars at a standstill, weaving in and out of the other pedestrians heading for the station. The streets were wet, shining with blue and green whorls of oil. She was already soaked to the skin as she arrived outside the great doric portico, staring up at the fire-blackened upper floors of the station.

And she saw him. He was waiting by one of the pillars, head turned away as he searched the passing crowds for sight of her. He stood there in his dark trench raincoat, his hands thrust deep in the pockets, with the rain running down his face. His dark hair was flattened to his forehead but he didn't seem to care. There was a kind of desperation about him as the clock behind marked the passing minutes of the hour that was lost to them.

Twelve minutes only. Twelve minutes in which to try and say all that was yet unsaid, all of her life in just twelve minutes...

She reached out for him and was drawn into a desperate searching kiss. There was no need for apologies, only regret for the time they had wasted. Arm in arm they walked into the station.

It seemed as though the whole of London had converged on Euston to take a train or see friends. There were men and women in uniform everywhere, army, nurses, Home Guard and Navy. There was even a Scots Pipers band playing a welcome to a detachment of troops just arrived off a train from the north. The plaintive note of the bagpipes was most affecting and Eileen held on to Gareth's arm more tightly, watching the soldiers as they marched past in their swinging kilts to the rhythm of the drums.

They found the right platform and the train that was ready and waiting to go, its funnel belching out clouds of steam, impatient to be gone. In the bustle and the noise Eileen felt a growing sense of panic at the thought of parting. They moved along the train but it was already very crowded, with no chance at all of finding a quiet corner to themselves where they might talk. There were soldiers and airmen all round, manhandling their kit, joking and talking with forced cheerfulness at the thought of heading back to their units after leave. Perhaps never to return.

Gareth dumped his bags in the open doorway of a carriage and then put an arm about her waist and walked a little way up the platform to get away from the noisy group round the train. There was so much to say and yet they spoke only of trivial, unimportant things, hating the lack of privacy, hating the time that was slipping away among strangers.

The shrill note of a whistle sounded above the noise on the platform. She buried her face on his chest, clinging to him tightly.

Doors began to slam along the length of the train. Gareth walked her gently back to the open carriage door. There was no more time. He pulled her to him and they kissed with sudden vehemence, full of a physical longing that was almost overwhelming. When he pulled his face away, he laid his hand against her cheek that was wet with jagged lines of tears.

He was deeply disturbed. He knew then that he should have left her alone. It was reckless and cruel to become involved. Touching her hair, still damp from the rain, he knew that he had plunged into this new assignment to bring an end to it all, to put the decision-making into the hands of fate. Perhaps if he came through it all, if he survived, then there would be hope for them...

He kissed her again, tasting salt on her lips, wiping away the tears that ran back into her hair. He saw the railway guard down the platform waiting for him to shut the door, and reluctantly he let her go.

'I love you. Remember I love you.'

The door slammed, separating them. He saw her half raise a

345

hand in farewell and that moment was frozen in time; he knew he would remember it always. He turned away with sad eyes, swallowed up behind the blue-painted windows.

She fell back along the track as the steam engine shunted slowly out, standing there in the gloom of the winter afternoon, lonely, vulnerable. The empty eyes of the darkened windows moved past, gathering speed as the train snaked out along the wet and shining rails, curving out of sight.

Alone on the deserted platform she felt numb with misery, forcing her steps towards the ticket barrier. She moved among the jostling crowds in the station without feeling. There was nothing left to her now but the memory of bitter hours and brief happiness. Now he was gone she knew what had been important in her life, but too late. The days stretched ahead, days to endure, living without him as though their love was dead.

Chapter Eleven

Iris first saw him as she approached the house. She was returning from a lunchtime session working at the pub and wanted nothing more than to put her feet up for an hour or two. The young man looked menacing from that distance. Tall and muscular, swarthy as a gypsy, he was wearing rough workman's clothing, all brown and blue, with large boots. She saw him hanging round outside the house, peering down through the railings into the basement window.

Her first thought was that he was trying to break in. But as she watched from across the gardens in the square, he seemed in no hurry to try the window. As she watched him it struck her that perhaps he was not a burglar at all. She wondered if he could have been sent to the house by her husband. She lived in dread that he would one day try and get even with her for what happened at Christmas.

For a long moment she was too frightened to go near, afraid that he might attack her. But then he turned suddenly around and she caught sight of his face and saw his expression, saw something in it that replaced fear with pity.

She crossed the square, aware that she had now attracted his attention. His dark eyes lit up at the sight of her approaching with all the eagerness of a child. His handsome features parted in a smile of such open relief that she had to smile back at him.

'Are you looking for someone?'

'My Gran.'

His innocent stare only confirmed her earlier suspicion. Why, he must have been into his twenties, a strong young bloke you

347

wouldn't want to get into a fight with. But looking into the clear empty gaze she recognised what was missing.

'And who's your Gran, love? What's her name?'

He chewed his lip, looking down at his feet uncomfortably. 'Just Gran.'

It was an absurd conversation to have with a man of his age, but Iris did not see it like that. Had not her own Uncle Sam been just the same? Forty he was and daft as a six year old. Something was missing upstairs. But a nicer, more gentle bloke you couldn't hope to find, and it was all there in his eyes when he looked at you.

'What's your name, then?'

'I'm Mike.'

'Mike what?'

'Mike Adams.'

Iris drew a long breath. 'And your Gran is called Lily, isn't that right? Have you got a sister, Mike?'

'Moira's gone away. A long time. I'm going to see Moira.'

'Oh yes?'

'Have I got the right number, missus? It's on this paper.' He thrust an old envelope into her hands imploringly. Iris turned it over and read the faded address on the back, the address of the house.

'Yes, love, that's right.' She handed back the prized envelope, nine years old by the postmark, and then got out her doorkey. 'Are you hungry, Mike? I'm going to cook myself a bite to eat. Come in and we'll wait for your Gran together.'

As she saw him tuck into her rations for the week with a man's healthy appetite, Iris wondered why she had never heard Lily mention a grandson, only of Moira her grand-daughter. She thought that she knew nothing really about Lily, hadn't wanted to probe too deep and be thought nosy. It was best to keep yourself to yourself. But she wondered if perhaps Lily was embarrassed having a backward lad in the family.

She heard Lily arrive, slamming the front door, just as Mike was mopping up his plate with a crust of bread.

'Mike?' She seemed incredulous, quite shaken at the sight of the young man in her kitchen. He stood up, blocking out the light from the window at his back. He towered over his grandmother, looking uncertain, rather apprehensive. He turned from Lily to the kind stranger who had taken him in.

'It's your Gran, love,' she told him.

'Gran!' He engulfed her in a bearlike embrace, the relief in his face almost pathetic.

'I haven't seen you since you were ten or eleven. What a fine boy you are, Mike!' She looked at Iris desperately. 'I can't think how he found me! All the way from Lincolnshire – How did you come down here, Mike? Is your mother with you?'

'Mum's at home.'

'Then your father?'

A shadow fell across his face.

'He's back there, he is.'

'Doesn't he know you're here, Mike?'

'You mustn't tell him! Don't tell him, Gran, he'll lather me!'

The fear was so obvious in his eyes that both women looked at one another.

'I won't tell anyone just now, darling, but you must tell me how you got down here.'

He perked up immediately and said rather boastfully,

'I got a lorry.'

'You mean you hitched a lift?' Iris was astonished. 'You came all that way just to see your Gran?'

'And Moira. I want to see Moira.'

Lily looked at Iris. 'She'll have to be told. She'll have to come up if she can get leave.'

'Bit of a surprise for her, eh?'

'And for me. Well, Mike, what are we going to do with you? Your mother will have a fit when she finds you gone.'

Moira succeeded in getting a 48-hour pass and came up to town the next evening. She was amazed to see her elder brother after ten years apart. She was as moved as Lily by the way he had changed so much in appearance, and as saddened by the way he had changed so little in intelligence. He was just the way she remembered him when they were children together, backs to the wall as she defended him against all comers as the butt of hateful school and farmyard jokers.

'He can't stay here,' she told Lily. 'His ration cards are back up

349

there. He'll eat you all out of house and home.'

'I'm more afraid that he'll get called up. He can't look after himself.'

'But he seems dead scared to go home,' said Iris. 'Poor little mite. What do they do to him up there?'

'Work him like a drudge-horse.' Moira grimaced, remembering. 'It's a hard life. Right out in the wilds. I daresay they need him now on the farm.' She met Lily's blue eyes full of pity. 'I used to stand up for him, you know? I used to take all the knocks until I was black and blue. I took as much as I could.'

'I know, I know. No one is suggesting...'

'He's my brother and I love the poor sod, but what can I do for him? I can't even look after myself let alone him.'

Lily saw that she was back at a low ebb and would have liked the leisure to be able to talk it out with her, but there was never enough time. Any moment now the sirens would be wailing.

'What about the raids? Mike has probably never been in an air raid. He'll be scared out of his wits.'

'I'll take him down to the shelter,' Moira suggested. 'Is Eileen coming back tonight?'

'Any time now. She'll be glad to see you.' She got to her feet. 'Well, we'll have to sort something out in the morning. We'll have to get him back there somehow. For the time being, at least.'

'I'll help you,' said Eileen when Moira had explained the crisis as they walked to the shelter that night. 'I can get a car and, as long as we don't stay there too long, we could do a round trip in the day.'

'Don't worry, Ei, I've no wish to stay a minute longer than we have to.' She slipped her arm through her friend's, with Mike on the other. 'What would I do without you? You've always been a real pal to me.'

They were both thinking of Veronica and the rift that had split their happy trio asunder, but it was neither the time nor the place to talk of it. Perhaps later, on the way back, Eileen thought, perhaps then I can try and bring them back together.

*

The weather was getting worse as they travelled north. Mike sat in the back seat, as proud as any wing commander being ferried around by his chauffeur. He seemed unaware that he was being taken home, oblivious of the uneasiness and regretful silence of his sister and her friend. He was too busy looking out of the window, pointing out people and cattle they passed, asking interminable questions all the way.

North of London the gentle hills were ringed with the ominous light of a coming snowstorm. Against the dramatic skyline, dark lowering clouds gave way to a lurid aura which stretched down on to a flat endless plain. The Fens. As they drove from the shelter of the hills a blizzard cut a swathe across the winter meadows, covering the land in a silent shroud of whiteness.

'Should we go on or try to find a place to stop?' asked Moira, her voice tense and full of alarm. The last thing any of them wanted was to be stuck in the middle of nowhere in a snowstorm.

'I'll battle on as long as I can. I'm afraid that if we stop now, we'll never get her going again.' She was concentrating very hard on her driving, wishing she had at least put a shovel in the boot.

The endless desolate fenland stretched on for miles in every direction, the bleak horizon only broken here and there by the spire of some distant village church. It was like the end of the world. Under the great rolling sky Eileen felt she was out on some vast plain that stretched to infinity, out where water and marsh met and no one could tell which was which.

'Is this where you were brought up?'

Moira turned to look at her, startled out of her own reverie, and the look in her eyes was answer enough.

How strange to be back here after so many years. She was thinking how she had planned and executed her own escape one biting February day, London-bound like Mike. In search of a new beginning, she too had turned up at the house in the square. But she had been taken in, not bundled into the back of a car and sent back again.

Guilt, like a wave of sickness turned her stomach. She looked at Mike expecting some sign of indignation, of betrayal on his face, almost disappointed to find none. He sat watching the white-flecked fields with total absorption, passively unaware of the fate that awaited him.

He caught her look and his handsome face broke into a radiant smile that reminded her painfully of Geoff.

One day, she pledged, one day I'll make it up to you, I promise.

Eileen followed the directions as they drove out of the one street town and the road divided into a confusion of twisting roads little better than lanes. They all looked alike to her, bleak decaying outposts, apparently deserted. Tilney Fen, Bilney Dyke, Fossdyke. Fourth Drove, Fifth Drove and grey isolated little farmhouses like islands on the plain.

They travelled the line of the dyke where it cut straight as a die across Ten Mile Bank, intersected by the tortuous black ribbon of road as it wound drunkenly across the fen towards the Wash. The aching desolation of the bleak landscape, unrelieved either by hills or trees, was a dismal winter scene in grey-green, grey-white.

Moira's family had a farm at Sea's End, apparently a good ten miles from any sea on reclaimed fenland. They could see the house for a mile or so before they arrived. Mike leant forward energetically over the front seats as he recognised his home, pointing and shouting with all the boisterousness of an untamed five year old. But it was not the house after all which had made him so excited.

'Mum! It's Mum, Moira!'

Eileen had been staring down the road towards the farm, but now she became aware of a group of figures in one of the huge fields that ran the length of the dyke. Against the speckled, half-frozen land, she saw one standing silhouetted, hand raised against the watery glare of the sun, looking at the car.

Moira looked at her brother for confirmation and was very agitated. Her face lost its colour as she stared at the woman standing out in the field. Bundled in layers of dark clothing, it was hard to tell that it was a woman except for the red cheeks and shock of dark hair which escaped her hat. In her hand she held a curved blade, something less than a sickle, with which she had been cutting turnips. Curious at the sight of the large vehicle, the fieldworkers had all stopped to stare, hands on hips, wiping the frost away.

Moira suddenly flung wide the car door and got out, immediately followed by Mike. But outside she stopped, unsure of herself and her welcome, very conscious of feeling alien in that desolate landscape. It was Mike who went forward, racing down the muddy track along the edge of the turnip field, calling something that was lost on the wind.

They watched as the woman climbed up from the field to meet him, shouting something and waving a hand at him. But when she joined him up on the track she suddenly pulled him into a tight embrace, angry at his going and yet relieved to have him back again.

They walked back towards the car with Mike pointing ahead, obviously telling her something of his adventures and explaining the presence of the women at the car.

'Moira? Is it you?'

Moira gave a strange choking cry and plunged forward, caught up in the emotional reunion. The scene brought a lump to Eileen's throat. She felt an outsider, intruding on such an intimate family moment.

'No, I can't stay,' she heard Moira tell her mother. 'I only came to bring Mike back. I have to be back on duty.'

The woman fingered the material of Moira's uniform.

'What's this you're in, then? Army, is it?'

'Air Force. I'm a WAAF now.' Moira turned uncomfortably to introduce Eileen, who had got out of the car to meet them. 'This is Eileen, a very good friend.'

The woman hesitated, peeling off her fingerless gloves before putting out her hand. It was as veined and red as her weather-beaten face, but the grip was warm and strong. As Eileen met her vivid blue eyes she suddenly saw that she was indeed Lily's daughter although her clothes, her face, her voice all spoke of the harsh life she had chosen.

'Get in the car, Mum, and we'll drive on to the house.'

'In the car? I've not been in a car since...' She looked wary of the strange vehicle, but then a twinkle came into her eyes. 'Where shall I sit?'

They put her in the front seat, with Moira and Mike getting

into the back but leaning forward to watch the delight on their mother's face. Eileen took it slowly, allowing her to savour every moment, touched by her delight at travelling in style.

'Oh Lord, look, I've got mud on your floor!' she cried, appalled at the clumps of earth deposited by her huge gumboots.

'It doesn't matter, really it doesn't,' Eileen reassured her but it seemed that nothing would comfort her. Her pleasure in the moment was gone, destroyed by a long-forgotten sense of propriety.

As Eileen drove in through the farmyard gates and pulled up before a wooden barn, they caught sight of a man coming along the side of the farm buildings, battling against the wind with his head down.

Mike began to tremble with fear as he approached. Moira remembered how he had always borne the brunt of their father's anger in the past. She remembered in particular that night he had been so drunk that one blow had sent the boy crashing through the glass door. Only the sight of the blood had sobered him up.

'Now, Jake.'

He pushed aside his wife's warning and glared in through the car window, totally ignoring Eileen sitting at the wheel. All his attention was focused on his son cowering in the back seat.

'Come back, have you?' All the muscles in his face were tight with restrained fury. 'Get inside before I give you what for.'

Mike needed no further encouragement. He flung open the car door and almost ran across the yard into the house.

'Now, Jake, don't be too hard on the lad.' She got out of the car and tried to lay a hand on his sleeve, but he was too agitated.

'Where's he been, then? And who are they? We don't want no official busybodies snooping around here.'

'They're not officials, Jake. Don't you recognise your own daughter?'

He glared at her as though she was crazy, but when he saw that she was serious he went straight over to the car and told both women to get out where he could take a look at them. Eileen he passed over with a cursory, dismissive glance, focusing all his attention on Moira. She bore it with a good grace, standing up to his scrutiny, chin tilted, eyes bold.

'Well, miss, what have you got to say for yourself?' He seemed rather taken aback by her calmness. 'Got yourself into uniform like the rest of them, I see. What kind of nonsense is that?'

'Air Force, Dad.'

'Air Force, is it? What's the matter, aren't there men enough to go round? What's the world coming to?'

'There's a war on, Dad, in case you've not noticed.'

'Oh, I've noticed all right, my girl. They're taking half my land for a blooming airstrip, that's what. And they expect all yields up. We've got the worst of it up here.'

'How many bombs have you had?'

'Bombs? Don't talk to me of bombs! City folks don't know they're born. They want to be up here in the fields dawn to dusk.'

Moira's mother quickly intervened.

'This is no way to treat guests, Jake. Let them come in for a warm and a bit of tea before they go back.'

'Back, is it? What, just a visit?' He seemed strangely disappointed.

'This time, yes,' Moira found herself saying. 'We're very busy at the camp.'

'Well, then, you best come inside, I daresay. What do you do at this camp?'

Eileen caught Moira's eye as they all moved across the mud and slush in the yard towards the house and barely restrained a smile of sympathy.

'Well, thank God that's over!' Moira settled back in the passenger seat and blew smoke rings.

'It wasn't so bad.'

'Come off it! Don't try and be nice about it.'

'I'm not just being nice and polite. I don't know why you feel ashamed, why you never spoke about them before.'

'Oh I don't know. I just sort of cut them out of my life. I chose another way. Is that so wrong?'

'No, but he's a nice boy, your brother.'

'My elder brother. I still remember him as a kid.' She shook her head. 'I just don't know how my mother puts up with it.' She turned to stare at Eileen as she concentrated on her driving. 'She chose to live like that, you know. She married him against all Lily's advice and pleading.'

'Perhaps she loved him.'

Moira gave her a look that was withering.

'There's no accounting for love,' Eileen added quickly. 'You can't judge from this distance. It's hard enough to tell yourself what love is.' She fell silent and Moira caught her mood.

'Yes, perhaps you're right.' She chewed her lip and stubbed out her cigarette. 'I was going to talk to you, Ei, about Geoff.' She sat back, taking the silence as her cue to go on. 'I suppose that you heard about the fight from Veronica. She said a lot of mean things to me that night, mean but true. She hurt me at the time but when she had gone I sat down and thought about everything. About the miscarriage, about Peter, everything. And I suppose I saw that I had been doing exactly what she said. I'd been throwing my life away, picking up and discarding people I didn't need any more. Yes, a bit like Mum and Mike.' She drew out her pack of cigarettes and began to fuss getting a new one out. 'It's very hard to talk like this.'

'Couldn't you talk to Veronica?'

'Not really. Oh, it wasn't that she wouldn't listen, it was because she was too settled. What with Tim and everything. I didn't think she could understand how I felt.'

'But I can?'

'I hope you can. You see, I love Geoff. We've nothing in common – or perhaps we've too much. He's a country boy born and bred. He loves nothing better than to get away somewhere quiet, fishing or just walking. He hates crowds, loathes parties, all the things I loved.'

'Past tense?'

'Perhaps that was the trouble. Perhaps I really am a country girl at heart.' She stared out at the bleak darkening skyline. 'I tried to change. I thought I knew what I wanted – until I met Geoff.'

'He's really special?'

'I thought I'd lost him when Peter said all those things about me. I was too scared to go near him for days. Peter got transferred off base. He rang up one night to tell me – and hurl another load of abuse. I just hung up on him.'

'The bastard.'

'Yes, he was, wasn't he? But I couldn't see it at the time. I suppose I was more interested in what he offered in the way of fun than what he might be able to offer as a man. But when Geoff turned up, I knew he was the one.' She caught a smile cross Eileen's face. 'Think I'm joking, love at first sight and all that? Well, it happened to me.'

'I was just thinking how it can happen the other way round, too. How you can know someone for quite a long time without ever really finding out how you feel about them. You sort of take them for granted.'

'And that's happened with you?'

'He used to irritate me and I never knew the reason why. I was so taken up with Jon, I suppose, and he wanted to bring me down to earth with a bump.'

'So it's over between you and Jon?'

'I didn't say that. I don't know any more. You see, he's gone away. It all seems out of my hands somehow.'

'No, I don't believe that,' said Moira firmly. 'I think you have to take your own decisions – however painful. That's the lesson I've learnt.'

'And Geoff?'

'I went to him. I couldn't hope that one day he would make up his mind to come back to me. So I swallowed my pride.'

'And it's worked out?'

'I'm keeping my fingers crossed. Let's leave it at that, shall we?' She took a long draw on her cigarette. 'But I still feel guilty about Veronica. I treated her badly.'

'She and Tim have set the date.'

'No!'

'I had a letter only yesterday. An invitation to the wedding, actually.' She looked at Moira sharply. 'Why don't you come along, too?'

'Oh, I couldn't do that. She didn't invite me.'

'She would have done if she thought you would come.'

Moira's face lit up. 'Do you really think so? She wouldn't be offended that I gatecrashed?'

'See if you can get the afternoon off. It's a week on Saturday at the Forces' Church in Greenwich, two-thirty sharp.'

Moira saw that she was really serious and a glow of excitement seemed to flow through her.

'I wanted to make it up with her. I'll get her a good present.'

'She'll be glad enough to see you there.'

'Yes? OK, Eileen, it's a date!'

At Greenwich they were queuing up to get married. It seemed that the war had made up many minds, and Tim and Veronica found themselves slotted in on a full afternoon schedule.

Veronica turned up with an elderly, rather sober couple in a large car. Her father was wearing a formal grey morning suit and looked very distinguished, if a little put out at having to queue outside the church. They waited in the porch for another service to finish, while his wife fussed with Veronica's costume. She did look lovely. No one thought of a traditional white wedding in wartime and, conforming to the times, Veronica wore a powder-blue suit with a spray of dressed carnations on one shoulder. She looked radiant. The classic lines of the suit gave her an air of springtime amid the gloom of the March day.

Eileen went over and gave her a quick kiss on the cheek, smiling at her parents, hoping she could get a chance to talk to her later at the reception.

Then suddenly the newly married couple appeared at the door, both in uniform, and their guests were spilling out of the church. Now it was their turn. Eileen went in and took her place, watching the door for a sign of Moira. But the music struck up almost immediately and Veronica appeared on the arm of her father to walk down the aisle.

Eileen turned her head, thinking that something was wrong, thinking that Tim had not yet arrived and they would have to stop the service. But she was wrong. There he stood across the aisle, head tilted to catch a word from his best man, smart and straight in army uniforms. He had been standing there all the time, but she had not realised it was Tim. As he turned his head to catch his first sight of Veronica, she saw that his face was whole and pink and full of wonder.

She knew that in her heart she had been expecting to see again the ravages of that day in Piccadilly. Even though she knew full well that for months now he had undergone operations, it was still a shock.

The service was preceded by an announcement by the vicar. He seemed a nervous, weary little man almost drowning in his white surplice. He told them in a high-pitched voice that he would be obliged to leave immediately if the air-raid sirens went, whether the wedding ceremony was completed or not. Then, as if he feared an outbreak of hostilities at any moment, he raced through the service, getting through the formalities in what must have been a record time.

'I do,' said Tim in his singularly attractive voice which carried round the church, while Veronica's response was lost. Then there was a hymn, one that Eileen had not heard for years, and she felt quite emotional as she sang,

'Hills of the North rejoice, Valley and Lowland sing...'

22 days without you, my darling. Oh Gareth, Gareth, where are you? I love you so.

Outside the church, as they squeezed past the next wedding party that was gathering at the door to get in, a faint watery sun cast enough light for Veronica's new father-in-law to get his camera set up.

Eileen found herself next to Tim and congratulated him, hardly able to take her eyes off the smooth skin of his face, unlined and soft as a baby's.

'You look marvellous!'

'I feel great. It's the happiest day of my life, Eileen, and we're both really pleased you could be here to share it with us.' He glanced over her shoulder. 'Who are those people with Veronica?'

She glanced back and saw a handsome couple talking to the bride, and her face broke into delighted laughter.

'It's Moira! She did come after all.'

Moira and Veronica had their heads together, clutching hands, half laughing, half crying. As Tim and Eileen joined them, Moira introduced Geoff, casual in his Air Force blue, bearing a gift-wrapped parcel under his arm. Moira took the present and thrust it into Tim's hands, then leant over to kiss him on the cheek, on the new side of his face.

'And I guess I get to kiss the bride!' Geoff added, promptly fulfilling a guest's privilege. 'And the bride's friend, why not?' He kissed Eileen soundly and then stood back, very pleased with himself. 'It's an old French custom!'

'Come along, everybody!' cried Tim's father. 'Form a group for the photographs!'

The party was a welcome relief from the grim routine of daily life. It was almost like being back in pre-war days, and to look at the newly-weds as they danced close together you might have thought they hadn't a care in the world.

Veronica cut the wedding cake after posing for more photographs before the magnificent three-tiered iced creation. Only once the pictures were taken did Veronica's mother carefully remove the cardboard mock-up to expose a single layer fruitcake, plain, uniced and eggless.

'Ah well, you can't have everything!' Veronica sighed, hanging on to Tim's arm, smiling at her friends.

'That is one happy couple,' Geoff concluded. 'Why don't you and I have a dance, Moira? Let's get in the mood.'

Watching both couples, Eileen felt her loneliness bite deep. She was happy for Tim and Veronica, and she liked Geoff more than she had expected. She hoped that he and Moira had a future together. But their happiness only served to reveal her own aching separation from Gareth. Amid the laughter and music of the party she struggled to keep down the surge of despair and desperation she felt, not knowing where he was or what he was doing, not knowing if they would ever be together again.

The day had gone well. She and Pat had made a journey out to Bletchley and while he was inside she sat in the car under the trees that were already budding with leaves, enjoying the early sunshine. She thought about her friends, feeling that their reunion was a sign of better things to come, a turning point. Perhaps now things would begin to go well for all of them.

Back in London she was down in the motor pool putting the car away after dropping Pat at the Ministry. She felt more cheerful and optimistic than she had for weeks. She was due to visit Jon, knowing that he was to be transferred to Roehampton mid-week and that he would be in a good mood. He had, in fact, been in a good mood ever since Gareth had gone away.

'You off then? Some people have all the luck.' The motor pool sergeant took a delight in baiting her, but she had learnt to ignore his jibes. Today she was feeling so good that she found a smile for him and a cheery goodbye, but she was barely out of the garage before he was calling her back.

'Not so fast! There's someone calling for you!'

As she turned she should have known that something was wrong. She saw Pat's figure standing just beyond the office, still panting from his search for her. He stood bareheaded, his arms hanging by his side, the message plain on his face.

'I thought you had gone,' he told her.

'No – you just caught me.' She was looking at him quizzically, trying to understand what he was saying with his eyes.

'I think we had better go back upstairs where we can talk.'

'No! What's wrong?'

'Let's walk then.' He was self-conscious in front of the listening sergeant, and took her by the arm, leading her out of the garage and into the wide street above. 'I'm afraid I have some bad news,' he said at last. 'It's about Gareth.'

She caught her breath, grasping the sleeve of his jacket as they stopped dead beyond the sandbag wall.

'His plane has not returned.' He was choosing his words very carefully, treading on glass. 'He went missing out over the sea. Off the Lincolnshire coast.' He watched her closely. 'There's been no word of him.'

Missing? She knew of two women whose men had gone missing. One heard news within a month that he was a POW, the other within five days that he was dead. And he too had been over the sea, his plane drowned.

Missing – presumed dead. That's what they said. Those were the official words. They rang in her head, words so familiar, seen so many times on official forms that they had almost lost their meaning.

'Lincolnshire?' She remembered the wild bleak landscape, the endless plain stretching to the sea. What, lost in that grey emptiness of marsh and water? Lost in that aching loneliness forever?

'I'm so sorry, Eileen.'

Missing – presumed dead. No return, no cruel injuries, none of those horrors she had tormented herself with in long nights. Gone, lost, not even his body. No body, no grave, nothing but memories left to her.

'Would you like me to see you home?'

She stared at him, wondering what he was talking about.

361

'Home? Oh no, I have to go to Bart's. Jon is expecting me.' Her voice seemed steady, with hardly a quiver to betray the hollowness.

'Even so – I don't think you should be alone.'

'I'm not alone, Pat. I'm going to see Jon. I told you.'

He looked at her, clearly confused by her reaction. Was he expecting her to break down, did he expect tears and all the outward display of grief? Because she could not share that with him, or anyone. She wanted to be alone now more than ever.

'I'll be all right, really I will.'

'Look, I'll call you later tonight, at the house, all right?'

She touched his arm, afraid that he would think her unfeeling. 'You're very kind. Thank you for telling me.'

His face twisted with anguish and he was reluctant to leave her, so finally she was the one to walk away.

Her step was brisk, although she hardly knew where she was going. She found herself suddenly in Parliament Square, the opposite way to what she had intended, and was drawn towards the river. Grey-green in the late afternoon, it surged below the Embankment wall, continuous rhythm, heart of the city. The sight of so much water brought the tears. She cried with great, aching tears, her chest heaving as she gasped for breath. She had to stop, leaning over the parapet below one of the bridges, eyes clouded and unseeing.

Her memories had haunted her, growing more vivid daily. She remembered his face as clearly as though it was only yesterday that he had left her. The afternoon sun, the thought of springtime, all had gone now, and with it all hope of happiness. Evening came rushing on, the sky lowering, not even a sunset. It grew suddenly cold, and all the colours of the day were washed away by the rising moon. A full moon, a bombers' moon.

Full realisation came to her then. She understood that he had known it all along. He saw no future for them, no hope. He had tried to tell her, tried to keep away, not wanting to hurt her.

'Thank God, thank God,' she said out loud, thinking of the brief hours together, hours stolen from all sense and duty.

For now she knew it had all been worth while. She had known what love was and nothing could take that away from her, not even his death. All the guilt they had suffered was now washed away. It did not matter any more because she knew what she must do now.

She began to walk on along the Embankment, watching the moon rise, feeling the cold night air strike her face. It was not so far now to the City. She thought if she did not go to the hospital tonight she might never go through with it. And besides, Jon had the right to know. She thought he was strong enough to bear the news of his friend's death, but would he understand what she must say? That she needed to be by herself, that she needed to go away from him, to understand herself before she could commit herself to anyone ever again.

St Paul's rose grey and silver in the moonlight above the dark street. Her footsteps echoed on the old cobbled street, broken and pitted from the constant barrage. The ruins swarmed with stray cats, brave and brazen in her path, running for cover only as the sirens wailed out across the City. The pigeons lifted from the buildings overhead, but Eileen kept walking, knowing that she could not have far to go now.

She was quite unprepared for the droning overhead. Suddenly there was a burst of blinding white light at the top of the street and she saw the road before her sway, the earth opening up like a giant wave. Two vivid rings of light, purple and red, rose the height of the buildings on either side and the bricks seemed to swell, stretching and expanding over the street as the glass flew out all about her.

She heard nothing, barely a whisper of wind warm against her cheek. But she felt the waves as they buffeted her, and she clutched at the stones on which she was lying, her fingers tearing at the earth for support. A grey curtain seemed to have descended and she fought hard to breathe. The air was falling to pieces around her and there was nothing but silence.

Chapter Twelve

'You have to give me full particulars, dear,' said the nurse kindly in her soft Scots accent. 'You see, you lost all your identification papers in the blast. We don't know anything about you.'

'So – no one knows that I'm here?'

'I'm afraid not. But we'll notify whoever you want, once we get your details. Now, let's start with your name, shall we?'

Eileen gave her name, uncertain whether she really wanted anyone to come to see her. The sterile white ward seemed impersonal, alien. She supposed that Pat would have to be told.

'You're lucky to be alive, you know. I've seen many blast victims in my time. Clothes in shreds, like yours, with never a mark on their bodies – but stone dead.' She busily filled in the last section on the official form.

'Was it a bad raid?'

'One of the worst. Full moon, of course.' She clipped her notes together and stood up. 'Brought down a lot of buildings round here. For a time I thought we'd be hit too.' She looked beyond the bed towards the windows. 'First the incendiaries, then oil bombs. The fires were pretty widespread.'

'And Bart's? Do you know what happened there?'

'Well, it's still operational, I know that. Why, do you know someone there?'

'Could you find out for me? It's my fiancé, he's a patient there.'

'Well, of course, dear. You'll want to know how he is. Just you give me his name and the ward number and I promise I'll do my best to find out for you.'

Eileen gave her the details and saw the sympathy on Nurse Graham's face.

'Don't you worry,' she told her as she was about to leave. 'I'm sure he'll be all right.'

But she was wrong. Eileen saw it at once by the way she stood talking in whispers to another nurse late in the afternoon. Nurse Graham wore her cape, ready to go off duty, and the bright splash of colour contrasted with the pallor of her face as she approached the bed. She drew the flowered curtains on the rail round her bed, shutting out her neighbour sitting up reading an old copy of *The Lady*, and Eileen knew then, if she had not known before, that her news was the very worst.

'He's dead, isn't he?'

The nurse stared at her, unable to say a word, all her neat prepared sentences fled.

'I knew. I had a feeling, a kind of certainty.' Ignoring the look on the woman's face she went on, speaking more to herself than to her. 'It seems right in a way. Gareth gone, then Jon. The only thing wrong is that I – I survived. A mistake, I suppose. It should have been all three of us.'

'You shouldn't say things like that.'

'Why not? It's true. It would have been the best thing that could have happened.'

'No, that's nonsense.' With her Scots accent it came out as a rebuke. 'You're only a slip of a girl. You have your whole life in front of you.' She took Eileen's silence for distress and her voice softened. 'I know well it must be awful for you, dear. You'll be feeling desperate just now, but I've seen a lot of people in exactly your position, and I know full well that with time . . .'

Eileen knew that she nodded, her throat tight and constricted, nodded to shut her up. She wanted her to go. She couldn't take any more of the soft look in her eyes, the alternating cajoling and buck-up attitude. She wanted nothing more than to be left alone.

When the nurse left her she slumped back against the pillows with an overwhelming sense of release. Her mind was whirling and behind the curtains she could hear whispered voices, knowing they were talking about her, about her loss. Throughout the day she refused all food, lying behind the patterned curtains, counting the flowers and longing for night. Night and another raid to rectify the mistake, to end her misery.

The blackout curtains could scarcely hide the bright lights from outside. Ironic that in the ward all should be darkness, here and there a muffled cough, a body moving in sleep, while beyond these walls another life and death struggle raged and people really cared about survival.

She was thinking of Vi, poor Vi killed in a raid when she had so much to look forward to. And George, alone now and grieving, moving like a man of sixty, shuffling back to war.

There was a bitter joker somewhere who took pleasure in turning the tables, in shattering the good times, dispelling any complacency.

In the brooding shadows, listening to voices inside her head she saw the situation clearly. Faced with a choice to be made between Jon and Gareth, fate had stepped in and taken the decision out of her hands, and she had lost both of them.

It seemed that you could have everything or you could have nothing. You gambled and you lost. But what was it that Moira had said to her that afternoon as they travelled back alone together in the car? She said she refused to believe in fate. She said you had to make up your mind to take your own decisions in life – however painful.

She knew that she must stop feeling sorry. It was herself for whom she felt regret and loss. She looked at her future alone and trembled.

The other women in the ward were very kind really. From the time that the ward orderly drew back her curtains in the pale dawn she was treated with a special consideration, aware of a cautious interest in the air, of knowing looks that understood. As the day wore on, she felt more than just gratitude. She felt a growing sense of awe that women who had suffered themselves had the time to care about her loss.

Looking at their battered faces, torn and scarred from glass splinters, she learnt the lesson of survival. She saw that life went on regardless, and sooner or later she must come to terms with it. Yes, she had suffered a great blow, but it was not the end of everything. Her life was not over. Now she must begin to think about herself.

It was hard to override the feeling of guilt, the sense of being selfish that she had become accustomed to. All her time had been so taken up with the demands of Jon and her job, of responsibilities, there had never been any time for herself. Yes, she had loved Jon, but knowing Gareth had shown her another side of herself. Each had their moment in her life, but it was not all, it was not everything. Love was not all absorbing. For the first time she realised she had to come to terms with the prospect of her own future – alone if necessary.

'Come on, chin up,' said the nurse. 'Worse things happen at sea.'

Eileen was struggling with the buttons of the dress they had found for her. In the blast her uniform had been destroyed, all except her shoes. She wondered what she looked like in the borrowed clothes, a civilian for the first time in more than a year.

'It will be all right when I get home.' She said it more to encourage herself than because she felt it.

'I still think you should have allowed us to fetch someone to help you. It's only been 48 hours after all.'

'I'll get a taxi at the gates.'

'I've already warned the porter.' She looked pleased with herself as though she had forced her hand.

'Well, then, it's all settled.' Eileen put on the heavy tweed coat, feeling the weight of it upon her back where the skin was raw. It had a large comfortable collar and huge patch pockets. She felt almost lost inside it, lost and rather vulnerable.

The nurse walked her to the door as she said her farewells to the other patients. In so brief a time she had come to know these women with an intimacy she had never expected. It was a wrench to leave them now, knowing they would not meet again.

'I want to thank you,' she told Nurse Graham out in the corridor, 'I want to thank you for all you have done.'

'That's all right, dear, that's what I'm here for. I'm sorry I had to bring such bad news.'

Eileen nodded, holding open the main door.

'Just you take it steadily,' the nurse called after her and stood waving at the open doorway.

She was grateful that the taxi driver did not expect her to talk. She was alone and afraid to be alone. Although they had given her

367

money for her fare at the hospital, even the task of paying off the taxi posed an enormous threat. She found even the slightest task exhausting, not physically although she felt stiff and sore, but mentally. Too much had happened too quickly. It was going to take a long time to regain her confidence, but she knew that Lily and Kitty and Iris would rally round. It was the thought of the house in the square that had kept her going. As the streets passed her by, a growing excitement filled her at the prospect of arriving home.

But she saw suddenly that she was in her own district and had not recognised it. She was lost, looking at the smoking buildings. She was very scared, staring through the window of the cab as it turned into the square past a road diversion where demo men were pulling down a bomb-damaged house.

'Is this the place then?'

She saw from his face that the driver did not like to leave her there. As he drew up on the far side of the square, she turned back to look at the row of houses, still black and stinking, still wet from the hoses.

'Yes, this is the place.' She stood out on the pavement, the smell of the fire bomb still in the air. 'It's all right,' she told him, handing over the fare. 'I'll be all right. I live here, you see.'

He gave her a long look, reluctant to become involved, and finally started up the motor again. She watched as the taxi trundled out of the square.

It was a very strange feeling to look at the ruins of the old house and know the sensation of insubstantiality. The house had stood there for more than a hundred years, surviving passing generations, unscathed. Now in a brief 48 hours the life of the house had been destroyed.

And Lily? And Kitty and Iris? Where were her friends?

Panic seized her and she felt sick. The stench of charred beams and the soft, yielding embers wet underfoot were like some disease-ridden remains over which she wandered, desolate and grieving. Were they all dead then? Gone with the house and everything she had come to love as her own family? And with them all hope.

Was this where the door had been? Black, flaking ashes stained her hands as she stretched out to touch the damp timbers. When had it happened? Why had it happened?

'Hey, miss, are you all right?'

He was standing above her, a tin hat looking down from the height of the pavement above. His overalls were blue.

'It's not safe, you being down there. The whole lot could come down at any moment. You better come on out. Give us your hand.'

When she got on the pavement she recognised Phil Laidlaw, one of the local wardens.

'Are you all right?' He was staring at her, obviously not recognising her; it was probably the civilian clothes that did it. She became aware she was still gripping his hand.

'What happened?' She met his eyes. 'You have to tell me, Phil. Don't you know me? I used to live here with Lily and...'

'Ah yes! Yes, I see.' What could he say to her? The strain on her face showed that she already knew. 'You'd best come down to the wardens' post. You can get a nice cuppa there.'

So it was the worst. She had to hold her breath as she walked with him, had to hold in all the fears and the despair wailing inside her head. All dead, was it possible? Everyone she had cared for taken from her in one cruel blow?

Phil entered the wardens' post ahead of her, having to coax her inside. The faces in the semi-gloom might have been familiar, but in that instant they meant nothing to her. The mug of tea pushed into her cold hands offered up more comfort than their hard, practical faces. She supposed they had seen it all before. Another night, another bomb. More grief and misery.

But Kitty, surely they should mourn for Kitty who had been at their side through every hour, sister, mother, daughter.

Did she want the truth? Looking at their faces, she knew they would tell her if she asked. With no frills, no fuss. But could she take it?

'Feel any better now, love?'

'It's just shock. You'll get over it,' added another. 'We had you down for dead for certain. Couldn't find no body, but you was missing, so...'

'I was caught in the blast. I've just come out of hospital,' she told them. She caught their exchange of glances.

'Then you were lucky, mate. You wouldn't have stood a cat in hell's chance if you'd been back here.'

'Then – everyone...'

'The old lady was up on the roof, fire-watching. Didn't stand an earthly. Rare old girl, that.'

'Crying shame.'

'I remember old Lily from way back. Won't be the same without her.'

Eileen did not dare to speak for the pain in her chest. Their words glanced off her, barely penetrating her consciousness. She understood that Lily had died, but she knew she would not really grasp her loss until she had time alone to think and to remember.

'You weren't with her long, were you, love? But I could see that you thought the world of her.'

Eileen looked up, thinking that they were talking to her, but she saw their heads turn towards the doorway and turned round on her chair to see for herself who stood there against the light.

'Kitty?'

'My God, it is you!' Kitty had her arms about her, with all her strength and compassion. Half-laughing, with tears on her cheeks, she held Eileen off to look at her. 'We all thought you were dead.'

'And I thought – when I saw the house...'

'We found her wandering in the ruins,' Phil added.

'Says she's just got out of hospital herself.'

'Hospital? Are you OK?' Kitty seemed to take in her appearance for the first time. 'Whatever are you wearing? And your hair?'

'Singed. They had to cut bits off.' She touched her head hesitantly. 'I was caught in a raid, thrown off my feet. I don't remember a thing until I woke up in hospital.'

Kitty dragged her down on to the wooden chair again, still gripping her tightly by the arm. Her face was lean and shadowed, masked by a new gauntness born of suffering. Only her eyes still retained the old sparkle, that vitality that had spelt fireworks. Kitty Russell, alive and safe. Eileen squeezed her hand, scarcely able to credit this sudden reprieve.

'I thought I had lost you all.'

'No – it was only Lily.'

'But, Iris?'

'She was working that night. As luck would have it, she and I

370

had set off together. We walked to the Angel, then she went her way and I went mine. It wasn't long after that the sirens went.'

'And Lily?'

'On the roof apparently. By the time I got back to the square it was all over. A direct hit.' She felt the pressure on her hand. 'It must have been quick.'

Tears rolled unashamedly down Eileen's cheeks. She did not see Kitty glare at their audience, or the male wardens begin to file out of the post and leave them in peace.

'Iris has got herself a new place,' Kitty was saying. 'She didn't waste any time, I'll say that for her. I've been grabbing a few hours here and there when I can. I didn't give a thought to finding a new place before. It didn't seem right, being on my own. But now you're still in the land of the living...' She saw Eileen raise her head and her intuition told her more than she would say. 'There's something more, isn't there? Do you want to tell me?'

'I thought I was alone,' she repeated. 'I had bad news too, you see.'

Kitty did not really see but the huge round eyes awash with tears spoke only of pain. She cradled her head against her shoulder.

'Well, now we've got each other. It doesn't matter what's happened, we're still alive. We've got a second chance, a chance to make a fresh start. What do you say? Shall we try and get a place together? Start again?'

Eileen sat up, wiping her eyes. 'You're a marvel, Kitty. You're so strong. I don't know what I would have done...'

'Don't think about it. Not now. We have to be practical, get things done. Now I'm on duty until three-thirty. We can try and fix something after that.' She frowned, calculating in her head all that had to be done. 'I'll deal with the welfare. I've only got the things I'm standing up in, and you must be the same.'

'Worse. These clothes are what they found for me at the hospital.'

'Lousy taste,' said Kitty with a ghost of a smile. 'Well, I'll see the Relief, see what can be done. Are you going to stay here, wait for me?'

'No, no, look, I had better get in touch with Pat. The hospital were supposed to tell him, but now he won't be able to find me.'

371

'Yes, we'll have to put up a notice or something to let people know we're still alive in case they come looking. Anyone arriving without warning at the house would have forty fits.' She looked concerned. 'Are you sure you're all right? You look a bit shaky to me. You're not thinking of going down to Whitehall, are you?'

Eileen shook her head. 'No, I thought I'd try and ring Pat at his home. Even if he's not there, his wife will take a message.'

'And you can give the post here as a contact point.' She fished in a pocket of her overall and produced some coins. 'You can use the telephone just up the road. It was still OK this morning. But come back after, won't you? I won't be away long.'

'Oh Kitty, it's so good to find you!'

'Strange how the bad times bring you closer together, isn't it? I suppose that's the only good thing to be said for this bloody war.'

It was true. Eileen thought she could search the wide world over and never find anything more sacrosanct than the comradeship she had found in war. Kitty, Veronica and Moira were still left to her. Friends that meant more than family. Real friends who would stand by each other no matter what came their way.

She saw Kitty on her way and then stood a moment in silence staring at the ruin of the square. The stark skeletal walls of the terrace were touched by sad sunlight. There was little pain in the scene now. She felt no ghosts, no nightmares. The faint warmth of the sun was gentle on her skin, harbinger of spring. A new beginning, yes, she felt it now, a faint stirring of hope.

She started to walk out from the square, heading towards the main road. She had not gone a block before she thought that someone called her name. She stopped, but before she could turn round she heard her name called again.

She would know that voice anywhere.

She turned sharply and saw him running up the street after her, and then he stopped, barely five or six yards away. He stood there, his coat open, his tie loosened at the neck. She saw that his face was hollowed by shadows, marks of sleeplessness and worry. But as his eyes met hers he suddenly began to smile and a look of incredulous wonder came over his face as he started forward to meet her.

As she went into his arms she knew she had made no mistake.

The wheel had come full circle.

'The thought of you kept me alive.' He began kissing her face, her eyes, her lips. She had to hold him in her arms a long time to believe he was really there with her. She had been so sure, felt so certain that he was gone forever.

'When I saw the house...'

'Yes, I know.'

'I tried to check the casualty lists at the police station but I couldn't find your name.'

'No, no,' she whispered, kissing the corner of his mouth, touching his unshaven face in wonder, feeling his warmth and strength.

'I came back to the house, thinking. I didn't know what I was going to do.' He stroked her poor hair, aware of her strange appearance. 'For a moment I didn't think it was you – I thought you were dead.'

His plane had come down, sinking into the marsh just off the Wash. It was only luck that he had baled out over the sea; better the open sea than the shifting sands of the coast. She listened in awe as he told how he was pulled out of the water after hours by a fishing boat, more affected by his escape than by her own. With no plane and no wreckage it was little wonder they had all thought him dead. But none of that mattered now. He had come back to her, like a bonus, an extra prize.

'I came straight here. I had to find you.'

When she had imagined all her supports were lost, when she was at her lowest ebb, compelled to attempt to make a new life out of the ruins, he had reappeared as though to prove that she had chosen the right path after all.

Uncertainty had gone. She saw nothing but joy and resolution in his face, and love that had been tested. On these foundations, come what might, she knew that the future existed for all of them.